Tamed by the Fire

by

Maxine Mansfield

Book Four of The Academy Series

Tamed by the Fire

Contact Information: info@thewildrosepress.com

Cover Art by *Diana Carlile*

The Wild Rose Press, Inc.
PO Box 708
Adams Basin, NY 14410-0708

Visit us at www.thewilderroses.com

Publishing History
First Scarlet Rose Edition, October 2013
Print ISBN 978-1-62830-168-7
Digital ISBN 978-1-62830-169-4

Published in the United States of America

A girl's deflowering is a once-in-a-lifetime event…

He didn't say a word as they walked from the great room or even as they made their way down the long hall. Not a *"hi, how are you?"* Not a *"how have you been?"* Not even an *"I've always been attracted to you, and I'm looking forward to doing this."* Nothing but silence.

When the door of her chamber clicked closed behind them, shutting them all alone from the rest of the world, Kitrina jumped at the sound of the bolt tumbling into place. She searched for something clever to say. Where was the speech she'd prepared just yesterday? The witty words meant to assure Zander that she was a woman full grown, sophisticated even? Words meant to put them both at ease?

They were gone, completely gone, and her mind totally blank.

Well, perhaps not totally blank. Even though she no longer faced him, she could still hear the depth of his breathing and in her mind still see the ripple of his muscles, the intensity of his gaze, the nearness of his lips. She gulped.

When his hands lifted her hair away and his fingers grazed the skin at the back of her neck, heat infused her from head to toe, and though certainly not cold, she shivered.

"Easy, my lady. Relax, all will be well. You shall see."

The closure of her gown suddenly gave way, and with a whoosh, the gossamer green material pooled about her feet. Kit stepped out of it, took a deep breath to steady herself, then turned to face him. The appreciation for what he saw reflected back to her from his heated gaze and bolstered her shaky nerves as nothing else on Albrath could have. Though his breathing appeared steady, his lips parted and his nostrils slightly flared.

Kitrina reached out and undid the clasp holding his kilt together. There was no mistaking his attraction to her as the plaid fell to the floor.

Dedication

To my niece Becky, the bravest woman I know.

Touched by the Magic,
Tempted by the Storm,
Taken by the Passion…
A new love is born.
Tamed by the Fire,
Tested by the Night,
Tried by the Desire...
A true love burns bright.

The Dragon Heart Opal
Hark unto thee both far and wide. A pact has been
made, a trust to confide. For dragon hearts are pure as
gold. And paladin hearts beat both worthy and bold.
They've formed a bond, they've given a token. A
promise in gemstone, never to be broken. An opal of
brilliance, an opal of trust. Worn by one whose soul is
found just.

Prologue

Zander cringed. "You want me to what?"

Barbarian Prince, Alex Zander Collin Hammerstrike, clamped his mouth shut in shock. He must've heard wrong. They surely hadn't just asked what he thought they had. After spending the last half turn of the hourglass at Castle Kuropkat listening to the speech from Sir Uthiel Dragonheart and his pretty wife, Lady Briarlarn, about the task they wished him to perform, he needed a few moments to let the impact of their request seep into his soul. Could he actually consider doing such a deed?

"Why me?" He shuddered. "There must be any number of men vastly more qualified for this particular job. Matter of fact, many make their living doing precisely this sort of thing."

The determined look Uthiel Dragonheart, leader of the human Paladins of Albrath, Protector of the Dragons, and Master of Castle Kuropkat bestowed on him didn't do a thing to alleviate Zander's tension. "The lass insists it be you."

Zander shook his head. He didn't wish to hurt their feelings. They were important people, after all, and close friends of his parents, but at the same time, the thought was terrifying. No, terrifying wasn't precisely the word he was looking for. It was downright exciting and titillating, but at the same time, not possible. Was it?

"Why on Albrath would she even consider me of all people to deflower her?" He didn't hear their response if they made one. Zander's mind raced with image after image of Lord and Lady Dragonheart's oldest daughter.

Kitrina, who from the very first moment she'd been placed in his arms as an infant, he had loved. And when she'd stared up into his five-year-old face with those trusting, stormy blue eyes and smiled at him, even though he hadn't understood what was happening, he'd been filled with such awe of her, it had rocked his very soul. She could never truly be his, but she was his heart's secret desire and always had been.

Kitrina, who he'd purposefully not laid eyes on for two years now. He had tried unsuccessfully to excise her from his mind and heart. Gone would be the innocent young lady of sixteen who drove him to distraction with her quick wit and sharp tongue, replaced by a woman of eighteen. Where had the time gone? Did she look much the same? Were her lips still as full, pouty, irresistible, and meant to be kissed? And did she still possess a body whose only purpose on Albrath was to drive a man insane?

He hardened and sat quickly at a nearby table as somewhere in the distance thunder rumbled. He tamped down his normally in-control spiritmaster tendencies. He prided himself on keeping his ability to manipulate the weather according to his mood and to sense danger when near well in check.

The last thing twenty-three year old Zander Hammerstrike needed at this moment was for Uthiel and Briar to realize what they were suggesting was the stuff that both his dreams and nightmares were made of.

Would they be so quick to offer up their daughter if they were aware that, instead of the routine, ceremonial breaking of a hymen, then withdrawal they expected, they would get the exact opposite? Zander had no doubt if he penetrated her once, even if his life depended upon it, he wouldn't be able to pull out and stop himself until he'd branded her upon his heart and soul forever.

A young black cat that had been playfully circling his feet since the moment he stepped through the doorway stopped, looked up at him, and jumped into his lap. Immediately, his spiritmaster sensibilities kicked in, and even though he knew without a doubt the cat posed no threat, still, there was something…odd about it. Something he couldn't quite put his finger on.

The cat circled his lap once and began making itself comfortable right on top of his erection. As gently as possible, Zander slid it to the floor, took a deep breath, and hoped a lightning bolt wouldn't strike him dead as he looked Kitrina's parents straight in the eye and bald-faced lied.

"We are talking about Kit, aren't we? Scrawny, giggly, hair-hanging-down-in-her-eyes, stuttering Kitrina? The same young lass who was forever in the company of my sister, Mia? My God Draka, I didn't realize she was even old enough for such a thing. I suppose I should've though, as she and Mia are about the same age. I'm flattered you would trust such an important occasion to me. Are you sure you wouldn't want to consider someone older and more experienced?"

Thunder crashed right overhead, and Zander gulped.

The kitten suddenly dug its claws deep into the tender flesh of Zander's ankle. With an "ouch," he jumped up and hopped away from the offending ball of fur. A flash of lightning illuminated the room. So much for the fur-covered hairball not being dangerous.

The light lilt of Briar's voice as she bent and quickly scooped up the cat was pleasant, but it didn't do much to calm the escalating tension in the room. Instead, she sounded forced, nervous, and strained. "I assure you, Zander, our daughter is well past the age for the ceremony. As a matter of fact, three years past. She's now eighteen, and as you probably know, most girls have their ceremonies at fifteen, sixteen at the latest."

Briar's smile faded. "For a while, we were afraid Kitrina wasn't even interested in such things. But it's mandatory for admission into The Academy of Magical Arts, and it's all she's talked about for a full phase of the second moon now. I'm sure you realize how important a Coming-into-Womanhood ceremony is to a young girl. After all, your sister, Mia had hers just a few seasons back. It's the night all young girls dream of."

She stroked the top of the furious cat's head as she continued. "You yourself must remember how excited you were for your own Seduction-into-Manhood ceremony. Don't you?"

Zander gulped again.

Briar got a faraway look in her eye. "I never had an

5

official deflowering ceremony myself, so I want this to be perfect for my daughter. All the pomp and glitter, presents and parties. How can we expect her ever to pass her sexual theory and practices finals if she doesn't get her deflowering out of the way? Prep schools are such sticklers. You wouldn't want to be responsible for holding Kitrina back. Now would you?"

Zander watched Briar stroke the half-grown black cat again who suddenly struggled furiously to get free. And though the animal had tried to do him bodily harm, he felt a certain empathy for the poor little creature. If he could escape like it was trying to do, he'd jump on the back of his steed this very moment and ride away from Castle Kuropkat as fast as he could.

He needed time to think. He needed time to decide how to let them down gently. Knowing that if he put off answering them long enough, they'd have no choice but to simply find someone else for the job. But to make his parents' best friends wait indefinitely for an answer would be rude. And if there was one thing Prince Zander Hammerstrike had been taught by those self-same parents was, never to be rude. So instead, he stood and listened, as Kitrina's mother went on and on and on.

"You are Kitrina's choice, not ours. Her heart is set on you, I'm afraid. We would've naturally preferred a nice, older professional deflowerer who would have experience enough to be gentle and patient, but she wouldn't hear of it. She demands it be you and only you, or no-one at all."

Zander smiled as the cat finally managed to escape Briar's grip and leap once more to the floor. Uthiel Dragonheart's wife didn't seem to notice, however. She didn't bat an eye or miss a syllable as she continued.

"We've both tried to talk her out of this, trust me we have. A girl's deflowering is a once-in-a-lifetime event, and we certainly want it done right. If not, God Draka knows she could end up traumatized. And, as you know, that's the reason deflowering and seduction ceremonies began in the first place, so young ladies and young men would never again have to feel the embarrassment and uncertainty of becoming an adult."

Mrs. Dragonheart's eyes filled with tears matching the rain now pouring outside, and Zander knew himself to be lost. "Will you do this one small favor for us, Zander? Will you do it for Kit, please?"

He sighed. Her choice? Why had Kitrina chosen him of all people? Could she possibly have the tiniest smidgen of the same feelings for him he'd always held for her? Did he dare to hope? And if she did, considering who he was and what his current circumstances were, was he within his rights to nurture it? Especially now?

Zander's heart pounded in his chest, and a lump formed in his throat.

Kitrina. Her name fit her well. Tiny and lithe, kitten-like even, with long flowing hair as black as a starless night and large questioning eyes the color of an angry sky. Kitrina, mostly human with just a quarter high-elf from her mother's side that showed in the slight point of her ears and the paleness of her completion. Kitrina, who was so very delicate she might break in two if a huge, hulking barbarian like himself actually got up the nerve ever to touch her.

In all of his years, he'd never seen another creature as fragile, as delicate, as lovely.

Zander shook his head. He simply couldn't do it, could he? Kitrina's parents had no idea what they were asking. Even for a barbarian, he knew certain parts of his anatomy were considerably more...well-endowed than average. A fact he'd relished and even bragged about with friends. Now he wished with all his heart to be counted among the simply average, if only for a night.

Could he do it? Would he dare?

What should've been a simple request was an extremely hard decision to make. Even if he could force himself to stop at just penetration, he feared he couldn't willingly cause Kit pain. Not even if she wished it, had asked for it. And pain he surely would bring her if he attempted to deflower her. It wasn't as if he could actually say that to her parents, though. How embarrassing would that be? But then, could he deny Kitrina Dragonheart anything?

With reluctant determination, Zander sighed and lifted his gaze to Uthiel and Briar Dragonheart. "If it's me she's determined to have do this for her, then I'll certainly give it my best shot."

Through one of the large windows in the hall, lightning streaked across the sky once more. Thunder shook the castle, and rain continued to pelt the ground. So much for control.

Briar smiled. "Thank you so very much, Zander. We'll see you a week from tomorrow at sunset. That's when the festivities are set to begin. You will remind your parents, won't you?"

The black kitten scurried from the room.

****

Scrawny. He still thought her scrawny and giggly

and...and...stuttering? She'd show Zander Hammerstrike just how wrong he was.

Kit laughed. Two years had been a long time, and the difference in her appearance had been nothing short of amazing. Zander didn't know that, however. He'd been away, studying at The Academy of Magical Arts. Well, wouldn't he be surprised?

She ran a brush through her long black hair until it crackled with energy and smiled at her reflection in the mirror. Oh, yes, Zander would be surprised.

Though she hadn't grown taller than the last time he'd seen her, other parts had filled out quite nicely. Her hips were more shapely and rounded, her breasts full and lush, and her ass, though not too big, was not too small, either. She'd been told by more than one admirer, her ass was just the right size to grab two fists full and hold onto.

But then she hadn't been the only one to change. He had, too. For one thing, he wore his hair longer. Thick strands, the exact color of burnt wheat, brushed the top of his shoulders. His eyes were an even darker, more intense shade of silver-gray than she remembered, and his mouth more kissable. Especially since it was surrounded by what looked to be a season's worth of beard growth. And then there was his chest, arms, and legs. Kitrina would never have guessed that in just two years' time Zander could become more muscled and more defined and...and simply more than his perfect barbarian self had been when last she saw him. But he had.

A tingling began between her thighs and spread inward until her pussy vibrated with it. It shot upward into her belly and then downward, all the way to her toes. She began to sweat. A week from tomorrow couldn't come soon enough.

Kitrina smiled as she stroked the length of the gossamer thin, pale green gown she'd wear for her deflowering. She'd made it herself for the event. Every seam had been stitched to showcase her curves and cause Zander Hammerstrike's eyes to pop right out of their sockets. Oh, yes, he was definitely in for a surprise.

Scrawny wasn't going to be what he thought when he entered her room next week. Though Kitrina was still technically a virgin and didn't have firsthand knowledge of how much pain would be involved, that didn't mean she wasn't experienced in the preliminaries.

She'd studied sexual practices and theory, among other things, thoroughly during the last couple of years at both Kuropkat Middle and High School and excelled in kissing, touching, teasing, and heavy petting. She had no intentions of letting Zander get away with the simple penetration and pull out move she'd been told most deflowerers practiced. Oh, no, she'd have it all or she'd have nothing.

After all, how much more could there be to the whole process that she didn't already know?

Chapter One

Kit cringed as a breeze from the castle door swinging open yet again had her nipples pebbling. This was the part of the deflowering ceremony she dreaded the most. To be placed upon a pedestal, naked except for a see-through gown, was not only degrading but disgraceful. But then who was she to argue with tradition? Especially when she herself had made the gown, and her father looked so proud as he greeted their guests while her mother smiled from ear to ear with tears of joy shining in her eyes.

"What the hairy hinny-hole on an over-weight ogress looking for her missing douche bag at the bottom of a pile of drunken trolls do ya make of that, Laycee? Briar and Uthiel's little girl has gone and grown up on us."

Kit smiled at the gnome antics. "Uncle Leeky, Aunt Laycee, I'm so glad you could make it. Where's Lumpy and Lavender?"

Leeky Shortz pointed toward the tables laden with food. "And just where do ya think ya'd find ya cousins? Eating, of course. I swear, that son of mine has a hollow leg ta go along with his hollow head. He can out eat three grown men any day of the week. And don't let him hear ya call him Lumpy anymore. Went and changed his name, he did. Goes by Pierced now. Pierced Shortz. Does kinda have a ring ta it. Now, where's the ale, lass? It was a long step through the portal from The Academy ta Castle Kuropkat, and I'm mighty thirsty."

Kitrina pointed Leeky toward the barrels at the other end of the room. As the couple turned to walk away, a grinning Laycee Shortz had a parting comment for her. "Nice tits ya've grown there, missy. I can remember when mine use ta stick up and poke out like that. Oh, nice dress, too. Have a humpin' good time this evening, dearie."

Kitrina didn't know what to say in response, so she continued to smile and didn't say anything.

Person after person approached and wished her well.

When Uncle Sarco and Aunt Lark made their way to her side, they both looked magnificent in matching purple robes. The wizard and leader of the elves, along with his barbarian wife, tried to engage her in conversation, but Kitrina couldn't think of a single thing to say to them. Finally, they simply patted her hand and walked away. How was she supposed to thank people for showing up to a party meant to celebrate the breaking of her hymen?

The longer she stood on the pedestal, the more nervous she became.

Every time the door opened, Kit was sure it would be Zander who walked through it and was disappointed when it was not. Not that she wasn't grateful for all the people who made the effort to attend, for she was.

She couldn't help but smile when she caught sight of Headmistress Seychelle, followed closely by her ever-present human companion, Ray. Though Kitrina wouldn't be attending The Academy of Magical Arts for three years yet, it was still an honor to have the headmistress come to Castle Kuropkat for such a function as this. It didn't even bother her when Ray began jumping up and down yelling "Ray loves cock" with his orange, knobby, sparkly dildo hanging from his mouth. Not a single person turned or gasped or even acknowledged him. It was so totally expected and simply who Ray was.

The door swung open once again, and Kit's heart pounded as Zander's parents made their grand entrance into the hall. King Adan Hammerstrike was still, without a doubt, a very attractive man. A muscled barbarian warrior from head to toe, he oozed masculinity and sex appeal. And his Queen, Lizbeth, with her striking beauty, toffee-colored hair, regal features, and poised stance, never failed to take Kitrina's breath away. No wonder Zander was more handsome, manlier, nobler, and simply more than any other man ever before him.

She was so riveted on his parents' entrance that she almost missed his.

Kitrina's breath caught in her throat. He stood tall, his rich, dark wheat-colored hair hanging loose about his shoulders. His eyes boring into her soul with their silver-gray intensity. His lips slightly parted in almost a smile. His chin proud and strong, his shoulders unbelievably wide, and his chest wonderfully bare. She throbbed all the way to her toes.

It took exactly seven strides of his incredibly long legs to reach her. She knew how many strides it had taken because she counted them. It was all she could manage, and it kept her rooted in place when every instinct screamed for her to run. She didn't run, though.

She'd asked for this, fought for this, dreamed of this, and would finally have this night.

Too insecure and embarrassed to look him in the eye, she watched the swishing of his blue and green plaid kilt about his knees. When he took her by the hand, though, she had no choice but to look up.

Thunder roared somewhere outside as his molten gray spiritmaster gaze penetrated her soul, melting her limbs as sparks of excitement skittered along her spine. His voice meshed with the thunder, became one with it as his words boomed for all to hear. "I understand we have business to attend to, my lady."

Applause broke out, mixed with hoots and cheers. The sound became a deafening roar.

Kit gulped once, nodded, then stepped off her pedestal and followed as Zander led her from the room.

****

He didn't say a word as they walked from the great room or even as they made their way down the long hall. Not a *"hi, how are you?"* Not a *"how have you been?"* Not even an *"I've always been attracted to you, and I'm looking forward to doing this."* Nothing but silence.

When the door of her chamber clicked closed behind them, shutting them all alone from the rest of the world, Kitrina jumped at the sound of the bolt tumbling into place. She searched for something clever to say. Where was the speech she'd prepared just yesterday? The witty words meant to assure Zander that she was a woman full grown, sophisticated even? Words meant to put them both at ease?

They were gone, completely gone, and her mind totally blank.

Well, perhaps not totally blank. Even though she no longer faced him, she could still hear the depth of his breathing and in her mind still see the ripple of his muscles, the intensity of his gaze, the nearness of his lips. She gulped.

When his hands lifted her hair away and his fingers grazed the skin at the back of her neck, heat infused her from head to toe, and though certainly not cold, she shivered.

"Easy, my lady. Relax, all will be well. You shall see."

The closure of her gown suddenly gave way, and with a whoosh, the gossamer green material pooled about her feet. Kit stepped out of it, took a deep breath to steady herself, then turned to face him. The appreciation for what he saw reflected back to her from his heated gaze and bolstered her shaky nerves as nothing else on Albrath could have. Though his breathing appeared steady, his lips parted and his nostrils slightly flared.

Kitrina reached out and undid the clasp holding his kilt together. There was no mistaking his attraction to her as the plaid fell to the floor. She gulped. Lord God Draka help her, his cock was huge. Bigger than she could've ever imagined. It stood proud, thick, and long. So hard and swollen, the pulsating of the veins running along its sides was clearly visible.

She'd felt various-sized cocks awkwardly rubbing up against her in sexual theory and practices class. Young men learning the arts of seduction just as she had. None of those cocks had ever been like this one, however. This was no boy's cock. This cock belonged to a man, and not any man, but Zander Hammerstrike, a barbarian god of a man. The throbbing between her legs that had begun the moment she'd first laid eyes on him this evening intensified to the point of demanding and almost painful.

"I…I leave myself in your capable hands." Warmth flooded her cheeks. "And…and other pa—parts, my lord." She stuttered and wanted to kick herself.

Zander chuckled. "It's good to see some things haven't changed, Kit. I've missed you."

That made her smile, but what he did next stole her breath.

With a single finger, Zander traced a path along her cheek, across her lips, her chin, and her collarbone, before circling a nipple and tweaking it between his thumb and finger. She gasped as tiny shockwaves of pleasure shot outward in every direction then exploded deep in her belly.

The moment her mouth opened, he captured it. She sighed into his embrace, into his kiss, finally where she knew she'd always been destined to be. How many times had she imagined this very moment, the first time his lips would touch hers?

No amount of imagination could have prepared her for this sensation, however. His lips were hard yet soft, gentle yet demanding. He tasted of power and lust, sunshine and sin. His tongue delved deep into the recesses of her mouth, driving out the last semblance of fear, and she kissed him back with all the passion her heart had been harboring for eighteen years.

The softness of the mattress beneath her back was Kitrina's first indication they were no longer standing, but Zander had laid them down upon her bed. The heat of his glorious weight along the length of her body, her second.

She took a deep breath and held it. His cock was rock-hard and positioned between her thighs at the junction of her most private parts. She scrunched her eyes tightly closed, and inside her mind, though she'd already done so this morning as she did every morning, Kitrina recited her Protection from Disease and Unwanted Pregnancy Spell.

Protect my body, protect my soul. Let not the specter of disease be bold. Protect my body, protect my soul. Let not the spirit of a babe take hold.

Then she waited for the pain, but it didn't come.

Finally, she opened one eye to see Zander grinning down at her. "You didn't really think I was going to lay you down and simply ravish you, did you?"

Kitrina shook her head back and forth, then nodded.

Zander wiggled his hardness playfully against her. "Though very tempting, my lady, that would be...barbaric. An innocent young woman, like yourself, must be properly prepared for such a thing, and we haven't begun...preparations yet. Ravishing is for the experienced, Kit. Ravishing is for...later."

His eyes bespoke a promise Kitrina's heart desperately needed to hear, and she pulled his head down for another kiss. Though grains of sand continued to trickle though the hourglass, for her, time slowed and stopped. His mouth devoured hers, and his hands laid claim to her soul as his fingers touched places no man had ever touched as he did. It was magic, it was mystical, it was like walking through fire and coming out unscathed. Though, after this night, Kitrina knew she'd never, ever be the same.

She touched him then, shyly at first, but with gaining boldness as Zander's muscles quivered beneath her fingertips. She ran her hands along the plains of his back, down past his waist, to finally grasp and hold onto his gloriously made ass, pressing her body against his.

She allowed herself the freedom of a lover, the freedom her mind had only been able to dream about for so long. Her fingers tingled as they swept over and down, up and around each muscle, touching, caressing, memorizing every inch of this man as she went.

He wasn't just lying there himself, though. Oh, no, Zander was quite busy, and Kitrina gloried in his endeavors. His hands and mouth were everywhere at the same time, yet still she craved more. First her mouth, then her neck. He sucked one nipple, then the other, before moving down and concentrating on her bellybutton and teasing her hip and lower, ever lower.

When he spread her legs and licked his way up the inside of her thigh, Kitrina was certain she was about to die. Her toes curled, and her pussy throbbed to a beat matching the pounding of her heart. Her insides contracted. Even the root shafts of the hair on the top of her head tickled, and there was no longer enough air in all of Albrath to feed her hungry lungs.

Then his tongue slowly slid up her folds, delved between them, and captured her clit. He took turns nibbling the hard little nub, then flicking his tongue in and out of her opening. Her juices flowed, and the world spun out of control. Even breathing became overrated.

She wasn't sure she actually heard his words or just felt them as he whispered against her heat. "I shall give you pleasure before the pain, Kit. This I promise."

She wanted to say something clever, really she did. Coherent thought had escaped her, however. Even if it hadn't, she probably couldn't have responded anyway. Her tongue had become too thick for her mouth, her lips too swollen from his kisses, and she was positive every drop of blood in her entire body coursed through her pussy at this very moment and nowhere else.

With the very next stroke of his rough, hot tongue across her tender clit, Kitrina came to the conclusion she wasn't going to survive this encounter. She was all right with that realization. After all, no matter how long she lived or what sexual experiences she might have in the future, nothing could or would ever compare to this.

She giggled, though not sure if it was from the euphoria of his touch or the simple lack of oxygen to her brain. Wouldn't that obituary be interesting to read? *Young woman succumbs while still a virgin. But don't be too sad for her, dear reader, for she died with a smile plastered on her face. One even the mortician couldn't wipe away.* Oh, what a wondrous death it would be.

A moment later, Kitrina really did think she'd died. The world around her splintered into a thousand pieces of light as uncontrollable spasms ricocheted throughout her core. Over and over, the tremors swept through her, like a tempest, leaving her boneless and quaking in their aftermath. The only thing still holding her together at all being Zander's arms.

It took her a few moments to quiet, but when she did, Kitrina realized Zander had slid himself back up her body and the head of his hard, hot cock once more rested at the opening of her still throbbing pussy. She pressed lightly against him, and Zander groaned.

"Easy, Kitrina. I'm big, and we must take this slow. I don't wish to hurt you."

She shook her head as she looked him straight in the eye, all fear and shyness a thing of the past. "I don't want to take it slow. I've been waiting all my life for this, and I want you, all of you, and I want you—no, need you—inside me now."

She arched against him once more. The very tip of his cock inserted itself into her opening. She wiggled with frustration, and it was Zander's undoing. "So be it. Your wish is my command, my lady" With one powerful thrust, he filled her completely.

Kitrina gasped at the fleeting pain but was then overcome with the most amazing sensation she'd ever felt. She wanted to laugh, and she wanted to cry. She wanted to shout, and she wanted to sing. Though she'd always been part of a family, never before had she been half of a perfect whole.

They fit together as if God Draka himself had fashioned them only for each other. Every breath he let out she took in, and every beat of his heart matched her own. His cock pulsed deep within her, and her pussy answered its need. It throbbed about his magnificent cock, sheathing it, cradling it, as the head touched the tip of her womb, promising a future that might someday be theirs.

He pulled back a little, and Kitrina feared Zander was going to do the break-the-hymen-then-pull-out move. She clutched him as tightly as she could and locked her legs firmly about his waist. "No, don't take it away, please. I...I...need."

Zander chuckled, but his voice sounded deep and

breathy as he answered, "If my very life depended upon my walking away from you this moment, my lady, I would rather die a thousand deaths." He laughed once more as he nuzzled her neck. "Remember the ravishing part?"

She nodded.

"Well, now's the time."

He did move then. He pulled out quickly and thrust back in deeply, over and over and over. Each stroke faster and faster, harder and deeper than the one before. The storm once more built in the recesses of her belly. The hot slide of hard barbarian cock along her virginal sheath sent tremors of pleasure to the very depths of her soul.

When the spasms came this time, she expected them, welcomed them, and gloried in them as the feel of Zander's hot cum spewed and sent forth his seed. Upward and outward, it traveled, coating her insides, marking her as his and his alone.

Through her ecstasy, Kitrina shouted. "I love you, Zander Hammerstrike. I always have. Oh, my God Draka, I love you so much, and I will until the day I die."

****

Though the hall was crowded, the face of her very best friend in all of Albrath was easily discernible from the rest. Princess Amelia Zoe Cassidy Hammerstrike, better known as Mia to her friends, was Zander's younger sister. She stood off to the edge of the crowd, looking her beautiful, kind self and nibbling a teacake.

Kitrina wanted to run to her. They lived a portal away from each other but had always attended different schools. It had been almost a year since she'd last laid eyes on Mia, and until this very moment, she hadn't realized how very much she missed her friend. She wanted to grab Mia, haul her off to her room, and give her every juicy detail of the wondrous things that had transpired. Well, possibly not every detail. After all, Zander was Mia's brother.

She couldn't do what she wished, however. Mia wasn't alone.

Her friend was casually chatting with the most beautiful woman Kitrina had ever seen. The tall barbarian stranger, who was probably not much older than she, had long blonde hair the exact shade of gold. Her eyes were as blue as a summer's sky, her lips a perfect peachy lushness, and she had a body with breasts, curves, and ass that could only be described as to die for. Even though Kitrina didn't wish to be rude and interrupt their conversation, she still found herself making her way toward them.

The squeal as Mia ran forward, grabbed her, and hugged her close warmed Kitrina's heart.

"Kit, I've missed you so. Oh, and congratulations on your deflowering…finally. I hope my brother wasn't a total barbarian." The girl giggled.

Mia's smile had Kitrina smiling also. But then Mia had always had that effect on her. "It's so good to see you, and thanks. I've missed you, too."

At the sound of someone clearing their throat, Kitrina turned. The beautiful barbarian female certainly wasn't doing any smiling. As a matter of fact, she looked…perturbed. "Aren't you going to introduce me to the guest of honor, Mia?"

The sound of Mia's gulp should have been a warning, but Kitrina was still flying too high from her experience with Zander to recognize it for what it was. Instead, she was taken completely off guard when her friend next spoke.

Mia's voice cracked and came out as not much more than a squeak. "Kit, this is Lady Asla, the daughter of the very influential Baron Ambrose Fistslammer. They hail from the barbarian city of Halla. It's even farther north than Alaria, if you can believe that, but a little more west...I do believe. She's...Zander's fiancée."

Kitrina must have heard wrong. She shook her head. "Fiancée? Zander's fiancée?" Her breath lodged in her chest, and her ears rang.

The beautiful barbarian lady held out her hand, and Kitrina took it. But it could just as well have been venom that dripped from the woman's mouth instead of words, for all the warmth they held. Lady Asla spoke loud enough for the entire room to hear.

"It's nice to finally meet the little human...friend of the Hammerstrike family. I'm glad my soon-to-be-husband could provide you with the pity fuck you so desperately needed...Kit—rina. Poor dear, your family couldn't afford a real deflowerer, I take it? I hope he did an adequate job. Though Zander is nothing if not thorough, especially in bed. He and I had such a chuckle about your situation. I mean really, eighteen and still a virgin. How wretched, pathetic, sad even."

She knew her face was red, for it burned as if it were on fire. Kitrina quickly glanced around the hall. Not a single person was talking, and everyone was staring...at her...waiting. Her father looked ready to commit murder, and her mother looked ready to cry. Zander, just looked...guilty.

Uncle Leeky finally broke the silence. "What the three-peckered, one-legged, two-toed ogre who's been trying ta buy a piece of tainted tail off a halfling harlot are ya talking about, lass? Of course, she knows it was nothing but a pity fuck. That's the way she planned it. Everybody knows Zander's next in line ta the throne and has *no choice* but ta marry a pure-blood barbarian lass. Even if'n the chit is a nasty piece of work."

Kitrina couldn't take her eyes off of Zander. It all made sense. She'd thought his initial attempt to reject her parents' request to be her deflowerer was just for show. She'd thought he hadn't wanted to appear overly anxious. She could see the truth of it now as he broke eye contact with her and gazed at the floor. What had meant more than the world to her really had been nothing more to him than a pity fuck. She wanted to run, she wanted to die, but Uncle Leeky just kept talking and wouldn't shut up.

"What safer choice could the lass have made? This way, the job's done right and by someone she trusts. And she doesn't have ta worry about sticky old mushy feelings like love and such. Our Kit's a right smart lass, she is."

Ray decided to add his own opinion to the situation as he began jumping up and down and yelling at the top of his lungs "Ray loves cock. Ray loves cock! Ray loves cock" before dropping his orange knobby dildo at her feet.

Kitrina couldn't breathe as she turned away from the room. She needed desperately to escape before she embarrassed herself and her family further. Slowly, she made her way across the great hall, and not a single person attempted to stop her. She didn't make eye contact with anyone, and she didn't say a word, but the moment she reached the hallway leading to her own chamber, she broke into a run.

She didn't miss the sound of footsteps following her or Zander yelling her name, but she didn't stop. She slammed the door to her room firmly behind herself, shutting out the rest of the world, and escaped into the one place she always went when upset or simply needing to be alone. Kitrina morphed into Cat, a black house cat.

A moment later, Zander flung the door open wide, and Cat scooted between his feet. It darted down the hallway, between the open doors, and out into the night air.

She had loved and worshiped him with all the hopes and dreams an eighteen-year-old heart could hold, and when she'd asked the most important thing in all of Albrath of him, he'd done what she'd asked and done it wonderfully. But he didn't love her. He never had, and he never would. She'd made a fool of herself, and she'd done so in front of every single person who knew her and even some who didn't. She'd embarrassed her family, she'd embarrassed herself, and worst of all, she'd embarrassed Zander.

Kitrina made her way to the fountain in the center of the garden. The one with the large bronze warrior who had stood silently for centuries, watching over Castle Kuropkat. She always came here when she needed to think or when she needed to cry.

Tonight, she wept.

Slowly, she morphed back, and the cat once more became the young woman. Perched on the fountain ledge, she hugged her arms about her knees and drew them in close to her body. Her mind screamed, "*Sid!*"

Before she took another breath, the huge black dragon landed silently at her feet. "*You have need of me, my lady?*" His voiced rumbled deep into the recesses of her mind.

Kitrina nodded and climbed onto the back of the majestic creature who'd been her friend and protector from the moment she'd been born. She looped her arms about his neck and laid her tear-streaked cheek against the coolness of his midnight black scales.

"*Take me away from here, Obsidian. Far away. Please.*"

Lightning streaked across an angry, dark, cloud-filled sky, and Kitrina flinched in response. Still, she urged Sid upward and away.

It didn't matter that Zander was obviously upset and was at this very moment unleashing his normally pent-up spiritmaster powers upon the skies. It didn't matter that thunder crashed so close it almost unseated her. And it didn't matter that wind blew violently, whipping her hair across her face and into her eyes, stinging them and blinding her. It certainly didn't matter that rain fell in a deluge, sheets of water soaking her, chilling her to the bone, and further obscuring her vision. No, nothing mattered anymore, and as far as she was concerned, it never would again.

Up into the night sky, Kitrina and her dragon flew.

Chapter Two

Three years. It had been three very long years since the fateful night of Kitrina's deflowering. And three long years since he'd last stepped foot onto the grounds of Castle Kuropkat.

Zander had no idea why on Albrath he'd been summoned here today, but he had, and as duty demanded, he'd come.

Not that this was his first attempt to contact the stubborn female. Hadn't he tried on more occasions than he cared to count to make right the wrong Kitrina thought he'd done her? He'd even run after her that very night, determined to explain. But did he get the chance? Would she even grant him an audience? No, she'd hidden herself away from him, and the stupid cat was all he'd ever found in her place.

He'd even sat there on her bed that night, for more than a turning of the hourglass pleading for her to show herself. The very same bed they'd made such sweet love on a short time before. She refused to come out, and she hadn't made a sound.

All of his attempts after that night had been met with the same scornful silence. Not even bribing his sister, Mia, to plead his case had helped.

In the end, Kit had adamantly refused to see or speak to him. He should probably be glad she'd shut him out of her life. Women, such emotional, unreasonable creatures…the world would be a better place without the lot of them most days.

So why today? There was no doubt in Zander's mind the summons hadn't come from Kitrina. She hated him. So who then, and for what reason? Kitrina's middle sister, Lara, was probably close to fifteen now, but if the Dragonhearts thought for a moment he would perform another deflowering, then, boy, were they in for a surprise. Taking one virginity had been more than enough to last Zander a lifetime. He was pretty sure he wouldn't survive a second.

The huge double doors of the castle stood ajar, and the moment he stepped through them, a servant silently escorted him down a flight of stairs and into a room Zander had never been.

Candles burned in sconces along the wall illuminating the recesses. The only furnishing in the entire area was an oblong table so big it took up the majority of the space. Around it sat at least a dozen chairs with all but two occupied.

At the head of the table was Uthiel Dragonheart, with his wife, Briar, to his left. To his right, stood one empty chair, and next to it were Zander's parents, barbarian King Adan Hammerstrike and Queen Lizbeth. Then Leeky Shortz and his son, Pierced.

Beside Briar, sat Sarco Sunwalker, lord of the elves, and his lady, Lark, who was Zander's father's sister, and therefore his aunt. Next to her were their twenty-three-year-old twin sons, Graydon and Gareth.

From the looks on all of their faces, this was no meeting about deflowering. Something serious had or was about to happen.

Zander's heart skipped a beat, and his breath

caught in his chest. Kitrina? What trouble had the lovely, obstinate woman gotten herself into this time?

There were only two seats left, one beside his parents and the one at the far end of the table, so Zander quickly took the one between his father and Uthiel Dragonheart.

The leader of the Paladins of Albrath and the sworn protector of dragons cleared his throat. "Kitrina has been sent for and should arrive momentarily. Please bear with us. We only have time to go over this once before decisions must be made and strategies discussed."

A moment later, if Zander hadn't been facing the doorway and watching for her, he wouldn't have known Kitrina had even arrived. She didn't make a sound, not even a whisper, as she entered the room and took the last remaining seat.

God Draka, she was so beautiful it hurt his eyes to gaze upon her. Even more beautiful, if that were possible, than when she'd been but eighteen.

Twenty-one now, the woman who'd entered as silently as a ghost held him just as enthralled as she always had. But gone was the long black hair of her teen years, and in its place were short, sexy, spiky tresses. If possible, her lips were even fuller, her eyes even bluer, and the curves displayed beneath the fabric of her tunic and the cut of her leather breeks even more lush.

Though she didn't glance his way, he wanted to reach out and touch her. He wanted to run his fingers through her hair, hold her, kiss her, take her away, and ravish her.

He hadn't realized how much he'd missed the sight

of her, the smell of her, the sound of her breathing. His cock hardened and Zander was glad, very glad, he was sitting down.

****

Kitrina schooled her features. What on Albrath was Zander Hammerstrike, of all people, doing here? But then, why were most of these people here? When she'd been summoned to a *family* meeting, there'd been no mention it would include people not directly related and certainly not Zander Hammerstrike.

She stole a glance at him from beneath her lashes, and her heart pounded. He was still mind-numbingly masculine, and so very, very handsome. She raised her gaze a fraction. There was something about his eyes that was different, though, older perhaps, wiser, sadder?

There was no time to ponder Zander or her reaction to him, however, as the deep rumble of her father's voice flowed throughout the room.

"Leeky, most of us know how *special* you are, but not all, especially not our children. Perhaps the discussion of what we now face should begin with you."

The gnome nodded and made a production of slipping off his lime green, going-ta-meeting-gloves as he held up a single finger.

"Ya see this?" The gnome slowly stripped off an overly large, dirty-looking bandage and revealed the tiniest of cuts. "What the stiff jock-straps and stained panties tossed willy-nilly in the corner at an all-night dwarf dandy convention do ya make of this, lass and laddies? Cut myself yesterday, and it-it-it bled." He held up more fingers. "At least four drops, and it hurt like the dickens. Knew right away I had ta call a

30

meeting."

Kitrina chuckled. "Seriously, Uncle Leeky? You had us summoned because of a paper cut?"

Leeky Shortz looked at her as if she were a simpleton he'd have to speak slowly to. "I bled! I'm not supposed ta bleed. I'm immortal, lass. At least, I was immortal. Pretty sure I'm not anymore, and since I'm no longer immortal, you, our little Kitten, are in danger."

Kitrina schooled her reaction, not allowing her face to give any indication his words had affected her in any way. They had, though. The stone nestled between her breasts warmed to an uncomfortable heat. She was about to casually ask Leeky what he meant by making such a ridiculous statement when her father, Uthiel Dragonheart, intervened.

"Leeky, our children haven't been told about your role in the war. They have no idea why Kitrina might be in danger. Perhaps it would be best if you started at the very beginning."

Leeky sighed. "A little over nine hundred years ago, during the war between the barbarians and the elves, right here at Castle Kuropkat, mind ya, I was one of the four top commanders."

A cough and the distinct sound of Pierced mumbling "Bullshit" into his hand broke Leeky's concentration for a moment. He glared at his son.

"What the too-tight trousers on the ample arse of an overweight, freckle-faced, troll trollop doing her shopping in the market square at midday is wrong with ya, Pierced? You've heard this story before. If I didn't know better, and if ya didn't look so much like me, or at least ya used ta before ya took ta wearing makeup,

I'd think yare mother used tainted sperm ta get herself pregnant with ya. How many times do I have ta tell ya it's not polite ta interrupt a gnome when he's storytelling? Everybody knows gnomes don't normally live over nine hundred years, but this is my story. Let me be telling it in peace."

Kitrina couldn't help but smile as the black-haired, snow-white-skinned, black-lipped, Goth-looking Pierced Shortz slumped in his seat but shut his mouth.

Leeky began again. "I've often been questioned about my ability ta be at that battle so long ago because although gnomes do have a fairly long life span, it isn't that long. I'll tell ya now. It's only because of Sarco's Great Uncle Arizon, God Draka rest his soul...finally, that I'm still here today.

Kitrina glanced at Sarco, lord of the high-elves, leader of Landis, and retired wizard instructor for the Academy of Magical Arts. The tall dark-haired man with crisply pointed ears and a ready smile had always been a part of her life. Though not related by blood, Sarco had been as much of an uncle to her as her mother's five brothers. He was one of her father's best friends in all of Albrath, and his wife Lark was like an aunt and the sister her mother had never had.

Kitrina was so lost in her own memories, she startled as Leeky's voice drew her back into the story.

"That fateful last day of battle, after Arizon made all his declarations concerning the barbarians and elves, humans, dragons, and such, he turned and pointed ta us four commanders, two on each side, and spoke the words I've no doubt still haunt all of us ta this day. I know they do me."

Tears filled the gnome's eyes. "'Ya four, who've

led others ta their graves but have cheated death of its sting, will know no eternal sleep of your own. Until the day every trace of blood has been washed clean from the land and every scar is gone from the landscape. Until the last tear has been shed for a life lost ta soon and every stone upturned has been put back in place, ya will walk this world and find no rest.

"'When this has all come ta pass, then and only then will ya be mortal again. When death does take ya, the sting of it will be as painful as if ya had died a thousand times before and forever will ya reside in the Valley of Torment. Only the one who holds the Stone of Anthion in his heart will escape death's wrath, be forgiven his sins, and walk victoriously through the gates of the gods.'"

He turned toward Kitrina and laid his pudgy little hand upon hers. "No one knows for sure where the Stone of Anthion lies, lass. Your Da gave me a piece of rock he thought was from the wall a few years back. Ta this day, ya aunt Laycee wears it around her neck on a chain. Uthiel thought it was one of those upturned stones Arizon spoke of, ya see? And as long as it didn't get put back inta the castle wall, me and the other three commanders would stay immortal forever. There'd be no need for anyone ta ever search for the Stone of Anthion."

His voice became no more than a whisper, and a single tear escaped his overly large gnome eyes. "But that was before yesterday, lass. All of what Arizon prophesized must have come ta pass, because I stand here before ya today mortal. And if I'm mortal, they're mortal. And if they're mortal, they'll come looking for ya."

Her hand flew to the stone attached to a thin throng of leather resting beneath her tunic. The heat of it comforted her soul as it always had. Slowly, she drew out the gemstone, her hand cradling the opalescent object as if it were more precious than her very life.

Kitrina held it out for all to see. "I still don't understand why. I don't have the Stone of Anthion. I only possess what is rightfully mine, the Dragon Heart Opal."

Leeky nodded. "I know, lass, but there are those who believe the two are one and the same."

Her only response was "Oh," but the rest of the room broke out into a heated discussion.

****

He didn't say a word. After all, what was there to say at this point? The air around Zander became uncomfortably thin, and his heart raced in his chest. If the Dragon Heart Opal and the Stone of Anthion actually were one and the same, not only would the commanders be coming to take it from Kitrina, they would be looking to take her very life, for that would be the only way the stone would ever leave her. That is, until the day she bore a child of her own, if she ever got the chance.

The Dragon Heart Opal. He'd seen it many times over the years. It had hung around Kitrina's neck since she'd been a baby. It had always been a part of who she was. Large and smooth, bluish-white and almost transparent, it was a teardrop-shaped, incredibly beautiful stone.

The story of the gemstone itself was the stuff of lore. The Dragon Heart Opal was rumored to have been a gift from the dragons themselves to the human who had slayed the very last nogard. A token of appreciation, so to speak. Fashioned from the still beating heart of a dying dragon, the stone had bonded to that first leader of the Paladins of Albrath and his firstborn child after him, and so on and so on.

Only three things could separate any part of the stone from its owner. When held in the hand of whomever the stone felt to be the owner's one true mate, it split into two equal parts and attached itself to both people. Then it would once more join back together when the first child of their union was born. The stone then bound itself to the child. And lastly, upon the wearer's death, if there'd been no children to pass it on to, the stone reverted to whoever was next in line until there was no one left to bond to.

Zander shuddered. The thought of killing people, and not just any people but such a wonderful, caring family of people as the Dragonhearts and for nothing more than a pretty rock, was beyond his capacity to understand.

The Dragon Heart Opal didn't even possess any truly magical abilities that he was aware of. It wasn't like it could give its wearer superhuman strength or stealth or even protection from evil.

Granted, it did pulse to the same rhythm as the owner's heart, and it did warm to the heat of the wearer's skin. And it couldn't be stolen or even misplaced. If left more than a matter of a few yards from its owner, the Dragon Heart Opal would simply dematerialize from wherever it lay and reappear where it should be. And now, perhaps the Dragon Heart Opal had acquired a brand new skill. It had just become a death sentence for the very person it meant to honor.

The sound of Kitrina's angry voice brought Zander back to attention.

"No, Father, in this you are wrong. We can't make a stand here. That would be suicide."

She stood and placed both her hands flat on the surface of the table while glaring down its length at the man who sat at the head.

"You can't worry about me. You must concentrate all your energy and that of the Paladins of Albrath on Mother, Lara, and Tawny. And...and on the dragons. It's your sworn duty to protect the dragons, for they will certainly die trying to protect all of you."

Uthiel wasn't having it. "You dare try and tell *me* my duty? You're my daughter. It's *my* duty to protect you. I will not argue this."

Kitrina paced before her seat, and Zander couldn't help but smile at her tenacity. She stopped, folded her arms across her chest, lifted her chin, and scowled. "I can take care of myself. I'm a rogue, taught by none other than yourself and Uncle Leeky. Remember? If nothing else, I know how to track them down and kill them before they can kill me."

Uthiel's face turned an ugly shade of purple. "No daughter of mine is going hunting after dangerous individuals and that's all there is to it. You will stay within the safety of these castle walls and let us men handle the situation. That is an order."

She was almost spitting fire and, for a moment, reminded Zander of the half-grown ball of fur he'd seen when last here.

"If you didn't want my opinion and you expect me to just sit here and do nothing while our family is slaughtered, then why did you summon me to this stupid meeting in the first place?"

Uthiel looked ready to explode, and Zander hurriedly intervened. "I have an idea."

All eyes turned his way.

"I have nothing but respect for you, Uthiel, and will follow whatever dictates you decide, but Kitrina is right about one thing. If she stays here, her presence puts not only herself but all of you in grave danger."

He took a deep breath, allowing himself a moment to arrange his thoughts. "Castle Kuropkat and its lands would be a prime target for attack from as many as three armies. But if I heard from my sister correctly, Kitrina plans to start her first year at The Academy next week, right?"

Uthiel nodded stiffly and Zander continued. "I say, have her go as if nothing unusual has occurred. Though I do suggest we not wait until The Academy is overflowing with people to get her settled in. I propose we leave first thing in the morning. I'll personally keep her at my side, and when that isn't possible, I'll make sure she's with someone we all trust. I give you my oath."

Uthiel shook his head and opened his mouth to speak, but Zander held up a hand.

"Don't you see? It's all about strategy, sir. Those other three commanders won't dare bring an army to bear on The Academy of Magical Arts. No matter how big their forces may be. Also, with Leeky, myself, Graydon, Gareth, and even Pierced there, we can keep her safe. I know we can."

He allowed himself a quick glance at Kitrina before looking at her father once more. "Kit is a rogue, and from what I've heard, a VoT of a good one. Give her a chance. Give us a chance. It would be a shame to once more spill blood where all trace of it is finally gone."

"She's my daughter." Uthiel's voice cracked. "It must be I who protects her."

Zander nodded. "Aye, she is your daughter, my lord, and much like you."

"I'm afraid I have to agree with the youngsters on this one, Uthiel." Sarco added his opinion to the discussion. "I'll help in any way I can, and I'll do whatever you ask, but Zander's plan sounds as if it might just have merit. We all know there's no safer place in all of Albrath than The Academy."

"What the drippy nose of a bare-assed troll trollop with saggy tits and a bad case of hay fever, are ya thinking by being so stubborn, Uthiel?" Leeky interjected. "There's something else ya obviously haven't taken inta consideration either. If Kitrina does come back ta The Academy with us instead of staying here, she can do research. Perhaps she'll be able ta find something we don't already know about the Stone of Anthion or even something new about the other three commanders. Two of them I never even set eyes on. It's doubtful, but she might even discover a peaceful solution ta this mess. Who knows?"

King Adan nodded. "You know me, Uthiel. I'd rather stand up and fight any day instead of waiting and watching from the background, but in this, I too have to agree with my son. Having Kitrina remain here is much too dangerous, not just for her but for your entire family."

The barbarian king turned and glared at Kitrina. "But you, young lady, you will not be going off to track down those commanders. You will stay with Zander at all times, and you will sit back, wait, and allow those bastards to come to you, or I'll personally drag you right back here myself, and I'll bring Zander's head along with me for decoration."

Zander didn't pay attention to his father's rantings. He'd heard the barbarian king's bluster too many times before. But Kitrina was a different story. He thought for a moment she was going to balk at his plan and especially at his father's declaration that she stay at his side. For the woman was glaring right at him, and it wasn't love he saw gleaming in her eyes.

Then Briar spoke and stopped any objections Kitrina might've been about to voice.

"I love both you and your father, but in this situation, I too implore you to do as Zander...Adan, Sarco, and Leeky suggests, Kitrina. Your father can't help but wish to protect you, and I fear he speaks with his heart and not his head." She leaned over and placed a kiss on Uthiel's cheek. "He is a wise man, however, and in the end, will listen to the sound counsel of those he trusts, and he trusts everyone in this room. You truly are your father's daughter, my dear, but you are also mine and you will go to The Academy just as you've planned."

She held up a hand. "I believe in your skills. I've seen what you are capable of, and I know you can handle yourself. I trust in your judgment emphatically. But in this particular situation, I implore your cooperation for one small point." Briar took a deep breath. "Though I realize it isn't what you may have wished for, I must also agree with Zander and his father about where you should reside. After all, one single room would be much easier to defend than a large dormitory and will put fewer people at risk. So, please, stay with Zander."

Kitrina opened her mouth, but Briar shook her head.

"I'm not finished. Sleeping in his room, being under his...protection doesn't mean you have to be under his thumb or even do things his way. You'll do what needs to be done, and you'll make use of your very own unique talents to do it. I know you will. And with the help of your friends, you'll defeat these...these monsters if and when they have the audacity to come for you."

Briarlarn Dragonheart smiled at her daughter, and the love and confidence Kitrina saw in that smile had tears prickling her lashes. She fought them back and refused to let them fall. She was a dragon-riding, stealthily sneaking, lock-picking, dagger-throwing expert. In other words, a rogue just like her Uncle Leeky and a woman full grown to boot. She was no longer a child, and there was no way she'd let these people see her weakness, see her fear. Especially not Zander Hammerstrike. Instead, she swallowed hard and listened to what more her mother had to say.

"Men at times don't easily comprehend the strengths we women possess. They think they must protect us, coddle us even. It is simply in their nature, so we must strive not to hold it against them. But this is your adventure, daughter, your life and your quest, and don't forget that. As for me, I have complete faith in you, my dear."

Lark Sunwalker and Lizbeth Hammerstrike both nodded and smiled.

Briar grinned even wider than either one of them. "Now that all of this...unpleasantness has been settled, for the moment anyway, I've had a meal prepared and little Tawny is anxious to sing for us. Shall we adjoin to the hall?"

Chapter Three

Kitrina watched the courtyard from the battlements just as she'd done every sunrise for as long as she could remember. Below, sixteen-year-old Lara and twelve-year-old Tawny ran headlong out the front gate and down into the valley below.

She sighed. She missed them already.

Lara, the young lioness, her hair all the shades of gold and brown just like the large predatory cat she'd been able to shift into since the tender age of three. With eyes the same forest green as their mother's and an ability to heal animals that already rivaled most full-grown druids, she was kindhearted and wise beyond her tender years. Kitrina's heart ached at the thought someone might hurt such a gentle soul.

And then there was Tawny. Though small for her twelve years, she was the feisty one of the bunch. What she didn't have in stature, she'd more than made up for in talent and spunk.

The earliest of the three to shift, by the time Tawny took her first steps she could morph into a tigress with a coat of bright red stripes matching the locks she'd inherited from Mother. That wasn't the only thing mother and daughter had in common, either. While in her human form, Tawny could already channel heal through her fingertips. A talent Briarlarn Dragonheart herself hadn't mastered until her twenties. And her voice, Tawny had the gift of song.

Kitrina smiled at the sight of the young lioness and the tigress cub frolicking in the dew-covered grass. They were so carefree, so young, so alive.

She loved being a part of this family, even if she had gotten the lesser share of magic, other than her father that was. Though a great paladin, Uthiel Dragonheart had absolutely no magical abilities. The capability to shift had come from his mother.

Jewels Stoutheart's grandfather had been half bahsheer, a race of cat-like people who'd sought sanctuary on Albrath when their planet had been overrun. The *gift,* as Father called it, was known to skip generations, and so, though his mother had been blessed with the skill to shape-shift into a sleek black leopard, he couldn't turn into anything. All three of his daughters could, though.

Not that she herself could shift into anything of consequence.

Kitrina shook her head. Her talent hadn't even manifested itself until she'd been five, and then it had scared her parents to death the first time they'd witnessed it.

That did make her smile. The memory of Uthiel and Briar Dragonheart chasing the tiny black kitten all over the castle and trying to catch her was a good one. Tormenting her parents by hiding in crevices too small for them to get their hands into had been her one guilty pleasure.

But then, what use was there in being able to become a common run-of-the-mill house cat? And what benefit could there ever possibly be when still, even at the ripe old age of twenty-one, there were times she couldn't control when it happened?

As a house cat, she certainly didn't frighten anyone, not even the castle mice, and as a house cat, she couldn't communicate with those around her, and as a house cat, she was vulnerable and didn't have the capacity to protect herself.

After all, what powers did a house cat possess? What was she supposed to do, meow attackers to death? Perhaps purr them into submission?

No, as a house cat, all she was capable of doing was lap milk, jump out and swat at the unsuspecting passerby, hide in small places, and roll in disgustingly smelly things on a regular basis. That thought, as always, didn't bring her much joy.

"I thought I'd find you here."

Kitrina jumped, so lost in thought she hadn't heard her father approach.

"Father?"

The man with hair almost as dark as her own and eyes her exact same shade of stormy blue smiled as he reached out and stroked her cheek. "Still mad at me, Kitten?"

Kitrina shook her head. "You know I can never stay angry with you for long."

Her father chuckled. "Perhaps not with me, but what of young Zander Hammerstrike? You do tend to hold a grudge, daughter. Will you be able to finally get beyond what happened in the past and work with him?"

"I hope so." She sighed.

Her father's hand resting lightly on her shoulder and giving it a gentle squeeze conveyed the warmth and caring his touch always had.

Kitrina held back the tears she'd been fighting

since the moment she awakened this morning. And though she dreaded the topic, she had no doubt he was about to bring up, she knew it needed to be discussed.

"He didn't marry that horrid barbarian lass, you know? Zander broke off their engagement that very night."

Kitrina nodded. "I know. Mia told me."

"He's a good man, Kitrina. Who he weds isn't his choice to make, never has been. He must join himself to a woman whose bloodline is at least mostly barbarian if he wishes to become king someday. It's his destiny. It's what he was born to do."

A single tear did escape then. "He could have told me, himself. He didn't have to let me find out the way I did. I made such a fool of myself, Father. I was nothing more than a joke between them, something to laugh about. And...and you speak of his destiny? You've always told me, we are masters of our own destiny. That's not true for Zander?"

Her father sighed. "Some destinies are harder than others to master, daughter. So, will you be able to reside with him? Trust him? Rely on him? Confide in him as to what you are, what you can become?"

The last question caught her off guard, and Kitrina had to think about it for a moment before she answered. "I will reside in the same dwelling with the arrogant barbarian because I gave you and Mother my word that I would, but I can tell you right now, I won't enjoy it. As far as trust...trust is earned, so we shall see.

"I am a rogue, Father, and it is those instincts I rely on the heaviest. Though I do promise to be not only open to Uncle Leeky's council but to Zander's also. And, of course, I'll take in consideration what Graydon and Gareth have to say. I'd be a fool to discount the opinions of not only a great rogue like Leeky, but also a powerful spiritmaster like Zander and two fire wizards like Graydon and Gareth. Their abilities will most assuredly come in quite handy."

She took a deep breath. "As for my capability to shape-shift into a house cat." She chuckled and shrugged her shoulders. "Someday, I'll tell the whole world perhaps, but not any time soon. A girl deserves to keep one teensy, tiny secret to herself, don't you think?"

****

Her heart filled with excitement, and Kitrina stared, awestruck as The Academy's high spires came into view. She smiled. No matter how many times over the years she'd come here with her parents, she always had this same reaction, as if seeing The Academy of Magical Arts for the very first time.

It truly was breathtaking. Five grand castles situated around a central courtyard and nestled within a beautiful valley. It was the center of higher education for all of Albrath. And what an education one received if one were lucky enough to be accepted into its programs.

The waiting lists were long and the rules strict. Students had to be at least twenty-one, they had to have passed all middle-, high-, and prep-school curriculums with above-excellent marks, including sexual practice and theory, and they had to have scored very high on the entrance exams.

The acceptance or not into The Academy of Magical Arts could make or break marriage contracts, business deals, land conversions, or even in some cases, who would or wouldn't ascend to a kingdom's throne.

And what a beautiful central place it was to get an education. In the backdrop to the north were the mountains of Landis where the high-elfin kingdom lay, and beyond them, the Dak Forest where her mother had spent her childhood. Even further north was the barbarian stronghold of Alaria, Zander's home.

To the west lay the desert, and beyond it, the troll swamplands of Karza. Far to the south and across the Tansian straight, the homelands of both dark-elves and ogres could be found. Between The Academy and the dark-elves were the fertile lands of the halflings. And to the east, the dwarves, and to the very, very far northeast, across the Tansian sea or just a quick step through the portal like the one they'd just made, sat her human home, Castle Kuropkat, the village, and the people she already missed.

She sighed, and Zander's arm tightened about her waist. A rush of heat flowed through her extremities, and Kitrina fought the tingles of awareness shooting outward from where his hand lay casually against her hip.

She hadn't wanted to ride before him upon his steed, she hadn't wanted to be positioned so snugly between his thighs, and she hadn't wanted to feel the heat he gave off seeping into her skin, making her too comfortable, making her think thoughts she shouldn't be thinking.

Kitrina had wanted to ride her dragon, but dragons weren't allowed at The Academy. Dragons frightened people, and in some instances, though not often and never without cause, they ate them.

She chuckled to herself. What an entrance they

could've made with her sitting atop Sid as he circled the sky before swooping in and making his landing in The Academy courtyard.

Large even for a male dragon, Obsidian was more than a little scary to most strangers. His scales were like the stone he'd been named for, black as the night until sunlight hit them. Then they turned as golden as the sun itself. And his wingspan was so wide, from the ground he looked like a demon coming straight from the pits of VoT. Oh, yes, Sid could be scary, but to Kitrina, he was a friend, and she regretted having to leave him behind.

"I felt you tense, my lady. Are you all right? I'm sorry if the ride isn't…to your liking, but rest assured, it will be over soon."

The whisper of air from Zander's breath upon the skin of her neck sent shivers skittering down her spine to land deep in the pit of her belly. She didn't want to react to him, not in word or in deed, but her traitorous body hummed with responsiveness. Her nipples hardened, and her pussy throbbed.

Kitrina took a deep breath. "I'm fine."

What on Albrath was wrong with her today? Hadn't the last three years taught her anything at all? What kind of woman would still long for the touch of a man who'd made a fool of her? Who had laughed at her with another woman? And not just any other woman, but the barbarian fiancée he hadn't even bothered to tell her he had.

But she did. Not only did she long for his touch, but she craved it as if it were a drug and she an addict. Her body still remembered the feel of his hands, his taste, and the glorious sensations his cock had given her when buried deep within her, thrusting, stroking, melding them into one.

Kitrina sighed again and stiffened her spine. She didn't love him anymore, really she didn't, and she wasn't ever going to love him again. But there was no denying the fact that, whether it was the very last kernels of that long lost love or simply a healthy dose of lust plaguing her right this moment, it was still going to be a very long semester if she didn't get herself under control.

****

If he didn't get off this damn horse soon, he was going to embarrass himself. Zander fought his cock's desire to harden like a man fighting for his very life. He tried thinking of naked trolls, ugly ogres, scary gnome sex games, and even his crazy ex-fiancée, Asla, but nothing helped. Kitrina's luscious ass brushed against the length of his partial erection with every step the horse took, and he was in a constant state of miserable ecstasy.

How could one tiny human female undo years of training in self-control, and with no more effort than it took to simply be who she was?

Lightning suddenly flashed across the sky and thunder rumbled in the distance. Clouds rolled in, and Zander was immensely relieved when, moments later, the stables came into view. Knowing in his heart that if this exquisite torture lasted much longer, he would lose his mind, throw Kitrina to the ground, and ravish her right then and there, in the middle of a downpour, like the barbarian he was.

Wouldn't that surprise Graydon, Gareth, Pierced, and Leeky? Zander chuckled. Perhaps not Leeky. He was pretty sure nothing could surprise Leeky Shortz.

Before the horse even stopped, Kitrina flipped her leg over its back and slid stealthily to the ground. He wanted to feel pride for her ability to move so effectively, but all Zander felt was anger. It was obvious she wasn't having the same difficulties he was as far as attraction. Oh, no, the little chit couldn't wait to get as far away from him as she could.

Zander shook his head. It was becoming blatantly obvious, if he wished to get any rest at all tonight, after he got Kitrina settled, he needed to make a visit to his friend, Talon. He needed a dose of the special treatment only the big barbarian could dish out.

Dismounting his horse, he tossed the reins to the stable lad and grabbed their bags. His mood grew fouler with each breath he took.

Zander didn't speak to Graydon, Gareth, Leeky, or Pierced as he stalked toward the wide double doors of the castle where his residence was located. Not an *I'll see you later*, not a *thank you for accompanying us*, not a thing. He didn't look back, and he had only two words to say, and they were meant for Kitrina. "Follow me."

Down a long hallway, they silently walked. Past first one door then another before stopping at the third door on the left. Zander pointed back toward door number two. "That's Graydon and Gareth's room." He then pointed across the hall to the door opposite his own. "That room is saved for two more of my cousins. They'll be here sometime before the beginning of the semester next week." Then he opened the door and ushered her inside.

****

Kitrina's breath caught, and a wave of dizziness

threatened to overtake her. When Zander had said this was his room, what he had really meant to say was this was his single room with a bed, barely big enough to accommodate his huge barbarian body, let alone hers. It was pushed up against the far wall.

The room did contain a fireplace for heat, and a tiny alcove for bathing and bodily functions off to the side. Even that, though, was only partially obscured from sight with a threadbare curtain of linen.

And the not-much-bigger-than-a-dungeon cell did sport a small table and two hardback chairs so a meal could conceivably be shared. It also had a tiny closet, a four-drawer dresser with a mirror hanging over it, one bedside stand, and that was it.

Not one single knick-knack, picture, or ornamentation of any kind. The walls were gray stone, the linens on the bed a gray mystery fabric, and even the shower curtain, though probably once pristine white, was a dull grey. How depressing, and even more importantly, where was she supposed to sleep?

He answered her question before she could ask it. "You take the inside. I can protect you better that way."

Kitrina bristled. "And just who's going to protect me from you? I'm not sleeping there. That wasn't part of the bargain. As a matter of fact, I wouldn't sleep in the same bed as you even if I had the hounds of VoT on my tail."

Zander ginned, but there wasn't anything humorous about it.

"Suite yourself, my lady, but if you thought my horse not comfortable enough for you, you'll find the floor downright miserable." He stomped on it as if to make the point. "Solid granite. And as far as those hounds from the Valley of Torment, well, honey, that's exactly what you do have coming for that sweet little ass of yours."

She had a retort all ready for him but was forced to stifle it when Leeky Shortz stuck his head in the still open doorway.

"What the gooey jam stuck betwixt the hairy toes of a drunk ogre trying ta ballet dance down Main Street at midnight in a pink tutu are ya doing, lass? Ya can put ya things away later. Aunt Laycee will be expecting ya to come and at least say hi ta her and Lavender."

Leeky took her bag and tossed it on the bed. "Anyway, I need ta talk with ya. Already told Zander, Graydon, and Gareth, all I know about the other three commanders, but ya had already gone ta bed last night. Come along ta my place, and I'll fill ya in. I'm pretty sure Zander here can find some way ta keep himself occupied till ya get back."

She didn't get a chance to answer. Zander did it for her. "That's a good idea, Leeky. You babysit her for a while. I do have somewhere else to be."

Then, without so much as a glance, he stomped off.

Along the hallway, she followed the gnome down one set of stairs and then another until they were in the very bowels of The Academy. Kitrina had been to Leeky's and Laycee's home on more than a few occasions with her parents, but today the silence was…creepy. With classes not starting until next week, The Academy was all but deserted.

To take her mind off the hollow echoes of the hallway, she thought about Zander. What did the arrogant barbarian have to be so pissed off about? She hadn't been the one to wrong him, and if he hadn't really wanted to help her, then why had he offered up a plan in the first place? He didn't owe her or her family anything.

Had his offer been just for show? She grudgingly shook her head. No, she had no choice but to admit, Zander, though perhaps a scoundrel of a deflowerer, was an honorable man. He always had been.

But then where had he taken off to in such a hurry? To some other woman probably. And, she'd bet her favorite dagger it was a barbarian woman and not an unsuitable human.

This very moment, he was probably entering her door, kissing her lips, sticking his tongue down her throat, fondling her breasts, and ramming his cock deep in her pussy. And where was Kitrina headed? She was on her way to an evening spent in weird world. For that was the kindest way to describe Leeky's household.

Kitrina fought back the tears she didn't even understand. Why should she care who Zander Hammerstrike fucked with as long as it wasn't her? She did, though, and the realization of that made her want to cry even more.

****

He hit the ground with an umph. Zander glanced up at the barbarian standing above him and raised a hand. "Help me up, Talon. Three or four more pummelings like that last one should just about do the trick."

The other man shook his head and sighed. "'Tis not the answer, my lord, and I'm telling you, it won't work. The only way to exorcise a woman from your head is to take her to your bed."

Slowly, Zander made his way to his feet. He

winced as he tried to take in a deep breath and realized the crack he'd heard on his last fall must have been another rib.

"That, my friend, is exactly what I'm trying to prevent. I promised her father I wouldn't take advantage of the fact she and I would be forced to share a bed. If anything happens between us, it must be initiated by her." He grimaced. "That's not likely to happen, trust me. She could barely stand to sit on the same horse with me for the short trip it took to pass through the portal. She won't be trying to seduce me anytime soon, so the only way I can see to keep my promise is if I'm in too much pain to move. You told me you'd help, so hit me again."

With a thud that reverberated off the walls of the arena, the barbarian who stood a head taller and twenty-five pounds of solid muscle heavier than Zander did just that.

Again, Zander struggled to stand, and this time Talon did help him up. When he was finally erect, Zander pointed to his left side. "I think you've done enough damage to this one. Let's work the other for a while."

Talon shook his head. "You may one day be my king, but you, my friend, are a damn fool."

Zander sighed. "Every muscle, Talon, every single muscle must hurt. If I'm left with even a fingertip that does not pain me, I'll reach out and touch her, stroke her, I know I will. She hates me, and with reason I suppose. I can't chance doing something that will dishonor myself further in her eyes."

The barbarian punched him again, this time in the gut, and Zander dropped to his knees.

"I still don't understand how doing what the lass asked you to do brought dishonor in the first place."

Zander grasped for breath but didn't try to rise. "It's not what I did. It's what I didn't do. I didn't tell her about Asla before I bedded her."

"Oh" was all Talon said before he once more helped Zander to his feet, then promptly knocked him back down again.

****

Kitrina took a deep breath and braced herself for the opening of the door to Leeky Shortz's apartment, knowing from previous experience there was no telling what she might see. But it was a waste of time. Nothing could've prepared her for what was going on inside.

"Mom...Lumpy and Steve are playing Ride-Em-Cowboy in the living room...again."

Sixteen-year-old Lavender Shortz sat on the colorful sofa made from panties her father had stolen over the years from female students. She was rolling her eyes and pointing toward the bizarre couple in the middle of the room.

A totally naked dark-elf was on his hands and knees, his snow-white hair hanging in his eyes, his dark indigo-blue skin shining in the glow of lamplight, and his bare ass up in the air.

Riding on his back—Kitrina gulped—not really riding on his back but rather attached to his ass with his stubby little feet braced against the back of the dark-elf's thighs, was a naked Pierced Shortz.

He had what looked to be a harness of some type around the poor man's neck, and he was...fucking him. His marble-sized balls slapped the elf's ass as Pierced yelled, "Giddy-up! Yee-haw! Buck me off if ya can,

Bronco Steve! Buck me off if ya can!"

Then while never slowing his stroke, he let go with one hand and pointed toward his sister. "How many times do I have ta tell ya? Don't call me Lumpy anymore. I'm Pierced, and I can prove it. I don't tell ya where ta play with your friends so just shut ya hiney hole about mine."

Then he turned his attention to the doorway. "Hi, Da. Hi ya, Kitrina. Meet Steve, my boyfriend." He smacked the dark-elf on the ass. "Steve, this is Kitrina, the human I told ya about."

Steve turned his head, grinned, lifted one hand, and waved.

It was then Laycee stormed into the room with a scowl on her face and hands on her hips. "How many times do I have ta tell ya boys, no Ride-Em-Cowboy in the living room? Take ya fun elsewhere. Ya know very well how hard it is ta get greasy lube stains outta the rug."

She turned toward the door with a wide smile on her face. "Kitrina, Leeky said ya was coming ta visit. Get on in here and make yaself comfortable. I'll have dinner ready in just a bit. We're having chili."

Then Laycee Shortz disappeared back into her kitchen.

Kitrina should have been disgusted by what she'd witnessed, revolted at the very least, but she wasn't.

She sighed. If the sight of gnome sex didn't act as ice-cold water splashed upon her libido, nothing would. And it hadn't either. As a matter of fact, if anything it made it worse. Her pussy virtually hummed.

It had been a very long time, too long since anyone had fucked her. As a matter of fact, not since she'd passed her final sexual practices exams over two years ago, and she couldn't even remember that partner's name or face.

She sighed once again. The dark-elf Steve might be gay, but that didn't mean he hadn't had an impressive cock. The length and width of which reminded her of Zander.

Even as she took a seat in an armchair close to the door, her clit reminded her that no matter what Zander might be doing right now or where he might be at the moment, he wasn't far enough away to dampen the throbbing between her thighs.

She tried to take her mind off the fact her heart was pounding, she was sweating, and her pebbly hard nipples were being taunted by the fabric of her tunic. Looking for something, anything to distract her current train of thought, Kitrina glanced toward Lavender and the other three occupants of the couch.

"I see you guys still have Laycee's blow-up doll, Tug McGroin, and Leeky's, Miss Bunny 2000, but is the plastic sheep a new addition to the family?"

Lavender, with her perky pigtails the same color as her name, giggled. "Yeah, that's cousin Baabette. Uncle Tug and Aunt Bunny adopted her."

Kitrina's only response was "Oh."

"What the purple poppies growing in a circle round a couple of troll transvestites doing the humpity-bumpity and the wiggly-giggle squirt in the moonlight are ya going on about, lass? This isn't the time for small talk. There'll be plenty of time for that later. We need ta be discussing commanders and strategy."

Lavender rolled her eyes again and stood. "Sorry, Kitrina, I can't sit through another of Da's old war tales right now. You're on your own."

Kitrina watched the teen gnome walk away and was suddenly self-conscious. She had done her best to put the Dragon Heart Opal, the Stone of Anthion, and what they meant out of her mind for most of the day, and guilt engulfed her for it. Her family was counting on her. If the three commanders weren't stopped here, it was her sister Lara they would be coming for next.

Leeky's voice drew her from her melancholy. "I know Bugger the ogre personally. We served together on the same side. He's a mean one and sneaky for an ogre. Oh, and he's a master of disguise. He once dressed up as a high-elf call girl, and I almost did him myself before I realized."

He leaned in close and whispered, "No matter what he's wearing, he can't seem ta hide his left hairy big toe. Dead giveaway."

Pierced chose that moment to sprint into the room still bare-assed naked. He grabbed up Baabette, the plastic sheep, and said only one word before turning and running back. "Ménage!"

Kitrina couldn't help but smile.

Leeky Shortz wasn't smiling, though. "Bugger's almost as good with a dagger as I am, but unlike me, he doesn't care who he sticks it in. The one thing ya have on ya side is, the ogre's impatient. He'll be the first ta come after ya. I can promise ya that. Ya just have ta be on the lookout for him."

Kitrina nodded, a lump of dread growing in her gut.

"As far as the dwarf, Wizzit, and the troll, Marquart, I've never seen them face ta face cause we were on opposite sides of the battle. But I do know that dwarf could be standing right beside ya and ya wouldn't suspect him. He's known ta be sweeter than honey, till he stabs ya in the back, that is. So, it's best not ta trust dwarves, any of them. Nasty bunch anyway."

Kitrina nodded.

"And as for the troll. For a female, Marquart is rumored to be so vicious, even the meanest male trolls under her command shudder when she walks by. Slayed over a hundred men barehanded I've been told, and that was on a slow day."

Kitrina was sitting on the edge of her seat. "So, how do we defeat an enemy we can't see coming and don't even recognize?"

Leeky snickered. "What the pink pasties on the nipples of a halfling harlot plying her trade down by the docks of the Tansian Sea do ya think we're going ta do, lass? We're gonna catch 'em, and we're gonna kill 'em, and that will be that."

The door to Pierced's room suddenly swung open and out popped a completely disturbing sight. There stood the dark elf, Steve, with Pierced impaled upon the head of his penis and Pierced with Baabette dangling from his own. Pierced yelled, "Surprise!" Then the trio disappeared back into their room.

Kitrina didn't know why. Perhaps it was the stress of the situation, perhaps it was the fear of what she knew was coming for her, perhaps it was the horror of the sight she'd just witnessed, or perhaps she was simply tired. But she broke out first into a fit of giggles, then a deluge of tears.

Chapter Four

Kitrina hadn't been back in Zander's room more than a quarter turn of the hourglass before the door crashed open and in walked the biggest man she'd ever seen in her life. He wasn't alone, either. He was half dragging, half carrying Zander.

"Unconscious, and with any luck, he'll be that way for a while, lass," was all he said before tossing Zander's limp form onto the bed.

"What happened? Who did this to him?" Kitrina was horrified. Zander's body, what she could see of it anyway—and that was quite a lot considering he wore only a kilt—was covered with red, angry-looking welts. Only his handsome face appeared to be untouched.

The man glanced over his shoulder as if the answer should be obvious. "I did, of course. Do you think just anyone could beat down Zander Hammerstrike?"

A heartbeat later, she had the razor-sharp points of her matching daggers pressed against the flesh of the stranger. One at his throat, and the other up under his balls. "You, then, must die."

Zander cracked open one eyelid. "No, Kit, don't. He only did as I asked."

She slowly took a step back and resheathed her weapons.

The big barbarian held out a hand. "Talon's the name."

She begrudgingly took the hand he offered. "Why? Why would he ask such a thing of you? What possible reason would a man have for willingly taking a beating such as this?"

Talon laughed. "You can't guess? 'Tis the only way the hardheaded man could assure himself he wouldn't touch you. He is a barbarian, lass."

Zander tried to sit but failed. "You weren't supposed to tell her that, you idiot."

Once more Talon chuckled, but Kitrina wasn't laughing. She stared in horror at the man lying on the bed. His once flawless chest was covered in big purple splotches. And his long, strong legs were a mass of knotted muscle, with deep bloody scrapes and scratches.

How he must either hate or desire her, to go to this length to keep his hands off her. If it wasn't hate, and somehow Kitrina knew it wasn't, perhaps her father had been right after all. Perhaps fulfilling his destiny was not an easy task and tormented him as much as it did her. Perhaps, even though he must someday marry a barbarian female, they could suspend time for a little while here and make memories to last them both through the coming years. Perhaps, if she didn't take advantage of this chance, there would never be another.

She turned toward Talon. "Thank you for bringing him home. I'll take it from here."

The big barbarian with dark, shoulder-length brown hair and laughing eyes to match nodded. "I'll be right outside the door. 'Tis another promise he made me swear. He did not wish you unguarded while he could not do the job himself." Talon winked at her. "He's right not to trust just anyone to guard you either. You truly are as beautiful as he said. It's plain to see why he wants you. Any man with blood running through his veins would."

Zander groaned. "Quit flirting, Talon, and get out. You've done enough damage for one night."

The big barbarian laughed. "I'll be right outside, lass." He pointed toward Zander. "After that one's asleep, if you want to see what it can be like with a real barbarian, just come on out and join me."

Zander opened both eyes and glared. "Don't make me get up from here and kill you, because I will."

Talon just chuckled as he backed out the door.

****

She watched him sleep.

Zander's eyes were closed in slumber, his breathing unlabored. After Talon had left them alone, they hadn't talked like Kitrina thought they would.

Instead, she'd simply heated a basin of water over the fire in the fireplace and silently cleansed his wounds. Then she'd made him a pain and sleeping potion from the herbs her mother insisted she always carry. Finally, she lay beside him, wide awake, watching him.

She'd been wrong when she thought his face was the only undamaged place on his body. When she'd removed his kilt to examine the rest of him, she found his cock to be unscathed also. And what a fine cock it was, even soft and resting between his thighs, it hung well past the halfway point to his knees, and even flaccid was still thicker than her wrist.

Her pussy contracted in response. She wanted to touch it, to taste it, to watch it expand and grow beneath her fingertips until it stood proud. She shouldn't, though. Zander needed his rest in order to heal. Didn't he?

With a sigh, she slid from the bed and paced the room. What was she thinking? She couldn't just reach out and touch him, could she? Touching led to other things.

Anyway, she hated him, didn't she? He'd broken her heart and crushed her tender little eighteen-year-old dreams. And after she'd planned them out so perfectly.

He was supposed to deflower her, then realize he couldn't live even one more turn of the hourglass without her. He was supposed to drop to his knees right then and there, declare his undying love, and beg her to be his wife.

She would've eventually accepted, after his third or fourth time of pleading, and they would've lived happily ever after at his castle in Alaria with their two children. One son, Prince Axel, one daughter, Princess Adriana, and of course, her dragon, Sid. But that didn't happen. Oh, no, the scoundrel had already been betrothed to that horrible Asla.

She stood beside the bed and watched him. She wasn't eighteen anymore, and she certainly was no longer a believer in happily-ever-after, and he was no longer betrothed. She now understood why she herself could never be his wife and he never her husband. Would it be so wrong then if they used each other during their forced time together, for pleasure, for comfort?

According to the principals and laws of Albrath, it wouldn't be.

Unless married, any man or woman was free to have sex with whomever they chose. It was considered good, clean fun, healthy activity, encouraged even.

She sighed, and her pussy tormented her. Why not have what she wanted, take it even? After all, Zander didn't look as if he could put up much of a fight.

With a chuckle, she climbed back in bed and snuggled up against the barbarian prince's side. Immediately, her breasts tightened and tingled. She ran her hand down the curves and concavities of her own naked body, stopping to tweak the perky, protruding nipples along the way.

Kitrina had never been one to wear clothing when sleeping. She hadn't liked the confinement and was glad for the lack of them now.

She didn't take her eyes from Zander's face as she slowly teased herself, sliding her hand down farther, parting the folds of her pussy, and allowing a single finger to circle her clit and slide the length of her dampness to probe her opening before once more making her way back up to stroke her hardened nub.

With her other hand, she reached over and lightly petted Zander's cock, glorying in the instant change in diameter, length, and stiffness.

He opened his eyes, and she could see questions in their depths. Questions she wasn't sure she had answers for.

"What are you doing?"

Kitrina shrugged. "Touching you. Touching me."

Zander grinned. "Aye, I can see that, but why?"

Her words came out almost like a purr, but she couldn't help it. "Because I want to."

Zander laughed. "Do you always do what you want, Kit?"

She didn't stop stroking either one of them, but her

voice did take on a more serious tone. "No, if I did, I would've been in your bed every night for the last three years."

He sighed. "I can't allow myself to fall in love with you, Kitrina, and you know why."

She did stop touching herself then and turned toward Zander. She switched hands and used the one she'd had on herself to continue stroking his expanding cock. She leaned up on her free elbow and looked him directly in the eye. "I'm not asking you to fall in love with me, for I certainly am not free to love you. I'm as bound by the Dragon Heart Opal and the choice it will someday make for me, as you are by the rules of the barbarian throne of Alaria. All I'm asking for—no, what I'm about to take from and give back to you is comfort and pleasure. There's no reason we should be tortured, either of us. Since we must share the same bed until this…situation is resolved, we should be free to do whatever we wish within the confines of this room. We can be, umm, fuck-buddies…so to speak. No strings attached, no hearts broken. I'm not a little girl anymore, Zander. I'm a woman." She squeezed his cock for emphasis. "I will have you, and I will have you now."

****

Oh, sweet Lord Draka, she was beautiful.

Zander watched in awe as Kitrina rose above him like a warrior goddess. The flickering light from the candles beside the bed illuminated every glorious inch of her, from the intensity in her eyes to the full lushness of her breasts, even the gentle concavity of her flat belly, the muscles of her thighs, and the smooth pinkness of her shaved pussy.

When she leaned down, pressed her lips to his, and

slipped her tongue deep into the recesses of his mouth, for the first time in his life, Zander forgot to breathe. When he recovered his composure enough to take a breath, he kissed her back with all the pent-up desire he'd held at bay for three long years.

Their tongues warred with first her the victor, then him. After the dropping of a smattering of grains of sand through the hourglass, she sat back up, frustration clear in her eyes. "I need more than kisses this night, Zander."

He chuckled. "The mind is willing, my lady, but I'm not so sure the body can comply. Talon did a thorough job. I can't even move my arms or reach out and touch you with my hands."

She shook her head, but she was grinning. "Oh, no, you don't, barbarian. You aren't getting out of this that easy. There's nothing wrong with your mouth or your cock. They're both in fine working order. Arms and hands are overrated in my opinion. I bet we can do this thing just fine without them."

He tried to nod, but the pain in his neck prevented it, so instead, he simply grinned back at her. "I'm willing if you are."

If he thought her rising before him moments before was a spectacular sight, when Kitrina turned her back to him and straddled his chest with her feet tucked up under his arms, her knees up close to his side, and her mouth mere centimeters above the head of his cock, the sight was mind-blowing.

She dipped her head ever so slightly and oh-so-slowly before licking her way across just the head of his cock.

Zander spasmed in response, and pain shot up the

muscles of his back.

"God, Kitrina, you're gonna kill me."

She had the audacity to giggle. "It'll be a fine death, Zander. I'll even speak well of you at your wake."

Then she took his whole cock in her mouth and down her throat. Zander forgot about pain. He forgot about everything around him as the most exquisite sensation he'd ever experienced rocked him to the core. It was like ripples of fire and quivers of ice, shivers of pleasure and tingles of excitement all rolled into one. She sucked and licked him along his shaft, around the underside of his cock's head, and she even probed the small hole on the top with her tongue, over and over and over again.

And above his head, just out of reach of his own tongue, poised the prettiest pussy he'd ever set eyes on. It was smooth, pink as bubblegum, and just as sweet looking.

He chuckled to himself. She was concentrating so hard on his cock, she'd obviously forgotten about her own pleasure. "Um, Kit, you're torturing me."

She lifted her head a moment, concern in her voice. "Am I really causing you pain? I'm sorry. We can stop...I suppose...if we must."

Zander chuckled out loud this time. "You're fine where you are. I just can't reach your pussy, my lady. Put it where I can get to it...please."

She laughed, wiggled her ass in his face, did what he'd asked, then went back to where she'd left off.

God Draka, her pussy was hot. She tasted of the forbidden, and her juices flowed sweet as honey. So sensual, alluring, scorching, and tangy.

He was like a man long denied and set before a feast. His tongue toyed with her clit and lapped along the length of her folds before delving as deep as it could into the opening of her slick channel as she rode his face.

And what a ride it was. They moved in opposite directions but in complete unison. She rocked forward and sucked the length of his cock all the way to its base as he licked his way up her folds, then she licked her way back up his cock as he latched on and sucked her clit.

Zander forgot about the pain every touch of Kitrina's skin upon his own caused and lost himself in the glory of the woman she had become. Her soft sighs filled his ears and overflowed into his heart. Her fingers about his cock caressed, her mouth upon it devoured, her knees up under his arms and against his side held him steady, and her pussy quenched his thirst like the sweetest of ambrosias.

His ass bunched in response to Kitrina's attention, and Zander was reminded of the beating he'd unnecessarily taken as pain shot up his back and down both legs. He stiffened, and Kitrina stopped and pulled away.

He groaned.

"Am I hurting you overly much?" she asked.

Zander breathed in the womanly musk of what was once more out of reach. "Was just a twinge. God Draka, don't stop now."

Kitrina laughed as she turned, faced him, and once more straddled his chest. Slowly, she slid down his body until his cock rested snug against her ass.

She rocked back and forth against it. "Are you sure

it's all right to go on?" She smiled, and her eyes gleamed with mischief. "I wouldn't want to make a big strong barbarian like you cry. Perhaps you need a break, Zander? Am I too much for you? Have you had all you can handle for the night?"

It took every bit of strength and determination Zander could muster to raise his arms, grasp Kitrina's waist with his hands, lift her, and slide her down the length of his cock until he was completely sheathed within her pussy, but he did it.

He was panting by the time he finished his task, but he didn't care. "You'll never see the day, my lady, when I will have had my fill of you. It's not possible. Now, be quiet and fuck me like a good wench."

She did just that, slowly at first, then picking up speed. Her back ramrod straight, the muscles of her thighs flexing, her head thrown back, her eyes closed, and her succulent lips slightly parted.

The fingers of one hand teased her nipples to tautness while, with her other, she sought her clit. She stroked the hard little nub, grazing his cock with every other downstroke, making him quiver.

Zander gloried in not only the sight before him but also the feel of her hot, slick pussy sliding up and down his throbbing shaft. The muscles of her sheath hugged his big cock tight, massaged it, caressed it, tormented and tantalized it.

Pressure built back behind his balls and low in his gut. His cock pulsed with pleasure, and his heart pounded. His breathing quickened as he bunched the sore muscles of his ass and added his thrusts to hers.

Kitrina's eyes flew open, and Zander locked gazes with her. He wanted to watch her come. He wanted to know it was he who was responsible for giving her release.

He saw the beginning of her orgasm a mere second before it happened. Her nostrils flared, her breath came in quick, short gasps, and her stormy-blue eyes glazed over as the first clenches of her inner walls enveloped his cock.

He redoubled his thrusts, pumping furiously into her, and never took his eyes from her face. He shuddered in ecstasy as hot liquid shot up his shaft. His ass spasmed, and his cock spewed forth its own release, coating her, claiming her as much as she'd just claimed him.

****

Kitrina stretched. The heat of Zander's body snug up against her own filled her with contentment and more than a few naughty thoughts. She could lie here in this bed with him forever and never get up.

She purred.

Last night had been wonderful, magical even. The memory of Zander's slick, hot tongue upon her lips and her clit elicited tingles of excitement that skittered along her spine and landed deep in her belly. And his cock, oh my God Draka...he had fucked her near to oblivion with that magnificent cock of his, and she had given her all to fuck him back in kind.

Kitrina giggled, though the noise she heard resonating from her throat sounded more animalistic than female. She smiled and licked her lips in anticipation.

Perhaps she would wake Zander with a little sunrise surprise. Perhaps she would lean over and take his cock inside her mouth, suck, lick, and kiss it until it stood rigid and proud. Perhaps she would then climb on top of the big barbarian, sheath herself upon him, and give him a proper good morning.

She was about to do just that, when his fingers lightly scratched her belly. It tickled.

"Where'd you come from, and where's your mistress?"

She smiled as she tried to answer his silly question with an equally silly answer, but all that came out was a "Meow."

Kitrina stiffened and glanced at herself. Her black fur was shiny, and she was curled up into a ball. Her paws were lightly kneading Zander's side. Her paws! All four of them!

Again, he petted her, this time his long strong fingers running the length of her cat body. An uncontrollable purr escaped her throat.

"You have the most amazing mistress. You do know that, don't you? And the things that woman can do with her…"

She locked gazes with him, and he chuckled.

"I suppose I shouldn't really be discussing such things with a cat, now should I? Let me up, if I can even stand this morning, and we shall go find her."

Kitrina jumped from the bed as the proud barbarian prince struggled to stand. When he had, he slowly made his way toward the door, still limping and bruised but just as gloriously naked as the day he'd been born.

She paced back and forth between and around his feet, rubbing her cat body against his legs and wrapping her tail around his ankles. How was she going to explain this?

"Don't trip me. I doubt I could get up if I fall."

She backed away.

Being able to shift into another creature was probably something lovers shouldn't hold back from one another. It was a matter of trust. But it was her secret and, at the same time, her worst shame.

Kitrina didn't think she could bear the look of disappointment or disgust in Zander's eyes when he realized her most special talent in all of Albrath was the ability to turn into a plain, ordinary house cat. Especially, since he himself was a powerful spiritmaster who could control the skies with thunder and lighting, rain and wind. And to boot, he was a decorated barbarian warrior and the heir to the throne of Alaria.

What use would he have for her if he found out? What would he think? Would he laugh at her like he had about the deflowering with Asla? Would he consider her a freak?

Their one night together wasn't enough to chance losing him now. She wanted more, needed more…time. No, Kitrina couldn't tell Zander.

She didn't yet know how she would do it, but she knew Zander must never find out. At least, not until the situation with the Dragon Heart Opal was done and their time together over. It was her secret, and she would keep it. Still, she felt a twinge of guilt for the deception.

Zander threw the door open and yelled at his friend. "Talon, where did Kitrina go?"

She couldn't see the barbarian guard from where she stood behind Zander's legs, but she had no problem whatsoever hearing his response.

"What are you talking about, Zander? Did the beating I gave you last eve affect your brain? No one has entered or left this room. Do you think me incompetent?"

What was she going to do?

Hurriedly, she glanced around, desperate for something, anything, to help her cause. She spotted the small bathing alcove and darted behind it. Quickly, she shifted back into her human form.

Holding the paper-thin curtain to her body, she stuck just her head out. "Zander, what are you doing? Close the door, I'm trying to bathe."

He shut the door and turned. "Where were you, and how did you get past me? Don't try to tell me you were in this room when I awoke the dropping of a few grains of sand ago. Only that black cat of yours was. By the way, how did *it* get here?"

She chuckled. "Remind me to make your next healing and sleeping potion not quite so strong, my lord. I've been right here, silly. As far as Cat," she shrugged, "she's here? That's just like Cat. Comes and goes as she pleases. There's no telling when or where you'll see her next."

Zander glanced around the room. "She was right here a moment ago."

Once more, she shrugged. "She probably darted out when you opened the door. Don't worry about Cat, she can take care of herself."

"You call your cat, Cat?"

Kitrina laughed. "Of course. That's what she is."

Chapter Five

Kitrina yawned and stretched the stiff muscles of her neck. Six straight turns of the hourglass in the dusty library, and she hadn't found much to help her cause. As a matter of fact, what she had found would've made even her believe the Dragon Heart Opal and the Stone of Anthion were one and the same if she didn't know better.

There were two books lying open before her, *The History of Human-Dragon Relations*, and *Great Warriors of Albrath*. Both were open to the description of the stones in question, and Kitrina had marked a particular section in each.

To make sure she hadn't been mistaken in what she'd read the first time, she reread the two identical paragraphs again.

"Usually described as a drop of rain suspended in time or the tear of a magical creature, plucked from its cheek and allowed to harden, the stone is forever captured in jewel form.

"Bluish-white in color, but at the same time, almost completely translucent, the gem has ribbons of all the shades of fire dancing within it. It pulsates with a heat of its own, as if almost alive."

In the next paragraph, there was no more than a slight variation in wording. In the book of human-dragon relations it stated *"The Dragon Heart Opal, gifted by a dying dragon, has been passed down from the leaders of the Paladins of Albrath to their heirs.*"

Whereas, in the book of Albrath's great warriors, the next sentence read, "*The Stone of Anthion, gifted by the great warrior Anthion himself to the man who defeated him, has been passed down to heirs.*"

The man who'd bested the barbarian warrior Anthion those many years before had been none other than a human paladin. No wonder, Bugger the ogre, Wizzit the dwarf, and Marquart the troll thought the two stones were one and the same. And it was no wonder all three would soon come looking for her.

Kitrina gazed at her companion and grimaced at the look on his face. Zander couldn't have appeared more uncomfortable if he were sitting in a flower arranging class.

"I'm sorry, Zander. You really didn't need to accompany me. It isn't necessary for you to sit here in pain. I'm a rogue, you know. I can take care of myself. Anyway, it's still a week before classes start." She flung out her arms encompassing the room. "Look around, there's no one here but us."

The stubborn barbarian simply shook his head. "Gave my word. You will never be without protection."

"You could have sent Talon in your place."

Zander scowled. "I would trust Talon with my very life any day of the week. I would even trust him with the safety of my mother…most days. There are even certain circumstances where I would trust him for short periods of time with my sister. But you, after the way he was looking at you last night, I won't soon trust that barbarian at any time where you are concerned."

Kitrina shrugged. "Want to help me with research

then? I'd like to get through at least two or three more books before we call it a day. It'll make the time go by faster."

Zander's reply was short and to the point. "I'd rather be slowly eaten by dragons, my lady, than be forced to read human history."

He leaned his chair against the wall, closed his eyes, and folded his arms across his bare chest.

"Dragons don't eat people. At least not barbarians. They consider them tough and chewy."

A "humph" was Zander's only response.

For a moment, she was tempted to shift into Cat and sneak from the room just to frustrate the arrogant barbarian, but something told her that, although Zander's eyes appeared to be tightly closed, an awareness of every nuance surrounded him.

Her suspicions were confirmed a moment later when he opened one eye and spoke. "Don't do it, Pierced. I'm warning you. If you do, I'll flay you upon the edge of my broadsword like the little peckerhead you are."

Pierced and Steve stepped out from behind a nearby bookshelf, and Kitrina gasped.

"Why'd ya go and do that, Zander? We only wanted ta surprise Kitrina and make her smile. Ya know, take her mind off things."

The barbarian shook his head but didn't say anything else. Kitrina, on the other hand, couldn't help but grin.

There they stood, both totally naked, but Steve was balancing Pierced on the very tip of his dark blue, rock-hard cock like a bizarre version of tight-rope walking. Or spring board diving. She wasn't sure which.

"I'm afraid to ask, but what are you guys doing?"

Pierced chuckled. "What's it look like? Strength training, of course. Ya can never have a cock ta stiff or be able ta stay that way for ta long, if'n ya ask me."

Steve vigorously nodded.

Pierced leaned in a little closer to Kitrina but pointed toward Zander, cupped his hands around his mouth, and whispered, "What happened ta him? He's got bruises on his bruises. Did ya go all rogue on him last night, Kitrina? Not that I'd blame ya, if'n ya did. I like it rough myself once in a while. All's fair in love and sex games, I always say. Ya might wanna take it just a tad easier on the poor little barbarian next time, though. It's hard ta perform if'n ya willy's been whacked ta many times in a row. Trust me, I know."

Kitrina laughed, but Zander answered, "No one whacked my willy, and there weren't any sex games. Go away and let Kitrina finish what she needs to do."

Pierced shook his head. "All those bruises, and ya didn't even get laid? How sad is that?" He reached back and poked Steve in the belly with a finger. The dark elf waved, turned, and they walked away.

Kitrina closed the book before her. Zander really did look like death warmed over, and he hadn't uttered a single word of complaint all day even though there was no doubt his last pain and healing potion had long ago worn off.

She dusted her hands against the soft fabric of her tunic as Zander eyed her. She smiled at the barbarian prince and held out a hand. "I think that's enough research for one day. You look more than ready for another potion. Anyway..." Kitrina yawned. "I didn't get much sleep last night for some odd reason." She grinned. "I do believe I could use a…nap myself."

Zander's eyes twinkled with mischief as he stood and extended a hand toward her. "Another potion would be appreciated, but sleep is for sissies. An afternoon spent *napping* with you beneath the sheets of our bed, however, sounds like a mighty fine idea, my lady."

Our bed. That phrase had such a nice ring to it. Heat wicked up Kitrina's cheeks and cascaded downward to land square between her thighs. She boldly took hold of Zander's hand and led the way.

Yes, a *nap* was certainly in order.

Before they even turned the corner of the hallway leading back to their room, Zander knew there would be no *nap* in his and Kitrina's immediate future. He sighed. No doubt in his mind as to who owned the distinctive voices booming off The Academy walls.

"I'm not taking the inside, you take it. I took the inside last year. It's your turn. Anyway, you fart all night, and they smell just like gouda. It's disgusting."

"You take that back! I do not fart, and if I did, they wouldn't smell like gouda, they'd smell like a fine, aged Limburger. I'm firstborn, remember. I call dibs on bed sides, and I choose the outer."

"You can't use the *I'm firstborn* card with everything we do. That's not fair. Being born a minute before me doesn't give you privilege in absolutely everything. It just makes you the heir. Even Mother says it's not right for you to get first choice all the time."

"She did not!"

"She did, too!"

Zander pinched the bridge of his nose, hoping to

stem the ache his head would soon be filled with. He thought he'd have more time before being forced to deal with them. At least a few more days. That wasn't to be, however. His cousins Ten and Levin had obviously arrived.

He'd thought they wouldn't come until next week or later this week at the very earliest. Silently, he cursed the fact he was part of a very extensive family.

Not that he didn't like his relatives, for he did, even Ten and Levin. There were just so many cousins, and they were always underfoot at the most inopportune times. It was as if his family could sense the worse possible moment to show up, and at that very turn of the hourglass they would be there. Especially these two.

There was no way around it. When this was over and he had his cousins settled in, Zander was going to have Kitrina make his next potion a double shot.

"Is that Ten and Levin I hear? They're the cousins you were saying would be in the room directly across from us? For the entire semester? Why didn't you tell me?"

Zander didn't even glance her way. He simply grimaced and nodded. Kitrina, though, she laughed and tugged Zander forward.

****

How long had it been since Kitrina had last set eyes on Ten and Levin Limburger? It had to be at least eight years if it were a day. As children they'd been closer, but distance and growing responsibilities had prevented many opportunities for their families to visit after a while.

How she had enjoyed Ten and Levin's halfling father Sherman and his stories. She could have listened to him all night. And she'd adored the cooking and ceaseless chatter of their identical twin barbarian mothers, Ally and Audrey, who were sisters to Zander's father King Adan.

Even though they weren't blood relatives to her, it felt like they were, and some of her fondest childhood memories were of sitting around her father's great table, listening to Sherman Bobert Limburger the Ninth tell tales of cheese making and dragon fighting while nibbling on hot, sweet tarts fresh from the ovens.

Then, she, Ten, and Levin would sneak away and play until the wee hours of the morning. It had been a magical time.

Kitrina rounded the corner and stood gaping in awe. Eight years had changed many things, and some not at all.

Sherman Bobert Limburger the Tenth, or Ten to his friends, really wasn't that much different as far as height from the last time she had seen him. He was still just a few inches taller than his father who stood just a hair over five feet. But his width, oh, my God Draka, his incredible chest had grown as broad as any of his barbarian ancestors, and his arms looked near to popping with all the bulging muscles they possessed. His hair was a crown of golden blond ringlets, his eyes a warm chocolate brown, and the handsomeness of his features rivaled even Zander's.

And then there was Levin. Or Sherman Bobert Limburger the Eleventh to be precise. Even though he'd been born one minute after his brother, and from which mother no one precisely remembered, Levin certainly hadn't wasted any time outgrowing Ten.

Levin was just as tall as any other barbarian Kitrina

had ever seen. Seven feet if he was an inch. That's where any resemblance to his mother's people ended, however. He had the same mud brown hair, bulbous nose, and bushy eyebrows as his halfling father.

They were a sight for sore eyes, and Kitrina rushed forward to embrace them both. They wrapped their arms about her and squeezed so hard she could barely breathe. Zander came to her rescue and pried her from his cousins' grasps.

"Awe, why'd you go and do that, Zan? We were just hugging baby girl here hello."

Kitrina smiled up at Levin, but Zander didn't look the least bit happy.

"What are you guys doing here already? I didn't expect you until the end of the week or even the beginning of next."

Ten puffed out his chest. "Your da sent a missive to our da saying Kitrina might be in danger and you were here at The Academy already trying to protect her. He wanted to come himself, but our mothers put a kibosh on that. They told him it's time for the younger generation to step up. So we came as quick as we could. What can we do to help?"

Kitrina's throat tightened. The thought that all these people, who weren't related by blood but were family by heart, would put themselves in danger for her was humbling.

She wanted to speak. She wanted to properly thank them, but she couldn't think of words strong enough to relay how deeply grateful she felt.

Zander, however, didn't seem to be lacking in communication skills at all. He straightened his spine, and his chiseled face became all that was serious.

"You're right. We can use all the men we can get. Kitrina must be guarded at all times. With classes starting next week, we should make a schedule. I, Graydon, Gareth, Leeky, Pierced, my friend Talon, and you two can take turns being at her side. It must be done without calling undue attention, though. We need to keep the element of surprise on our side."

"Surprise?" Ten asked.

Zander nodded. "Yes, surprise. Get settled, and later I'll fill you in on the details."

Ten and Levin slipped into their room and closed the door.

Zander nuzzled her neck. "Now, how about that nap we were talking about before my cousins arrived?"

Kitrina gulped and nodded. She didn't trust herself to speak. She was afraid if she did, she would say something that would drive Zander away, and she wasn't ready to let him go yet.

Guilt filled her, and her heart ached with it. It wasn't as if she didn't understand he could never be hers. That he truly was destined to be the next king of the barbarians and someone else's husband. But until she'd witnessed with her own eyes and heard with her own ears him giving orders to Ten and Levin, like the king he would someday be, the finality of it had never sunk in.

She should put a stop to this attraction between them while her heart was still mostly whole. She should encourage him to seek out other women to lie with. Women more suitable to his station. Barbarian women, strong and tall, dark blonde like himself, beautiful like he was. Women with blood pure enough to claim a prince and hold a throne. And most importantly of all, a woman worthy of producing an acceptable heir. A woman like the horrid Lady Asla.

Not a dull, drab human like herself whose greatest claim to fame was the ability to throw a dagger in a straight line and shift into a stupid alley cat.

A single tear made its way down her cheek, and she quickly swiped the evidence of it away. Even though the hallway wasn't the least bit drafty, she shivered.

Zander mistook the reason behind her sudden chill. "You are cold, my lady. Allow me to escort you into our room and warm you properly." He tilted her chin, and his lips captured hers. Sparks of excitement skittered along her spine and exploded deep in her belly.

Kitrina sighed and smiled against Zander's lips. How could a girl be expected to resist a temptation like that? Later, she would worry about her heart, his kingdom, and the threats they were facing, but for now, the idea of just how warm Zander Hammerstrike could make her was the only thing on her mind.

****

Zander pulled Kitrina into his arms and held her tightly against his heart the moment the door closed. After a long afternoon of strange but pleasant companionship, what had just happened? What had caused that sudden look of pain to fill Kitrina's beautiful eyes a heartbeat before his lips sought the sensitive spot upon her neck he knew drove her wild? Why had she shivered? Why had her kiss tasted of tears?

He wanted to ask her. He wanted to insist she answer. But at the same time, he couldn't. There was much between them better left unsaid, mutually forbidden by their fragile truce to even discuss. Kitrina had been right when she'd told him she was as bound by the demands of the Dragon Heart Opal as he was by the barbarian throne. He needed to leave it alone.

She sighed against the bare skin of his chest, and for a moment, Zander's heart forgot to beat. If all they were destined to have was the here and now, he wasn't going to waste another single grain of sand dropping through the hourglass of the time he had left. He would show her with his touch what he couldn't say out loud, what he could never promise but wished he could. He tilted her chin until she had no choice but look him in the eye, then he kissed her, lightly, teasingly, then drew back.

She gazed up at him, as silent as he. Her lips trembled. Her eyes misted.

"Don't." Zander shook his head. "Don't think about any of our problems right now. There'll be more than enough time to dwell upon them later." He stroked her cheek. He kissed her forehead gently. "Let me love you. Love me back."

Lifting her into his arms, Zander laid Kitrina upon the bed and quickly divested them both of their clothing. His muscles ached and burned from the beating Talon had given him the day before, but he didn't care. The sight of Kitrina opening her arms and spreading her legs in invitation made him forget about all his other aches except one.

His cock throbbed with expectation, heavy and pulsing, stretching, taut. He needed to feel himself sheathed deep inside her sweet pussy more than he required his next breath, and he had to be inside her now. Hoping she was as ready as he, Zander slid between her thighs and, with one powerful thrust, entered her.

Oh, my God Draka, he had surely died and was now receiving his eternal reward. Hot and slick and tight, the walls of Kitrina's pussy were. They hugged him close, they massaged, they stroked, they caressed and cocooned his cock. Over and over, he violently slammed into her body as he tugged on the short spikes of her hair and kissed and bit her lips, her neck, and the hard little nipples of her breasts.

Somewhere in the back of his mind, Zander knew he was close to losing his grip on reality. He needed to slow this down. He needed to back off. He couldn't allow himself to do this. Not this way. He couldn't hurt Kitrina. He wouldn't.

Never before with anyone else had he come so close to what his ancestors had described as the lust fog. A barbarian need so deeply seated it possessed the soul and did away with self-control. Gulping in deep breaths, he forced his strokes to slow, to gentle.

"No." She clawed at his back. "I'm not some frigging flower, damn you." She rammed her pelvis up against his. "You won't break me, Zander. I'm sturdier than I look. Fuck me, barbarian. Fuck me hard. Fuck me like you mean it." She growled and bit him on the chest, her teeth sinking deep. He felt blood trickle down between them.

He did lose control then, but he did it with the full knowledge that she was right there with him. For every powerful thrust he plunged into her, she answered with a forceful momentum of her own. He drove forward and she pushed back. He plundered her pussy, and she pillaged his cock. He lunged and captured her lips, and she parried his kiss into more, so much more.

Their sweat mingled and their bodies slid in a furious rhythm as the panting of their breaths and the slapping of his balls against her ass rang in their ears. She bit down on his shoulder hard as her inner walls suddenly clenched tight around his cock, and the rippling spasms of her pleasure convulsed their way up his length.

That's when he truly lost his mind. That's when everything went black and the head of his cock exploded. With a shout and a grunt, he once more lunged deep, and his hot seed coated her still quivering sheath.

Chapter Six

Kitrina glanced around the arena at her fellow hand-to-hand combat classmates, wishing she were anywhere but where she was. Her very first real class of her very first day of her very first semester at the Academy of Magical Arts, and just who did she have the odious privilege of sharing her class with? None other than the contemptible Lady Asla Fistslammer, Zander's ex-betrothed.

The snooty barbarian female sat directly across the bleachers from her and had been staring daggers in Kitrina's direction while whispering behind her hand to the girl setting next to her since the moment class began. Why hadn't she realized Asla would still be a student here at the Academy and they would undoubtedly come face to face sooner or later? After all, there wasn't that much difference in their ages, only a year or two at the most. But in a hand-to-hand combat class? Who would've guessed?

The beautiful barbarian, with her long golden hair braided down her back and her startling blue eyes glaring, whispered something once more to the student sitting beside her. The troll female glanced up quickly and bestowed a look of pity on Kitrina before quickly turning her gaze away. Asla giggled.

Kitrina cringed as heat surged up her neck and flowed across her cheeks. God Draka, how she hated being so fair complexioned and so frigging female. She wanted to walk across the room, grab Asla up by the collar of her tunic, and shake her. She wanted to yank every strand of her blonde hair from her head and poke her eyes out with a sharp stick. She wanted to punch her in the face and kick her in the shins. She wanted to—

"Miss Dragonheart? Kitrina?" A voice from the front of the room bellowed.

She took a deep breath and glanced at her instructor. Wally didn't look happy. "Yes, umm, Mr. Titwilder?"

It was hard to remember to call him that.

"Do stop glaring at the other students and attempt to at least pretend yout want to be in my class. Anyone who knows yout knows yout skill level is above most of what I'll be teaching this semester. But if yout just attempt to even act like yout are paying attention, yout might surprise youtself and learn something."

Kitrina grimaced and nodded, feeling guiltier for being caught not being attentive than for not clinging onto every word Wally had to say. She glued her gaze upon his face and tried her best to listen.

"Now class, let's discuss the various blocks yout will be…"

Walaford Thaddeus Titwilder, Wally to his friends and family, had been another one of those numerous cousins who hadn't really been a blood relative to Kitrina at all. The son of Aunt Laycee's brother, the great gnome diplomat Thaddeus Titwilder and the illustrious leader of the troll nation, Karla, Wally had been a welcome guest at Castle Kuropkat many summers when they had all been young.

With Wally being basically the same age as Zander

and she and Zander's sister Mia being almost inseparable, they had all four spent more holidays together than Kitrina could count. They rode dragons, vanquished foes, and fulfilled many a quest while their parents did whatever it was that grown-ups do while their children weren't under their feet driving them mad.

Kitrina knew Wally had always enjoyed himself during his time at Castle Kuropkat. While there, he could be himself. Not just the shorter than average half-troll, half-gnome kid who others of his clan teased and laughingly called a trome. He didn't have to be the boy who was forced daily to prove his worth and prowess to a tribe full of big, strong bullies. And he was free to run to his heart's content and dream and explore just like any other child.

But with childhood now a long ago thing of the past and having no choice but to be a grown-up for the rest of his present and future, Walaford Titwilder had buried any time or patience he'd ever had for childish pursuits. He no longer laughed freely or smiled often. It saddened Kitrina to realize her once joyful friend was much too serious for his age.

Not that he seemed to be lacking because of his too-serious nature. Wally was a well-regarded troll warrior and a future leader. A man who had earned the right to one day take his mother's place and rule over most of the troll tribes throughout the vast Karzan desert. He was the youngest troll to have ever graduated a four-year course in less than two years and the youngest man ever of any race to have been given the position and distinction of Professor of Defense at The Academy of Magical Arts. He took his position and his responsibilities seriously, very seriously.

Still, Kitrina missed the old Wally.

"Okay, class. Let's see what yout got." Walaford Titwilder stated.

Students slowly made their way toward the mats scattered about the floor of the arena. Levin tugged on the sleeve of Kitrina's tunic and shook it playfully. "Come on, baby girl. Didn't you hear Wally?" He winked. "You're on mine and Ten's team."

Ten and Levin. Kitrina sighed. They were her sworn bodyguards for this class. Though she loved them dearly, this was a waste of their time. When it came to hand-to-hand combat, she could take care of herself.

Ten suddenly stopped, turned, and made a production of pumping up his biceps and then kissing each of his bulging arm muscles before beckoning her to follow. Kitrina rolled her eyes.

Zander, the stubborn barbarian, had adamantly refused to believe that she could not only take care of herself but could probably take both Ten and Levin down with one hand tied behind her back. Even when she offered to show him her skill, he'd just stood there grinning at her as if she were a simple child and said, "Now Kitrina, we both know they'd let you do whatever you wanted to them. Honey, real men don't hit girls. Not if they can help it, anyway."

She'd wanted to hit him. She'd wanted to smack that condescending look right off his face. She hadn't though. She knew that deep down Zander had her best interest at heart, and she had given her parents her promise that she would cooperate. But that didn't make playing the weak little helpless female any easier to swallow.

For every single class, every single meal, every single trip through every single hallway and even every single moment she slept until the commanders had all been dealt with, no exceptions, she would be followed and watched over. Zander, Talon, Graydon, Gareth, Ten, Levin, Leeky, Pierced, and now even Wally had taken a blood oath to lay down their very lives if necessary to see her protected.

At the rate things were progressing, she'd be lucky to get to take a shower in peace or even go pee without someone being at least within hearing distance. God Draka help her if she developed a bad case of farts.

Kitrina took a deep breath, trying to alleviate the suffocating feeling of her situation and rose. Quickly, she joined Ten and Levin on their mat and faced the opposing team standing before them.

She felt the tug of her first genuine smile of the day as the corners of her lips lifted. Their opponents were none other than Lady Asla, the troll female who had been sitting beside her, and some random male dwarf with a red beard that reached the floor. Perhaps this class wouldn't be so bad after all.

Kitrina positioned herself directly in front of Asla while Levin stood before the female troll, and Ten across from the dwarf.

Kitrina grinned. "Shall we?"

Asla snarled. "Bring it, bitch."

Levin poked Kitrina in the side. "Isn't that the barbarian lass Zan almost married?"

Kitrina nodded without taking her eyes off her opponent. "Yeah, that's her all right."

"Wow." Levin sighed. "She's the prettiest thing

I've ever seen. What's wrong with Zander's brain? I'd have married her in a heartbeat."

Kitrina wasn't sure which of them she wanted to hit first, Levin or Asla.

Ten made the decision for her a moment later when he socked his brother. "Keep your mind on what we're doing here. Don't be letting your cock do your thinking. You know good and well why Zan didn't marry her. The chit's a known troublemaker."

Levin chuckled. "Maybe he just wasn't using the right, umm, incentives to keep her in line. Bet we could make her so tired she wouldn't have the energy left to cause any mischief."

Asla exploded with rage. "Don't flatter yourselves, freaks. I'd never. Not ever. Not for anything. I'm a purebred lady."

Asla swung a fist at Levin, but Kitrina stepped between them and intercepted it. "No one hits my cousins without going through me first." She doubled up her own fist and punched Asla right in the nose. Blood spurted and the beautiful barbarian screamed. She rushed headlong into the much smaller human female.

The fight was on. Fists flew and punches landed, legs tripped, and bodies rolled. The troll female who had been standing back watching jumped on Levin and bit his ear while the dwarf launched himself at Ten.

Levin yelled and yanked the female troll away until she dangled about a foot off the floor in front of him and at arm's length. She kicked him in the balls, and the big half halfling, half barbarian dropped her on her ass as he doubled over in pain.

"That wasn't very sporting of you, troll." Levin

groaned.

Kitrina, Asla, Ten, and the dwarf all stopped fighting midswing and stared.

"The name's May...cee. Not troll." She glared. "I wasn't trying to be sportsmanlike. I detest being...restrained. I meant to make yout release me. And I did."

Levin chuckled even as he clutched his crotch with both hands. "That you did, lass. That you did."

Asla whipped her head around, and the end of her braid slashed viciously across Kitrina's right cheek. Pain sliced through Kitrina's face as she quickly jumped out of the way of Asla's next spin. Though she covered her cheek with her hand, blood flowed through her fingers and down her chin to drip onto her tunic.

Wally grabbed Zander's ex-fiancée by the arm and pulled her even further away. "That's enough, class dismissed."

Grabbing the end of the braid and examining it, he sighed. At the very end of her hair, tied tightly within the ribbon holding her braid together, was a short, thin, curved razor. "What's this," he demanded.

Asla laughed. "You call yourself a professor of defense? It's a barbarian ula shank, of course, you idiot." She shrugged her shoulders and grinned. "All the women in my city wear them and know how to use them. It's...tradition."

Walaford Titwilder unsheathed his dagger and with one quick, clean stroke whacked off her braid, the entire braid. "Hand-to-hand combat means just that, Lady Asla. And as one of my students, yout hands are the only weapons allowed in this class."

Asla turned a strange shade of green and promptly

fainted.

****

If Kitrina had thought she wished to be anywhere but hand-to-hand combat class, that *anywhere* did not include where she was right now.

Leeky Shortz paced back and forth within the small confines of his rogue instructor's office while she and all the men who had taken a vow to protect her stood waiting to hear what the gnome had to say about what had just happened. He yanked off the dark gray gloves he'd just donned to teach his advanced rogue class, stuffed them into his pocket, and fisted his hands at his side. His entire head blanched white before turning a bright red.

"What the red, splotchy grunge growing betwixt the chubby arse cheeks of a buck-nakey ogre temptress on the third day of a five-day ménage with a duo of unsuspecting dwarf dandies were ya thinking, lass?"

Kitrina took a seat on the edge of his desk and grimaced as she held a cloth laced with her own mother's healing herbs to her cheek. "Sorry, Uncle Leeky." She shrugged her shoulders. "I guess I let my guard down for a moment. It won't happen again."

He shook his finger at her and sputtered. "I should hope not. I taught ya better." He held up his hands. "Isn't it bad enough that ya've got assassins on ya arse and ya ain't even taking that seriously enough? But, but, but…ya let a lass cut ya. A lass with no real warrior training ta boot, for God Draka's sake. And…and…she still breathes. Have ya no shame, no honor?" He hung his head.

Kitrina lifted her chin and glared. "I told you it won't happen again."

He turned on Ten and Levin. "And ya two. Ya better find a really good place ta hide ya worthless carcasses if Kitrina gets so much as a hang nail on your watch again. What the slimy slop set before the wedding feast of a troll trollop and a backwards-walking ogre opera singer was ya thinking?" He turned toward Wally. "No offense ta trolls meant, nephew."

Wally didn't say a word. He merely nodded.

Though Leeky was obviously mad as a hornet and poor Ten and Levin were shaking in their boots, she wasn't really concerned with any of them. She chanced a quick glance up at Zander who stood silently by her side and wished she hadn't. If Leeky Shortz could be considered angry, then Zander could only be described as livid. His thick barbarian arms intersected across his chest. His once luscious full lips were a hard straight line. And his silver-gray eyes were the color of overly full rain clouds.

With that thought in mind, Kitrina jumped as thunder rumbled and crashed somewhere in the distance.

"Why the VoT didn't you have your protection spell up?" Zander demanded.

She met his angry gaze. "It was hand-to-hand combat class, Zander. That means you use your hands to best your opponent. Just your hands. Nothing else. No one has need of a personal protection spell in hand-to-hand combat class. It isn't done. It would be considered an insult."

He glared right back. "Well, there was more used today than just hands, wasn't there? From now on, you will have your protection spell up at all times, no exceptions." He paused for a moment and tapped his chin. "I wonder how long it would take my mother to make you a talisman of protection. Perhaps I'll look into that. Until them, I'll keep you at my side…safe."

She shook her head. "Don't be ridiculous. You know as well as I do that in order to draw out those three commanders coming after me so we can eliminate the threat I'm going to have to take risks. I'm a rogue, a good one, Zander. I know what I'm doing."

She looked pleadingly toward Leeky. "Tell him. Tell him how skilled I am, and that he really has nothing to worry about."

Leeky shuffled back and forth and scratched his jaw. "What the stinky pits of a big-nosed ogress braiding her underarm hair in the shade of a palm tree do ya want from me, lass? I'll admit ya're good, even really good, 'cause I taught ya myself. But in this instance, I gotta agree with Zander. It's protection spell up and ya attached ta the hip of the big lad here. We men'll take care of this, lass. Just behave and leave the rest ta us."

She opened her mouth to reply but didn't get the chance to be heard as everyone else in the room talked over her.

"Perhaps we should increase the number of her guards," Graydon said.

Gareth shouted. "I'd do double duty. I don't mind."

Talon growled. "I'll rip the head off any person who dares touch her again. Be it female or not. Even if it's another barbarian like that witch, Asla."

Pierced, in true Pierced fashion, presented a completely different solution. "Maybe she should just drop the classes she could get hurt in and take non-violent ones. You know, like flower arranging and singing. Oh, and dance. Dance is good. Though, I do suppose she could fall." He frowned.

She wanted to scream. She wasn't a child, and she was VoT tired of being treated like one. Jumping off the edge of Leeky's desk, Kitrina headed for the door.

"Just where do you think you're going?" Zander yelled.

She glanced over her shoulder and glared. "To take a shit. Do you mind?"

Apparently not, for no one followed.

****

Kitrina slammed the door to the room she and Zander shared so hard the walls shook with the force of it. She didn't care. The whole prison of an Academy could fall down around her ears into a huge pile of rubble as far as she was concerned, and she wouldn't lift a finger to rebuild it.

Drop any classes she might possibly get hurt in? Keep her protection spell up at all times as if she were a simpleton? Double her guards? Take a frigging flower-arranging class? Never!

She lay upon the bed, threw an arm across her face, and tried to think. What was she going to do? If she wasn't careful and a whole lot smarter than she'd been lately, her protectors were going to get her and probably themselves killed with their kindness. A fact she couldn't even begin to hope to get through their thick skulls. She could see it in their faces, in the arrogance of their eyes. They felt they were doing what was best for her, especially Zander.

But they weren't. Even Leeky who knew her abilities to be exceptional was acting as if she were made of porcelain and as inexperienced as some green first-year rogue student who had never even held a dagger, let alone knew precisely how to poison tip one.

How was she ever going to draw out the three commanders coming after her and deal with them if the men in her life lost their minds every time she got a tiny little scratch? Let alone allow her to do her job when it came time to use herself as bait? With the bloodhound pack mentality they were all exhibiting today, she'd fail. They'd scare away anyone who came within ten feet of her. They'd scare them all the way to Castle Kuropkat, to her parents, and to her little sisters. That couldn't be allowed to happen. Something had to change.

How though? They didn't respect her as an equal. How was she going to get through to them? How would she make them listen?

She was a rogue, for God Draka's sake, and a VoT good one. If she'd been born male like they were, none of this would be happening. Not only would she have had the authority behind her as the heir to the leadership of the Paladins of Albrath, but none of them would've thought twice about offering her up as bait. Yes, if she were a man, it would've been her calling the shots and making the decisions. Instead, no one paid any mind to what a lass said, let alone what one thought.

Then a conversation she'd once overheard between her parents came to mind and Kitrina grimaced. It had been a dreadfully cold afternoon a couple of years back in the dead middle of winter, and they'd all been huddled before the roaring fire in her mother's solar, trying to stay warm.

Her mother and father had been arguing for what seemed like forever about the need to better insulate the castle. Her mother being on the side of modernization, and her father, preferring to keep to the traditional style he'd worked so hard to rebuild.

Her mother had raised her chin and looked her husband straight in the eye. "Perhaps you're right, dear. After all, what's the warmth and comfort of your children compared to the importance of preserving this keep as originally built? The girls can always put on thicker layers of clothing, I suppose. Or even wear blankets around. They won't mind and winter won't last forever. After all, what's a little sniffle and chest congestion as long as you're happy?" Then she'd smiled a gentle smile, went back to the garment she was mending, and never mentioned it again.

Kitrina had been so angry with her mother. She couldn't understand why an adult, any adult, wouldn't just come right out and say what they wanted without dancing around a subject and using female wiles and manipulation to get their way. She herself had always been a blunt person and preferred others to be just as direct with her. It kept life simple. But being blunt obviously wasn't working for her now.

Before spring even had a chance to think about thawing the frozen landscape around the grounds of Castle Kuropkat that year, every seam between every stone forming the entire keep had not only been insulated but tightly sealed. The castle was ridiculously warm.

Kitrina pondered the choices before her. Since being blunt hadn't worked, and she was, after all, female and couldn't change that fact about herself even if she wanted to, would it be so terribly wrong to practice some of those feminine wiles her mother was so good at? Perhaps it would be worth a try. What she'd done up to this point certainly wasn't working.

Rolling to her side, Kitrina yawned and snuggled into the thick fur that covered the bed. Though it had been her father she'd spent most of her time looking up to as she grew into adulthood, perhaps she should've spent more time emulating her mother. Kitrina sighed. She sure wouldn't mind a little advice and some words of wisdom from the woman who had given her life.

****

The door banged open, startling her awake, and Kitrina bolted upright.

"Come out here and face me, you little she-devil." He roared. "You can't hide forever, Kitrina. I will find you." He ran his hand through his hair as his eyes darted around the room. "This isn't funny anymore."

She glared up at Zander and opened her mouth to tell him to stop being an idiot, when all that came out was "Meow." Kitrina gulped and looked down at her cat body. Not now. *Fuck.* How was she going to get out of this one?

He sat heavily on the edge of the bed, picked her up into his arms, and stroked her fur. "So, where's your mistress gotten herself off to this time, Cat?" He pointed to the clothing lying across the bed that she'd been wearing when she'd fallen asleep, then caressed the fur of her neck. "It looks as if she's at least been here and changed."

All Kitrina could manage was to curl closer into his embrace and purr as Zander's long strong fingers ran the length of her spine all the way to the tip of her swishing tail. Her fur crackled with energy beneath his touch, and warmth infused her all the way to her claws.

Lord God Draka, this was wonderful. This was amazing. She didn't want it to stop.

Even as a child, she'd never really been petted. While in cat form, her parents had occasionally patted her on the head, but for the most part, other than chasing after her when she was doing something dangerous or trying to bribe her to come out of a tight hiding place, for the most part, they'd allowed her to frolic and play as any kitten would. As long as she stayed within their sight.

She glanced up at Zander. He looked worried, and she wanted to comfort him. Kitrina did the only thing she could think to do except shift back into human form. She licked his chin. His salty, sensual essence coated her rough tongue, and she rubbed her head against his hand.

He chuckled. "I wish your mistress liked me as much and trusted me even half as much as you do, Cat. I swear she's going to be the death of me yet." He nuzzled the fur around the cat's neck and sighed. "What am I going to do with her? How can I keep her safe if she keeps running away from me?"

Kitrina lifted a paw and stroked Zander's cheek, and he laughed.

"You're bored I take it and want someone to play with, don't you? Perhaps later. Right now, I need to continue my search for your owner." He sat Kitrina back on the bed and picked up the tunic she'd been wearing. She watched fear fill his eyes as his fingers touched the bloodstains left from the cut she'd gotten earlier.

He glanced at her once more and sighed. "Just between us, Cat. I…care for that stubborn woman so much I can't seem to think straight most days. I always have." Zander shook his head and sighed. "My head knows she can never truly be mine. We both have responsibilities we can't avoid. But some days, my stupid heart refuses to accept it. What am I to do?"

Kitrina meowed, and her heart pounded in her chest. He...cared for her? Was that anywhere near to loving her as she did him? And what if it was? What good could it do either of them? He was right. They both had responsibilities that ultimately would keep them worlds apart.

Zander tossed the tunic back on the bed and backed away toward the door. "Oh, and Cat. Let's keep this little discussion between us, okay? God Draka help me if she ever finds out how I really feel. I can hardly get her to be cooperative as it is. I'd sure hate to give the little minx more power over me than she already has."

Again, Kitrina meowed. It was either that or burst into tears. Earlier, she'd almost decided to come clean with Zander. To tell him not only of her feelings but also about her ability to shape-shift. Both were out of the question now. This quest was difficult enough without adding in the distraction of a fledgling love that had nowhere to go or seeing the look of betrayal on Zander's face when he found out just who he'd been confessing his feelings to.

The door had no sooner shut before Kitrina shifted back into human form. She grabbed up the Dragon Heart Opal that had slid mostly beneath her pillow while she'd dozed and slipped the leather thong it was attached to securely over her head. It settled safe and warm between her breasts, nestled itself against the heat of her skin, and thrummed softly to a beat matching her heart.

Thank Draka Zander hadn't seen it. If he had, he would have known for certain Kitrina was near, or he, at the very least, would've thought her to be. Since he wasn't aware of her cat form, there was no way he could know what happened to the stone when she shifted. It was the only time the Dragon Heart Opal felt no particular affinity for her.

Kitrina's legs suddenly wobbled and her knees threatened to buckle as the ramifications of what she'd just realized hit her. She sat on the edge of the bed and gripped its side to steady herself. A thought more terrifying than her own death shuddered through her. What if? What would happen to the stone, to her family, if she somehow became trapped in cat form…again?

It had happened once before, and Kitrina had tried her best to drive it from her memory. Only in her nightmares did she relive it. She'd been fifteen and simply playing as children do. Hiding from her little sisters, teasing them, tormenting them.

It had only been a game.

The space behind the two loose slabs of stone at the back of the pantry had been much too tempting to resist. Kitrina knew if she moved the slabs to the side and shifted into Cat, she could hide there as long as she wanted or until her sisters finally gave up looking for her.

So, that was what she'd done.

She'd been so smart, so clever. She'd even remembered to drag the Dragon Heart Opal and her tunic into the hole with her so no one would see them and guess where she was. At least she thought herself smart. Until a maid came into the pantry to retrieve something, noticed the stones were not quite straight, and fixed them.

Darkness enveloped her to the point Kitrina had been sure she would suffocate from it. She tried to push the slabs back out, her tiny paws becoming sore and torn with the effort. But in kitty-cat form, she wasn't strong enough. She tried to shift back into a human over and over, but the small space prevented it. She meowed until her throat ached, and she scratched until she was beyond exhausted, but still no one came.

Just when she was about to give up hope, the panty door opened and someone tossed in a bag of potatoes. They hit the back wall, knocking one of the slabs askew, and Kitrina squeezed through the small opening. She took deep gulps of air into her feline lungs before her legs took control of her brain. She ran as if demons from within the Valley of Torment were hot on her tail. Through the pantry door and across the stone tiles of the castle, she skittered. Out into the open bailey and over the meadow, she sprinted. Down into the valley and up onto an outcropping facing the mountains, she scampered. Only then did she slow, only then did she stop, only then did the panic begin to subside.

She sat there, staring out until the sun dipped low in the sky. She simply breathed in and breathed out, over and over until her small, black fur covered legs no longer trembled and her heart no longer raced. Then, she headed for home.

It was only after she'd returned to the castle and entered her own chamber that it hit her. The moment she shifted back into human form, the Dragon Heart Opal materialized about her neck. But the stone hadn't sought her out at all while she'd been a cat, no matter how far away from it she had run.

So, what would happen if one of the commanders discovered her secret? If they somehow got their hands on the Dragon Heart Opal while she was in cat form, could they then possess it without it dematerializing and attaching itself to the next in line? Of course they could, as long as they prevented her from becoming human again. After all, she wouldn't be dead, just trapped.

Kitrina shuddered. Since the day of the game when she'd become trapped, she now had a desperate fear of small, closed, tight places. Even the thought of being locked away for a short period of time and not being able to get out had her heart pounding. What would it be like to be imprisoned for the rest of her life?

What if the Dragon Heart Opal and the Stone of Anthion really were one and the same? They certainly could be.

Though surrendering herself to the enemy would take every ounce of courage she could muster, it would be a reasonable solution to the dilemma if somehow they failed to stop the coming threat.

But then, did she truly have that much courage? Could she actually go through with it if presented with no other choice? Would she be strong enough to sacrifice herself to a lifetime locked in a cage if it was the only option left to safeguard her family?

Kitrina stiffened her spine. Of course, she could, and if it came to that, she would. Her family meant everything to her, and there was nothing on Albrath she wouldn't do to protect them.

Still, she couldn't prevent the tears from coursing down her cheeks. She had never told her parents the stone didn't follow her when she was in cat form. She'd always been afraid they would forbid her to shift if they knew.

The tears fell harder with the knowledge that her family probably would never know what really happened to her if she did have to give in to the demands of the commanders the only way she could. And though she had no doubt they would search for the rest of their lives for her, it wouldn't be a stray cat locked in a cold dark cage they would be looking for.

And Zander, would he search? He'd at least want to and probably would for a while. She was certain of that. But when he didn't find her, when the years went by, would he simply go back to his castle in Alaria and take a barbarian bride. Of course, he would.

And that is just as she was when, a moment later, the door once more opened and Zander found her.

Buck ass naked, except for the Dragon Heart Opal around her neck.

Sprawled in the middle of his bed, on top of the fur covering.

Crying.

Chapter Seven

Zander shut the door, quickly crossed the floor, and wrapped Kitrina within the safe confines of his arms.

She sniffled.

He stroked her hair and kissed the top of her head. "It can't be as bad as all that, my lady." He whispered against her cheek. "Where were you? I've looked everywhere, Kitrina. I was worried."

She stiffened, and Zander took a deep breath before tilting her chin upwards and forcing her to look at him. Tear-misted eyes stared back at him, and they held such desolation the sight broke his heart. "Talk to me, Kitrina, please."

She shook her head. "I don't want to talk about it right now. I can't." She laid her fingers against his lips. "Make love to me, Zander. Fuck me so hard I'll forget all about obligations and stones and dreams that can never come true. Just for a little while. Then we'll talk."

He sighed as his lips captured hers. How could he deny her anything? He knew he couldn't. As efficiently as possible, Zander divested himself of his tunic, breeks, and boots. His cock was already throbbing, wanting, ready. He fought the demands of his own body and tamped down his desires. This time was for Kitrina, and before he was through, there would be no doubt in her mind that, even though he could never make her his wife, she was and had always been his queen. This day, she would know she'd been worshiped.

He kissed her forehead, her eyes, and then her nose, her chin, and then her ears. He captured her lips, then nuzzled her neck. Over and over, he made love to her face, her neck, her shoulders.

His lips and tongue teased her compliant mouth, then kissed and darted into her ears before his teeth nipped the point on her neck where her pounding pulse was visible. She shuddered beneath him, and he smiled. God Draka, she was beautiful.

His hand cupped her right breast as his lips tormented her raspberry-red nipple into pebbly hardness. She bucked against him and squirmed. He licked and nipped the other nipple even harder and sucked it until his balls tightened uncomfortably and his cock expanded more than he thought possible against her undulations.

Her legs wrapped around his, and her pussylips stroked the length of his cock, seeking. Still, he forced himself to go slow. He fondled her hip and grabbed her ass, squeezing, kneading, massaging.

"For the love of God Draka, Zander. Quit torturing me, and put that VoT thing where it belongs," Kitrina growled.

Zander chuckled. "You wish is my command, my lady." He flipped her over until her face rested against the pillow. Her elbows at her side, her knees firmly against the mattress, ass straight up in the air. And what a sweet ass it was.

Smiling, he positioned himself behind her and kissed the curvy cheeks of her ass, then gave a quick nip to both before parting the folds of her moist pussy and thrusting his cock to the hilt.

He pounded into her mercilessly, and she answered with forceful lunges of her own. Time lost all meaning, and nothing else in all Albrath mattered as they fucked, hard. Him giving all he had to give and her receiving the gift of what his body offered.

The door flew open and Talon walked in...almost. He gaped in the doorway for a moment before clearing his throat. "Umm...I see you found her." He pointed over his shoulder. "I'll just go tell the guys we can stop searching now." Then he backed out, shutting the door as he went.

Kitrina chuckled. "I think we may have traumatized your friend."

Zander resumed his stroke, but slower this time, more methodical. "I doubt it. Not much surprises Talon. But if we did, he'll get over it." Leaning down, he licked a path up her spine and between her shoulder blades.

She shuddered.

He feathered kisses along the path he'd just licked, then nipped her, hard.

She gasped and wiggled her ass. "Quit playing around and get back to the real fucking, barbarian. You know what I want, what I need."

Zander slammed his cock just once, hard and deep into Kitrina's pussy before leaning forward and whispering into her ear. "As always, my lady, your wish is my command."

He gripped her hips tightly and gave freedom to his lust. Faster and faster, he ground his cock into the hot, wet sheath of her pussy. His balls smacked her sweet ass as her inner walls caressed, massaged, and squeezed tight his shaft.

Pressure built up behind his sac and deep in his belly. Only moments at most remained before the ecstasy would drive him over the edge and into oblivion.

He quickly slipped his fingers between the lips of her pussy, finding her clit. Rolling the hard nub between his thumb and forefinger, he flicked, rubbed, and stroked.

No more than the dropping of a single grain of sand before his semen shot forth and coated her insides, he felt Kitrina convulse around his cock and quiver in his arms.

Just as his cock produced its last spasm of ecstasy, Zander pulled from her pussy. He lay beside her and tugged her protectively into his arms. Her head lay on his chest, close to his heart, her legs entwined with his. He stroked her back and kissed the top of her head.

Taking in a huge gulp of air, he let it out slowly. "Well, my lady, you have now been soundly and thoroughly fucked, so it's time to talk." He glanced at the hourglass. "It's almost time for the midday meal, and I doubt you bothered to break your fast this morning before hand-to-hand combat class, so out with it. You can't afford to miss another meal."

Kitrina leaned up on an elbow until she looked him in the eye. "What would you like to know?"

He sighed. "You know precisely what I'm asking. Why did you run away and where did you go?"

She lay back down and snuggled against him. Her breath puffing softly against his chest sent spirals of pleasure shooting straight to his cock. *Oh no, no, no, not this time, you little minx.*

He cupped her chin and tilted it upward until not

only could he look her in the eye, but she couldn't look away. "Kitrina?"

She took a deep breath. "I had to get out of that room. I felt like I was suffocating. I came here, changed my tunic, and…umm…walked the halls for probably a quarter turn of the hourglass, then came back. I was just getting ready to take a quick nap before midday when you…found me."

She'd looked just slightly downward both times when she'd hesitated, and then again when she'd said the word found. Zander's spiritmaster sensibilities awakened, and he wondered what she wasn't being completely honest about. But he decided not to pursue that line of questioning…just yet. After all, she was female. They were known to be prone to keeping secrets. Instead, he schooled his thoughts on how better to explain her need to stay close to her guardians.

"You mustn't run away again, Kit. Give me your word you won't."

She closed her eyes and shook her head. "I can't do that. I don't want to make a promise I might have to break." She opened them once more, and Zander's heart skidded to a stop at the pain he saw in their depths.

"Why, Kitrina? What would tempt you to break a promise to me?"

She swallowed hard, but her gaze didn't waver. "There is nothing I wouldn't do to safeguard my family, or you, or my friends, Zander. Nothing. I'm no longer the same naive little lass you knew three years ago. I'm a grown woman, a rogue, and a good one. I know how the world works. I will lie, I will cheat, and I will kill without hesitation to see those I care about kept safe. And I will lay down my life if need be."

He started to speak, but she held two fingers to his lips. Zander waited.

"I know all of you want only to protect me and my family, but you are going about it the wrong way."

Though he wanted to shake his head and demand she listen to reason, he didn't. Instead, he captured the hand she held at his mouth within one of his and kissed her fingers. "Then, my lady, tell me what you see as the right way to do what must be done."

She chewed her bottom lip a moment, and looked so vulnerable he had an almost undeniable urge to kiss her. He didn't, though. This discussion was too important to allow his lust to interrupt.

"Correct me if I'm wrong," she said, "but we have three ex-commanders coming to The Academy with the sole intention of taking the Dragon Heart Opal from me any way they can, right?"

He nodded.

"And since surprise is our only true advantage, how are we to keep them from realizing we know their intentions if I'm constantly followed and guarded, pulled out of class every time I get a little bump, bruise, or scrape? Trust me, they will know."

Zander kissed the tip of her nose, stalling. He didn't want to admit she was right, but she was. "Okay, my lady, I see your point. Perhaps we have been slightly...hyper-vigilant. So, what would you suggest? Within reason, that is."

She rolled her eyes. "I am nothing if not reasonable. All I ask is back off just a little bit. Have the men stay on guard but not right on my ass. I'm the only one who can draw those commanders out. You have to give me the breathing room and trust in my abilities to do what only I can do."

His heart hammered in his chest at the thought of putting her in danger, and he hugged her close, inhaling the musky fragrance of the love they had just made that clung to her skin. "The thought of you hurt scares me more than you can ever know. But you're right." He pulled back enough to look her in the eye. "I'll make a deal with you. If you agree not to run away from me ever again, I'll relinquish the leadership of this quest into your capable hands and follow you. I'll make sure everyone else does also. Do we have an understanding, my lady liege-lord Dragonheart?"

If he had known that offering to let her call the shots while he did the grunt work would make her eyes glow brighter than the sun, he would've insisted on it from the very beginning.

She smiled brightly and hugged him tight. "You've got a deal, my first-in-command Sir Hammerstrike. You won't be disappointed in me, Zander, you'll see."

He chuckled and squeezed her back. "Oh, and Kit? No more secrets between us either, okay? If this campaign has any hope of succeeding, we must be completely open, and trust each other emphatically."

He not only heard her gulp but felt it against his chest. "Of course, no problem. No secrets here. Just openness and trust."

But her answer didn't ring quite true to his ears or his spiritmaster senses.

Zander closed his eyes and concentrated on calming the pounding of his heart deep in his chest. What the VoT had he just agreed to?

****

Though the hallway was crowded due to the fact it

was now midday and between classes, Kitrina was acutely aware of every face, every body, every sound, anywhere near her and Zander. Her eyes searched for anything out of place, and her ears sought any unusual nuance of sound. She found none. Still, her fingers lightly gripped the steel handle of the dagger resting beneath the edge of her right sleeve, and the coolness of its razor-sharp blade against her wrist comforted her. A good rogue was always prepared, a careless one soon dead.

Slowly, they made their way through the crowd and toward the cafeteria. Her stomach grumbled, and she hoped Zander hadn't heard it. No such luck, though. He smiled down at her and gave her an *I told you so look* before chuckling. She swatted at him playfully, and he laughed out loud.

It was no wonder she was hungry. She hadn't eaten a thing since last evening's meal. And considering the exercise session she'd gotten this morning with Zander, it was no surprise she found herself ravenous.

"Don't do it," Zander calmly stated.

Out of the corner of her eye, Kitrina saw the gnome and dark elf no more than a heartbeat before they jumped out directly in Zander's and her path.

"Surprise," Pierced yelled, and Steve grinned.

She sighed and shook her head. She had to be more attentive, or she was going to be dead. That fact didn't sit well with her, and she glared at the gnome and his boyfriend.

Pierced was dressed in an all-black ninja costume. Except some of the material had been cut away in the back and his pasty white ass cheeks stuck out of the holes. He balanced precariously on the naked, except for a pink cape, dark elf's jutting cock, and he held a blade almost bigger than himself in his hands. He swished it back and forth menacingly. "On guard," he shouted.

Zander growled. "Not now, Lumpy."

The gnome lifted his chin. "Those are fighting words, barbarian. I'm Pierced, and I can prove it."

Zander simply shook his head.

Kitrina closed her eyes and counted to ten, not wanting to hurt Pierced's feelings, but at the same time, not wanting to stand in the middle of the hallway and chat with him either. She was hungry. She still had two classes to attend after midday meal. She didn't need this right now.

The gay-Goth gnome suddenly giggled. "Ah, come on, Zander. Lighten up. Have some fun. Smile once in a while. Ya take life much ta serious."

A flash of something metallic in her peripheral vision caught Kitrina's attention, and she turned toward it at the same time Zander did. There stood Ray, not five feet away. In his hand, he held his usual orange, knobby dildo, but there was something different about it and about him.

"Ray loves cock," he said.

Her spine tensed. Ray's voice sounded gravelly, as if he were suffering from a cold. And something wasn't quite right about his eyes. They weren't as dull as they normally were. As a matter of fact, they shone with more intelligence than she had ever seen before. Her gaze traveled down his length, all the way to his feet, and every nerve ending in her body roared to life.

With a flick of her wrist, she buried the blade of her dagger straight into his heart a mere second before

Zander completely removed his head with one swipe of his broadsword. Blood poured onto the hall as Ray's body slumped. His tongue lolled out of his gaping mouth, and his lifeless head rolled across the floor.

Pierced jumped off Steve's cock. "Oh, my God Draka, you've killed Ray."

A high-elf female and her two dwarf companions screamed, a troll debutant fainted, and Steve stopped grinning.

Kitrina shook her head and was about to respond, but she didn't get the chance.

"What the sticky snot balls stuck deep in the pockets of an over-indulged ogre panty sniffer getting high on the crotch rot of a troll transvestite's week-old thong are ya talking about, son? They didn't kill Ray."

Leeky walked over and kicked the headless body over until it lay on its back. The body began changing, morphing right before their eyes. He pointed to the still very hairy left big toe. "Yep, that's Bugger the ogre, all right. And if ya check that dildo he was carrying, I'd bet my favorite nut sack ya'd find a pair of knives hidden in it. That was his way." He winked at Kitrina. "Nice job. One down, lass. Two ta go."

She cringed and couldn't stop shaking.

The warmth of Zander's arms wrapping around her helped alleviate some of the cold that had seeped into her soul the moment the dagger left her hand. She'd never killed a real live person, not even someone who'd left her no choice. She didn't like the feeling.

Zander leaned in close and whispered, "The first time is always the hardest, my lady. But, God Draka willing, you'll never have to take a life so often that it gets easier."

She shivered, and her stomach rolled, any thought of food or enjoying a pleasant midday meal with Zander a thing of the long forgotten past.

****

"The lacing of cerebral toxins on the tips of arrows or daggers can be especially useful in…"

Kitrina tried her best to concentrate on the lecture that Professor Daymeon Nightstrider, her dark elf poisons instructor, was giving. It wasn't much use, however. His indigo-blue skin and shoulder-length snow-white hair still became nothing more than a blur before her eyes.

She shuddered in her seat.

She'd killed a man.

It didn't matter that she'd almost convinced herself it had been a case of simple self-preservation or even that she was duty bound to protect herself and her family from harm. She'd taken a life. She'd killed a living, breathing person who, a moment before she'd released her dagger, had been going about his business of thinking and hoping and dreaming like everyone else on Albrath. It didn't even matter that his business had included doing her bodily harm. All that had really mattered to her was that Zander could have been harmed trying to protect her. God Draka help her, she really was still in love with the barbarian. And not simply in love with him but deeply in love to the point she hadn't given a second thought to taking another's life to protect his.

Not that the thought of killing was new to her, for it wasn't. On many occasions, she'd joined not only her father but also both of her grandfathers on hunting excursions. She'd even brought down more than her share of Alarian water buffalo, Kuropkat elk, and even Dak Forrest pheasant with both arrow and dagger. And she'd done it with a sense of pride and accomplishment.

But never before had she taken the life of another person. To kill a two-armed, two-legged child of God Draka with a soul was completely different than hunting animals for food.

No matter if it was justified, it felt wrong.

Her stomach turned and bile rose in her throat. Tears stung the backs of her eyes, and Kitrina wanted her...mom. The thought startled her. She'd never really been a momma's girl. She'd always preferred the more blatantly honest, non-syrupy masculine company of her father.

But right this moment, she'd give almost anything on Albrath for the feel of her mother's comforting arms about her shoulders and to hear that gentle voice telling her all would be well even if it wasn't the truth. And she longed for the touch of her mother stroking her hair, rocking her back and forth slowly, kissing her brow, and healing her soul as only her mother could.

"Hemotoxins on the other hand must be used very sparingly as they are known to..."

She sighed, wishing this class and the next were already over and done with so she could return to the small room she shared with Zander.

And do what...hide away?

That thought more than any disturbed her.

Kitrina wasn't a coward, had never been. Or was she? If not, then why did she want more than anything to slink quietly away, unnoticed? Why did she wish the leadership of the quest to protect the Dragonheart Opal rested back upon Zander's shoulders instead of her own? And when had she become such a whiny little sissy lala? For that's exactly what Pierced and his ever-present sidekick, Steve, would call her if they could see her face right now. They couldn't, though. They were sitting directly behind her, assigned guard dogs for this class.

The thought angered her, and she drove back the threat of tears, stiffened her spine, and sat up ramrod straight. She very well may have killed a man today, but it wasn't without good reason. And, God Draka willing, she'd never have to repeat that particular action again. But deep in the recesses of her heart, Kitrina knew she would kill again, without a second thought if left with no other choice.

She wasn't a coward, she wasn't a sissy lala, and she didn't need constant guardians shadowing her every move. She was the daughter of Sir Uthiel Dragonheart, for God Draka's sake, the leader of the Paladins of Albrath, and she was a damn fine rogue in her own right. It was high time she started acting like it.

The last grains of sand filtered through the hourglass, and poisons class ended. Kitrina rose from her seat, squared her shoulders, and headed for the last session of the day, elemental wizardry.

****

Kitrina pushed yet another student, this time a halfling, out of the path of a flying ball of fire. Graydon and Gareth Sunwalker could both go straight to the Valley of Torment as far as she was concerned.

Weeding out the weak...really? A class tradition from the past when their father, Sarco Sunwalker, Lord of the Elves, had been the wizard instructor here? Whatever.

What her two dark-haired, pointy-eared, mostly high-elf, identical pseudo cousins were really trying to do was decrease the number of students they'd have to contend with in their class. But instead of just coming out and saying there were way too many wanna-be wizards interested in learning how to control and use the magic of fire, they'd devised this totally unfair little exercise and had called it weeding out the weak.

In reality, though, what the co-instructors of elemental wizardry were doing was unfairly matching their skills against the poor unsuspecting throng of students and…and…enjoying it way more than they should.

The twins both took turns throwing low-level fireballs at random intervals. Any student unfortunate enough to receive a direct hit was then immediately tossed out of the class.

She wanted to throttle them.

They were supposed to be aiming at all of the students. They weren't, though. They were cheating, and it was obvious to anyone with eyes and the time to spare a look in her direction. Even after twelve fireballs being thrown in rapid sequence, not one single flaming orb had come anywhere near her.

So much for discretion in their task of keeping her safe. And so much for not showing apparent favoritism.

Gareth grinned at her as he angled his arm off to the right. Kitrina glanced sideways and saw who he was aiming for. It was the troll female from this morning's hand-to-hand combat, and if she wasn't mistaken, the girl had also been in her poisons class. With a quick jump and lunge, Kitrina knocked her to the ground a heartbeat before the fireball would've hit her square in the chest.

"Thanks, I think." The troll smiled.

At least, she thought it was a smile. With the large tusks sticking out the corners of the troll's mouth, it was hard to tell.

Kitrina smiled back, just in case. "You're welcome. After the way we got off on the wrong foot this morning, I figure I owed you. I mean, it's not your fault you're friends with Asla. She hates me in case you didn't know." She held out a hand. "I'm Kitrina Dragonheart."

The troll female grasped it within her dark green appendage. "Everybody knows who yout are. I'm Maycee, just Maycee. Nice to officially meet yout. And just for the record, I'm not really friends with that barbarian chit. I was just unfortunate enough to sit next to her. We'd better get moving. Looks like our instructors are winding up to throw again."

Another fireball, this time from the hand of Graydon Sunwalker, barely missed Maycee, and the scent of singed hair filled Kitrina's nostrils. She gagged. "God Draka, I already hate this class."

"Why'd yout take it then?" Maycee asked on the run.

"I had this crazy notion I could tip my daggers and arrows with fire magic along with the poisons I already use. You know," Kitrina shrugged, "a kind of deadly triple whammy."

Maycee laughed. "Me, too. Yout know what they say, don't yout?" She grinned even wider. "Great minds think alike."

Kitrina nodded as she once more blocked a fireball meant for her new friend. "Yes, they do. Now, all we have to worry about is surviving this challenge."

"I sure hope so." Maycee grinned. "'Cause it's almost supper time, and I'm hungry enough to eat like I've got something to celebrate."

Kitrina's stomach suddenly grumbled, reminding her she hadn't fed it since the night before. "Me, too."

Chapter Eight

"What the open oozing pustules on the bare arse of a nose-picking, booger-chewing, bellybutton-lint searching, ogre organ player do ya think about that? Our lass looks ta be getting a might ta friendly with the troll lass if'n ya ask me. Why, that green-skinned, greasy-haired female could very well be one of Marquart's minions for all we know."

Zander rubbed his thumb and forefinger along the stubble of his jaw as he leaned back into the recesses of the hiding place from which they had chosen to watch the weeding out of the weak.

The last thing he wanted was for Kitrina to catch a glimpse of him and realize he was following her, watching her. Especially after he'd told her just a couple of turns of the hourglass ago that she could lead, that she could run the show. If she saw him, the fragile bond of trust they were just beginning to forge would be irrevocably broken. The thought worried Zander more than her choice of new friends.

"She knows what she's doing, Leeky. We have to trust her, give her the benefit of the doubt…at least for now. That is, until she gives us a reason not to, which I hope doesn't happen. She knows she has to put herself out there, make herself the bait for the trap. How else will we draw out the dwarf and the troll commanders? Make them come to us? Make them make the first mistake?"

The gnome shook his head. "It may make sense, lad. But that doesn't mean I've gotta like it."

****

God Draka, Kitrina was hungry. She attacked her plate as if she hadn't eaten a bite in a week instead of just a day.

"I think Professor Titwilder is ever so dreamy, don't yout?" Her female troll companion sighed as she twirled her black greasy hair around her green pinky finger and stared blatantly at the full table of men next to theirs.

Kitrina stifled a giggle and almost choked as she stuffed yet another forkful of wild rice and Academy-grown Brussels sprouts into her mouth. It surprised her that she'd had that reaction to Maycee's words. She'd never been the giddy, giggly type. Even as a preteen, when most girls were known to be silly and it was expected, she hadn't been. She'd always been focused and serious. What was it about spending time with this particular female that had her dropping her guard and actually enjoying herself when she knew she needed to remain vigilant?

She too quickly gulped a drink of water, and Zander stared at her with concern as she coughed.

"I'm fine," she assured him as she followed Maycee's gaze to Walaford Titwilder, their hand-to-hand combat instructor. "I guess I've never thought of Wally as dreamy." She chuckled. "I've only ever thought of him as one of my many not-by-blood cousins. But more power to you if you think he's dreamy."

Maycee sighed again. "Oh. I do. Just look at those

big, long, thick tusks. Yout know what they say about the size of a man's tusks, don't yout?"

Kitrina shook her head, but Maycee just kept on talking as if she didn't notice. "That's why I took his class in the first place, just so I could be close to him. It's not like I'd ever have need of hand-to-hand combat with my bow skills. But I still wouldn't mind having him around to protect me. After all," she laughed, "I'm just a weak, helpless little female."

Kitrina flinched. "I disagree. Women these days need to know how to protect themselves, even without the help of a man or a bow."

Maycee shook her head. "Oh, I wasn't implying that we don't. I was just…" Her voice trailed off. "Yout were amazing today, by the way. I saw what yout did in the hallway…with yout dagger. Unless a true friend was in danger, I'd never have the nerve to do something like that." She shrugged. "But then again, perhaps I'll gain some courage of my own by hanging around with yout."

The female troll's smile was so sweet and genuine it almost brought tears to Kitrina's eyes. She'd missed this, the companionship of another female, more than she realized. Though Zander's sister Mia was her very best friend in all of Albrath, and the one person who knew all of her deepest, darkest secrets, Mia couldn't be here with her at the Academy.

The barbarian heir to the throne and the spare weren't allowed to be in the same place at the same time for more than a few hours, unless of course they were both at their castle home in Alaria or at a formal gathering like her deflowering. And since Zander was needed here at The Acadamy for the entire semester,

Mia couldn't be.

And her sisters, Lara and Tawny. God Draka, how she missed them. But they were safe at home where they belonged, at Castle Kuropkat, and she wouldn't have it any other way.

The sound of Maycee's voice drew Kitrina from her musings. "Oh, I was told Professor Titwilder has a sister, though not many people have actually seen her face to face. I even heard she's deformed or something. That she isn't truly green and doesn't have even the beginning of a nub where proper tusks should've grown. Is that true?"

The question surprised Kitrina, and she dropped her half-eaten pheasant leg onto her plate, her appetite suddenly gone. "Yes, he has a sister. Her name is Cerra, and I don't consider her deformed in the least. But I won't discuss her. That would be impolite."

Maycee wouldn't let it go. "But is she really a tuskless, pale excuse for a troll? That's all I want to know? I'd hate to say something I shouldn't in front of Professor Titwilder if I ever do get the nerve to actually speak with him...privately."

Kitrina shivered though she wasn't cold. She didn't know what to say to Maycee. She'd only ever seen Cerra on a couple of occasions and both times the young girl had been covered from head to toe with what had looked like a burlap bag with holes cut out for her eyes, mouth, and arms. Was she tuskless? Was she hideous? Was she even green? Who knew and who cared?

But the few glimpses she had gotten of Cerra's tormented brown eyes had told Kitrina that, even if she wasn't hiding some kind of deformity under that sack cloth, she was certainly hiding something. Something she wanted kept private.

To Maycee, she simply replied, "I just wouldn't mention his sister at all if I were you."

Zander stood and beckoned to Kitrina. She was happy for the reprieve. Not that she hadn't been glad for the female company, but the day had been long and she was more than ready for a different form of communication. One that didn't require so many words.

****

Marquart Maycee Strumgrund, once immortal troll commander and now irritatingly as capable as anyone else of dying given the right circumstances, opened the door to Asla's private suite as if it were her own and made a beeline for the bed chamber. If she still didn't need the stupid female so badly in order to carry out her mission, she'd slip a knife between Asla's ribs, gut her from side to side, and rip out her stupid heart.

She couldn't do that though. The sweet ecstasy she always experienced after committing a particularly vicious murder would simply have to wait. Right now, she still needed the female barbarian's assistance.

That thought irritated Marquart more than any other she'd had for weeks. For more than nine hundred years, she hadn't needed anyone for anything and now she was dependent upon the talents of a blonde barbarian bimbo? Life wasn't fair.

Not bothering to knock, she flung the door wide open and stepped inside. There upon the big four-poster bed lay the little chit, magnificently naked with her rose-hued skin glowing in the soft light of the three moons of Albrath. And she wasn't alone. Nestled snugly between Asla's thighs and sucking noisily on her glistening clit was her dark elf chambermaid. Her very sexy, female, dark elf chamber maid.

The sight of all that indigo blue skin mixed so enticingly with Asla's rose petal pink perfection had Marquart throbbing as if it were her own cunt the dark elf was munching on and not the barbarian's.

This would never do. Especially not after the mess Asla had made of the hand-to-hand-combat class earlier in the day.

"Is this really what I'm getting for all the hard-earned platt I paid yout daddy, the baron? Yout getting a cunt licking while I get...nothing?"

Asla jumped so quickly the dark elf, who had been servicing her, completely lost her balance and ended up ass first on the stone floor. But Asla didn't even look in the maid's direction as she grabbed a sheet from the bed and covered herself. "Wha...what are you doing here? These are my private chambers. You can't just barge in whenever you wish."

Marquart chuckled as she made her way to the big bed, poofed up a couple of pillows, climbed up, and settled in. "I thought perhaps now would be a good time to discuss strategy." She glanced at the dark elf chambermaid who stood, rubbing her ass cheeks and glaring. "That is, unless yout truly are too busy. If that's the case, I'll simply take my influence elsewhere. Perhaps Daddy really won't mind so much after all if Zander Hammerstrike ends up belonging to the little human."

"Oh, no, no, no," Asla insisted. "Father is counting on me...I mean us, and I'm never too busy for you. You know that. You simply...surprised me."

Marquart smiled. "I still have no idea as to what

yout or yout father see in the barbarian prince, and why on Albrath yout would even want him after he threw yout over the way he did. I think the man is odious. He doesn't even have a decent pair of tusks."

Asla looked as if she were about to cry…almost. "You know exactly why I must have him. Father wants me to be a queen, needs me to be a queen, and…and…I'll do whatever is necessary to please him. Father…disappointed, isn't a pleasant sight."

Marquart scoffed. "Well, if this morning was any example of yout idea of doing whatever's necessary, then I'd hate to be around yout when yout intentionally screw up. Bating Kitrina Dragonheart? Starting a fight? Drawing attention to youtself? Really, Asla? What part of any of that disaster did yout father or I request yout do?"

The barbarian chit had the audacity to glare.

Marquart took two deep breaths and forced her hands to remain flush against her sides instead of lashing out and squeezing the life-giving air from Asla's throat. "Play nice, that's what I said. Make friends, especially with Kitrina's bodyguards, those two half-witted halflings. I need them at ease. I need them to let their guards down. I need an opportunity to get close enough to inspect that stone Kitrina is known to wear constantly around her scrawny little human neck."

She took another really deep breath and clinched her fists. "But did I get that opportunity? VoT no, I didn't. What I got was picked up and shook like a rag doll by an overgrown halfling. Yout will do better tomorrow or else."

Asla looked about to respond, but Marquart lifted a hand. "No comments, no excuses. Either yout do as I say, or I will tell Daddy how uncooperative yout've been and find someone else who will do my bidding. Now, leave me."

"La...leave?" Asla stuttered. "But...but...but this is my chamber, my room."

Marquart smiled as she patted the bed. "Not anymore, it isn't. I like this bed. It's comfy. So I've decided we'll be roomies for the duration. What better way to keep my eye on yout. Yout can have use of the spare bedchamber down the hall."

Asla nodded and motioned to her chambermaid.

"Leave the dark elf," Marquart snarled. "My cunt could use a good licking tonight. It's been a while. That is, unless yout rather be the one doing the honors."

Asla left alone.

****

"What are you doing, Kit?"

Kitrina smiled at the gloriously naked Zander Hammerstrike as she cinched the knot about his wrist tighter and attached the other end of the silk cord securely to the solid wood post on the left side of the bed. "What does it look like I'm doing, barbarian. I'm tying you down, and then I'm going to have my way with you. Most assuredly more than once. Probably all night long."

He shook his head. "Umm, I don't mind you taking the initiative and doing all the work, but as far as the tying me, I don't think so, my lady. How am I to do my job and protect you if I'm bound?"

She winked at him as she attached his other wrist to the opposite post. "We both know Talon's right outside the door, on guard, just as he has been every single night since we first arrived. So, that means all you have to do is relax and leave the rest to me. The ropes are simply a...gentle reminder of who's in control, and who isn't."

He laughed. "You do know, it'll take a lot more than a couple of ropes and a tiny female to control me, don't you?"

She didn't answer him right away, and she didn't even look up as she made quick work of securing both of his ankles just like she'd done his wrists. There was no way to explain why she wanted—no, needed—to be in control tonight and how she needed to feel something, anything, other than the coldness that had settled deep into her soul the moment the dagger left her hand earlier in the day. She needed his complete submission. She needed to prove to herself that he was safe with her and always would be, and she needed to prove that, though she'd taken a life, she was still very much alive and intended to stay that way.

Zander tugged at his bindings, then gulped. "Umm, Kitrina, these ropes are getting kind of tight."

She did look up at him then. "Relax and don't struggle, you'll be fine." Licking her lips, she smiled. "Special rogue knots, taught to me by our very own Uncle Leeky himself. I'd tell you how they work, but then I'd have to kill you." She chuckled. "And the last thing I want is you dead. Trust me, Zander I don't like my meat...cold. On the contrary, I like it sizzling hot and dripping with juices."

Though he didn't say another word, Zander Hammerstrike's eyes widened, and he smiled.

She slowly slipped her tunic up and off, tossing it to the floor as she gloried in the site of his nostrils flaring and his breath quickening. His cock thickened before her eyes and rose to attention, its head purple and angry, the veins traveling along its length pulsing with life. Her pussy thrummed with excitement and anticipation.

She thought about blowing out the candles and plunging the room into total darkness. Not only would she be depriving Zander of his ability to move, but also to see. Then his other senses would have to take over. But she didn't. She couldn't. She wanted to show and tell him with her body what she couldn't say in words, what they'd both agreed to not discuss but was there between them just the same, and she wanted him to watch every single moment of it.

"If I do anything you feel uncomfortable with, just say Leeky and I'll stop." She leaned in close and whispered. "It'll be our safe word."

He chuckled. "Leeky, why on Albrath would you choose him of all people?"

Never breaking eye contact, Kitrina slowly crawled her way up Zander's body and straddled his chest. She lightly kissed his lips, nuzzled his chin, and then nipped at his neck. "Don't get me wrong, I love Uncle Leeky to death, you know I do. But can you think of anything else in all of Albrath that could cool one's ardor faster than the thought of Leeky Shortz?"

Zander didn't argue the point.

Instead, he gasped as she took his left nipple between her teeth and lips. First, she sucked and then she bit down, hard. Wet heat mixed perfectly with a combination of pleasure and pain. His balls clenched and unclenched as his rod hardened even further in response. His ass lifted from the coolness of the sheets, and his cock rose, seeking, but finding no relief.

She had the audacity to giggle, and Zander groaned. "Minx, I can only take so much teasing. Be a good lass. Slip that sweet pussy of yours down my cock and ride me."

Her response was to bite him once more, this time, harder, but on the soft skin of his neck just below his right ear. A bite that had tendrils of excitement skittering down his spine, through his ass, and straight out the head of his cock. It would no doubt leave a visible mark on him in the morning...her mark.

The thought made him pause. What would he give if life really were that simple? How easy would it be to just lie back and allow Kitrina to place her unique mark upon him, to claim him as her own, to simply forget about who he was and who he was destined to become? He couldn't though. A love bite was one thing, but there had to be no question of anything else between them.

He sighed. "Though I wish it were different, you can't claim me, Kit. You know I can never be yours any more than you can be mine."

For a moment, her eyes clouded with what looked like pain, and he longed to take his words back. He wanted to enfold her within his arms and promise her anything.

Before he could demand she release him from his bonds so he could do just that, however, she whispered, "Shh, I'm no longer a child with silly dreams. This is just foreplay, nothing more." She took a deep breath and locked gazes with him. "I know the rules we both live by. If I stake a claim on you at all, it is only for this night. We both have nothing more to promise each other." She smiled, and her eyes glistened with what he hoped was mischief instead of tears. "Now, hush and let a girl do what a girl is of a mind to do."

Then, without another word, she turned, and straddled his chest once more. But now she faced his cock with her feet tucked up under his arms and along the side of his head so that the backs of her knees rested against his armpits. Her sweet pussy hovered mere heartbeats above his lips.

She smelled of honey and lust, refreshing life-giving manna, and soul-burning spice. His mouth watered and his heart pounded.

Oh, my God Draka, with every breath she took her moist, pink little clit poked its head from between her folds, teasing him, daring him to capture it, begging to be licked.

He stuck out his tongue as far as it would go, striving to snatch the promised nectar. He growled in frustration as no matter how hard he tried, she managed to keep her pussy at least the distance of a breath out of his reach.

Then she placed a hand on each of his thighs, leaned forward, and slipped her mouth over the head of his cock and down its shaft, all the way to the base and back up again and again. His ass bucked off the bed as his body endeavored to follow the path her mouth was taking. He didn't want to lose the sensation for even a moment before she started her path back down again.

How had that tiny rosebud of a mouth managed to take in the entirety of him? Kitrina was small, especially compared to him, and he…well, he was not. His cock alone was at least ten full inches if it was one. After all, he was male, and like all the other males he had ever known, he'd measured it. And at full hardness, his cock was thicker than his wrist, he'd measured that, too.

A moment later, though, he lost his train of thought as her tongue teased the underside of his cock's head before lapping its way up and dipping into the hole at its top. Her fingers stroked up and down between his cheeks, playing with his balls and toying with the opening of his ass.

He squirmed.

With her next upswing, she leaned to the side of the bed and grabbed up a tube of something laying on the nightstand. Zander didn't have a clue as to what his sexy little Kit was up to until she once more attacked his cock with vigor.

On the very next pass down, she slipped one of her now-lubed fingers inside of him, just to the first knuckle initially, then to the second, then all the way in. She held it there.

He almost said Leeky. It was on the tip of his tongue. He'd never had anything put in his ass before, not even during sexual practice and theory when it was common and acceptable to experiment. The thought just hadn't appealed to him. But then, his sexual practice and theory class hadn't been with Kitrina.

Quickly, she pulled her finger almost all of the way out then plunged it back in to the hilt while nipping the head of his cock and sucking it all better. Saying anything, especially Leeky, became the last thing on his mind as she repeated the process.

His brain seized, his balls contracted, and his heartbeat became as erratic as his breathing. Though he'd had sex with many partners over the years, he had never truly been fucked himself before this night. He was now, and as long as it was Kitrina doing the fucking, he liked it.

She was in total control of every sensation his body experienced since he was tied down and couldn't move. It was wonderful, it was magical, and it was freeing. All he need do was lie still and completely submit to her. Allow her free rein. Permit her to do whatever she pleased to pleasure him.

Pressure built deep in his lower back, and his ass spasmed once, then twice, shooting off tiny spirals of delight into every direction. In response, she added a second finger to the first and fucked him faster. Her mouth sucked his shaft hard, and with her other hand, she cradled his balls out of her way, rhythmically squeezing them, fondling.

Zander struggled against his bonds. He wanted to grab her. He needed to flip her over and plunge his cock deep into her sweet little pussy that, even at this very moment, was still so tantalizingly out of his reach.

"Kit, release me now, for God Draka's sake. I need to fuck you so bad."

She continued to ass-fuck him, but had the impudence to giggle as his cock popped forth from between her lips. "You aren't getting loose until I'm ready to set you free, so be a good boy and come already."

Then her mouth devoured his cock once again.

The little imp. So much for letting her have control even for a minute. He'd show her. He didn't come on demand. If he came at all, he'd come on his own terms, not hers. He was the man, after all. He was the one in charge here. She just didn't know it. It was how it had always been and how it should always be. He'd only let her tie him down on a whim, and it would be a freezing cold day in VoT before Zander Hammerstrike came when told to.

Then she added a third finger, pumping his ass ruthlessly while she squeezed his balls with her other hand and sucked his cock as if she here pulling a really thick milkshake up through a straw.

It wasn't frosty cream she got for her efforts, however.

Before Zander could take another breath or think another thought, his mind exploded as his ass, balls, and cock all contracted at the same time and hot, steamy cum shot upward and out. She swallowed it down as fast as it spurted forward, and the very last thing Zander heard before his mind went totally blank was, "Now see what doing as you're told gets you? What a good boy you are."

All he could manage to do was smile like an idiot and wonder how deep the snow covering the ground this very moment in the Valley of Torment really was.

****

"What the pissed-on—"

Kitrina jerked upright as she caught herself a heartbeat before her head would've hit the top of her desk.

"—polka-dotted panties gracing the ample arse of a buxom barbarian beauty do ya think the three most important dagger tosses are? Come on, lads and lasses. It's not that hard. This is first year material."

She shook her head. The very last thing she needed today was for Leeky Shortz to catch her sleeping in his class. She rubbed her eyes, yawned for the fifth time in the last turn of the hourglass, and cursed herself for her lack of intelligent decision making. Would this day never end?

The pudgy little gnome slipped off his gold dagger-throwing gloves and held up three fingers. Slowly, as if speaking to simpletons, he dropped a finger back in place with each point he made. "There's the overhand, the underhand, and the flick of the wrist, of course. At least, tell me ya recognize them."

No one responded, and Kitrina couldn't help but chuckle to herself as the little gnome hung his head. Leeky replaced his gloves and fisted his hands at his waist. When he glanced back up at the classroom, there wasn't anything funny about the look in his eyes. "What the putrid pork belly hanging off the oversized middle of an ogre okra eater dancing the hokie-pokie on a barrel of malted barley do ya take me for? Every last one of ya will be staying right here in this room until someone demonstrates a proper dagger toss. And I don't care if it takes ya entire lunch period ta do it."

Stay until someone threw a dagger properly? What had she been thinking doing and redoing Zander all night long? It had seemed like such a fine idea at the time, and it had certainly been loads of fun to fuck his brains out until he begged for mercy, but right now, she'd give the left side of her still numb clit for a quarter-turn-of-the-hourglass nap, and the only way she was going to get one was during lunch.

Kitrina raised her hand and let her dagger fly. It landed with a thud, sticking straight out from the wall, a heartbeat to the right of Leeky's ear.

He didn't even flinch. "Let me rephrase that. Every last one of ya will be staying right here in this room until someone, other than Kitrina, who can do them in her sleep, I might add, demonstrates a proper dagger toss."

Kitrina groaned. So he had noticed her drowsiness. Could the day get any worse? Even hand-to-hand combat class had been too weird for words this morning. Though it had been nice to see Maycee's smiling face, it had been Asla's demeanor that was truly disturbing. The woman had been positively...friendly. Not only had she smiled, even at Ten and Levin, but she had giggled and flirted and laughed at their jokes. It was creepy.

Finally, Zander raised his hand and stood. He looked even more tired than she felt, but he took aim and tossed his three daggers in quick order. The first one overhand, the next underhand, and finally, the last with no more than a flick of his wrist. She let out the breath she wasn't even aware she'd been holding.

Leeky applauded. "Well done, Prince Hammerstrike." He glared at the rest of the room. "Ya pecker-heads better practice before tomorrow. Now, what the VoT-roasted tail feathers of a plucked bare-arsed homing pigeon are ya waiting for? Get on outta here and leave a gnome in peace. Class dismissed."

****

The quick half-turn-of-the-hourglass nap during lunch hadn't been nearly long enough time to offset the effects of Kitrina's not so gentle ministrations of the night before. Zander stifled a yawn into his hand as he and Leeky spied on her from the shadows afforded by the depths of the arena. He shook his head. They weren't spying exactly. It was more simply a matter of being cautious. Nothing wrong with that.

Though he emphatically trusted both of his cousins

Graydon and Gareth Sunwalker to keep Kitrina safe during wizard's class, a second and third pair of eyes in a session filled with random balls of fire flying anywhere and everywhere couldn't hurt. Especially as long as the hardheaded, willful little chit didn't know she was being watched.

She was with the troll again, that Maycee chick, and they were laughing and giggling like silly schoolgirls. What the VoT was Kitrina thinking? The pair was standing close enough that if Maycee was of a mind to, the troll could slip a dirk right between Kitrina's ribs before Zander could even think about reaching her.

He didn't like it one bit, and he'd voiced his concerns to the stubborn female not a quarter of a turn of the hourglass ago. And had she taken his misgivings into consideration? Obviously not, because she wasn't paying the least bit of attention to what Maycee was doing now. The troll female had maneuvered herself until she was directly behind Kitrina, leaving the woman he loved completely open and vulnerable to attack.

The woman he loved? Zander groaned. He couldn't, could he? Had he somehow let the guard he kept firmly around his heart down and allowed himself to fall in love with the one woman he knew could never be his? He sighed as the truth of it hit him square in the gut. He had fallen in love with Kitrina, hopelessly and completely. And when this was all over and done with, no matter how it ended, losing her was going to hurt worse than death itself, because lose her he would. It would be better for both of them if he started backing away from her emotionally. It would make it easier to walk away when the time came. Wouldn't it?

"What the tainted, ingrown toenails of a hung-over halfling hula dancer trying ta entice a human horticulturist ta munch on her hair pie is wrong with ya, lad? Ya sound as if ya're dying."

Zander thought about telling Leeky exactly what was bothering him, but the words died unspoken. After all, what was there to say that could possibly change anything?

Chapter Nine

The last two weeks since the death of Bugger the ogre had dragged by at a snail's pace, and Kitrina was tired of constantly looking over her shoulder, of being on guard, always watchful, always ready for an attack from the remaining two commanders that hadn't yet come. She longed for something, anything to move this quest along and get it over with. And if the bickering in hand-to-hand combat class this morning was any indication, the others involved in the quest to keep her and the Dragon Heart Opal safe were just as on edge as she was.

"It's not your turn to spar with Asla, it's mine. So, back off...you...you overgrown buffoon, and let the firstborn show the lady how it's done right." Ten punched Levin in the gut hard enough to cause him to lose his balance and end up flat on his ass in the middle of the floor.

Levin, the half-halfling, half-barbarian behemoth jumped to his feet, his face blood red, his bushy eyebrows drawn together, and his hands clenched into tight fists ready to fight. "You sparred with Asla first yesterday, so just keep your paws to yourself, short stuff. It's my turn. And don't be trying to pull that firstborn crap on me. In class, we're equals. Mothers said so."

"They did not," Ten countered.

"They did, too," Levin argued.

Out of the corner of her eye Kitrina watched Wally moving toward them quickly, and she stepped between the brothers in hopes of defusing the situation before it got out of hand.

"Is there a problem here yout need me to settle for yout?" Walaford Titwilder was obviously just as antsy as the rest of them, and if the look on his face was any indication, he was as ready for a fight as they were.

Kitrina needn't have wasted her time, though, as Asla took care of the disagreement without so much as lifting a finger or her voice. In no more than a whisper, she pleaded, "Ten, Levin, stop, please. I'll spar with both of you at the same time, I promise. I don't want you guys fighting over me. It hurts my...feelings, and it's drawing Professor Titwilder's attention."

Both men immediately backed away from each other and grinned at the blonde barbarian female as if she were the last woman on Albrath and they were both her devoted servants.

"Nope," Ten answered for them both. "Wall—I mean Professor Titwilder. No problem here."

Kitrina didn't get it. Why was Asla still acting as if she actually liked anyone who wasn't a high-born barbarian, especially Ten and Levin? It wasn't just out of character for the coldly beautiful female, it was creepy. It was almost as if Wally Titwilder's whacking off her long blonde braid during that first day of hand-to-hand combat class had also somehow removed her ability to be nasty. It simply didn't make sense.

And it wasn't just Ten and Levin she was working her charms on either. Zander's ex-fiancée was being pleasant to everyone around her. In the last two weeks alone, Kitrina herself had been on the receiving end of more smiles and apologies for past bad acts than she could possibly begin to keep track of. It made her skin crawl.

Even Maycee had made comments to the effect. "Isn't it nice to see Asla making the effort to fit in and play nice with others?"

Well, Kitrina didn't believe it, and she wasn't buying Asla's act for the time it would take a single grain of sand to slip through an hourglass. If there was one thing life had taught her long ago, it was that a leopard didn't change its spots mid-leap and a mean, spiteful female didn't suddenly change her ways either.

Ten and Levin could trust Asla and play along with her games all they wanted. But one thing was certain, Kitrina wasn't going to be that easy to convince or that gullible.

****

Zander wasn't sure exactly why, but he had been following Kitrina around from class to class, watching her every move from the luxury of the shadows for the last week. Not that he didn't trust her or those he had set to guard her, for he did. It was just that he knew the longer this quest continued and the more prolonged the wait for the two remaining commanders to show themselves became, the task grew more and more tedious and the chances of becoming complacent and careless increased. He cared too VoT much to take chances with Kitrina's safety.

Not that he had allowed her to be privy to his worries or to what he'd been up to. Oh, no, he knew better than to permit Kitrina Dragonheart, rogue extraordinaire and leader of this quest, to find out he'd been…spying on her. After all, by delegating leadership to her, he'd put himself in the role of her underling. Underlings did not spy on their liege lords. It wasn't done.

But then sometimes circumstances dictated the necessity to step outside convention and simply do what must be done. And there really was no need to inform Kitrina of his suspicions until there was something tangible he could give her as proof. After all, it wasn't her he didn't trust. He had complete faith in Kitrina and her abilities. It was that VoT irritating troll, Maycee, he had a problem with. The green-skinned, greasy-haired, yellowed-tusked pain in his arse seemed forever to be underfoot and way too close to wherever Kitrina was during every waking moment of the day.

And no matter how many times Kitrina assured him that the friendship between the two women was nothing more than a camaraderie of like minds with no sinister plots being planned or hatched on Maycee's part, he wasn't buying it.

Though Kitrina was, without question, a smart, savvy rogue and could take care of herself in almost any situation imaginable, she was also…well…female and just as vulnerable to the absence of other female company as the next girl.

Female companionship had been lacking in Kitrina's life lately. With the constant testosterone overdosed association of not only Zander but also Talon, Leeky, Pierced, Steve, Graydon, Gareth, Wally, Ten, and Levin, any chance of the influence of female hormones in the vicinity had been extremely rare.

And it had become blatantly apparent to Zander that Kitrina trusted Maycee and didn't believe for a moment the troll had ulterior motives for seeking out her company. They'd even argued about it...heatedly and repeatedly.

But Zander's spiritmaster sensibility had been screaming at him for the last two weeks that Maycee's motives were not to be trusted. A deafening roar in his mind so loud that it made his eyes hurt and his heart heavy. A warning that had never once been proven wrong and wasn't likely to be now.

And his spiritmaster sensibility didn't stop with just the troll, either. Even now, with his ex-fiancée surrounded by both Ten and Levin, he still wouldn't put anything past Asla.

The barbarian female with the short curly blond hair might succeed in looking innocent and pulling the wool over his cousin's eyes, but not his. No, Zander had been the recipient of Asla's poisonous personality, and he'd seen up close and personal just how far the woman would go to get what she wanted. Never again would he be stupid enough to trust her.

He watched them spar, though, Ten, Levin, and Asla, while always keeping an eye on Kitrina, who was grappling with a klutzy-looking, little dwarf fellow.

Zander smiled. The Limburger brothers really were quite good. For being so bulky and short, Ten was amazingly agile and fast, ducking and weaving, spinning and kicking. And while Levin couldn't compete with Ten's speed, he more than made up for his lack of quickness and finesse with his brute strength. The two brothers moved in tandem, first right, then left, back, then forth, and even though Asla didn't have a prayer of a chance of actually defeating either one of them, she was certainly giving it her best shot.

As for Katrina...now there was a fighter. Zander grinned as she swayed and jabbed, bobbed and sidestepped the dwarf, only to catch him off guard time after time and knock the man flat on his arse. God Draka, he was proud of that woman.

Suddenly, she glanced in his direction, as if she somehow sensed he was there, and Zander slipped just a hair farther into the shadows and out of sight. Oh, yes, with the way things had been strained between them lately, the last thing he needed was for Kitrina to catch him spying on her.

The dwarf surprised him by suddenly bowing out and backing away. Maycee the troll took his place facing Kitrina, and a trickle of apprehension skittered along Zander's spine. Even Ten, Levin, and Asla paused in their match to watch. And not only did they pause, but so did Wally Titwilder and the entire rest of the class.

Zander's palms itched, his breathing hitched, and his heart pounded as Maycee ducked Kitrina's first swing and landed a solid uppercut to her chin. Kit's head snapped back, and for just a moment, her eyes glazed over. Somewhere in the distance thunder crashed, and it was all Zander could do to remain in hiding and not join the fray. This was not good.

Back and forth, they sparred, fists flying, feet tripping, and eyes ever darting back and forth, watching, gauging, always on guard.

Grudgingly, Zander admitted to himself that the two women were evenly matched. Though he didn't want to be, he even found himself mildly in awe of Maycee's skill.

He and Kit had fought for fun a few times since

they'd come to The Academy of Magical Arts, and he knew how very talented and sneaky a combatant the petite human female really was. There was no doubt about it; Leeky Shortz had taught Kit well, very well. And for Maycee the troll to be holding her own so easily against Kitrina right this moment meant only one thing. Someone, somewhere, at some time, had taught the VoT troll how to fight, too.

But then Kitrina wasn't having any real problem keeping pace with Maycee either. Her lithe body moved like that of a well-choreographed dancer as she pivoted, turned, lunged, and flipped the big troll right up and over her shoulder as if the green-skinned female weighed no more than a gnome.

Before Zander could catch his next breath, Maycee lay flat on her back with Kitrina straddling her.

That position didn't last long, however. Kitrina offered Maycee a hand up, and the troll took it. They bowed to each other and then were at it again. Back and forth, they scuffled, neither gaining nor losing ground, nor giving an inch.

He was so enjoying the match that, at first, Zander didn't realize the danger present. But then his spiritmaster sensibility zinged. His head felt ready to explode with it, and his fingertips heated to the point of discomfort. Tiny sparks of lightning jumped back and forth between each digit, and a buzzing rang loudly in his ears.

He couldn't believe it. He'd let himself become so engrossed in the action that he'd completely missed the potential danger to Kitrina. He quickly scanned the room, every person's face, every person's body language, and every person's proximity to her. From the corner of his eye, he saw it, the glint of steel, where the glint of steel shouldn't have been.

And not just steel, but a steel dagger. A dagger in the hand of the troll, Maycee.

He rushed forward out of the shadows, horrified as Kitrina's eyes found him and locked with his own. Maycee's arm raised, and Zander prayed he'd reach Kit in time. He hoped desperately that the look of betrayal he saw in her eyes this very moment wouldn't be her last impression of him.

He wasn't going to make it, though, and he knew it. His heart stopped dead in his chest as Maycee cocked her wrist a scant breath before Zander reached Kitrina.

The troll flung her dagger. It flew right past Katrina's right ear and his left, so close that the current of air it rode upon puffed at his hair as it continued its path across the room. He blinked once as he spun, then watched in amazement as the blade landed with a sickening thud directly between the wide open eyes of the very startled, klutzy little dwarf. The very same dwarf Kitrina had been sparring with only minutes ago.

The dwarf's own dagger fell from his raised hand and clattered to the floor no more than a moment before his body followed.

Zander's knees buckled with relief, and he hung his head in shame. Kitrina had been in a real and present danger, and all the while, he'd been hiding in the shadows and watching the wrong person. He'd been keeping his eyes trained on Maycee, doubting her reliability, her trustworthiness, when it should've been the dwarf he scrutinized.

Someone—Zander had no clue who—ran out of

the room and brought Leeky back with him, and it was the gnome who confirmed what everyone else who was privy to the situation and the quest suspected.

Leeky searched the dwarf's body, flipping it back and forth, going over every inch before finally lifting the hair away from the nape of its neck. He gasped as he pointed to a small tattoo of a capital K in faded black ink.

"What the turquoise tramp stamp above the hiney-hole of a street-walking ogre temptress with a preference for dark elf meat do ya make of that, lads and lasses? See that there mark?" He lifted his own tuffs of graying hair out of the way to reveal another tattoo identical to it. "I'd forgotten all about these. I knew the commanders on our side each had an identifying mark like this in case of death during battle, but I didn't know the other side used the same strategy. That K's for Castle Kuropkat. Makes sense, though. No doubt about it, that dwarf's Commander Wizzit, for sure."

He turned toward Kitrina and grinned. "Two down, one ta go, lass."

Zander lowered his head in shame. In the end, it had taken a troll he didn't trust, a troll he didn't even like, and a troll that, if he were being honest with himself, he had to admit, he was more than a little jealous of to do what he should've done himself.

He would never live this down. It had taken Maycee of all people to succeed in protecting Kitrina where he himself had failed. It was a very bitter pill to swallow.

What was even worse, though, was the realization that his spiritmaster sensibility had somehow failed him. Well, perhaps not totally failed him. After all, there had been a danger present.

Zander shook his head. Something about his spiritmaster abilities was definitely off kilter lately, and he didn't know if it was because he didn't want to trust Maycee or because he cared so much more for Kitrina than he had the right to. Whatever the reason, it stung to realize he could no longer completely trust a skill he'd honed and counted on his entire life.

If that wasn't bad enough and if he really was right about the intensity of the fire, rage, and betrayal he saw gleaming in Kitrina's eyes right this moment, he wasn't going to easily get away with being worried for her safety as a valid excuse for spying on her, either. At least, not without a whole lot of groveling.

Zander hated groveling.

****

"Oh, for God Draka's sake." Kitrina sighed. "Give it a rest, will you? Maycee hasn't done anything to warrant this level of distrust. At least not yet." She closed her eyes and rubbed the back of her neck, trying unsuccessfully to alleviate the tight knots of tension her muscles had formed.

It had been more than a complete rotation of the second moon since the killing of the dwarf commander, Wizzit, and during that entire time, Maycee hadn't done a single thing anyone could consider even remotely suspicious. Unless, of course, being practically stuck up Kitrina's ass every waking moment of every VoT day could be deemed suspicious.

As a matter of fact, considering what Maycee had done with her dagger toss, Zander Hammerstrike should've been heralding her as a hero instead of ranting like a lunatic...again.

Kitrina shook her head. Why couldn't she get the hard-headed barbarian to listen to reason just once without a fight?

"I can't afford to give it a rest, Kit, and neither can you," Zander roared. "What if you're wrong about her? She's a troll, for God Draka's sake. And we both know that a *female* troll commander is the only threat left. So what if she's not actually Marquart? Perhaps she's in cahoots with her? After all, you can't dismiss the fact that at the end of the day, she is and will always be a troll."

Kitrina forced a smile. "Well, Wally's a troll. Do you think he's in cahoots with Marquart, too?" She held up her hands when he glared at her. "Just kidding. Sheesh, lighten up, will you?"

Zander didn't smile back.

He paced the space of their room like a caged animal, and she wished he would just sit down for the time it would take a handful of sand to trickle through the hourglass and listen.

He'd been sullen for weeks, to the point they rarely spoke or even touched, except at night, in the dark, and then without words, and hurried as if they were both afraid it would be their last chance.

What was wrong with him?

No matter how many times and in however many different ways she asked, she always got the same response back. *"Nothing, I'm fine."*

She sighed. As if the space between them wasn't wide enough, this new unwarranted outburst certainly didn't help matters. It only added to her frustration. She was so sick of fighting.

He didn't sit as she'd asked, though. He just kept pacing back and forth and yelling. "I get that Maycee is like some kind of hero to you now. After all, it was Maycee who saved your ass where I failed. It was Maycee's dagger who took the dwarf commander's life and prevented him from taking yours." He held up a hand. "And before you say anything, I agree, I shouldn't have even been there watching you from the shadows in the first place—"

"Spying on me," she interjected.

Zander shook his head. "Whatever. What's important is that I shouldn't have allowed myself to become distracted, and I swore to you then and there it wouldn't happen again. But too much is riding on the outcome of this little venture you're proposing to suggest leaving behind the one person you know without a doubt has your back in favor of that...that...troll and...and...my ex-fiancée of all people."

It was her turn to pace. "You can't come. You make them nervous, Zander. VoT, you make me nervous. You scowl and grumble and bluster at anyone anywhere near you, and...and...lately you're almost unbearable to live with."

She stopped directly before him and locked her gaze with his, daring him to look away. "This...trip was set up to be a just-us-girls kind of outing, but if you insist, I'll take Ten and Levin along. Asla certainly seems to like them well enough lately, and they don't get on Maycee's nerves...often."

He looked as if he was still going to argue, and Kitrina stomped her foot. "It's just a frigging day trip to the central library on the Isle of Shak-spere, for VoT's sake. You know as well as I do, if there's any proof the Dragon Heart Opal and the Stone of Anthion are not one and the same, it will be found where the majority of human history is stored. I'd really like to prevent more bloodshed before it happens if possible."

"A day trip, that's what you call it?" he shouted. "The Isle of Shak-spere is on the other side of the world, Kitrina."

She took three deep breaths and blew them out slowly. "Zander, you gave me the lead in this quest, remember? Stop being so melodramatic and let me do my job. It's nothing more than the matter of stepping through one portal and back out another and we both know it."

She cupped his chin and forced him to look at her. "I don't know for sure if Maycee is or isn't Marquart or at the very least working for her. Do you? I mean, it's not as if we can hold her down and shave her head to look for a tattooed K, can we?"

He shook his head.

"Then," she whispered. "There's no other way we're ever going to find out for sure before Yulemass is upon us in just a couple of weeks and our families are close enough to be put at risk unless I make myself seem vulnerable to her. You have to trust me in this and let me do my job."

He started to speak, but Kitrina placed a finger gently against his lips. "I'll be careful, I promise, and I'll be back before the start of hand-to-hand combat class tomorrow morning, proof or no, I swear."

She stroked his cheek. "Wasn't it you who first told me to keep my friends close and my enemies even closer?"

He nodded.

"Well, that's exactly what I plan to do until I'm certain if Maycee is friend or foe."

****

"What the rosy red rash on the bare backside of a nose-dripping, sweat-covered, eyes-itching, buck-nakey dwarf with a head cold attempting a blowjob on an unsuspecting dark elf passerby for two platt and change is wrong with ya, lad? Ya let her go where and with who?"

Zander glared at Leeky. "Do you realize the length of your 'what the's' are directly proportional to your level of agitation?"

The gnome balled up his lime-green gloved go-to-meeting-clad fists and shook them in the air. "I'll show ya a 'what the' right in the kisser and don't ya be thinking for the time it takes a single grain of sand ta slide through the hourglass, I won't. I might not be immortal anymore, but I'm not afraid ta take on the likes of a wet-behind-the-ears, pecker-headed barbarian like ya."

Zander backed up a step and held up his hands. "It was just an observation, Uncle Leeky. Kitrina went to the human history library with Maycee and Asla. She took Ten and Levin along with her. She'll be back by morning."

The gnome's entire face turned a bright red, contrasting garishly with his lime green gloves. "It's not the where she went that bothers me and ya know it. It's the who she went with. What the...the...ahh, VoT, now see what ya've done ta me, I can't even talk right. What were ya thinking sending our lass off with that...that troll?"

Zander felt the first genuine smile he'd had for days grace his lips as Leeky quickly glanced toward Wally who sat cross-legged on the floor across the room, right in front of Talon and between Graydon and Gareth.

The gnome gulped. "No offense meant taward trolls, of course, nephew. Some of my favorite people happen ta be trolls."

Wally simply shrugged.

Talon didn't remain silent like the others, though. "I'm afraid I have to agree with Leeky on this one, my friend. What were you thinking?"

Zander sighed. "As Kitrina so very eloquently pointed out to me just this morning, I did hand over the reins of this quest to her, and at some point, we're all going to have to trust her judgment. She's quick, she's smart, and ultimately, it's her neck in jeopardy if she fails. We need to at least give her the benefit of the doubt."

Leeky puffed out his chest. "Well, I did teach her everything she knows, and she's a VoT fine rogue even if I say so myself. Guess it wouldn't hurt ta give the lass a little leeway." He pointed a finger straight at Zander. "But what the strings of rancid reindeer sausage stuck betwixt the buckteeth of a bohemian barbarian bystander during a dwarf dandy potluck do ya think will happen ta ya if Uthiel Stoutheart's little girl gets so much as a hangnail?"

No one was smiling now.

"Meeting adjourned" was all Zander had to say on that subject.

Chapter Ten

Kitrina read the passage before her, then reread it once again. Though probably not useful for her needs, it was beautiful, and it made her feel as if she really were a part of something very special.

The Dragon Heart Opal:

Hark unto thee both far and wide. A pact has been made, a trust to confide. For dragon hearts are pure as gold. And paladin hearts beat both worthy and bold. They've formed a bond, they've given a token. A promise in gemstone, never to be broken. An opal of brilliance, an opal of trust. Worn by one whose soul is found just.

Tears stung her eyes. Was her soul even close to being just? Was she truly worthy to wear the Dragon Heart Opal? Probably not. She was simply a female, after all, and by human law, wasn't even allowed to become a paladin. Did it really matter? Even though the original presentation of the gemstone had been to the chosen leader of the Paladins of Albrath, the stone moved from heir to heir, regardless of what kind or gender of soul inhabited the body.

Kitrina shuddered. Not that it had ever been worn by anyone evil, for it hadn't. She knew without a doubt that every single recipient of the Dragon Heart Opal had been a good and just paladin and had passed the stone down to their good and just sons.

Uthiel Dragonheart, however, had been the first of the long line of leaders of the Paladins of Albrath not to have a son to pass the stone down to. So, around the neck of his eldest daughter the gleaming treasure laid. Could a female be worthy to wear the treasure in truth, even if she could never become a paladin?

Kitrina knew in the recesses of her soul she would just as quickly lay down her life to protect the dragons that'd brought magic to Albrath as any man would. And though it didn't count because she was female, she'd even sworn the blood oath before Obsidian, her very own dragon, when she'd been but six summers old.

The words of the sacred oath of the Paladins of Albrath floated back through her memory, filling her heart, feeding her soul.

"From this day forward, 'til time is no more. I pledge you my dagger, I pledge you my sword. I pledge you my service, I pledge you my brawn. I pledge you my heart 'til my last breath is drawn."

She had meant those words with all the conviction a young girl's soul could hold on the day she'd sliced her finger and mixed her blood with Obsidian's, then crossed her heart, kneeled before the huge black dragon, and recited them out loud. Though she was now silent, Kitrina meant them even more today.

She sighed as she closed the volume she'd been searching and reached for the next book in the tall stack before her. She still hadn't found what she was searching for, and oath or not, sunlight was wasting.

Kitrina hesitated a moment before she opened the next volume. Was this the one? Perhaps this very text would hold the answer. And what if it didn't? What then? What if not one of the books in this huge library, or any library anywhere, could positively prove that the Stone of Anthion and the Dragon Heart Opal weren't one and the same?

Would she then be forced to take the life of someone she'd begun to care about as a possible friend? She hoped with all her heart Maycee was exactly who she said she was and not who Katrina suspected her to be. But there had been little clues in her research, glimpses of unguarded looks, private whisperings with Asla, feelings like the ones she experienced even now. Animosity flowed in her direction from across the room where Maycee sat. It was like a wet steady breeze, chilling to the bone, and as cold as death.

She pushed back her concerns and flipped the first page. Be she paladin or no, be she female instead of male, and be Maycee friend or foe, in the end, it didn't matter. An oath was an oath, and as long as she breathed and wore the Dragon Heart Opal about her neck, she would do whatever needed to be done to protect not only every dragon on Albrath but also everyone she held dear. And God Draka help anyone who dared stand in her way.

****

Marquart watched Kitrina nonchalantly read, as if she didn't have a care in the world, and seethed with hatred. Even with Ten and Levin close by, it would be so easy to end her worthless life right here and now. The stupid chit's back was completely open and vulnerable...again. Like so many other times over the last few weeks. She'd deserve it, was practically begging for it even.

It took all the willpower Marquart could muster not to simply toss her dagger and bury it deep in the heart of the useless human female and grab what should rightfully be hers.

She didn't, though. Even if she'd been sure she could've taken out both Ten and Levin afterward and gotten away cleanly, it wasn't yet time. She'd carefully plotted Kitrina's untimely death over and over in her mind in multiple scenarios. She'd hoped for it, planned it, and dreamed about it but couldn't afford to carry through with the execution of it. At least not until she found a way around the stupid stone's affinity for the human.

If there was one thing she had learned from her forced closeness to the wannabe rogue paladin, it was that if Kitrina were to die, the gemstone she constantly wore about her neck would magically disappear. Poof, gone, no longer within reach.

According to what Marquart had researched about the Dragon Heart Opal/ Stone of Anthion, the process of ingraining herself into the trust of the next heir in line would then have to begin all over again. She shuddered at the prospect.

She was so VoT sick of being nice to anyone let alone…humans, and she certainly didn't want to deal with any more of them than was absolutely necessary. Except perhaps at the end of her blade or locked away in her dungeon for entertainment.

That brought a smile to her face, but it didn't take care of her current problem.

There had to be some way around the link between the stone and its wearer that she simply hadn't discovered yet. And it wasn't as if she could glean that information out of Kitrina without getting her alone or vulnerable enough to really question her. Or in the very least giving her a good enough reason to reveal the information willingly.

They should've been alone right now. Tonight's carefully thought out plans depended on privacy.

Marquart glanced at Ten and Levin, the half barbarian, half halflings, or as she liked to think of them, the barfling brothers, and her temper flared even hotter. They weren't supposed to be here. This was supposed to be an all-female outing. But was it? VoT no. The two thickheaded bodyguards sat on either side of the little human chit, so close not even a mosquito could get between them.

Getting Kitrina completely alone and vulnerable any time in the near future was going to be a trick with Zander, the overly possessive barbarian, making sure his precious little gemstone wearer was always well guarded even when he wasn't around. But then Zander Hammerstrike hadn't counted on Marquart's ingenuity and perseverance, now had he?

She laughed out loud, and the barfling brother's heads turned. Marquart smiled innocently and batted her eyelashes at them. They quickly looked away.

Yes, she had a very good idea how to go about discovering just what knowledge she needed in order to procure the Stone of Anthion for her own use. And if she didn't succeed tonight, then another opportunity would, without a doubt, present itself. One always had and one always would.

After all, she was special, always had been. From the moment she was born, she had been destined for greatness and power. She'd even received the honor of becoming one of only four immortals on Albrath. An honor that lasted for almost nine hundred years. If that wasn't a sign that the gods wanted her to succeed, then what was? Nothing was going to stop her. Not the passage of time, not death, and certainly not the stupid human chit, Kitrina Dragonheart.

But what if her plot for this evening didn't bring about the results she was counting on?

A backup plan began to form in her mind. It grew, it expanded, and it took shape. So if she didn't manage to succeed tonight and failed to find an opportunity to get Kitrina alone at The Academy in the very near future, she'd just have to give the worthless human an irresistible reason to sneak away unguarded.

She couldn't really afford to wait much longer. Even now, she felt herself aging. Everyday a new wrinkle, a new ache, a new pain. She didn't have time to play nice. She couldn't and wouldn't waste what few years she had left being miss proper troll, Maycee, when there were other...options.

After all, Yulemass was less than a quarter turn of the third moon away, and another entire season would be gone without her possession of the only object that could ensure she'd have an easy death when the time came. And not simply an easy death, but a one way ticket, no questions asked, straight ride through the gates of the gods into paradise.

With the numerous atrocities she'd committed over the last almost nine centuries, Marquart had no doubt that possessing the Stone of Anthion was the only way she'd ever be invited into the Haven of Souls. The only other option, being cast into the Valley of Torment, wasn't on her to do list. And since she'd never been one to bow before or ask anyone, even a god, for anything, especially forgiveness when she wasn't sorry for taking what she felt was rightfully hers to take, why should she have to? Guilt and regret were for the weak. Not for her.

No one had ever dared call Marquart weak.

Yes, Yulemass could very well be the answer to all her problems if it came to that. It would be perfect timing and oh so fitting. After all, wasn't it the normal time of the year to reunite with family and loved ones? Wasn't it an occasion of goodwill and giving of one's self? A time of unmitigated cheer? A moment to stop and remember what was really important in one's life?

Just what would Kitrina be willing to give up or do in order to save those who weren't fortunate enough to wear the Dragon Heart Opal around their necks? In the spirit of Yulemass, of course?

Marquart cackled, though there wasn't anything remotely funny about the sound.

Kitrina, Ten, Levin, and even Asla turned and looked at her in surprise. Their confusion only served to make her laugh harder.

****

Kitrina yawned and quickly covered her mouth to stifle it as the third wave of to-the-very-marrow-of-her-bones tiredness enveloped her. She gave up and closed the book she'd been so diligently trying to study and laid her head upon the cool leather of its binding.

What on Albrath was wrong with her?

It wasn't that late. And she hadn't worked that hard. The sun had barely begun to set, and the three moons of Albrath were not yet remotely visible through the wide open windows encircling the library's high walls. And still, she couldn't seem to keep her eyes from fluttering shut time after time. As a matter of fact,

it had been all she could do to make it through the end
of the short dinner break she'd taken with her friends
less than a single turn of the hourglass ago.

Kitrina forced her eyes open once more and
glanced toward Ten and Levin. They were both so
deeply asleep that they were snoring in tandem. Asla
was draped across Levin's lap like his personal security
blanky, and his arm was flung haphazardly around her
waist. Her feet were nestled in Ten's crotch, and a
satisfied smile graced the first-born and heir to the
Limburger dynasty's face.

A thin line of drool upon her chin was the only
thing to mar Asla's near perfect barbarian continence.
Even though they had become, if not…friends, then at
least not out and out enemies, the thought brought a
smile to Kitrina's face.

Turning her head, she searched for the one missing
group member, Maycee, and finally found the female
three rows away with her head resting upon her arms on
the top of the table. A book lay open before her, and the
troll's breathing seemed regular and relaxed.

Perhaps too regular and relaxed?

Kitrina yawned again and tried without success to
keep her eyes fully open. Something wasn't right here.
Something she couldn't quite put her finger on.
Something just beyond her scope of understanding. But
since all of her companions were also apparently as
affected by this sudden, overwhelming tiredness as she
was, perhaps it really was nothing more sinister than the
effects of too much good food and way too much free
flowing wine.

What would it hurt to give in just this one time and
let her guard down for a few moments? After all, they

were all alone here. Not even a fulltime librarian was on site. Even though it had been built less than fifteen years ago, the central library on the Isle of Shak-spere had become so sacred to everyone, not even the most evil citizen of Albrath would dare harm a single page of a single book within its walls. And the only other possible threat to her person was if she were wrong about Maycee, who was apparently as sound asleep as Kitrina wanted to be.

She shook her head. No, she shouldn't give into the fatigue. Something was definitely wrong. She could sense it. It would be a mistake to succumb to the exhaustion, and Zander would be angry if she did. She should fight it.

But always being the responsible one, the strong one, the self-reliant one, was more of a tedious task today than Kitrina was up to. And a teensy quarter turn of the hourglass nap just might be what she needed to clear the fog in her brain. Couldn't it? And who would be the wiser?

Yes, that's what she'd do. One quarter, no more than a half turn of the hourglass nap at the very most, and then right back to being responsible, vigilant, and alert.

With the decision made, Kitrina smiled as warmth filled her. It flowed as freely as the blood coursing strongly through her veins. Peace enveloped her, blanketed her, snuggled her in close, and held her tight, safe. With a deep breath and a single long sigh, the memory of Zander's angry face, the library, the dangers she faced, the quest, even all of Albrath itself, slipped silently into oblivion.

Kitrina slept.

****

Zander woke from a sound sleep with a start and jumped to his feet. Quickly, he dressed, slid his dagger snug into the sheath on his belt, and slipped his broadsword through the scabbard on his back as he headed for the door. Thunder roared somewhere far off in the distance.

Something was wrong. He knew it, could feel it. His spiritmaster sensibilities were once more bombarding him from every direction like tiny pinpricks of lightning shooting straight through his skull.

Even though he was tempted to ignore and not trust them after what happened with the dwarf Wizzit, he didn't. He'd learned long ago what the consequences of doing that could be. His best friend, Talon, still carried the scars of the one other time he'd failed to pay heed to his gift when he should've.

Though he'd never attained the ability to truly read minds like his Aunt Lark could, he had received an almost eerie knack of knowing when someone was lying to him, or if a person he cared for was in danger. And right now, Katrina wasn't just in a little danger. She was in a dire situation and wasn't even aware of it. As a matter of fact, he had the oddest feeling that right at this moment, Kitrina wasn't aware of much of anything.

He had to get to her, and he had to get to her now.

"What the VoT?" Zander cursed as he tripped over what could only be Talon Starkweather's big feet.

Talon immediately woke. "Going somewhere?"

Zander growled. "What the VoT are you doing lurking out here in the hallway? Why aren't you in your own bed? You know as well as I do there's no need to guard my door tonight. Kitrina isn't here. Go get yourself a decent night's sleep for once."

Talon chuckled. "Hmm. And just what has you up and about at this hour, Zander? Missing her, going to check on her perhaps? Give it up, you've been caught. Just where are we off to?"

Zander opened his mouth but Talon shook his head. "And before you try, don't even bother with some half-baked story that's only going to insult my intelligence and piss me off. We've known each other much too long for that crap."

Zander sighed. "You're right, my friend, we have. Now get your big ol' barbarian's arse up off that floor and let's get moving. Time's wasting and Kitrina's in trouble. I...feel it. "

No more questions were asked.

****

Once the room was completely quiet except for the rhythmic breathing of slumber, Marquart listened for the space of another ten grains of sand through the hourglass before slowly lifting her head from the table top and glancing in Katrina's direction.

"It's about VoT time," she grumbled.

It had certainly taken the stupid little human chit and her companions long enough to fall into a mindless stupor. Next time she'd add two healthy dollops of the elixir, Oblivion of Truth, to each bottle of wine instead of just one, and she wouldn't care if they overdosed and never woke up. That is, if another round of questioning became necessary. She hoped it wouldn't. Marquart hated wasting time, especially hers.

On tiptoes, she made her way to the barfling

brothers and poked Asla in the shoulder to get her attention. "Get up," she whispered. "It's time."

The stupid barbarian female had the audacity to swat her hand away and snuggle deeper into the lap of the one called Levin.

Marquart pinched her left arm...hard.

Startled, Asla jumped. "Oww! Why'd you do that?" she cried.

Marquart clamped a hand over her mouth. "Shut up. If yout wake these two idiots, I swear I'll kill every last one of yout."

Asla became deathly quiet.

Marquart studied her for a moment. "Yout drank some of the wine, didn't yout? Even after I warned yout not to."

At first, Asla shook her head, then she nodded. "Just one sip, though, I swear. I didn't want anyone to become suspicious."

Marquart sighed. "God Draka, save me from fools. Let's get started. This stuff only lasts so long."

Together, they made their way to Kitrina, and Marquart handed Asla a smudged piece of parchment. "Ask her the first question and be quick about it."

Asla grimaced. "Why me? If you want to know something, why not just ask her your—"

Marquart leveled her blade against the smooth skin of the barbarian female's throat. "I wouldn't want Kitrina to remember later that it was I asking questions. And, yout father promised yout help, but if yout aren't any good to me in this, then what good are yout at all?"

Asla gulped, gripped the parchment tightly, and read the first question. "Is the Dragon Heart Opal and the Stone of Anthion one and the same?"

Kitrina mumbled something unintelligible in her sleep.

Marquart seethed. "What the VoT did she say?"

"How should I know?" Asla shrugged.

A heartbeat later, Marquart had the tip of her dagger pressed against the pulse point of Kitrina's throat instead of Asla's. "I'm so fucking sick of this shit. If the stupid human can't or won't answer my questions, I'll simply kill her worthless ass right now and go on to the next in line. With her out of the way, I bet her little sister, Lara, wouldn't be so reluctant to give me what I need."

Asla grabbed Marquart's hand and pulled the blade from Kitrina's exposed skin. "No, please, don't kill her. I'll get her to talk. I swear I will." Her face reddened and she stuttered. "Not that I re-re-really care if K-Kitrina Dragonheart lives or dies, mind you, but Ten and Levin were sent here specifically to guard her and they would be b-blamed if she's harmed."

Marquart laughed. "What do yout care what happens to the barfling brothers?"

Asla's face lost all trace of color and she gulped. "I don't, not really."

Marquart cackled. "Yout like them, don't yout?" She shook her head. "Perhaps even more than just like. My, how far the lofty have fallen."

Asla's eyes filled with tears. "So what if I do? They treat me like I'm a real person, like I'm special to them. No one has ever been as good and kind to me as they are. I just don't want to see them hurt, that's all."

Marquart sneered. "Then, unless yout wish me to inform yout father of yout propensity toward those two mutant halflings, I suggest yout do my bidding and do it quickly. And if yout don't do a better job of asking my questions and getting my answers, the pain all of yout will feel is going to be excruciating and much worse than anything Daddy has ever thought to do to yout."

Asla gulped and lightly shook Kitrina's shoulder. "You must answer me, please. Are the two stones the same?"

When Kitrina spoke, it was barely a whisper, more of an audible sigh. "I honestly don't know. I wish I did."

Marquart shook her head and pointed to the parchment. "Just get on with it. We're running out of time."

Asla read. "Is there any way to separate yourself from the Dragon Heart Opal?"

Kitrina nodded and smiled. "With the birth of my first child, the stone will bind to him...or her." Her smiled faded. "Or upon my death. Then the Dragon Heart Opal would simply pass to the next in line, to Lara."

Marquart stomped her foot. "I knew it. That's what all my research told me. I might as well kill her right now and move onto her sister. They must run out of relatives at some point."

Asla put a finger to her lips. "Shh, she's trying to say something else." She patted Kitrina's arm. "Go on. What?"

The words tumbled unheeded from Kitrina's mouth with a giggle. "Or, of course, if Kit becomes Cat. Because when Kit is Cat, the Dragon Heart Opal doesn't care about her, nobody does. Not even the oath, not even the dragons."

Marquart shook her head. "What the VoT does she

mean? She's not making any sense. I must've given her too much of the elixir. Her brain's scrambled."

Asla shrugged. "Perhaps." Then she asked. "What oath?"

Kitrina smiled in her sleep. "From this day forward, 'til time is no more. I pledge you my dagger, I pledge you my sword. I pledge you my service, I pledge you my brawn. I pledge you my heart 'til my last breath is drawn." She sighed. "The paladin's oath, of course."

Just then, the sound of boots clacking as they hurried along the cobblestone floor of the library rang as loudly as thunder.

Marquart snatched the parchment from Asla's hand and hurried back to her seat. "Betray me, and I'll do worse than kill yout. I'll tell yout father what I know."

Quickly, she laid her head upon the table and closed her eyes…almost but not quite.

Asla wasn't as lucky or as fast. The barbarian female turned to scamper away, but Talon engulfed Asla within his firm grasp and held her tight.

Zander roared as he knelt at Kitrina's side and scooped her into his arms. "If one hair on her head has been harmed, Asla, as God Draka is my witness, you will pay."

"I didn't hurt her, I swear." Asla squealed and swatted unsuccessfully at Talon's grasp. "I was just trying to wake her."

Talon didn't release her.

Marquart chuckled softly to herself. Asla wouldn't tell Zander or the other barbarian anything of her involvement. Of this she was certain. The silly chit was too concerned with protecting her own ass.

But perhaps she should suddenly appear to wake.

She could cry foul and accuse Asla of a misdeed, and Zander might just be honor bound to do away with the female barbarian for her. After all, did she really need Asla anymore? She had served her purpose and outlived her usefulness, hadn't she? And it would save her the extra added inconvenience of cleaning up that particular loose end later.

Marquart chuckled, just a hair louder but not so loud as to be heard. No, she wouldn't go quite so far as to insure the disposal of dear little Asla just yet. Who knew what tasks needed to be done that she herself didn't wish to waste her time on?

Instead, slowly, she lifted her head and shook it back and forth, as if trying to clear it from a fog. Glancing up at Zander who still held the sleeping human female snugly within his arms, Marquart cried, "No, please, not on my watch. What's happened? Has Kitrina been injured? I'll never forgive myself if she has."

Chapter Eleven

The irate little gnome paced back and forth before the woman Zander loved with every fiber of his being, and he wished there was some way to protect her from what was coming. He couldn't, though, and wouldn't if he could. If he himself hadn't been able to convince Kitrina of the unnecessary dangers she'd put herself in, perhaps the red-faced, purple-glove-wearing, lecture-giving Leeky Shortz could.

"What the constipated cramps, bouts of bilious burping, and fits of festering farts plaguing a dwarf dandy who consumed more than his fair share of pickled, peppered water buffalo penises were ya thinking, lass? I thought I taught ya better. A rogue, any rogue…even a really bad rogue, doesn't let herself get caught sleeping on the job with her panties flapping in the wind and at the mercy of her enemies."

Kitrina hung her head. "I know, Uncle Leeky. I know. I failed you. I failed myself. And worst of all, I've failed my family. I don't deserve to lead this quest. I should turn it back over to Zander."

Zander scowled. "No, you shouldn't."

He didn't understand this Kitrina. Where was her fight, her fire, the determination he so loved? He didn't know this woman who sat so still and defeated only a few feet away. He wanted to cross the room and shake her. He wanted to scoop her up safely within his arms once more and never let her go. He wanted to kiss every inch of her body until she burned, until she once more became the Kitrina he recognized. He needed to assure himself she was still in there somewhere. Right now, though, he wasn't so sure she was.

Even though this Kit's voice sounded like the Kitrina Dragonheart he knew and loved, that was where the real similarities ended. This woman looked as Zander had never seen his Kit look. Not even the day of her deflowering when she'd been so deeply humiliated. This Kitrina Dragonheart looked...as if she'd died in that library instead of simply succumbing to the effects of a potion.

Her normally spiky midnight-black hair hung limp and dull about her ears. Her stormy blue eyes were cloudy and red rimmed. Her lovely peach skin had lost its luster. She was so washed out, she appeared almost bloodless.

He shuddered. His heart stuttered and, in a moment of fear, slammed to a stop before once more resuming its pounding. He should do something, say something, anything, but what?

Leeky Shortz's face pinkened, and he quickly patted Kitrina's hand. "Now, don't go being ta hard on yaself, lass. Wasn't all ya fault, ya know."

He made a production of crossing the room and kicking the shins of the very repentant Limburger brothers. The action brought the first real smile of the day to Zander's face.

"What the smelly bellybutton lint marinating for a month in the dusty, crusty navel of an ogre onion farmer were ya two dunderheads thinking? Ya were sent ta protect our Kitten here, not laze about daydreaming of pizzle-twiddling Zander's ex. And don't ya dare insult my intelligence by denying it. I've seen the way ya both look at Asla."

Ten opened his mouth to speak but then shook his head in defeat and shrugged his shoulders.

Zander had plenty to say on the subject of his ex-fiancé. "I caught her standing over Kitrina. I'm not sure what she was doing, but I have a very strong suspicion she's up to her teeth in mischief. I don't trust her."

"No, she's not." Ten loudly insisted, with Levin nodding his head right beside him. "Asla's not like that. You don't know her the way we do. We'll vouch for her innocence. If anybody's to blame for what happened at the library, it's that troll, Maycee. I'd stake my family's secret cheese recipe on it."

Kitrina shook her head. "No one's to blame but me. This was my quest, my responsibility, and I let my guard down. It won't happen again, I swear." She took a deep breath. "Since we didn't take those bottles of wine with us from here, we must assume that the drink could've been tampered with long before we ever got to that library, by whomever for whatever reason. And since we confiscated those bottles without permission for our own use, we shouldn't accuse anyone of wrongdoing without solid proof." Her spine stiffened and a hint of a spark lit Kit's previously dead eyes. "But, God Draka help Asla or Maycee or anybody else who tries to harm me or those I care for, ever again. I'm done playing nice, and I'm VoT tired of following the rules when others don't."

Zander nodded. Kitrina Dragonheart might very well have suffered a setback today, and she might very well have a ways to go to get back on her A game. But if the gleam now shining in her eyes was any indication, there was one thing Kit wasn't. She was no longer defeated.

****

Zander's lips grazed the sensitive spot right below her left ear, and Kitrina sighed. After the meeting with Leeky and the guys finally ended, they'd made their way back to Zander's room and quickly undressed each other without either one of them uttering a single word. A fact Kitrina was very thankful for.

The last thing she wanted right this moment was to discuss what was or wasn't found and what did or didn't take place at the library. What she did want, what she desperately needed, was to be held tightly in this man's arms, touched by this man's hands, and kissed by this and only this man's lips until every memory of the day, real or imagined, faded into oblivion.

He nipped the pulse point at the base of her throat and desire shot like lightning straight through her chest landing deep in her belly. Her nipples hardened, and her pussy ached with a want to be filled.

Still, they didn't speak, not a syllable, not a groan, not even a moan, but she had no problem understanding exactly what Zander Hammerstrike was telling her with his hands, his mouth, his body, and his heart. He loved her, and she gloried in that knowledge.

The fingertips of one of his big hands grazed a nipple while the other held the back of her head steady and firm. His lips teased and flirted with first one eyelid and then the other before fluttering kisses upon her nose and cheeks. His leg slid its way up hers and wedged between her knees, parting her, opening her, readying her for what they both wanted, needed.

His cock rubbed her hip, hard and hot, first slow, then fast, and then slow again. His breath mingled with hers as he finally captured her lips in a kiss.

And God Draka, what a kiss it was—hot, hungry, and demanding, his tongue warring with hers, plundering her mouth, stealing her breath, and capturing her soul. He tasted of comfort and safety, of coming home, of desire, lust, laughter, and love all combined into one glorious flavor. A promise without words meant to last a lifetime and beyond. She kissed him back with a reverent silence she could only hope he understood.

Her heart hurt. Why him? And why did their destinies have to be so polar opposite and unchangeable?

He kissed away tears she hadn't realized she allowed to fall and whispered against her hair. "Shh, forget everything else for just a while, my lady, and let me love you."

And she did.

His entire body became a dazzling force of nature as his mouth, his fingers, his legs, and especially his cock all meshed into one magnificently functioning instrument of pleasure. Her skin tingled everywhere he touched her, and her heartbeat pounded in her ears as he slid over her and nestled his hips between her legs.

Time and place lost all meaning as, with one powerful thrust, his cock slid home. Her pussy clenched around him, her breath mingled with his, and her very heartbeat matched the cadence of his as their fingers intertwined.

She closed her eyes and concentrated on the different textures, the sounds, the very essence of the man with her, above her, and most enjoyably inside her.

Ever so slowly and thoroughly, he fucked her. God Draka, he was big and hard and wonderful. The ridge of the head of his cock slid expertly along her pussy wall, leaving spirals of pleasure in its wake, while his thick shaft pulsed within her with a heat that lusciously burned from the inside out. His stroke was firm but controlled. Every clench of his thigh muscles, every undulation of his hips perfectly orchestrated to eke out the most pleasure possible…for her anyway.

But what of him?

She swatted his shoulder. "Let go, damn you. How many times must I say it? I'm not some fragile little flower. I won't break. Fuck me like you mean it, barbarian."

Zander chuckled. "I've never thought of you as a flower, Kit, fragile or otherwise." He slid his cock home once more and she shivered. "A sleek tigress or a snarling leopard, even a cunning lioness, perhaps," he whispered. "But never ever something as passive as a mere flower."

Tears stung her eyes, and Kitrina gulped. "You have no idea how much I wish you were right."

His response was to slip a hand between them and locate her clit. Once, twice, then a third time he stroked it, and Kitrina gasped as waves of delight washed through her. Her breath quickened, her thighs tingled, and her stomach tightened.

He leaned in close, nuzzled her neck, leaving tendrils of excitement shooting outward in his wake. "You, my lady, are my wild cat, and in charge of me and our quest. And in that quest, your wish is certainly my every command. But as to this endeavor," he stroked her once more, "I'm the one on top at the moment and in charge of this particular fucking. I'll see to it as I see fit. Though, I am a reasonable man and willing to compromise. Would you like to practice the art of compromise with me, Kitten?"

He enunciated his question with a quick deep thrust of his cock and a playful pinch to her clit that left Kitrina trembling and incapable of any answer but a nod.

Zander chuckled. "So, my lady truly is a little wild cat, isn't she? And she really does wish to…copulate liked a barbarian?"

Again, she nodded.

Zander's eyes lit with a mischievous gleam, and what could only be described as a wicked, wicked smile curved his lips. "It's time for a change of strategy and pace then, I suppose."

Kitrina held onto the man above her for dear life as gone were his slow sure strokes replaced with quick, wild, deep plunges. The fingers of his one hand flicked and stroked the super sensitive membranes of her swollen clit while his other hand stole away behind her and those fingers found the opening of her ass.

He smiled lecherously. "Turnabout's far play, my lady, don't you think?" Slowly, gently, and carefully, he inserted the tip of his middle finger into her ass, slipped it out again and back in. All the way back in.

She held her breath at the unexpected invasion, waiting for the beginning of a pain that never came. What did come was a deliciously overwhelming assault on her senses. Her pussy throbbed and quaked with every stroke of his cock. Her clit hummed and her ass tensed and tingled around every stroke of his fingers.

Pressure built higher and higher, starting in the pit of her belly and radiating outward. Consuming, engulfing, scorching her pussy, her clit, and her ass to the point she had no choice but give into her body's demand or die from the simple gratification of it.

But still, Kitrina fought to stave it off. "No, no, not yet," she cried as spasms of pure white heat flowed and rolled and pulsed through her.

When the orgasm was done, she lay panting in his arms. His cock still deep and hard within her body spurted forth its seed. She'd known it was about to happen, but her orgasm had come as a surprise and was, in a way, a disappointment. Not that her release hadn't been just as marvelously magnificent as she'd known it would be, because it had been.

It was just... She wasn't ready to give him up for even the remainder of this night, let alone...forever. She gulped.

Never, ever, in all of the times she'd lain with this man, whom she loved so dearly, and shared with him the ecstasy of her body flying apart into so many different pieces, had she ever regretted their lovemaking coming to its natural conclusion. But this time she did. This time had been too fast, too final. This time had felt, in some ways, almost like a goodbye. She wasn't ready. She needed more time. She needed Zander for a lifetime. She'd need him forever.

"Don't even think about falling asleep on me yet, my lady. I've only begun to take my pleasure of you this night."

Kitrina blinked back tears, smiled into the darkness, and wiggled her ass in invitation. "What a wonderful mind reader you are, barbarian. Carry on."

Zander's cock hardened within her sheath, and he began to fuck her once more. Her pussy thrummed about his cock, and she put away her fears and worries of the future. The anticipation of what lay before them this night was more than enough to occupy her mind, and it had her heart pounding and her thighs clenching him tight.

A smile that not even the threat of being cast into the pits of the Valley of Torment could wipe away graced her face, and she fucked him back with all the enthusiasm her heart contained.

No more words were said. No more words were needed. But she was gifted with four more orgasms, two more for him, before the first rays of a new dawn broke across the horizon and they closed their eyes in slumber.

****

Kitrina stretched. The muscles of her inner thighs ached, but she didn't care. Last night's wonderfully wild lovemaking session with Zander had been more than worth the few well-earned friction burns and scattered bruises that graced her body.

She gazed at the man she loved slumbering so contently beside her and couldn't help but smile. Temptation to reach out and shake him awake for an encore filled her. She didn't, though. For waking Zander might very well mean another bout of fun-filled frolicking, but it would, without a doubt, mean it was time to answer questions he hadn't asked last night. Questions, she wasn't so sure she was quite ready to answer.

She sighed, lay back, and snuggled up against the warm flesh of his chest. Not that she'd willingly admit it to him, but Zander had been right. What had she been thinking traveling to the library of human history with only Ten and Levin for protection? Not that anything really bad had happened, had it?

Kitrina chewed her bottom lip as glimpses of a memory or a dream, she wasn't sure which, invaded her mind. Asla standing over her with Maycee in the background, asking... Asking questions she hadn't wanted to answer but couldn't seem not to. Questions about the Dragon Heart Opal. Questions about its properties, its possession. What had she told Zander's ex? What had she said? What secrets, if any, could she have possibly divulged to the pair?

A big warm arm suddenly engulfed her, and Kitrina smiled up at Zander. He wasn't smiling, though. A look of confusion marred his handsome face.

"Though a cute but strange little pussy you are, you're not who I expected to find in my bed this morning."

He rubbed her back and Kitrina frowned. It was on the tip of her tongue to ask him who he had been expecting when his rubbing caused a purr to escape her throat.

A purr?

Kitrina gulped and looked at herself. Not now. Not this morning?

Zander sat up. "Where's your mistress, in the shower?" He kicked off the covers and rose. "Kitrina...Kit," he yelled as he stepped into the legs of his breeks.

The door opened and Talon stuck his head through. "What are you bellowing about in here?"

Zander grumbled. "Kitrina, where is she? Where'd

she go? To class? Have I really slept half the day away and not even known it?"

"Kitrina hasn't gone anywhere." Talon shook his head. "She couldn't have. She has to be in here somewhere."

Zander made a production of looking under the bed and even throwing open the curtain surrounding the private bathing alcove. "Well, if she is, then she's learned the art of invisibility. Other than the two of us, the only living, breathing thing I see in this room, is her stupid cat."

Talon took umbrage "I know my duty, Zander, and I'm telling you she didn't get past me." He fisted his hands at his side. "Do you really think I'd let Kitrina go wondering around The Academy unguarded, especially after what happened yesterday? No one, and I do mean no one, has left this room since you and she entered it last night and closed the door. And no, it's not that late. It's midmorning, and there aren't any classes today. It's the holy day before the Yulemass break, remember."

"I don't care what VoT day of the week it is." Zander didn't simply speak or yell this time, he roared as he gestured about the room. "What I do care about is, where is Kitrina?"

He paced. "You had one job, Talon, one simple job, and that one job was to watch out for that stubborn-assed woman's well-being while I slept. You've failed her, and you've failed me." Zander grabbed up his tunic and slipped it over his head. Not bothering with boots, he headed out the door.

Talon followed. "Now just a minute, Zander, you aren't being fair or reasonable. I'm telling you, no one, especially not Kitrina, not even that stupid cat of hers, came in or out of that door during my watch last night. I swear it."

"Well, she's not here now, is she? And she certainly didn't walk through a wall or disappear into thin air, did she? Perhaps I should've appointed the stupid cat to watch over her while I slept. It couldn't have done a worse job."

Kitrina cringed at Zander's reply as both men stalked off together, and all she wanted to do was cry. God Draka, what an idiot she'd been.

Shame filled her to overflowing, suffocating her with guilt. What was wrong with her? She should've had the courage to just shift back into human form right then and there in front of them both and prevent their horrible argument from starting in the first place, but she hadn't. She'd lost her nerve.

After yesterday's fiasco, she couldn't bear to see the added hurt and disappointment in Zander's eyes when he realized she'd been holding out details about herself that, she had to admit, he had every right to know. And not simply withholding the knowledge she had the ability to shape-shift into a…stupid cat but that she had also utilized that stupid cat form to willingly become a sounding board to confidences he thought he was sharing with a creature he could trust not to divulge his secrets.

Kitrina shifted back into human form and sat cross-legged in the middle of the bed, tears stinging her eyes. What was she going to do? Somehow, she had to make this right, but how? The moment both men walked away, the chance to tell the truth was past and the damage done.

She shook her head. Even if she followed them this

very moment and told Zander she was a shape-shifter, he'd hate her for making him look like a fool and so would Talon. And the worst part was, she couldn't blame either one of them if they did.

But then simple hate she could live with. She'd deserve it. But there was a big difference between warranting someone's hatred and living with the knowledge Zander would realize she'd broken his trust. A trust he'd given her freely and without question. Being untrustworthy was unacceptable. To guard the secrets of those in one's care was the single true quality a rogue valued above all others.

So, what to do?

She loved Zander enough to let him go when this situation was all said and done, for he was destined to become the barbarian king someday and she...well, she was destined to be simply Uthiel and Briar Dragonheart's daughter for the rest of her life. And she loved him enough not to let him see how much losing him yet again would rip her heart into a million pieces and toss them to the wind.

But did she love him enough not to clear her conscience and protect him from the pain of her betrayal? Kitrina sighed. Yes, she did. After all, what was one more tiny lie at this point? Especially since, when this quest was over, she and Zander would go their separate ways. None need be the wiser.

She'd didn't have any clue what excuse she'd come up with, though, but she'd fabricate some feasible reason for not being where she was supposed to be this morning. A reason that would make sense to both men, and in the end, preserve their friendship. After all, the preservation of the bond Zander and Talon shared was what was truly important. Talon would be at Zander's side long after she was gone.

Then it hit her, and Kitrina hurried to the medicine bag her mother always insisted she have in her possession. Quickly, she rummaged through the contents until she found the small silver box containing the mixture of burundanga root, henbane, and ground jimson weed, commonly known as the Powder of Forgetfulness.

Smiling to herself, she sent out a hasty thank you to God Draka and her mother for not only Briarlarn Dragonheart's knowledge of herbology but also her tenacity for drumming into the brains of her three daughters the use of every VoT twig, leaf, root, bud, and stalk of every VoT plant known to Albrath, whether they wanted the information hammered into their skulls or not.

Hastily Kitrina dressed and rushed from the room, not considering her safety, not considering that the last commander hunting her—Marquart, could be anywhere, even around the very next corner. And she didn't waste energy contemplating the quest in her care. There'd be plenty of time to worry about it later.

But right now, there was no more time to waste. It was imperative she find Zander and convince him of Talon's innocence in her actions. Yes, she'd find them both, and she'd make this right. And it didn't matter what cost her lies exacted on her soul. In the end, it would be worth it. It had to be.

****

Marquart Maycee Strumgrund, high commander of a formidable troll army and seeker of the Stone of Anthion, stood in the shadows of the hallway leading to

Kitrina's and Zander's room. She had watched the scene before her unfold.

It seemed not all was well and peachy-keen in the confines of the chambers of The Academy of Magical Arts this gray, stormy morning. How appropriate. She smiled.

She liked chaos, thrived on it even. A peaceful life was dull, boring, and without imagination. And she should certainly know. Hadn't she lived a marginally sedate existence for the last five centuries of her nine hundred years or so? Always hiding away from prying eyes, always watching from the bleachers so to speak, forever ordering others to do the fun stuff she wished she could openly do herself.

For to be immortal without those around you learning you were immortal and trying to somehow learn the secret of it in order to take advantage for themselves was a full time job.

How many times had she caught one of her generals looking at her a little too closely, trying to find a way to take her place? None had succeeded, but that had meant staying in the shadows, never trusting anyone, and changing her personal guard long before they had the chance to realize she never aged and never suffered injuries. It really was a thankless, tedious job.

Why, if one took the time to give much thought to her long life at all, under the circumstances she'd be considered in some circles virtually a saint. After all, she'd hardly executed more than a handful or couple hundred or so pathetic specimens of mortal contention with her own hands, and then only those who gave her absolutely no other choice. Those who had gotten too close to her secret or openly defied her orders or attempted to thwart her plans. It was the only real entertainment she'd allowed herself over the years. That, and the occasional cunt licking from a stable of sex slaves.

But—she shuddered—she was just like all the rest of them now...mortal and...and...vulnerable. There could be no trusting anyone but herself with the importance of this mission.

She'd hoped to recruit Walaford Titwilder to her side. That hadn't happened, however. The hand-to-hand combat instructor hadn't so much as looked her direction without just cause. And he certainly hadn't succumbed to her vast charms. On the contrary. It was as if the man loathed the very sight of a well-made tusk. Maycee sniffed. It didn't matter. She didn't need him.

What did matter, however, was she needed the VoT stone. She must have the stone, and she must have it soon before one of those underlings of hers realized she'd been weakened by mortality and was as dependent on her next heartbeat, her next breath, as they were.

She glanced from side to side, letting the quiet fill her, and smiled. Her tusks, comfortingly rubbing the worn skin of her cheeks. The incessant posturing and yelling from the two male barbarian idiots about Kitrina being missing and of all things a stupid cat had finally ceased with their departure and the hall lay empty before her and silent.

It was finally time to move, time to proceed, time to get a peek in Kit's room.

So Kitrina had somehow managed to slip away and elude her guards, had she? How very interesting, and convenient. It would make her plan of searching the human chit's chamber for any tidbit of useful information so much simpler.

Marquart bristled. But where the VoT was Asla today? She'd personally taken on the task of retrieving the Stone of Anthion, but that didn't mean she should waste her time on such a menial task as this one when there were those under her command who should be ready and willing to do her bidding. It was beneath her.

Asla would pay for her insubordination.

A commander of her standing shouldn't have to lurk in drafty hallways and dirty her hands sneaking through other people's...things, searching for clues.

So what if she hadn't been able to ask one of her generals to come along with her and do these little errands because they would've been insulted and a little more than suspicious. At least she should've been able to put this particular job off on Asla. It was a chore worthy only of a grunt, and Marquart Maycee Strumgrund certainly was no grunt.

Oh yes, before this little project was well and truly over, Asla would pay, and pay dearly.

She was almost to the open doorway when Kitrina suddenly rushed from the room and headed down the hallway in the same direction Zander and Talon had taken.

Marquart jumped back into the shadows.

How odd. How could Kitrina have been in the room all along and the two barbarians not see her? And if she had been, then why hadn't she let them know she was there?

When Kit is Cat the Dragon Heart Opal doesn't care about her.

Marquart shook her head. Last night, she thought

she'd overdosed the chit and Kitrina had been speaking nonsense. But, what if?

Marquart made her way through the still open doorway. "Here, kitty, kitty." She looked under the bed and behind the curtain as her mind filled with the possibility. Could the answer to all her problems really be that simple?

For good measure, she tried one last time. "Here, kitty, kitty. Come out and show youtself, yout little ball of fur yout."

There was no answer, and Marquart laughed as she headed to the library to do a little research of her own. Yes, the old adage really was true after all. If yout want something done right, do it youtself.

Chapter Twelve

"I swear, Talon, if any harm's come to Kitrina, I'll never forgive myself. Though I trust you with my very life and always will, I had no right to commit her safety to anyone but myself. I'm sorry I put you in that position." Zander didn't slow his forward momentum as he hurried down the hall, but he did lower his head. "What was I thinking? I should've stayed alert and vigilant for at least one night."

He locked gazes with Talon and knew he was going to sound like he was looking for reassurance. He probably was, but, it didn't matter. Only Kitrina's safety did. "You don't think perhaps someone…took her, do you?"

Talon scoffed. "I already told you, Zander, no one got past me, and I mean no one. Nobody, not even you, can stay awake for hours on end, so stop blaming yourself. I'm telling you, there must be some other explanation. I have no idea what, but something we're both missing."

Zander shook his head. "If no one got past you, then where the VoT is she? The only thing I can figure is, you must have gotten knocked out or something and don't remember it. Or drugged perhaps?"

Talon stopped dead in his tracks, and Zander was forced to stop, too.

"Do you really think I'd forget something like

getting punched hard enough to knock me out? With my skills...with my thick skull? Seriously?"

Zander did feel a little silly for suggesting such a thing. In all of his twenty-six years, he'd never once seen anyone big enough or strong enough to knock Talon Starkweather on his arse, let alone rattle his brain so much he forgot it even happened. It was on the tip of his tongue to say just that when the sound of the voice he feared he'd never hear again stopped him in his tracks.

"Zander, Talon, slow down."

He spun so fast he stumbled and lost his balance for a moment. God Draka, this woman was going to be the death of him yet.

"Kitrina." His voice broke, and he swallowed back the lump that had been forming in his throat since the moment he awakened to find her missing. "God Draka, where have you been?"

Quickly, he took in every aspect of her visage. Every hair was neatly in place, her eyes were the same stormy blue they'd always been, her lips still just as kissably lush and pink, and she didn't appear to be bleeding or bruised or broken in any manner.

No, on the contrary, Kitrina looked...fresh, vibrant, and completely innocent of any wrongdoing on anyone's part, especially her own. Which could mean only one thing. The sneaky little rogue had slipped away from him...again...on purpose.

Rage took the place of worry, and Zander took a moment to tamp it down. There must be a good reason. There had to be. If there wasn't, he was going to kill her or at least make her wish she were dead. "Kitrina, where have you been?"

Zander was proud of himself. He hadn't yelled. He'd spoken in a calm voice, and he hadn't yet grabbed her up and shaken the life from her like his fingers itched to do. But somewhere close by thunder rumbled. The walls of The Academy shook with it.

"Um, I thought I'd be back before you woke, sorry," she mumbled.

He could feel his right eye twitch, and he fisted his hands at his sides to keep them in place. "That isn't what I asked you, my lady. Where were you, and how did you get past Talon?"

She had the audacity to chuckle. "Oh, that part was easy. I drugged him."

"You dr—drugged me? Impossible," Talon howled

It was all Zander could do, not to choke her that very moment. She'd drugged Talon? And then laughed about it?

The sudden deluge of rain outside was so loud he could plainly hear it through the walls as the drops hit the cobblestone walkways. He took deep breaths, trying to calm himself. It didn't work. Instead, he watched what he really wanted to do unfold in his mind. Yes, he could do it. He could and should choke her to death, if for no other reason than to preserve his and everyone else's sanity. He'd slowly wrap his big barbarian fingers around her delicate little human neck and squeeze until Kitrina Dragonheart was no longer capable of driving him crazy and making his life a living VoT.

Instead, he had to ask. "Kit, why would you do such a thing? How would you?"

She raised her chin a notch and spoke as if she were explaining the art of walking and chewing bubble gum at the same time to an idiot. "I did it because he would have prevented me from leaving, and I didn't want him to."

She held out a small silver box. "Powder of Forgetfulness, comes in handy and works quickly without leaving any nasty side effects. I got it from my mother."

Kitrina had the nerve to poke him in the chest, hard. "Zander Hammerstrike, I'm ashamed of you." She pointed toward Talon. "You didn't really think your best friend let me go wondering off alone without an incentive he was powerless to resist, now do you? You, of all people, should know him better than that."

She stomped her foot. "And I'll have you know it even took a double dose of this stuff to make him set back down, go back to sleep, and forget he'd even seen me."

Zander held his breath. It was that or give into his urge and kill her. When he could no longer keep it in, he let the air out in a whoosh. "I thought we had an agreement, Kitrina. I thought you were not to wander off by yourself anymore, remember? We had a deal."

She did look almost repentant. Her eyes lowered, and she hugged herself before starring up at him with pleading in her eyes. "I'm sorry, Zander." Kitrina pointed to Talon. "I know I promised to take someone with me whenever I go anywhere, but it really was just a quick, simple task. I didn't want to wake you, and when Talon insisted he accompany me…well…he just looked…so very tired. I simply didn't have the heart to disturb what little rest he gets on that cold hard floor outside our room every night."

Tears glistened in her eyes, and though he knew

she was probably lying to him, it was all Zander could do not to wrap her in his arms. He didn't, though. He had to hear the rest of her story. "What task was so important it couldn't wait?"

"I...I think you might possibly be right about...about...Maycee," she cried.

A single tear welled up and slowly slid down her right cheek. Zander captured it with the pad of his thumb and wiped it away. He sighed. Yes, there was no doubt about it; Kitrina Dragonheart was definitely going to be the death of him someday.

"I was right about what, Kit? And you still haven't told me where you went or why."

She took a deep breath, and the words tumbled out of her mouth quickly. "I went to the library. I had to research something. There's no class today, remember? It's a holiday...kind of. So, I didn't think anyone else would be there this early in the morning. And I was right, it was empty."

She paused for a breath, and Zander's patience snapped. "For God Draka's sake, Kitrina, quit beating around the bush and just spit it out."

She glowered at him. "If you'd give me a chance to tell you without interrupting me every other second, I just might be able to."

Zander made a point of glowering back at her, but he shut his mouth, crossed his arms, and waited.

"Well," Kitrina said. "When I woke this morning, I remembered something that happened while I was, umm, drugged. Something I think might be important."

"Must be nice," Talon scoffed. "I don't remember a thing."

Kitrina cringed. "Sorry."

Zander shook his head. "Talon, hush. Kit, get on with it."

She nodded. "I know it was Asla who you caught standing over me, and I'm certainly not ruling out any involvement on her part, but I swear I remember Maycee prompting her to ask me questions. Questions about the Dragon Heart Opal." She paused for a moment. "I think Maycee was threatening Asla if she didn't do what she told her to, but I can't be sure. It's all jumbled."

Kitrina swallowed a loud sob, and Zander reached out to gently stroke the same soft warm neck he only the dropping of a few grains of sand through the hourglass ago had wanted to choke the life out of. He felt ashamed.

"Take your time," he whispered.

Then he made a quick promise to himself. Kitrina didn't deserve his anger. She deserved his patience. Never again would he give credence to thoughts of violence against her in any way, no matter what trials the sometimes infuriating little bundle of feminine rogue put him through in the future.

"I went to the library to check Maycee out," she continued. "I wanted—needed to see what I could find out about her past. Even though I know it's common for many trolls not to use a last name and that makes them hard to keep track of, what it takes to get admitted into The Academy of Magical Arts really isn't that hard to pursue. I found the scores of her entrance exam. I even found recommendations from more than a few high-placed individuals, including three troll generals and Asla's barbarian father of all people."

Zander's spiritmaster sensibility zinged to life in a

whole other direction, and he stiffened at her side, dreading to hear more, wishing he'd been wrong about Maycee. Being right should've felt...better than this did. It didn't, though. It just felt...scary.

Kitrina didn't seem to notice his change in demeanor, however. She kept on explaining, just as he'd asked her to. "But what I didn't find was any trace of personal history before this year or before her application to enroll in this institution. It's as if Maycee didn't exist before we all met her here at The Academy. I find that...odd. Don't you?"

Zander nodded. "I think we'd best call a meeting."

****

"Surprise!"

Marquart stared at the two obviously disturbed individuals standing before her and wondered if they had any idea how close they'd just come to being dead? She resheathed her dagger and made a point of glaring at Pierced and his piss-poor excuse of a grinning, dark elf boyfriend. What a waste of bone, blood, and muscle. "Go away, I'm busy."

They didn't leave. No, that would've made way too much sense, and there was certainly no one on Albrath ignorant enough to accuse Pierced Shortz of having anything as common as sense.

"Ah, Maycee, don't ya at least want ta know what we're up ta today?"

She really didn't. But she had to admit, considering how they looked, there must have been some kind of really disturbing story behind whatever the two of them had going on.

The strange little gay-Goth gnome was perched upon smiling Steve's jutting rock-hard blue cock, and he was as naked as the day he'd been born, which wasn't unusual, except today, he was also wearing a blond curly wig, had a red cape slung across his shoulders, and was carrying what looked to be a picnic basket of some sort in his hand.

And Steve? The dark elf was just as equally bizarre, if not more so. He was stark-assed naked, too. But his normally clean-shaven face was framed by not only his usual snow-white locks of hair but also a furry-looking beard to match. He was wearing round, rimmed, old lady spectacles, and had an absurdly long, whiskered blue snout on his indigo blue face.

She wasn't going to ask them what they were up to, though. She wasn't. No matter what antics the pair came up with or what they said to provoke her curiosity.

Instead, Marquart forced herself back to her task, once more buried herself in the book on paladin genealogy, and smiled. All along, the answer to her dilemma of how to procure the Stone of Anthion from the grasp of the stupid human chit had been right at her fingertips, and she hadn't even realized it.

Well, she realized it now.

It amazed her how one little word in one single sentence of one obscure text could so alter the outcome of her entire existence. And that one word was bahsheer.

Sir Uthiel Dragonheart, the leader of the Paladins of Albrath, the Protector of the Dragons, the Master of Castle Kuropkat, and Kitrina's father was part bahsheer. His mother's grandfather had been a full blooded bahsheer, which made Uthiel Dragonheart part bahsheer, which made Kitrina not only a descendant of the race known as bahsheer, but also, apparently, a recipient of their unusual recessive gene.

Maycee grinned as she read on. Bahsheers, a race of cat-like people, who, when their blood mixed with those who weren't bahsheer themselves, sometimes produced offspring with the capability to shift into various cat forms. Perhaps even cats like the one who the Dragon Heart Opal apparently didn't care about.

"Little Red Riding Hood, that's what we're doing."

Marquart glanced up. "What?"

Pierced placed both his hands on his hips. "I said we're playing Little Red Riding Hood. I'm Red." He pointed over his shoulder to Steve. "He's the big bad wolf, and he's gonna punish me for being naughty and eat me all up and other stuff."

Pierced giggled, and the sound echoed off the walls.

Marquart realized that since most of The Academy was virtually vacant today because of the stupid Yulemass celebrations starting, she could easily kill these two idiots with none being the wiser. Not only would it decrease the number of bodyguards constantly surrounding Kitrina, but there would be two fewer pains in her ass to contend with later when the little human chit disappeared off the face of Albrath and the hunt for her began.

Blood lust filled her. It had been a very long time since she'd had the pleasure of killing anyone, let alone these two who so deserved it. Marquart unsheathed her dagger. Why not indulge her urge? It was a win-win situation.

"There ya two are. Da sent me ta find ya."

Marquart spun and starred straight into the face of

a young purple-haired female gnome. What was it with all these people sneaking up on her today? She hadn't managed to live nine centuries by being careless. And yet today, two idiots and a gnome youngster had managed to do something many grown men had failed at in the past and subsequently paid for with their lives.

It wasn't to be tolerated.

"What's he want now, Lavender? Can't ya see Steve and I are right in the middle of Little Red Riding Hood?"

The female gnome stomped her foot. "He's not going ta care what ya are or na in the middle of and ya well know it. He told me ta tell ya what the whatever pickled something or other on a wood-elf choirboy's backside, and there's an emergency meeting and ya'd better come quick."

"VoT, VoT, and double VoT," Pierced swore. "I swear Da has a sixth sense. He always seems ta pick the most inconvenient moments ta interrupt our fun."

The library door swung open and in walked Asla. "Maycee, I was told you were looking for me?"

Steve grinned and waved goodbye as he walked right past her with Pierced still balancing precariously on his stiff cock, as if he didn't have a care in the world.

Lavender followed them both, and Maycee resheathed her dagger.

Too bad. Killing those three would've no doubt been a useless endeavor, but oh so fulfilling. But then, another opportunity would present itself. It always did.

Right now, though, there were more important matters to contemplate.

She glared at Asla. "It's about time yout showed

up. Go get packed. We need to leave."

****

"What the chewed-up and spit-out crunchy balls of wax from deep in the ear canals of an overly friendly ogre streetwalker with a penchant for dirty little dwarf boys who like ta dress up as donkeys and bay at the three moons of Albrath while doing the humpity-bumpity wiggly-giggly squirt do ya make of that? It's ta bad really. I was just starting ta…kinda like that troll."

Kitrina swallowed back her guilt. She should've shared her suspicions concerning Maycee with her friends earlier much earlier. And she certainly should have never lied right to Zander's face.

She realized that now. It'd been a mistake, a big one. She should've had the guts to own up to the fact she was a shifter, even if the only thing she could shift into was an embarrassingly useless, and as Zander had so eloquently put it, stupid cat. But she hadn't.

What if he found out later she'd deceived him? He'd never again trust her, he'd never ever forgive her, and she wouldn't even blame him.

"I say we track Maycee down right now," Zander said. "Bring her back here. We need to interrogate her. Perhaps we could even finally get a good look at the back of her neck and see if there's a K tattooed there. It's time we got to the bottom of this."

Pierced jumped up from his seat in the middle of Steve's lap and waved his hand in the air. "Oh…oh, I know where she is or at least where she was. Steve and I talked to her in the library just before coming here. You can ask Asla. She was there, too."

Kitrina sighed. The library. Of all the places on Albrath to set her lie to Zander and Talon, why had she picked the one location that could be so easily disproved?

Everyone knew it was a requirement to sign the ledger in the lobby before entering or leaving the library. A ledger Zander definitely wouldn't be finding her name on this morning. And Maycee had been in the library at the exact same time Kit had told Zander she'd been there? And Asla, too? Why? And if asked, would they expose her deception?

Kitrina swallowed hard and tried to breathe calmly.

Not that her entire story had been one big fat fabrication, for it hadn't. The part about going to the library and checking out Maycee was one hundred percent true. It just hadn't happened quite when and the way she'd said it had.

Her real visit to The Academy's library had taken place more than a week before, and what she'd found or really hadn't found had been the true catalyst behind planning the trip to the Isle of Shak-spere in the first place. She'd wanted a chance to draw Maycee out into the open, test her, make her comfortable, and at the same time make herself appear vulnerable in hopes the troll would finally show her hand.

She sighed again. Well, that whole fiasco hadn't gone quite as planned, now had it? But then, lately, nothing seemed to.

The sound of raised voices snapped Kitrina out of her introspection.

Zander's voice boomed. "Speaking of Asla, I for one don't trust her, and it's not just Maycee we need to be concerned with. Let's not forget, it was Asla that Talon and I found standing over Kitrina. Women or not, if we find proof they're trying to do Kit or her family harm, they're both dead as far as I'm concerned."

Ten's face turned a frightening shade of red. "Don't be trying to put this off on Asla. She's innocent, I tell you. I'll vouch for her." Levin nodded in agreement with his brother and stood with his hands fisted at his sides.

"Innocent," Zander scoffed. "Asla hasn't been innocent a day in her life. At least not since the moment she learned to speak."

Levin bristled. "Take it back, Zander. That's the woman Ten and I love you're speaking ill of."

Zander laughed, though there was no real humor in the sound of it. And then he simply shook his head. "Well, I feel sorry for the both of you if you really and truly are in love with Asla. Because the only person Asla Fistslammer is capable of loving is Asla Fistslammer."

"That's not true," Ten yelled. "You don't know her like we do."

It was Zander's face that turned an angry shade of red this time. "I don't know her?" he bellowed. "I was engaged to the crazy barbarian baron's daughter for what seemed like two eternities. Don't tell me I don't know her."

"Stop," Kitrina implored. "This bickering isn't going to get us anywhere except at each other's throats."

Leeky Shortz pointed toward Ten and Levin. "Ya two just sit down and keep ya short-n-curlies out of a bunch before I box both yar ears and send ya back home ta Sherman and your mothers." He shook his head. "Love, bah, makes a man plum stupid."

Then he gestured toward Talon, Wally, Graydon,

and Gareth. "And ya four lads? Ya heard Zander. What the pox-infested oozing pustules on the outer lips of a stinky, overly used vagina tucked betwixt the legs of a high elf harlot strutting the streets in search of her next unsuspecting prey are ya waiting for? An invitation ta dance? Go find Maycee and Asla and bring 'em back here. But don't tell them we suspect anything just yet. Don't want 'em high-tailing it off before we get answers."

Leeky waved them on their way. "Now, get going. We'll be waiting, umm, patiently. Zander's right. It's well time we finally know the truth."

****

Zander couldn't put his finger on the reason Kitrina looked so...guilty. He knew it deep in his gut just as sure as he recognized the difference between the sound of her voice and the feel of her soft sigh against his skin in the middle of the night.

Over the last few weeks of their forced confinement, every nuance of Kit had become so familiar to him that, at a single glance, he could differentiate even the most subtle of variations in her moods and expressions.

Today, however, she had him...stumped.

He wasn't exactly sure if the sly little rogue was remorseful about an act she'd already committed or feeling guilty about something she was yet contemplating. One thing was certain, though, the woman's mind was running an out-of-control race reminiscent of an Alarian water buffalo stampede.

Not that anyone else would notice. To the remainder of the room, Kitrina Dragonheart probably appeared just as calm, cool, and aloof as she did most days, but to Zander's eyes, she was anything but.

She sat waiting, just like the rest of them, but there was nothing still or calm about Kit under the façade she presented to the rest of the world. She'd fidgeted with the edge of her tunic to the point the hem of one section lay frayed, and even though she was being discreet about it, her eyes darted back and forth like a caged animal searching for an escape route, and the left corner of her bottom lip was chewed raw.

Oh, yes, there was no doubt about it. Kitrina was definitely covering something up or devising a plan that would put herself, if not all of them, in imminent danger.

Zander wasn't sure which he wanted to do first, grab her up and demand the truth straight from her luscious lips or wrap her within the confines of his arms and make sure she knew that, above all else, he'd keep her safe...always.

He didn't do either, though. Just as he hadn't confronted her earlier when she'd stood before him, looked him straight in the eye, and lied right to his face about drugging Talon and then sneaking off to the library. After all, God Draka knew Kitrina Dragonheart could be an extremely exasperating female on her best day, and today certainly wasn't one of her best.

Recognizing her lie was yet another example of his strange spiritmaster abilities. But today, that gift made his heart ache. She obviously didn't trust him enough with her safety, with the safety of her family, or even with his ability to see this quest through to be truthful with him in all things.

Zander had no idea what had caused her to so doubt his skills, his loyalty, even his word, but she obviously did. The only time he'd ever even been remotely untruthful with her had been concerning the Asla-being-his-fiancée debacle. And that hadn't really been a lie. It had been nothing more than a simple case of omission so as not to offend her tender little eighteen-year-old view of the world around her. Women, they were illogical creatures, and if he lived to be a thousand, he'd never completely understand their thought process.

He did understand certain nuances of Kitrina, however. After all, she was one hundred percent woman from the top of her head to the very tips of her delicate little toes and every delightful inch of her in between. And as a member of the female gender, it was taken for granted that she had her own motives for keeping secrets. Reasons that were private, incentives that obviously made sense only to the feminine brain.

After years spent in the company of his mother and sister, it was an unstated privacy that Zander comprehended he had no right to breach. Especially since, when this quest was all said and done, and the Dragon Heart Opal and those who would wear it were once more safe, there would be nothing of permanence he could offer Kitrina except for his friendship.

Still, he watched her while waiting for the others to return with Maycee and Asla in tow. Wishing there was something, anything, he could do to prove to the woman he hopelessly loved with all of his heart that he truly was worthy of her trust. And the longer he observed her, the more he was sure of his suspicions. Oh, yes, Kitrina Dragonheart was definitely hiding something. Something big.

The door banged open and a frowning Talon,

Wally, Graydon, and Gareth walked through it. Zander was relieved the waiting was finally over, but since there was no Maycee or Asla accompanying them, he also dreaded what he was about to hear.

Talon took a deep breath before looking him straight in the eye. "I'm afraid I'm destined to disappoint you yet again today, my friend. We searched every nook, cranny, room, and tower of this entire Academy. I'm sorry. Maycee and Asla are both gone, vanished, not even a gown or a hairpin or a shoe left behind to attest to their existence. It's as if they've never been here."

Zander fumed. It wasn't bad enough the two women had escaped and they would have no choice but hunt them down, but the room itself had grown cold with the spreading apprehension. And Kitrina's face…it had gone from blank to startled and then resigned in the space of time it took no more than three grains of sand to sift through the hourglass. That sight alone scared him more than not knowing where the two missing women were or what they were plotting.

And then there was Ten and Levin. With Talon's proclamation, both men lost all semblance of color and looked white as death as they each stoically swiped a tear from their eyes before the offending droplet had a chance to dribble down their cheeks.

Damn Asla, damn Maycee, and damn the Dragon Heart Opal for causing all of these problems in the first place. And God Draka help Maycee and Asla if he was ever lucky enough to get his hands around either one of their throats.

Chapter Thirteen

Asla dragged her feet once more, and Marquart snarled. "If yout don't move yout ass faster than that, I swear I'll cut yout pretty little neck where yout stand."

"I don't care," Asla responded. "I want to go back to The Academy, to Ten and Levin." She sniffed loudly and broke out into yet another bout of tears. Her third such fit in at least the last ten minutes. It wasn't to be tolerated.

Marquart shook her head. "Yout don't care, and yout want to go back to...to...to the barfling brothers?"

Why her? Why was it always her who was forced to endure such idiots?

Marquart put that thought away for a moment, not wanting to dwell on her past or her deeds. The sorry fact was, she did still need Asla's cooperation in order to carry out two more very specific tasks, and until those tasks were fulfilled, she'd simply have to do a better job of coercing the stupid little chit.

After all, this was a new day, and the wait was almost over. Marquart knew exactly what she needed to do and how she was going to go about procuring the Stone of Anthion. All she had to do was ensure the opportunity to put her plan into motion came to pass.

And with the portal stone standing right before them and The Academy of Magical Arts at their backs, all she wanted from the blonde barbarian bimbo was a modicum of assistance to get the ball rolling.

She cleared her throat and took a deep breath. She could do this, she could play nice...really she could. "Asla, be reasonable. In just a few days, this will all be over and yout will be free to go wherever yout wish. But right now, I need yout to convey a missive to yout father from me. It's of the utmost importance."

The stupid chit had the audacity to shake her head. "No, I won't do it, Maycee. I'm done helping you, and I don't care what you threaten to do to me anymore. I...I don't hate Kitrina like you do. As a matter of fact, I even kind of like her, and I don't wish harm to befall her or anyone else. And...and...I refuse to betray Ten's and Levin's trust in me. They love me and I love them."

Marquart chuckled. So much for playing nice. But then, she'd never really liked nice anyway. It was so...tedious, boring even. "Perhaps yout don't care about anything I can do to yout per say, but what about...what Daddy can do? Especially if yout leave me no choice but to inform him as to what a bad little girl yout've been."

She shook her head. "Tsk...tsk. Yout no longer hate, as he does, the very woman who, for all intents and purposes, ripped yout father's hard-earned grasp of the barbarian throne right from his fingers? Falling in love with useless halfling mutants, two of them, really? At the same time? And worst of all, they are men without a practical title between them that yout father could use to his advantage? Now, won't those accomplishments just make yout father so very proud?"

Asla's face turned a bright shade of red, and Marquart leaned in close and whispered, "I know what he's done to yout when yout've proven to be a disappointment to him in the past. Yout do remember of what I speak, don't yout? The deliciously vile things he's achieved...in the dark, in his dungeon, late at night, behind locked doors and walls so thick no one ever hears yout screams?"

Asla shuddered, all color draining from her face.

Marquart cackled. "Oh, yes, I know everything. Of that, have no doubt. Not only have I got eyes and ears all over Albrath, my silly little barbarian, but I've also seen yout scars and I've even played with his...tools."

She laughed again as she handed Asla a rolled up parchment and pushed her toward the portal. "Now, take this message to Daddy and be quick about it. And if yout know what's good for yout, yout better be with yout father when he and his men join me at Castle Kuropkat by this time tomorrow or else."

****

God Draka, she was sick to death of waiting.

Kitrina paced the small confines of the room she shared with Zander and contemplated her next move. It had been four days, four very long days since Maycee and Asla had disappeared into thin air without a trace. And it had been three equally long days since a missive had been urgently sent to Castle Kuropkat, explaining her concerns and strongly suggesting her family join her here at The Academy for the annual Yulemass celebration instead of traveling home for the holidays herself as planned.

There had been no word from any of them, however. Not that she'd expected to hear from Maycee and Asla so soon, though she had no doubt they were anything but done with her and she'd definitely be informed of their intentions in the future. But what really concerned her was the fact she'd not heard a single word from her father or her mother and not even through the psychological link with Obsidian, her dragon.

She understood Sid was probably still a tad miffed at her for leaving him behind, but not to answer her mental summons? It wasn't heard of. And her parents? Never had they neglected to ease her fears. Oh, yes, something was wrong, very wrong, and it was high time she found out just what it was.

Making up her mind as to what she needed to do, Kitrina hurriedly dressed. She'd just donned her traveling tunic, breeks, and boots, when the door swung open and Zander walked in.

"Going somewhere?"

Kitrina chewed her bottom lip. She didn't want to lie to him...again, but there was no way around it. She couldn't afford to tell him the truth. If there really were something wrong at home, it would be much more dangerous to her family for an entire group of huge men to march through the portal of Castle Kuropkat and arrive on her father's doorstep, than it would be for one itty bitty rogue to sneak through unnoticed and check the situation out first.

"Ah, I see you've caught me," she laughed. "I was just about to go out in the woods and search for some...herbs. I'm getting low on some of the supplies Mother swears I must keep stocked. We'd hate to be caught needing something I don't have, now wouldn't we?"

She picked up the small medicine bag, slung it over her shoulder, and headed toward the door.

Zander not only barred her way with his body, but

he stopped her all together with a single shake of his head.

She stomped her foot. "Why do you always have to be so unreasonable?"

"Why are you being untruthful with me about your destination, Kit? You may very well be the leader of this quest concerning the Dragon Heart Opal, but, you're not in it alone, and it's still my duty to protect you. Even from yourself. And especially if you are contemplating running off to Castle Kuropkat as we both know you are."

Heat wicked up her neck and filled her cheeks. "I am not co-co-contemplating anything," she stuttered. "And how dare you call me a liar, Zander Hammerstrike? I-I-I do need fresh herbs. But what I don't need is a protection detail from you or anybody else just to go for a quick hunt in the woods to find a bunch of leaves, seeds, and stems. Now, let me pass."

The infuriating man had the nerve to grin at her while shaking his head. "Not on your life, Kitten."

She was so mad she was seething. Kitten? She should really show him a kitten. It would serve him right if she shifted this very minute and darted between his legs and out the door. The only thing that kept her from doing just that was the sudden appearance of Talon right behind him.

"Kitrina, Zander, I'm glad you're both here. Leeky just called a meeting, and you'll never guess what it's about." He grinned. "Asla's back. Gareth caught her trying to sneak into The Academy, and he, umm, escorted her up to Wally's classroom so we'd have privacy. She looks like she's been through VoT and back, but I bet even Ten and Levin won't feel sorry for the back-stabbing little barbarian after we get to the truth out of her."

They hurried along the hallways, and though it was difficult to keep pace with the two huge barbarians in front of her, to Kitrina's mind, they were all traveling at no more than a snail's pace. She felt each and every crack in the rough cobblestones beneath her slippered feet, and noticed every subtle color change in the gray stone walls she walked past. Why? Why had Asla suddenly returned, and more importantly, if Asla was here, then where was Maycee?

She didn't have long to ponder her questions, however, as Zander flung the door wide open and Leeky Shortz's voice flooded the corridor.

"What the pissed-out-of pecker on a pox-ridden dwarf dandy trying ta entice some poor unsuspecting high elf debutant inta a closet for a game of touchy-feely and honey-bunny-in-ya-cunny do ya mean we gotta wait for Kit ta get here before ya'll talk?" He shook his fist at Asla. "Trust me, lass, ya'll talk."

Kitrina stopped in her tracks, right inside the doorway. Though she knew the woman standing across the room surrounded by an entire group of angry men was most absurdly Asla, there was little resemblance left to the barbarian female she'd almost come to, if not exactly like, not completely despise anymore.

This woman looked so defeated and alone in the world. Even Ten and Levin stood off to the side…waiting. Her lovely golden blonde hair hung in untidy short clumps about her head. Her once startling blue eyes appeared empty and dead. Her always pristine tunic was ragged and torn in various places. And what looked like deep scratches or, God Draka forbid, burns marked both her arms and legs. What on Albrath had happened to Asla Fistslammer in the last four days?

Ten and Levin didn't even glance at each other as in unison they both moved until they stood on each side of the barbarian female. Kitrina wasn't sure why, but she was proud of them and grateful for their show of support to a woman who had most probably betrayed them all and wished her harm.

"Sheesh, Uncle Leeky," Ten implored. "Give her a break." He pointed toward the door where Kitrina still stood. "See, Kit's here now, and I'm sure Asla will explain everything."

Levin added his own plea. "Yea, Uncle Leeky. You'll see. I bet Asla has a perfectly good reason for taking off like she did."

The woman they were talking about looked up and gulped. Was that guilt, shame, remorse, or a combination of all three Kitrina saw starring back at her from the depths of Asla's eyes? She wasn't sure. The woman's gaze darted back and forth between Ten and Levin. She sighed, took two more deep breaths, and swallowed. As if finally coming to a decision, Asla once more locked gazes with Kitrina and her eyes hardened. She stood up straight, stiffening her spine, and spoke as if reciting from a script."

"Kitrina Dragonheart, you are to return to Castle Kuropkat this very day, and you are to go alone. If you refuse or fail in any way to follow these instructions, there will be dire consequences. Your family has been taken prisoner, and the dragons your people are so proud of protecting have been rendered useless to your plight. You now have exactly twelve turns of the hourglass to comply or else."

Kitrina gasped as pandemonium broke out in the room. She didn't hear a word, though, as Zander gripped her arm, leaned down close, and whispered, "Don't even think about it, my lady. You aren't going anywhere without me."

She ignored him or at least tried to. No matter how much she struggled, there was no getting loose from the stubborn barbarian's grip. She settled for putting Zander's dictates out of her mind for the moment and decided since she had no choice but remain at his side, for the time being anyway, she might as well attempt to get answers to the questions running rampant through her mind.

"Is my family unharmed?" she shouted over the roar of everyone else in the room. All talking suddenly ceased. Only the breathing of the occupants could be heard in the silence that followed.

The hint of tears glistened in the eyes of the woman across the room, but she nodded her head. "I do believe your father was…beaten and your mother and sisters were, umm, threatened, but other than the fact they are…caged at the moment, they all seem well enough. Though, I do not know how long that will last. You must hurry."

Kitrina held her breath, wanting desperately to scream, to yell, to strike out at Asla and bury her dagger so deep within the barbarian traitor's heart she'd never again have the opportunity to bring such news to another. She didn't, though. She forced her mind to calm and continued her interrogation in a fashion that would've made her father proud if he could've been here to see it.

"Since Maycee disappeared the same day and time

as you did, I take it she is also involved in this scheme?

Asla nodded. "She is the catalyst."

The barbarian female suddenly turned first to Ten then to Levin and sobbed. "I didn't know she was Marquart the fourth troll commander at first. I swear I didn't. I would have never helped her if I'd known. No matter what Father..." She hung her head.

Asla's father? How interesting. What did the Baron Fistslammer have to do with Marquart and the crazy troll's obsession with the Dragon Heart Opal? There was more to that story than had yet been told, but now was not the time. There were far more pressing questions.

"You said the dragons had been...subdued. H-how?"

Asla's eyes filled with terror. "It was horrible. The troll army destroyed many of their eggs, and with Uthiel Dragonheart in chains before them, the dragons didn't even try to defend their nests." She paused for a breath. "You see, Marquart had threatened to kill him if the dragons interfered."

Asla sniffed. "Your father was so brave, though. He ordered the dragons and the other paladins present to ignore Marquart's threats and attack the troll army anyway. I think they were going to do just that, but then the trolls uncovered the golden egg."

Kitrina gasped. A golden egg? Really? It could only mean one thing. A new male dragon had been conceived and would soon hatch.

Male dragons were rare, very rare. As a matter of fact, Obsidian was the only male dragon successfully hatched in over a hundred years. He was the undisputed future of the dragon race, and with the existence of a brand new golden dragon egg, it appeared he was well on his way to living up to that expectation.

"They took the golden egg and placed it at the foot of that great big statue in your castle's courtyard." The words flowed quickly from Asla's mouth now. It was as if once she'd gotten started, she could no longer stop. "My father's barbarian solders are standing guard around it at all times. Marquart calls the egg her insurance policy that your father, the dragons, and even the other Paladins of Albrath will not interfere with her plans for you."

Asla took a deep breath and locked gazes directly with Kit. "Oh, and Kitrina? Avoid Castle Kuropkat's dungeon at all costs, for the certain death of your family awaits you there."

Kitrina gasped and knew what she needed to do. There was no doubt in her mind now. She somehow had to get away from these men who had sworn to protect her with their very lives and make her way to Marquart…to the dungeon. Even though Asla had warned her, she knew offering herself up to the troll commander was the only chance she'd have to save her family. And though she was a female and therefore not a true Paladin of Albrath, she also had to find some way to save the precious new male dragon.

Zander's grip on her wrist tightened. "Don't even think about it. We'll find another way."

She took a deep breath. "You and I both know there is no other way. At least let me scout ahead and bring back word. Trust me, if I know Maycee, I mean Marquart, she'll have a whole gaggle of troll warriors waiting for us right on the other side of the portal. I really am a very good rogue, Zander. Perhaps if I go first, I can sneak through their lines and find where they have my family. I must try."

He shook his head at her. "I can't allow you to take that risk. You're too important to us, too important to me. I pledged to protect you and protect you I will. Even from yourself if need be."

She gazed into the handsome face of the man who held her heart in his hands and sighed. So, it had finally come to this.

Kitrina reached up and with her free hand stroked the stubble-covered cheek of the man she loved. She could do this. She was brave enough. She had to be. Her family and the dragons she'd sworn to protect needed her to be strong.

Zander had spoken about his pledge to protect her, but it was an entirely different vow she thought of now. The promise she'd made, what seemed like a lifetime ago and forged in not only word but also blood filtered through her mind.

From this day forward, 'til time is no more. I pledge you my dagger, I pledge you my sword. I pledge you my service, I pledge you my brawn. I pledge you my heart 'til my last breath is drawn.

Carefully, she slipped the Dragon Heart Opal up and over her head and placed it gently into Zander's free hand. She securely closed his fingers around it.

"Please, keep this safe for me until I...or Lara can once more claim it."

He shook his head no and started to speak, but Kitrina shushed him with no more than a single fingertip against his lips.

"In a moment, you are going to be very, very angry and disappointed in me," she whispered. "And," she swallowed hard, "justifiably so. There are...things I should've shared with you but didn't."

She squeezed Zander's hand. "But I hope someday, in the future perhaps, years from now, you'll find it in your heart to forgive me my little deception."

"If and when this situation is all said and done," she pleaded. "And you wonder if I ever truly cared for you. Please, if you believe nothing else of me, know in your heart that I now and have always loved you with all that I am. And there has never been another in all of Albrath to whom I'd gladly trust more with my life...with my very soul."

She cleared her throat. "But this isn't just about me or even the lives of my family anymore, Zander. Though I am female, in my soul I'm as much a Paladin of Albrath and a protector of the dragons and the magic they bring to this world as any man has ever been. It's my duty. One I freely chose long ago." Then she smiled. "Remember me fondly if you can...please."

Before another heartbeat passed or a tear could fall, Kitrina shifted into Cat, darted right past Zander, and fled through the still open doorway.

His roar faded as she quickly sprinted toward the portal. The secret dragon portal. The portal heading home. The portal she knew would take her straight into danger.

****

Zander stood astonished, unable to move, unable to speak, unable to draw in a decent breath. She was gone...gone. And Wally's classroom had grown deathly silent around him. Silent, that was, except for the startled gasps that still echoed throughout the chamber and competed with the pounding roar of his heartbeat. The Dragon Heart Opal still clutched within his fist pulsed fast and hot. He gripped it tighter.

He couldn't believe what he'd just seen. Kitrina Dragonheart, the woman he'd loved all his life, the woman he thought he knew every detail and secret about, had just somehow…shifted, morphed…changed into a…a cat?

He shook his head and, for a moment, wondered if he should perhaps pinch himself to make sure this wasn't all some kind of bizarre nightmare. After all, he'd eaten turnips at supper last night, and they did at times cause him issues.

Though he wished it weren't so, Zander knew without a doubt he was wide awake and what he'd just witnessed was real, too VoT real.

Kitrina had actually become a sleek little ball of black feline fur right before his very eyes. And not just any ball of fur, either. She'd turned into Cat, her cat, the very same stupid cat who'd been underfoot all semester, and even worse, the very creature to whom he'd confessed things he would've never willingly said to Kitrina's face. And worst of all, she'd smiled at him right before she'd done it and had even had the nerve to wink before leaving him standing, all alone, without so much as a glance back in his direction. He was going to kill her if Marquart didn't do it for him first.

The sound of Leeky Shortz's voice did what probably nothing else could've at that moment. It pulled him from his state of shock.

"What the pimply, pasty-white arse cheeks on the backside of an overaged ogre temptress whose tits hang ta her bellybutton and whose pubes have gone gray do ya think of that, lads? Ain't our little Kit a sight ta behold when she goes all bahsheer on us and stuff?" He sniffed and swiped at his left eye where a teardrop had formed. "Been a while since I've seen her do that. Makes a rogue proud, I tell ya."

Zander shook his head. "You knew? You knew this...this...bahsheer thing about her and you didn't bother to tell me?"

The gnome had the balls simply to shrug his shoulders. "Wasn't my place ta tell. Anyways, I thought ya knew. It's not like her grandmother being part bahsheer was ever a big secret or anything. Everybody who's anybody knows the Dragonheart lasses all inherited the ability ta shift inta one cat form or another. It's in their genes, ya know."

Zander searched the faces of the other men in the room, and though he'd heard their gasps when Kitrina had...shifted, he saw the truth of Leeky's words written on every one of their faces. They knew, all of them. Well, not all perhaps, Talon did still look as if he were about to either faint or piss himself.

He couldn't just let his suspicions lie, however. He was a glutton for punishment and simply had to confirm what he'd rather not know. Zander began with the two cousins he'd trusted most in all of Albrath, Graydon and Gareth, the half high elf, half barbarian twin sons of his Uncle Sarco and his Aunt Lark Sunwalker.

"You knew? You knew what Kitrina was capable of and you never once thought to let me in on it?"

Graydon sighed. "We thought you already knew. I mean, we've known since we were little kids. VoT, Zander, she used to get the biggest kick out of shifting right in front of us and using her cat form as a way to cheat and win at hide-and-seek."

The elf had the balls to laugh, and Zander had to force himself to not pick Graydon up by the collar of his tunic and shake him like a rag doll. He didn't, though. He stood stiffly and awaited the rest of the explanation.

It didn't take very long for his smiling cousin to continue. "Watching Kit become Cat never got old, no matter how many times we seen her do it." Graydon's smile faded. "How were we to know you weren't privy to what just about everyone else in Albrath was? Don't blame us for your lack of paying attention to what went on right under your nose."

Heat spread its way up Zander's neck and face. He put his anger aside for the moment, however, and turned his gaze toward Ten and Levin. "And you two? I suppose you guys knew, too?"

They both nodded, but it was Levin who answered. "We didn't know that you didn't know. I swear we didn't. We would've told you if we had...probably."

The big halfling rubbed his hands nervously along the sides of his legs. "Sheesh, Zander, how could you not have known? When Kit was little, she was that sneaky-ass cat almost as often as she wasn't. She used to jump out from every dark corner she could find and scare the, umm, you-know-what out of me and Ten just for the fun of it. Didn't surprise us in the least when she became a rogue full time. After all, she'd been sneaky all her life."

Levin shook his head. "You were at Castle Kuropkat as much if not more than we were. Seriously, how could you not have noticed?"

Zander sighed and thought to question Wally and Pierced next but changed his mind. There was no need.

The knowledge was written all over their faces, and anyway, he'd heard more than enough. He hung his head in shame. They were all right. Not knowing was his own fault.

How many trips had his family made to Castle Kuropkat over the years? The festive holidays? The long, lazy days of summer? They were too numerous to count. And of those trips, how many of them had he really paid attention to what little Kitrina Dragonheart had been up to? Not many, that was for sure. And he'd done it on purpose.

After all, she was five years younger than he, and she was his sister Mia's friend, not his. And then, of course, there was the sad fact that the older he and Kit both became, the harder it was for him to keep his hands—and other body parts—to himself.

The heir to the barbarian throne did not embarrass himself or his family by chasing after a girl, any girl, especially the lovely, oh so very temping Kitrina.

Though he could never remember a time he didn't love her with all his heart and didn't desire her with every fiber of his body, being the heir to the barbarian throne meant keeping himself aloof, apart, especially from the one female he'd already been assured he could never have for his own.

Not that he hadn't allowed himself the opportunity to join in on the merriment...occasionally, for he had. Especially when that frolicking had included the more acceptable and safe male companions, like Wally, Graydon, Gareth, Ten, Levin, and even Pierced. Oh, the hours they had spent riding dragons, questing, and saving fair maidens in distress. He would never forget it.

So, why then, in all the times they had actually spent time together, had she never once shifted in front of him? And more importantly, why had she trusted all of the others with her secret, but not him?

As if the fact she'd shared her ability with the pseudo cousins, except for him of course, wasn't bad enough, from the look he saw in Asla's eyes, Kitrina turning into a VoT cat and scampering away hadn't come as any huge surprise to her either.

He glared at the woman who'd once been his fiancée, daring her to think about lying to him. "And you? I take it she told you?"

Asla gulped. "No, I swear, she...she didn't tell me. At least not directly. Maycee—I—I mean, Marquart did."

The Dragon Heart Opal pulsed even faster and hotter within his grasp, and Zander squeezed it tighter, trying to maintain a grip on his temper and his sanity. "Kit told the—the troll, but not me?"

Asla shook her head. "No, no, no, it wasn't that way. May—I mean, Marquart found out all on her own. I swear."

"How?" Zander roared.

Asla gulped. "I don't know. You'll have to ask her, I guess. She doesn't exactly take me into her confidence. I just know that Kitrina said the Dragon Heart Opal doesn't care about her when Kit is Cat, and I overheard Marquart tell my father that Kitrina has the ability to shift. That all the Dragonheart girls can. I don't know for sure how, but I do know she plans to use that information to get her hands on the Stone of Anthion."

"For the love of God Draka," he yelled. "It's not

the VoT Stone of Anthion."

The Dragonheart Opal pulsed ever faster within his grip, and the heat of it became unbearably warm. All of this trouble over a hunk of calcified mineral, and for what? If the stupid thing didn't mean so much to Kitrina and the entire Dragonheart family, he'd throw it so far away it would never again be found.

Zander shook his head. Throwing the Dragon Heart Opal away wouldn't work, and he knew it. The stone was bound to Kit and followed her wherever she went. There had never been a time he could remember when it hadn't hung around her neck. Why then did she leave it behind now? In his care? Could Asla be right? Did the Dragon Heart Opal not care about or follow Kitrina when she was…Cat?

Slowly, he opened his fist and stared at the opalescent wonder he'd seen so many times but never really paid that much attention to. After all, the Dragon Heart Opal had simply been a stone hanging at the end of a piece of leather, a necklace, a bauble, a shiny object worn around the neck of the loveliest lass in all of Albrath, and he'd always considered it dull in comparison to its wearer.

But he paid attention now as ribbons of all the shades of fire danced within its tear-shaped form. The heat and the pulse of it flowed through his fingers like the surge and ebbing of a tide.

Turning it back and forth to catch the very best light, the form of a dragon spreading its wings preparing for flight suddenly appeared. And then, just as quickly as the dragon was there, it was gone, replaced by a light show of rainbow-colored shooting stars.

Zander brought it up to eye level, marveling at the play of light and fire. He rolled it between his fingers, caressing it, turning it, testing its weight and hardness. He was mesmerized.

Then, without warning, a fissure of brilliant blue light formed down the very middle of the Dragon Heart Opal, and the stone simply split in half.

He gasped.

Leeky Shortz cackled. "Well, what the prickly barbs sticking straight up and out from a pet porcupine's arse do you make of that? Looks like our little Kit's finally gone and got herself a mate."

The gnome strutted across the room and high-fived him up as high as his pudgy little purple-go-to-meeting gloves would reach. His hand landed right above Zander's knee. He grinned. "Congratulations ta ya both, lad."

Zander shook his head. There must be a mistake. There had to be another explanation for what had just happened. The Dragon Heart Opal couldn't have divided on purpose. The whole splitting-when-choosing-the-owner's-mate thing was simply a legend, wasn't it? Though he'd never questioned what he'd been told about the stone before, he certainly did now.

Not that he didn't want Kitrina as his wife, for he did, with all his heart and soul. He'd dreamed about such a chance, hoped for it, and mourned the loss of that dream when he'd learned he had no choice but marry an at least mostly barbarian female instead.

But they'd both known becoming one could never be an option for them. After all, there were obligations they each had at Alaria and Castle Kuropkat and people neither one of them could stand to disappoint.

He stared at the two perfect halves of what used to be the very singular Dragon Heart Opal. It couldn't be true. Perhaps he'd simply squeezed the stone too tight and...and damaged it? That was feasible, wasn't it? Perhaps he could force it back together.

Zander closed his hand around the two pieces of stone, took a deep breath, and squeezed with all of his strength. Both halves now pulsed at a separate rate, and with different degrees of warmth.

He sighed. He couldn't be Kitrina's mate, he just couldn't. He was destined to become the king of the entire barbarian race, not...not...the sideline-sitting husband of the oldest daughter of the leader of the Paladins of Albrath.

His heart ached for the impossibility of the situation. Kitrina was without a doubt the most amazing woman he'd ever known and certainly deserved a man who would walk proudly beside her for the rest of their days. A man she could stand toe to toe with in an argument, a man who would gladly father their children, and a man who, when they were both old and grey, would still see the forever young girl still shining in the light of his wife's eyes.

And Kitrina Dragonheart deserved a man who was ready and willing to be the partner of a too-brave-for-her-own-good, pain-in-the-arse rogue female, who could turn him into a blubbering idiot with nothing more than a smile and a wink before turning herself into a frigging cat, of all things, right before his very eyes.

But that man couldn't possibly be him. Could it?

Zander was so lost in his introspection that he almost missed Talon's comment.

"Ok, I get it. The stupid rock chose you, and you're

now first in line to become Mr. Kitrina Dragonheart. But what I'd like to know is, what's the plan to keep your little kitty cat alive long enough to actually drag her sweet ass to the altar? 'Cause drag her is what you're going to have to do to get her there. She's not going to just let you quietly give up your throne, you know."

Zander took two deep breaths and let them out. What were they going to do? He'd worry about the fate of the barbarian throne later, but standing around The Academy twiddling their thumbs certainly wasn't going to solve anything, and everyone in the room was looking at him...waiting.

He made his decisions quickly, cleared his throat, and addressed the men who, along with himself, had sworn to protect Kitrina and her family with their very lives.

"Graydon, you and Gareth head to Landis and get Uncle Sarco and however many elf warriors he can spare. Leeky, you, Pierced, Steve, Talon, and Wally meet me on the Alarian side of the portal...the other portal. I'll go to Alaria and rally my father and our warriors and meet you guys there." He chuckled. "We'll use the dragon portal and not the regular one. We'll sneak right onto Castle Kuropkat lands before anyone even knows we're there."

Ten stepped forward. "What about me and Levin?"

Zander sighed and pointed toward Asla. "Someone's gotta stay here and guard the prisoner."

The color drained from the barbarian female's face. "No, you don't understand. I must go back."

Zander shook his head. "There's no way in VoT you're going anywhere except to a deep forgotten cell in the bowels of my father's Alarian castle when this is all said and done."

Asla stood up straight. "You don't have to worry about me betraying any of you or repeating a word of what I've heard...or seen. And don't waste your breath, Zander. You can't scare me with threats of being tossed into a dungeon. Been there, done that, many times. And as long as it's not in my father's castle, I really don't care."

She looked at him pleadingly. "But if I don't return as I promised Marquart I would, she and my father will torture and kill Kitrina's youngest sister, Tawny. Please don't doubt for the time it would take a single grain of sand to sift through the hourglass that they won't. The child isn't necessary to their plans."

Though tears glistened in Asla's eyes, Zander didn't believe her concern was genuine, but what choice did he have but trust her? It was either send her back and take the risk she'd do exactly what she promised not to and repeat everything she'd heard, or take the gamble little Tawny wouldn't be sacrificed before he could get to her. That was a chance he wasn't willing to take.

He had one more question he needed an answer to, however, before he could decide on what course of action to take. "What's to stop the bastards from killing Tawny whether you return or not? If they haven't already?"

Asla shook her head. "They wouldn't. They have no reason to."

It wasn't what he wanted to hear, but Zander knew he had no other choice. "Ten, Levin, would you be willing to escort Lady Fistslammer as far as the portal to Castle Kuropkat?"

They both nodded, but it was Ten who answered. "We'll not only escort her to the portal, but we'll walk right through the VoT thing with her."

Zander shook his head. "No, it could be a trap."

"I know none of you trust Asla," Levin said. "And, in the past, it was probably with good reason. But she's changed, I swear she has, and we trust her, we love her, and we believe in her. If we're right, then Ten and I will meet you guys on the Castle Kuropkat side of the portal. And we'll make sure it's clear. If we're wrong..." He shrugged. "Then the next time we meet, you're welcome to take our heads. If we're still in possession of them."

His two half-halfling, half-barbarian cousins stood one on the right and the other on the left of Asla. As if of the same mind, they each took one of her hands in theirs and tugged her forward. She followed.

"Be careful and watch your backs. We'll see you again before this day is through" was all Zander could think to say. His mind and heart were already looking ahead, focused only on Kitrina and getting her back into his arms where she belonged.

Chapter Fourteen

Kitrina ran straight through the rarely used dragon cave portal without so much as a blink of an eye. But landing on the other side, in the oppressive darkness, with the sound of the breath of a thousand huge beasts all bearing down upon her was a whole different matter. Her cat fur prickled in awareness, and her cat eyes scanned first left and then right for the sight of the well-worn path she'd traveled so many times as a child. She had the creepiest feeling that today, though, she was being watched for an entirely different reason...stalked even.

She needed to get out of this cave, and she needed to get out fast.

The dragons knew her as the human Kitrina, and as such, she trusted them implicitly and knew they'd never willingly harm her. But as Cat, she had no way of directly communicating with them, and it was a well-known fact that there had never been a dragon born who'd been known to turn down a warm-blooded fur-covered snack, not even her very own dragon, Obsidian, if hungry enough.

Being a dragon's, any dragon's midmorning morsel wasn't in her plans for today. There were more important tasks ahead.

Even as children, she, Lara, and Tawny had been warned not to play in the dragon caves when in feline form. Not that all of the dragons hadn't been introduced to them as cats that were off limits, especially as dinner choices, for they had. And when out in the open and easily distinguishable from others of their feline species, not once had she ever felt remotely threatened. It was just that here, in the darkness of the dragon caves, in the deepest recesses of their private domain, instincts were, at times, known to overrule reason.

She'd considered taking the more direct Castle Kuropkat portal from The Academy but had decided against it because she'd been positive it would be heavily guarded. She wasn't yet ready to be seen or to take the chance she'd be turned over to Marquart. There were questions she needed answers to first. Questions like, how many combatants now occupied her home? What had they done with the rare male dragon egg to ensure the cooperation of the dragons and the other paladins? And most importantly, was her family secure? And if so, where in the castle were they being held?

She fleetingly thought about shifting back into her human form, at least until she could safely clear the cave, but decided against it. If she shifted now, the Dragon Heart Opal, her only bargaining chip to save not only the baby dragon but her own family, would once more be about her neck instead of with Zander, where it was safe, where he could use it to hopefully accomplish the task if she failed. Or, at the very least, help Lara complete it.

No, she couldn't afford to shift into her human form yet, especially to protect her own skin. For what then would happen when she had no choice but to become Cat once again? And she would.

She needed to sneak in and explore the castle in order to find her family, and the only way to get past the guards and get into the deepest recesses of Castle Kuropkat was by continuing to be the stupid cat.

No one paid a moment's attention to a plain, ordinary house cat, not even a black one. And as Cat, she had no doubt she could walk right through the wide open doors of Castle Kuropkat without so much as raising an eyebrow from anyone, especially troll guards.

Kitrina took five steps forward and froze as the ground beneath her paws suddenly rumbled with movement. Dragons. And they were close by. She almost lost her nerve. She almost shifted back into Kit. But she didn't.

She knew without a doubt that if she morphed now, and then back into Cat once she was free of the cave, the Dragon Heart Opal would be left behind, somewhere…discarded…unprotected...and potentially lost, if for some reason she was prevented from becoming human again.

She rubbed her neck with her paw, missing the warmth of the stone that normally hung there, missing its weight, missing its presence. She couldn't do it, not even to save herself. There were too many variables involved in her plan as it was to risk losing the legacy of the Paladins of Albrath.

Yes, it was too risky by far. If she somehow became trapped in cat form, the beautiful stone wouldn't be available to save her family, and as Cat, she wouldn't be able to tell anyone where to begin to search for it.

That wasn't a chance Kitrina was willing to take.

She'd rather be eaten by dragons. At least that fate would find the rare male dragon egg still safe, her family still alive, and the Dragon Heart Opal around Lara's neck where she could then use it to save them all...hopefully.

She took a deep breath and stepped forward once again. First things first. If she was going to save anyone or anything, it was imperative she make her way out of this cave, down the mountain, across the valley, and into Castle Kuropkat. And in order to do so, she had to safely navigate these rocky cliffs and corridors first...in one piece...with her fur intact...preferably.

Around one bend, down two dark corridors, across the expanse of a walkway bridging a wide gaping chasm, and over what seemed to be miles of debris beneath her paws, the origins of which she really didn't wish to speculate, she ran.

Kitrina's heart pounded hard in her chest, the muscles of her legs cramped and ached, the pads of her paws stung and burned, and the quick sharp breaths tore at her lungs. But she didn't stop, she didn't even slow down, and she didn't look back. Not even when she felt the eyes of an entire covey of dragons boring straight through her.

Up ahead the cave's opening suddenly loomed, and Kitrina let her breath out in a whoosh. She'd made it. Just a few more yards, and she'd be out into the sunshine and among the cover-affording foliage she so desperately needed in order to stay hidden.

Her right paw had just cleared the cave entrance when not only her path but the sunlight she was running toward was completely blocked. Slowly, Cat look up and up, and then up some more. Finally, she saw them.

The large, unblinking, peridot-green eyes of a dragon. And not just any dragon, but a huge dragon covered with blood red scales.

At first, the sight of those particular peridot-green eyes filled her with excitement. They were almost as familiar and comforting to her as the gazes of her parents. It was Carnelian, Obsidian's mother, and the very dragon who was bound heart and soul to both Uthiel and Briar Dragonheart.

Then she remembered she was Cat, not Kit, and she shivered. The red scales of the dragon's face flattened out as ever so slowly Carnelian brought her great head down close to Kitrina's face and sniffed.

Kit closed her eyes and held her breath. The ability to contemplate shifting into human form fled her mind. Her only thought, her only hope, was for the end to come quickly and as painlessly as possible. Her mind raced with the possibilities of how it would end. Would the great female dragon roast her with her flaming breath before eating or simply swallow her whole like a berry plucked from a bush? She couldn't decide which scenario would be worse.

Then Carnelian licked her, and Kit was sure her heart was going to stop. She waited for the first bite, and waited…and waited. Finally, she opened her eyes, and though she was sure she'd never seen a dragon actually smile, that was exactly what Carnelian was doing. With a jerk of her massive dragon's head, she motioned Kit south toward Castle Kuropkat, toward home, toward the real danger.

Kitrina didn't take time to thank God Draka for the fact she was still breathing and in one piece, unharmed. And she didn't bother scratching a patch of dirt to cover the spot where she'd peed herself when she thought she was about to be eaten, either. Instead, she quickly nodded her understanding of the situation to Carnelian and took off, racing down the mountain in a flash of black fur and pink-padded paws.

****

Zander was the first of his group to pass through the portal into the dragon's lair. He moved off to the side to make room for the others who would follow, and the skin on the back of his neck prickled with awareness.

How many times had he stood in this very spot without an inkling of trepidation And how many times over those long ago summers had he ridden on the backs of one dragon or another without a hint of fear? Clinging to their scales, gripping the sides of their necks with his arms and thighs, shouting his excitement to the four corners of Albrath?

He couldn't begin to count.

And how many times had he simply lain in the tall grass surrounding Castle Kuropkat, stretched out with his cousins, watching the dragons at play? Dreaming of stalking them, capturing their leader, conquering them for a quest? Again, too many times to count.

But today, today was different. Zander Hammerstrike was no longer a child, and this was no longer play. Dragons were known to have long memories, and he certainly hoped they would remember him fondly, but he also knew they were extremely protective of not only their own, but of the residents of Castle Kuropkat and of the Paladins of Albrath. Anyone fool enough to blindly trespass upon sacred dragon ground, especially when the dragon's eggs were in danger, did so at his own peril.

Zander was no fool. He was simply in a hurry. He couldn't risk walking through the Castle Kuropkat portal and storming its gates without reinforcements. And he wasn't yet ready to show his hand. He had to locate Kitrina first. He had to get her and her family to safety before he'd be free to put a stop to all this nonsense about the Dragon Heart Opal and the Stone of Anthion by removing Marquart's head from her horrid troll body.

For beheading the evil, lying, conniving, hate-filled troll commander was exactly what it was going to take to stop the threat. And it didn't matter to him that she was female. He couldn't afford to let it. After all, the woman had chosen her path and her fate the day she'd decided to jeopardize Kit's well-being.

The cave's antechamber filled quickly as Zander's father, King Adan, and an entire contingent of barbarian soldiers followed him through. Then came Talon and Wally with Leeky and Pierced bringing up the rear. They would meet up with Graydon, Gareth, and their father, Sarco, at the Castle Kuropkat portal.

At the last minute, Steve had been left behind at The Academy to make sure Laycee and Lavender weren't left without protection. A task he'd willingly agreed to, but one that had finally managed to wipe the dark elf's always-in-place smile from his face. It couldn't be helped.

"What the dirty bare feet of a hoe-down stomping, obese oboe-playing ogre in a too-tight tutu do ya make of this place? Dragon caves give me the heebie-jeebies. Make yaself useful and get a torch lit, Pierced? It's darker than dehydrated donkey piss in here."

Pierced struck a match, lit a torch, and the cave flooded with light.

A sudden intake of air echoed through the cavern as every eye present locked onto the huge black dragon standing right before them. Close enough to incinerate them all with a single burst of his fiery breath if he so wished.

Zander stepped forward and bowed. "Obsidian, it's good to see you again, old friend. We've come to help."

The dragon's stare locked with his own, unblinking, probing, as if it could read his every thought and feeling. The two halves of the once whole Dragon Heart Opal pulsed in Zander's pocket and grew warmer than it had been before.

He wasn't sure why, but he hadn't told his parents about what happened with the stone yet. It simply hadn't seemed the right time or the right place. Getting to Kitrina was more important. There would be time later when all was said and done to contemplate the meaning behind the Dragon Heart Opal breaking.

At least, hopefully, there would be.

As Obsidian continued to stare, an unfamiliar warmth filled Zander's mind to overflowing. Not soothing, yet not uncomfortable, simply there where it hadn't ever been before. Then he heard it for the very first time, the voice of a dragon, and not just any dragon, Kitrina's dragon.

"Zander Hammerstrike, barbarian mate of my lady, Kitrina, chosen by the Dragon Heart Opal and destiny, you and your friends are welcome here, and so is your help. But first, considering what you now are to my kind, we will share blood with you and hear the Paladins of Albrath oath from your lips."

From seemingly everywhere and yet nowhere in particular, the ground beneath his feet rumbled, and before Zander had time to blink an eye, the cavern filled to overflowing with dragons, hundreds of them. Some big, some not so much, of every color imaginable, and as similar as siblings yet each as uniquely distinct as any other race who'd ever inhabited Albrath.

The men behind him, even his own father, backed toward the still open portal. But Zander didn't move. Instead, he asked a question. "Why do you need the oath from me? We'll help without it."

Once more Obsidian's voice filled his mind, but this time it was mixed with the undertones of every other dragon in the room. *"As mate to the wearer of the Dragon Heart Opal, you are now heir to the leadership of the Paladins of Albrath, after our Lord Uthiel. You will one day be our leader, our protector, our future, and the father of the children our lady Kitrina Dragonheart will bear."*

Zander shook his head and in his own mind answered, *"I can't be what you wish me to be. I'll do all I can to help, but I'm not destined to be the leader of the Paladins of Albrath. I'm destined to be the Barbarian King of Alaria."*

Obsidian chuckled and the sound of it vibrated the walls. *"Ah, if life were only so simple, that all we need do is follow the path to which we were born. We have no power to choose our own destinies, young Zander Hammerstrike. Have you not yet realized? It is destiny itself that chooses us, not the other way around."*

The warmth of a hand on his shoulder distracted Zander from his conversation with Obsidian. "Why do they demand an oath from you, son? They never have before."

His father's words ripped the very heart from his chest. He couldn't do it. He couldn't tell his father, who had always stood by his side with pride shining in his face, that he might actually consider giving up his throne and joining himself to a human female instead of a barbarian one. And why would he consider such a thing? Simply because he loved her with every fiber of his being and not because a stupid chunk of rock had chosen him for her when it had broken in two while he held it in his hand.

But then again, how could he not? His father deserved the truth, and Zander himself needed his father's infinite wisdom and understanding more now than he'd ever needed it before.

Zander didn't say a word, however. Instead, he dug deep into the pocket of his breeks and pulled out the two very separate and distinct pieces of the once singular Dragon Heart Opal.

King Adan gasped. "I see."

Zander nodded, and though he prided himself on being tougher than steel, tears stung the back of his eyes. He forced them away. "I don't know what I'll do. I can't even think about what this means yet. I just know I have to save her, save all of them, even the stupid egg. VoT, especially the male dragon egg. That's what Kitrina would want, and that's what I must do or die trying."

It was his father's turn to nod. "Then take the oath, son, and we'll all take it with you. For today, we're all Paladins of Albrath."

Zander pulled his dagger from its sheath and sliced

his finger before kneeling before Obsidian and handing off the blade to his father. Every single man in turn, from the king of the barbarians to the king's lowliest warrior, and even the great rogue Leeky Shortz himself and his son Pierced, and then finally Talon followed Zander's lead.

Obsidian in turn, sliced his talon. Drops of dragon blood welled and mixed first with Zander, then with every other man present.

Warmth once more filled Zander's mind, and not just his own but the collective intellect of every man present. He heard their struggle for breath mixed with his right before Obsidian's voice boomed within their psyche. *"Do you know what words to say?"*

Zander shook his head.

"Then repeat after me." Obsidian took a deep breath, as did every other dragon in the room. And his voice boomed loud and clear in their minds as he recited the promise that had existed for centuries between man and dragon. *"From this day forward, 'til time is no more. I pledge you my dagger, I pledge you my sword. I pledge you my service, I pledge you my brawn. I pledge you my heart 'til my last breath is drawn."*

On bended knee and without blinking, Zander and his companions repeated the oath. When they were done, Obsidian had one more thing to say. *"Zander Hammerstrike, from this day forward, though you may have been born more barbarian than human, you now and forever will be my human and I your dragon."*

****

Down the steep mountain and across the wide valley, Kitrina ran. Sharp rocks slashed at her tender cat paws, and thorny thistles pricked her once shiny fur. Still, she didn't slow, and she certainly didn't think about stopping. For the towers of Castle Kuropkat rose upon the horizon, beckoning her onward, calling her home.

Trolls of every size and shape were everywhere she looked. They were patrolling the cobblestones of the roadway, marching the fields, and even slinking along the riverbank close to the waterfall.

Though in cat form and though she was probably safe from notice and capture, she avoided direct contact with the troll soldiers as much as possible. For a moment, she was once again tempted to morph into a human just for the pleasure of pushing as many of Marquart's minions as she could get her hands on over the waterfall's edge and watching them go splat at the bottom. Perhaps later, perhaps after this quest was all said and done and her family and the dragons were safe.

Instead, she watched and waited, darting ahead and ever closer to the castle with every opportunity afforded her. Through a copse of trees, across an outcropping of rocks, down one path, and then around a bend in another road she ran. Each step of her paws drew her closer until, finally, Castle Kuropkat's outer bailey came into sight. She did stop then, and she stared open-mouthed and slack jawed.

Oh, my God Draka, what the VoT had Marquart done to her home?

Kitrina couldn't tear her gaze from the fountain in the center of the garden. The one where the large bronze warrior had stood silently for centuries watching over Castle Kuropkat and all of its inhabitants. He wasn't there now. His body laid in pieces, his weathered face broken, and his appendages no more than scattered piles of rubble. And in the midst of all that wreckage stood six bigger than life barbarian soldiers, guarding a single, suspended golden dragon's egg.

The egg hovered a few feet off the ground. The crackle and hiss of a magical bluish aura surrounded it, telling Kitrina all she needed to know. There was a spell upon the dragon's egg, a powerful one, and not one that would easily be broken or gotten around without damaging the precious contents inside.

Off to the left, in the periphery of her vision, stood a dark green female dragon, and Kit's heart went out to the creature who was obviously the egg's mother. She looked so defeated. Tears filled her big diamond-colored eyes to overflowing and leaked down the green scales of her cheeks.

No, not Jade, not her child. Kitrina's heart skipped a beat. Of all of the female dragons in the covey, why did it have to be Jade's egg that was threatened? Hadn't she already paid a high enough price, and for long enough?

Jade, Obsidian's love mate, and a covey favorite who had finally produced a viable egg. Even though she'd valiantly tried season after season without success, she always kept her head held high and had never given up hope.

Now, that same dragon slumped just out of the reach of the barbarian guards, her once majestic wings folded in surrender, her sharp as razor claws completely retracted, her head hung low.

Though Obsidian had had no choice but mate with every female available and ready in order to preserve and increase their species, Kitrina knew, though his loyalty belonged to her and his covey, his heart, his very soul, had always belonged to Jade and Jade alone.

What would he do now if it were demanded of him in order to keep his and Jade's child safe? Their male offspring, their future? But then, what could they both possibly be capable of that they'd never been before, now that their son, their very species, and the magic the dragons brought with them to Albrath was in danger?

Kitrina didn't wish to contemplate the possibilities. But for the first time in her life, she felt fear instead of comfort at the thought of what Obsidian, her friend, her confidant, her protector from the moment of her birth was capable of.

Perhaps she should wait for Zander to arrive. In her heart she knew he, Leeky, and all of her pseudo cousins would be right on her heels and would be here any time now. Perhaps it would be wiser to sit here and wait at least a little while longer before making her move? After all, wouldn't she be silly to go rushing headlong into danger without…backup?

Then Jade emitted the most sorrowful sound Kitrina had ever heard. Not a wail precisely, more a deep, soulful hurt-filled moan of loss. Kitrina could not wait the passing of one more grain of sand through the hourglass to act.

She shook her head and tucked away her fears. There was no more time for trepidation, no more time for delay. In her heart and with the words of her blood oath forever burned upon her soul, she was now and would forever be a Paladin of Albrath. After all, she *was* the first-born daughter of Uthiel and Briarlarn Dragonheart, not a coward and not simply a female to be placated and pampered and ignored. She wouldn't shame those who needed her help with her silly apprehensions, not any of them, not her parents and certainly not the dragons who were counting on her help.

The blood oath she'd sworn burned with a vengeance in her veins as she scurried across the bailey and right between the feet of the barbarian soldiers. Her heart pounded furiously in her cat body as she skirted past one obstacle then another in the crowded and cluttered courtyard until, finally, her paws took her straight up the steps of Castle Kuropkat and through its wide open doors.

Oh, yes, the time for fear and contemplation was long over. The moment had arrived for action and, if need be, sacrifice.

Kitrina took a deep breath and forged ever forward. She would not cower in the shadows for the dropping of one more grain of sand, and she would not hesitate the passing of another heartbeat to do her duty. Her family was being held hostage somewhere in this castle against their will, and there was a baby dragon, still in its shell, being held captive in the courtyard who needed her help.

By God Draka, she was going to do whatever it took to complete this quest or, with her very last breath, die trying. And when the smoke had cleared and the danger was past, she'd see them all safe and sound, and…hopefully happy, no matter what trials and tribulations her own future might hold.

Chapter Fifteen

Zander and his companions skirted the boundaries of Castle Kuropkat lands as quickly as they could without revealing their presence to the horde of troll soldiers patrolling the perimeter. It was imperative they get to the portal and welcome the, hopefully, already waiting Sarco, Graydon, Gareth, and the contingent of elfin soldiers they were bringing along with them before alerting Marquart and her army of their impending arrival.

Their luck had run out, however. The moment the portal came into view, Zander's heart pounded in his chest. For there, directly in front of the gateway between Castle Kuropkat and the rest of Albrath stood only his two half-barbarian, half-halfling cousins Ten and Levin...alone...not an elf in sight.

Alone that is, except for the troll soldiers who were now advancing upon Ten and Levin's position.

The two brothers stood back to back with their booted feet planted firmly upon the ground and their swords held ready, high above their heads, as more than two dozen trolls rushed toward them.

Zander ran, as did the rest of his men, but there was probably no way he was going to reach his cousins before they were cut down. Still, he desperately tried. He redoubled the cadence of his sprint, his heart pumping, his feet pounding the ground, and his blood burning with a lust for death as it coursed through his veins.

Then, suddenly, the portal burst wide open, and Uncle Sarco, cousins Graydon and Gareth, and an entire contingent of high-elf soldiers spilled through.

The trolls began backing away even quicker than they'd been advancing, but it did them no good. Screams of agony and rage rent the air as the trolls were trapped between Ten, Levin, and the elves before them and Zander's men behind. Swords, daggers, staffs, wands, and flaming balls of fire quickly sliced through the troll numbers until not a single one remained standing…or breathing.

"Well, what the infested, unshaved hoochy-coo of a backwards-strolling ogre streetwalker with an insatiable appetite for bald-headed dwarf dandies in lime green G-strings do ya make of that, lads?" Leeky wiped the blood from his dagger with the fingertips of his black-as-the-night, go-to-warring gloves. "If'n Marquart didn't know we was here before, she's sure ta know it now."

Zander ignored Leeky for a moment and glanced toward Sarco. "Thank you for coming, Uncle."

Sarco chuckled. "Did you think for even the dropping of one grain of sand that you could've kept me away even if you'd wanted too? Uthiel Dragonheart's my friend, he's family. Many has been the time we've come to each other's aid over the years. Family sticks together, nephew…always has, always will."

Zander smiled. Then he turned toward his half-barbarian, half-halfling cousins. "Ten, Levin, where's Asla?"

They answered in unison. "Up at the castle, where you told us to send her."

Zander nodded. "Do you think she's responsible for these soldiers being here?"

They both shook their heads.

"I know you don't completely believe us yet," Ten said. "But Asla's no traitor, Zan. She's on our side, Kit's side. It was Asla who helped us get safely through the portal in the first place. She went through ahead of us and distracted the guards so we could get a jump on them. This mess," he gestured toward the carnage at their feet, "was simply a case of wrong place, wrong time. I can guarantee you, those trolls just happened along while we were waiting for Sarco and his soldiers to arrive. Another few grains of sand dropping, and they would've never even seen us."

Zander nodded again. "Well, then, I guess we'd better get moving before more of them decide to show up."

Walaford Titwilder poked him in the shoulder, then pointed to the dead troll soldiers littering the ground. "What d'yout think about me procuring one of their uniforms. Bet I could easily pass myself off as one of them if need be? Might come in handy. Yout can never tell."

Zander grinned. "I like how you think, Wally. It just might at that."

****

The inside of the castle was even worse than the outside. Tears stung Kitrina's cat eyes as she passed through the entryway of what used to be her lovely home on her way to the dungeon, the most likely place she'd find her family.

Wilted flowers lay scattered throughout the hallways and shards of glass from various broken vases cluttered the floors. The once lovely tapestries she, her mother, and both of her sisters had so diligently stitched and lovingly placed on the walls had all been yanked down and trampled upon. Though it was probably an improvement over her own needlework, to see her mother's intricate handiwork so callously used stung her heart.

In the great hall, the huge trestle table was the only thing left standing and around it sat at least a dozen barbarian soldiers and...and...of all people, Asla's father, the Baron Fistslammer. The man sat at the very head of the table, swilling Castle Kuropkat ale, eating Castle Kuropkat food, and issuing orders from Kitrina's father's chair, as if he belonged there...as if it were his place...his right. And Asla sat at his right side, looking as regal as any lady of any keep had ever looked.

Kit wanted to kill him. She wanted to kill them both. She wanted to sneak behind Ambrose Fistslammer in her cat body, leap up, and slash his traitorous barbarian throat with her sharp claws and teeth before he had the chance to know what hit him. And then she wanted to repeat the process with his daughter. Instead, she completely skirted the great hall and headed toward her mother's solar, toward the stairs that led downward.

There would be time later for revenge against Baron Fistslammer, Asla, and Marquart...hopefully. If not by Kit herself, than certainly by Zander when he got his hands on them. Either way, the baron, his daughter, and the troll would all pay for their treachery, someday, somehow.

When Kit entered Briarlarn Dragonheart's solar, it took her a moment to move. Couches had been ripped to shreds, bookshelves overturned, and carpets slashed. Even Mother's delicate elfin china with its dragon's breath and cherry blossom pattern, a wedding present from Grandpa Midan, which had always been saved for only the very most special of occasions and guests, had been smashed and scattered. The very same china that would've come to Kitrina on the day she wed. The tears did fall then, fast and hard.

Kit stopped in the middle of the room swiped her cat paws across her cat eyes and shook the fate of the family heirlooms away. Determination instead of loss and self-pity filled her. Things were only things, no matter how precious, and as such could be replaced. Family couldn't. And it was her family, not the things they'd collected over the years, who needed her to be strong now.

Kit scampered toward the stairs that would take her down into the very bowels of the castle. Down to the long-unused-for-anything-other-than-storage dungeons.

****

How strange. The stones of the stairway leading downward chilled the pads of her paws, and Kit shivered. She couldn't remember the squares of granite ever being so very cold before. At least not since Mother had gotten her way and Father had weatherproofed the entire keep.

Well, the steps were cold as death now, and Kitrina couldn't be sure if it was due to nature or dark magic. She didn't dwell on either possibility, however. It didn't matter which was responsible, because either way she was still going down the stairs. Her family was there, she could feel it, feel them, and something as silly as cold feet wasn't going to stop her from getting to them.

Onward, she ran.

It was dark as night, but with Kit's cat eyesight, she could see well enough. Even though it had been years since she'd last played games with her pseudo cousins down here, every crack in the walls, every crevice between every stone upon the floor looked and felt familiar. Even the scent of the dusty, musty air brought back feelings of nostalgia. She shook them away. This was also no time for a walk down memory lane.

Forward, and as quietly as possible, she crept the narrow passageway, past one open cell and then another. The long rusted open metal bars of each one gaped just as they always had. Boxes, crates, trunks, sacks, pots, and baskets of goods still cluttered their floors.

Visions of long ago games of hide-and-seek invaded her memory, and then she knew exactly where her family was being kept prisoner, where she herself would've locked them away if she'd been Marquart.

The Cell of Certain Death.

Kitrina shivered again, but this time it wasn't because of the temperature of the room. How many times as a child had she found herself locked within the confines of the chamber christened the Cell of Certain Death by her best friend and Zander's little sister, Mia?

Too many to count.

The Cell of Certain Death, though no one had actually ever died in it, as far as Kit knew anyway, was situated below the very last chamber in the huge dungeon. Smaller than the rest, the cell that housed its secret compartment was deceivingly innocent looking and completely empty of any debris, even dust. Its missing bars, its shadowed corners still almost deceptively welcoming.

The cell didn't need bars in order to trap its victims, however. The stone floor itself was somehow spring-loaded and, with the weight of the very first step inside, gave way. Whatever or whomever had been unfortunate enough to trigger its latch found themselves falling into the dark, hidden-away space below. The only way out was for someone else to place enough weight upon the floor above to once more spring the trigger.

The chamber had probably been first used as a safe place for the lord of the keep to stash his most precious valuables, but to the children who had romped through Castle Kuropkat's dungeon on their many quests and during their endless games of summer, it had been the spot that had been the most fun to lure their unsuspecting victims into.

Kitrina herself had spent the greater part of an entire day within the stiflingly confining walls of the Cell of Certain Death, and just because she'd been too smart for her own good while hiding from Ten and Levin. She'd probably be there to this day if she hadn't been able to mentally alert Obsidian to her distress.

But then, if her family really was being held down there, how had Marquart come to even know of the chamber's existence?

Then it hit Kit, the reason why she had known without a doubt exactly where she'd find her family was because Asla had all but told her in the cryptic warning she'd issued back at the Academy. But how had the barbarian female found out about the cell and its secrets?

Kitrina sighed. Ten and Levin must have confided in Asla about the Cell of Certain Death in their innocent stories of growing up, in their stories of summers spent at Castle Kuropkat. Getting to know each other stories that all men and women share with the person they're trying to woo, trying to impress. Never once suspecting, they just might be delivering a dangerous weapon right into the hands of the enemy.

With her sharp-sighted cat eyes, Kitrina scanned the dungeon, ever watchful for something, someone, or any sudden movement that shouldn't be there. She didn't see anything out of the ordinary, though, so closer to the cell she crept.

"Meow," she signaled and was rewarded with the sound of human gasps coming from beneath the floor. Her heart raced. Yes, they were here. She'd found them.

Then her father's warning filtered up through the stones. "Kit, run. Get out now. It's a trap!"

She didn't do as he'd commanded. She hadn't come all this way to simply turn tail and flee. Instead, Kitrina shifted back into human form as she raced back to the cell that held the heavy sacks of grain and dragged one of them forward with her.

Though her naked skin was chilled due to the low temperature of the room, sweat beaded her forehead as she pushed, prodded, and heaved the sack up and onto a corner of the floor of the Cell of Certain Death. The stones suddenly gave way, and her father, her mother, and her sister Lara climbed up and out.

But where was Tawny? It was on the tip of

Kitrina's tongue to ask when her father pulled off his tunic and handed it to her. "Here, daughter, you need this more than I. It's…cold down here."

Blotchy black and blue bruises covered his chest, and one eye was almost swollen shut. Her heart ached for him, and Kitrina longed to wrap her arms around her father and ease his pain. She didn't, though. She could see the determination gleaming in his eyes. Now was time for action. Later there would be a chance to tend to wounds, old and new…hopefully.

Kit nodded and gratefully slipped the warm, soft, doeskin shirt up and over her head. The hem of the garment struck her well below the knees. For a moment, she almost smiled. She must've really looked a fright for her father to give up his very favorite tunic. All naked and wild eyed to be sure.

Instead of smiling, however, she asked, "Where's Tawny?"

Her family didn't get the opportunity to answer, as the very air around them began to shimmer. From seemingly out of nowhere, Marquart, with a dagger to Tawny's throat, appeared along with six very big, very mean-looking trolls.

The commander cackled. "I haven't lived for nigh onto nine hundred years without learning a few little black-magic tricks along the way. Trust me, they've come in handy…many times." Then she laughed again. "Have yout by chance misplaced a member of yout family, Kitrina? Tsk, tsk, how very irresponsible of yout. Perhaps I can help with this…unfortunate situation?"

For emphasis, Marquart caressed the flat of her blade along the tender skin of Tawny's small neck, and the fear-filled gaze her sister shot her had Kitrina's heart pounding hard in her chest.

"Remember poisons class, Kit-ten? Remember cerebral toxins and just what they are capable of doing? Well, that's exactly what I dipped this dagger into, and unless yout do exactly what I say, I'll slice little Tawny's sweet throat with it. She'll be dead before even three grains of sand have time to shift through the hourglass, and there won't be anything yout can do to prevent it."

Kitrina gulped. Marquart would do it. Of that, she had no doubt. She could see the insanity shining in the woman's eyes, feel her adversary's animosity, her desperation flowing toward her, oozing from every pore.

Kitrina knew exactly what Marquart was after. Still she asked. "What do you want?"

The troll chuckled. "Do yout think I'm playing a game here, Kit? Really? Don't insult me by pretending yout don't know exactly what it is I'm after." Marquart pointed. "I'll trade the dagger I have at yout sister's throat for nothing less than what now hangs around youts."

****

Zander lifted his hand in warning as he and his group came within sight and sound of the outer bailey. The wailing of a large, dark green dragon rent the air, and the nervous shuffle of the barbarian soldiers surrounding what was obviously her egg filled their sight.

Obsidian's voice sifted through all of their minds at the same time. *"You will have to forgive Jade. She is in mourning. Our egg is encased by a spell that even with our knowledge of magic, we cannot break. A spell so dark and powerful that any disruption of the force field surrounding our child could immediately crush the egg's fragile outer shell and destroy the growing male dragling within."*

The dragon sighed, and Zander felt Obsidian's pain and frustration reverberate through every pore of his body.

"She knows there is probably no hope. In the end, we must fight for and with the Paladins of Albrath and against the evil that is Marquart and the Baron Fistslammer. The safety of our humans...and all humankind must come before the needs of our own." He sighed again. *"Still, she is his mother and cannot help her grief."*

Zander shook his head. "No spell is unbreakable, Obsidian, even those forged of dark magic. There must be a way, and if there is, we will find it."

It was the huge black dragon who shook his head this time. *"To save the egg would be to sacrifice the life of an innocent, and that we cannot do. Someone would have to surround the egg itself with their own essence. They would have to block the dark energy, absorb it within themselves, and somehow repel it outward away from the egg. The force of the dark magic alone would probably kill them. Still, I would gladly do this task for my son...but dragons cannot touch dark magic. That is why Marquart chose it."*

Zander nodded. "One way or another, we're going to at least attempt to save that dragling, dark magic or not. But first, I need to get inside the castle and make my way to Kitrina before she does what I'm afraid she's about to do."

He slipped his hand deep into the pocket of his breeks, searching for the small comfort found in the two halves of the once whole Dragon Heart Opal. As long as there were two pieces, then Kit was probably safe, still probably hidden. But his fingers only found a single half of the stone, his half, the half that wasn't attached to the thin strip of leather he'd always seen hanging about the neck of the woman he loved.

Zander's heart pounded and his spiritmaster sensibilities roared to life. Kitrina's half of the stone was missing, and that could mean only one thing. Kit had shifted from cat form into a human, and if that was the case, knowing Kitrina Dragonheart as he did, he had no doubt that, even as they were all standing around discussing how to proceed, she was, this very moment, inside the castle negotiating a deal with the devil herself in the form of Marquart for the safe release of her family. A negotiation that was doomed to fail.

Zander turned quickly to his father and his best friend, Talon. "Along with our soldiers, please see to the left flank."

Adan Hammerstrike smiled. "It'll be our pleasure, son. Any barbarian who dares draw a weapon on his king deserves nothing better than death."

Zander then faced his uncle, Sarco Sunwalker, his cousins Graydon and Gareth, and the entire contingent of elf soldiers they'd brought along with them. "And if you don't mind, Uncle, take the right."

Sarco grinned. "I've always been partial to being on the right side of a battle."

Leeky Shortz cackled as he twirled his twin daggers in the palms of his black as the night, go-to-warring gloved hands. "What the rusty, crusty, pink-polka-dotted panties on the wide arse of a streetwalking banjo-playing, dark elf pretty with a taste for medium rare, sweet-ta-the-very-last-bite tube steak do ya make of that? Looks like the rest of us get ta take it down the middle."

Zander nodded. "If you don't mind." Then he hesitated. "But not me and not Wally." He took a deep breath. "Kit's in real trouble. I sense it. Do whatever you need to do to take back Castle Kuropkat. But give me and Wally a few minutes to get inside the castle before you start. We'll worry about how to save the egg when this is over." He ran his fingers haphazardly through his hair. "I'm going to have Wally, umm, escort me right past those guards as his prisoner. And hopefully, our ruse will get us all the way to Marquart herself before anyone's the wiser."

Levin stepped forward. "Our help isn't needed out here with these few. Ten and I are going inside with you."

Zander shook his head. "No."

Levin wasn't having it. "I wasn't asking. I was telling. Asla's inside that castle, too, just like Kitrina is, and we're going in after her. There's no telling how many barbarian and troll warriors are waiting inside, not to mention the baron. Four's better odds of getting them both safely out than two will ever be. Wally's just gonna have to escort a couple of extra prisoners to Marquart, and that's all there is to it."

Zander wanted to argue the point. He didn't want to put anyone else in danger, especially not his kindhearted, lovesick cousins. If Wally Titwilder hadn't been half-troll and the perfect person to use as a guard, he wouldn't have suggested using him, either. But he was.

There was no time for debate. And he knew there was nothing on Albrath anyone could ever say to him to convince him to wait outside while the woman he loved was in danger. He wasn't about to insult Ten and Levin by trying to do so now.

If his plan had any chance at all of working, Zander had to implement it soon. So, he simply nodded in Ten and Levin's direction as he once more faced Leeky Shortz. "We could use a little diversion, if you could manage it. Just enough distraction to make sure those barbarian guards don't look too closely at any one of us in particular. If you know what I mean?"

Leeky rubbed his chin. "Oh, I hear ya, Lad. It's times like these I wish I hadn't stopped bringing my Miss Bunny along with me on day trips. Sorry, it's been a while since I've had need of her help. Guess I really am getting old, after all."

Pierced hopped up and down excitedly as he pulled something plastic from deep within his front pocket. "Baabette," he said as he popped out her stem and began forcing air into her limp body. "Had ta bring her," he interjected between bouts of blowing. "Couldn't trust the little hussy at home with Steve. I've seen the way she looks at him. I've no doubt she'd like ta have him shear her wool and nibble on her lamb chops." Pierced gave two more really deep, hard blows, and then closed off Baabette's stem. "It's about time my slutty little cousin was good for something other than enticing other people's boyfriends with her come-hither smile."

He kicked off his boots and breeks and positioned Baabette on the tip of his little gnome penis. He rammed the blow-up sheep down all of his one and a half inches and slapped her on her plastic ass. "Ya take it baby, just like that. Ya know ya like it rough. Ya know ya want daddy ta drive it home."

For a moment, Zander thought he must be losing his mind, because he could've sworn Baabette's plastic plastered-on smile and eyes got even bigger than they normally were. He shook his head to dispel the troubling image.

For a moment, Leeky distracted him. The pudgy little gnome's voice broke as he exclaimed, "What the puckered pimples in the stinky armpits of tutu-wearing ogre temptress do ya think of that, lads? He's a chip off the old block, I tell ya. There's no doubt about it; he knows just how ta make his old da proud."

Pierced grinned. "If'n ya liked that, then just watch this."

Out into the open bailey Pierced Shortz danced as if he didn't have a care in the world, with his bare gnome arse shining in the sunlight, and Baabette bobbing up and down on his little gnome cockling.

The barbarian soldiers stared with their mouths gaping open.

King Adan Hammerstrike cleared his throat. "Now that is what I call a diversion. But Zander, what do you say to a little change in the weather? Just enough so the enemy can't tell how many strong we are or see us coming until it's much too late."

Zander nodded. "Good idea."

He closed his eyes, clasped his hands together, and lifted his face toward the sky. Thick dark clouds rolled in, rain pelted down in cold heavy drops, and fog swirled, covering the ground.

It was now or never.

Zander motioned for Wally to take his end of the rope tied securely around Zander's waist and lead them on. With Ten and Levin also loosely bound to him, they set off.

Chapter Sixteen

Kitrina grasped the leather throng holding the Dragon Heart Opal and slipped the gemstone over her head. "If you expect me to hand my legacy over, then you need to set my family free."

In response, Marquart nicked the tender skin of Tawny's neck enough to spill a single drop of blood. The young girl flinched, and then went completely limp in the troll's arms.

Kitrina gasped, but Marquart simply raised an eyebrow.

"Cerebral toxins, remember? If less than a single drop can render her helpless for a few moments, just imagine what a *full* dose will do?" The troll commander grinned, and her sharp tusks gleamed in the flickering candle light. "Now, be a good little human and do as yout're told or else."

Kit handed over the stone, and it was Marquart's turn to gasp. "Where's the rest of it? What kind of trickery is this?"

At first, Kitrina didn't understand what Marquart was talking about, but then she glanced once more at the stone the troll held in her still wide-open palm. It was smaller. And not just by a little bit but by half.

Her heart raced, and her breathing quickened. There were only two reasons for the Dragon Heart Opal to *ever* change shape, and since she knew for a fact she hadn't born a child for the stone to attach itself to, there was only one other possibility. The stone had split into two equal parts. The Dragon Heart Opal had chosen her mate.

But who?

Who could Zander have entrusted with the safety of the Dragon Heart Opal other than himself? Her mind filled to bursting with speculation. Then, with a soul-deep certainty, she knew. There could be only one man the stone would've chosen for her. For, there had only been one man who'd ever held her heart.

Alex Zander Collin Hammerstrike, prince of Alaria, future king of the barbarian race, would've never willingly handed over a responsibility he felt was his own to another man. Any other man, no matter how trusted. The stone, the Dragon Heart Opal, had without a doubt chosen Zander, the one and only man in all of Albrath who could never, ever fulfill the role of being her mate.

A sob lodged in her throat, but she refused to let her family or the horrid troll, Marquart, see her pain. She doubled her resolve and stiffened her spine. Not only would she do what she must to save her family, but now, she'd do what needed to be done in order to save Zander from ever having to make a choice. For a moment, however, she wondered. If circumstances were different, which path would've he chosen, her or the barbarian crown?

"I asked yout a question, human." Marquart's words put a stop to any further speculation.

Kitrina didn't look at her family as she lied. She couldn't, she didn't have the heart. "You've never held the gemstone before, Marquart. It looks bigger on me, a small human, than it does in the hands of a great big troll."

The commander grinned as she slipped the leather throng holding the precious treasure over her head and allowed the jewel to settle between her large green breasts. "Is it always so uncomfortably...warm?"

Kitrina nodded, knowing as she did, it was Zander's heat, his life force, the stone was now emitting against the cold-hearted troll's skin. But "I'm afraid so" was all she said.

Marquart picked up a small cage and held it out at arm's length. "Now, shift into Cat and get into yout new home. I'm not stupid, yout know? I've been watching. I know the stone won't remain in my possession unless yout are very close to it or can no longer become human."

Her mother gasped. "No, don't listen to her, daughter. Don't do it."

Kitrina didn't look at her mother. She didn't even acknowledge that she'd heard her speak. Instead, she simply shook her head. "Not until my family is away from here and safe."

The troll laughed. "Oh, I think yout will. It's either that or watch yout family die, one by one."

Kitrina shook her head once more. "As you've said, you can only truly possess the Dragon Heart Opal, the true Stone of Anthion if I am Cat and do not have the space available to shift back into human form. If you want my cooperation, then release my family. For without them being safe and away from this place, away from you, there is no reason for me to ever acquiesce."

Marquart put her dagger to Laura's throat this time.

"I'll do it. I swear I will kill her. I don't have time for foolishness. Now shift."

Kitrina stiffened. "If you harm her, if you harm any of my family further, I will never again become Cat, and you will never truly possess what you so desperately need."

The troll commander growled. "How can I be sure yout will do as yout say if I do release them?"

Her father struggled against the troll soldiers restraining him. "Don't do it, Kit. We'll find another way."

Kitrina didn't acknowledge her father either. Instead, she looked Marquart straight in the eyes. "I'll give you my oath as a Paladin of Albrath. You can ask anyone, it is a promise that, once given, can never be broken as long as the one it was given too still breathes."

Uthiel gasped. "No, no, don't, Kitten. You mustn't."

Marquart smiled smugly. "Agreed, give me yout pledge and shift now."

Kitrina shook her head. "Not until I see proof of their safety."

The troll commander smiled. "I'll have them taken to Alaria. That should make you happy. I'm sure King Adan would be more than happy to send back one of his many barbarian soldiers with the news of their safe arrival."

"No." Kitrina shook her head once more. "There are barbarian warriors all over the place here. Send them to Landis, to Sarco Sunwalker, and have him send back an elfin emissary. Then, and only then, will I believe my family safe and do as you ask."

"So be it. What do I care where they are taken." Marquart motioned to a group of three troll soldiers. "See the Dragonheart family safely escorted through the Castle Kuropkat portal and into Landis. Then return to me with the elf dignitary."

****

The barbarian soldiers had been so busy watching the Pierced and Baabette show and trying to get themselves out of the sudden downpour that they hadn't wasted much more than a single glance or two in the direction of the random troll soldier marching what were obviously his three prisoners toward the keep.

Zander almost chuckled. He would have to if he hadn't felt the eyes of at least a score of very dry, very alert troll and barbarian soldiers on him and his companions the moment they stepped through the doors.

But instead of allowing even a hint of a smile to curve his lips, he kept his head down and followed as Wally navigated the group through the hallways of Castle Kuropkat. The closer they came to the great hall, the louder the sound of raised voices grew. One in particular had the small hairs on the back of Zander's neck rising in protest and the fingers of his hands clenching and unclenching into fists.

Asla's father, the Baron of Halla, traitor to not only King Adan but to the entire race known as barbarian, sounded as if he were issuing orders from Sir Uthiel Dragonheart's place of honor. It wasn't to be abided.

Zander took deep breaths and soothed his rage. The time would come for revenge, but first he must find Kitrina and her family and see them to safety. And then he must deal with Marquart and see her dead and out of their lives forever. Then and only then would he be free to make sure Baron Ambrose Fistslammer never got the chance to betray anyone ever again, especially his king.

He schooled his expression as they entered the hall, prepared to face whatever sight awaited him with calmness. But he couldn't help but notice Wally suddenly tense. Zander glanced up and immediately knew why.

Wally dropped the hand he lightly held the lead rope of his prisoners with and grasped both Ten and Levin in a virtual death grip of sorts while he addressed the room. "I have a gift for Commander Marquart! Someone she's been expecting."

Zander thought he'd prepared himself for the sight he would see when he himself looked up, but he hadn't. He couldn't prevent his shock or his grimace. For there sat the Baron Ambrose Fistslammer in all of his glory, not only in Sir Uthiel Dragonheart's seat, just as Zander had feared, but also at the very head of Sir Uthiel Dragonheart's table. He was completely surrounded by at least a dozen of his personal warriors.

It was who the baron had confined at his side, sitting right on his lap, with what looked like a…a…dog collar fastened tightly about her neck while he held loosely onto the end of a leash, that had Zander's stomach turning, however. It was Asla, the man's own daughter, his own flesh and blood. But it wasn't an Asla that Zander had ever seen before. This woman's gown was filthy and hung haphazardly upon her slouched frame, her face was smudged, tear streaked, and bruised. Her eyes were devoid of any spark, cold, unseeing, and even her breathing seemed robotic, more forced than a natural expression of life.

Zander chanced a quick glance at Ten and Levin. They both looked ready to bolt from Wally's grasp and slay Asla's father or die trying. He couldn't let them do it, not yet anyway. Instead, he gave his head a slight shake, just enough to convey the silent promise of a later retribution.

It took Ten the space of twenty-six long heartbeats to nod and even longer for Levin. Then the baron opened his mouth, and Zander was almost positive his effort to restrain his cousins from taking immediate action would be in vain.

"Do you see who has come to visit, pet?" The baron cackled with glee while tugging Asla's chain. "It appears our troll friend here has escorted a guest into our hall. Or was he invited at all? If not, then he is nothing more than a trespasser and must be severely dealt with. Oh, and looky here. It seems he brought friends along with him. Won't Marquart be so very pleased to see royalty has come to pay her their respect?"

Asla didn't respond, and the baron tugged on the chain connected to the collar about her neck, hard. "Why so quiet, my dear? Don't you wish to properly greet your ex-fiancé, Prince Zander? King Adan's whelp? The man even you, with your vast charms, couldn't manage to entice into a marriage, into your bed?"

Asla shook her head, without even looking up.

"Where's your father, boy?" The baron glared directly at Zander.

He couldn't help himself. Zander simply had to stir the viper's nest. "That's Prince Zander to you, Baron. Not boy. You will do well to have respect for your betters. And as for my father, he is just where he should be. He is home, on his throne, ruling his kingdom, ruling the entire barbarian race."

The baron spit on the floor and wiped his chin with the sleeve of his tunic. "My betters? Do you really believe yourself above me? Ha! I'll show you better. Before Marquart and I are done, it'll be me sitting on the throne of Alaria, and Adan Hammerstrike's head will be on a pike in *my* bailey. I have my own barbarian warriors behind me, and the promise of a huge troll army at my back to boot. Prince...bah." He spit again. "I'll show you just how valuable your being a prince is."

The baron yanked once more on Asla's chain. "Sit up straight and pay attention, daughter."

Asla's head jerked.

The baron growled. "Who are these other fellows with the *prince*? Tell me quickly and don't lie. I'll know if you do, and you won't like the consequences." To make his point, the baron pulled his daughter's chain in close until Asla's face was even with his own. He kissed her roughly with a loud smacking sound right on the lips.

Asla gagged and recoiled as if she'd been slapped instead of kissed, and the baron smiled.

Zander wanted to gag, but he held his breath and his tongue while Wally did his best to hold back Ten and Levin.

Now was the moment they would all finally find out just where Asla's loyalties lay. For God Draka knew she not only recognize them, but in the case of Ten and Levin, she could easily spout some very intimate details if she was of a mind to.

She looked her father eye to eye. She didn't smile. She didn't frown. As a matter of fact, as far as Zander could see, Asla gave no indication whatsoever of what she was thinking or what she would say. Slowly, she turned from her father and locked gazes with each man in turn before glancing back at the baron and simply shrugging her shoulders.

"I may have seen the troll guard in the bailey once or twice. I'm not sure. There are so many of them wondering about this cold, dreary castle, and they do all look so very similar to each other." She shrugged again. "As for…Prince Zander's companions? Sorry I can't be more helpful, Father, but I've never laid eyes on either one of them before today."

The baron nodded and gestured toward Wally. "Well then, I suppose you'd better quit loitering and see our guests escorted to our mistress. You know as well as I do, Marquart gets testy when kept waiting."

Wally nodded. "Can yout tell me, baron, just where may I find the commander?"

Baron Fistslammer's eyes narrowed. "You don't know?"

Wally shook his head. "I've been stationed at the Castle Kuropkat portal since the moment we first arrived, just as the commander ordered. I've not been privy to her movements."

Zander fingered the hilt of one of the daggers concealed beneath his tunic, just in case.

The baron waved his hand in the direction of the far hallway. "She's down in the dungeons with her Dragonheart family captives, of course. Where else would she be? "She's been watching and waiting for that oldest daughter to arrive for hours, so she can finally collect her rock and be done with this nonsense. I do hope the girl's stupid enough to show her face soon. After all, I have a king to dethrone, a land to overtake, and a kingdom to start running."

It took every ounce of patience Zander had left to stand still and simply wait for Wally to turn and lead them away, just as any other troll guard worth his salt would. And if there was one thing Zander was positive of, it was that Wally Titwilder, his friend, his pseudo cousin, his partner in crime was worth much more than something so common as salt.

They were so close to their goal of finding Kitrina and getting their hands on Marquart. He could feel it, but it was also imperative they not make a single misstep.

Zander waited while Wally bowed low before the baron, and he waited while his friend gathered the tether ropes he, Ten, and Levin were attached to. And he even allowed the other three men to walk slowly before him, as if they had all the time in the world.

Still, the moment they stepped into the hallway, it was hard not to hurry, and it was hard not to take over the lead himself and rush ahead toward Briarlarn Dragonheart's personal solar and the stairs they knew would lead them to the dungeons below.

Zander's palms itched, and his head pounded as his spiritmaster senses screamed danger. He didn't stop, however. He didn't even slow down. Somewhere, in the bowels of Castle Kuropkat, the only woman he'd ever love was at this very moment facing Marquart, offering herself up as replacement for her family. Zander knew it as well as he knew his own name.

"God Draka, save me from VoT stubborn females

who think they can take on the whole frigging world without help from anybody," he mumbled. "Wait till I get my hands on her. If Marquart doesn't kill her, I just might."

Wally turned and whispered back, "Did yout say something?"

Zander shuddered and shook his head. "Not that I want to repeat in front of witnesses. Just be on the alert. We're getting close to the solar, and you never know how many troll warriors Marquart will have stationed along the way."

Wally nodded, and the group continued.

They were through the doorway of the solar and no more than a few feet from the stairs when they heard a voice that was not much louder than a whisper itself but still very familiar.

"I'm not an idiot," Uthiel Dragonheart said. "No matter what Marquart may have promised Kitrina, I know she has no intention of letting me or my family go free now that she has Kit captive and the Dragonheart Opal in her possession. But I do implore you. Do what you wish with me. I don't care. But do not harm my wife and daughters. They're innocent in this. I'm sure, deep down, somewhere, even trolls have honor, don't they? See them safely off Castle Kuropkat lands and to Landis as Marquart promised. That's all I ask."

The sound of laughter filtered up the stairs. "Yout females are innocent, yout say? Those little hellions of youts almost took my head clean off with their sharp claws when they shifted into those crazy mean cats when we first caught them. And yout wife? She VoT near choked poor old Baron Fistslammer to death before we could pry her hands off his throat. And just cause he was playing a little touchy-feely with his daughter at the supper table two days back. Innocent, my shiny green arse."

The troll laughed. "I'm looking forward to making sure none of yout get the chance to cause my commander any more trouble. And yout are right, Marquart does mean for us to kill yout all, so make yout peace with yout god if yout can. She said what she said to get the chit's cooperation. And it's her direct orders we follow without question. Not some misguided antiquated ideas of honor. There's no such thing as honor. There is only duty and victory."

The sound of a grunt filtered up the staircase. "Now, shut yout mouth and quit begging. It's undignified. If yout just keep climbing these stairs like good little humans, we'll get all this unpleasantness over with, quick and clean like."

Zander heard Uthiel's voice once again. Closer this time, and stronger. "So be it."

The rate and strength of Zander's pulse doubled, and the air of his next breath lodged in his chest. Silently, he motioned toward the other three men to move. The Dragonheart family would soon crest the top of the stairs, and they were obviously in imminent danger. Even worse, Kitrina wasn't with them. She was still somewhere below, alone with Marquart.

Though he would've rather rushed headlong into the fray, Zander forced himself to stay put and took up position in the shadows to the right of the entryway. He placed his back flat against the wall, and Wally did the same at his side. Ten and Levin mimicked their movements and stance but on the left of the stairway.

As if of one mind and one heart, all four men unsheathed their previously hidden weapons and waited.

Within the space of fourteen heartbeats and one breath, the first two trolls immerged from the stairway. It was sixty-three heartbeats and four more breaths before the Dragonheart family walked through the opening, followed by one more troll soldier.

Zander knew precisely how many heartbeats and breaths had passed. He'd counted them. Every single one an eternity. He waited until the entire party was halfway across the room and a few feet from the doorway of Briarlarn Dragonheart's solar. He had to be certain no more trolls were bringing up the rear before he made his move.

Suddenly, Uthiel Dragonheart spun. Even with his hands tied behind his back, he somehow managed to grab a dagger from the hand of a very surprised troll. A second later, that same man lay face down in his own blood.

It was the most amazing thing Zander had ever seen. With a quick flick of his own dagger, the second troll hit the floor. All four men moved in tandem, and before Uthiel, Briar, or their daughters had a chance to face the one remaining troll warrior, all three lay dead at their feet.

Uthiel didn't look surprised to see them as Zander cut his bonds and freed his hands. "About time. Kit's still below. I'm going after her."

Zander grabbed his arm to keep the man from rushing back down the stairs. "No, wait."

Uthiel shook his head. "Get my family out of here and to safety. Take them to Alaria if possible. I'm going back for Kit."

Again, Zander prevented him from moving. "There are too many soldiers, barbarian and troll alike, between here and the portal to accomplish getting your family through without a nasty fight. I'm sorry, but we need your sword arm if we hope to have a prayer of succeeding."

Uthiel shook his head. "I've seen you fight. VoT, I helped train every single one of you. You can do it. I know you can. I can't just leave Kit down there all alone in the dark. You don't know what that...that...Marquart might do to her. What she's already done to others. What she's capable of."

He jerked away from Zander's grasp. "You don't understand. I know you like her, are protective of her, may even love her at least a little, but Kit doesn't mean to you what she does to me and her mother. She's one of our daughters, for God Draka's sake, our blood, our firstborn, our future, and my responsibility. I love her. I will save her. Trust me in this."

Zander didn't lay hands on the man he'd respected all of his life again. Instead, he reached deep into the pocket of his breeks and pulled out his half of the Dragonheart Opal and held it for Uthiel to see. "You think I don't understand what Kit means to you? Perhaps I don't. But I can tell you what she means to me."

He took a deep breath, steadied the shaking of his hand and, for the very first time, completely accepted with his heart and soul the truth he'd known and had tried to avoid all of his life. "Kitrina is *my* future, too. My mate, *my*...everything. Not just chosen by this chunk of rock, but by *my* heart. She's *my* destiny. I love

275

her more than anything or anyone else in this life or the next, and I'd gladly exchange my next heartbeat for hers this very moment if I could. But we both know that isn't possible. Only Kit can do what she is doing right this moment, and we must do what we can to help her in *her* quest.

"Together, we can fight our way through this castle and get the rest of your family outside where Father, Uncle Sarco, Leeky, and quite a few others are waiting to help win the day. Marquart doesn't want to harm Kit, Uthiel. She wants Kit alive." Zander hesitated a moment, then continued. "No, she doesn't just want; she *needs* to keep Kit alive. For if she fails to do so, she loses the one thing she thinks she must possess, the Stone of Anthion."

He slipped his half of the Dragonheart Opal back into his pocket, then ran his fingers haphazardly through his hair. "I really hate to admit it, but Marquart's presence, Marquart's side is probably the safest place your stubborn-arse daughter could be right this moment."

Uthiel slowly nodded. "You might be right in your assessment of the situation. Kit has always been known to be a tad obstinate at times and even careless when it comes to her own well-being. She's much like her mother, I'm afraid."

Briar made a very unladylike sound, but if Uthiel noticed, Zander couldn't tell. Instead, the man slapped him on the back and motioned toward Wally, Ten, and Levin. "Let's go clean this nest of vipers out of my castle and get Briar and the girls somewhere safe. Then we will deal with Marquart and get our girl back." Uthiel chuckled. "Oh, and welcome to the family, son.

Do Adan and Lizbeth know?"

"I showed the stone to my father just a little while ago, though there really was no time to discuss its ramifications. But as for my mother, she does not yet know, sir." Heat crept up Zander's neck, but he ignored it.

"And I take it," Uthiel suddenly looked serious, "the stone splitting in two is a fairly *new* development? Have you even discussed this incident with Kitrina yet?"

Zander shook his head.

Uthiel chuckled again. "Well, I know your parents, and they'll no doubt be disappointed, but in the end, they'll understand. They will want only your happiness. But I do wonder which discussion is going to be the more heated? The one we're about to have in the great hall and the bailey with our uninvited guests or the one you're going to have with my daughter? She's not just going to sit back meekly and watch you abdicate your throne without a fight, you know?"

Zander sighed. "With your daughter, my lord, I've learned that most things are a fight."

Briarlarn Dragonheart wasn't chuckling. As a matter of fact, she was scowling directly at her husband with her hands fisted at her hips and her foot tapping fast and hard. Zander stepped back. He'd seen that same exact expression on Kit's face often enough to know to get out of the way.

"Enough!" she hissed. "There will be time to hash out details once *we've* taken back *our* castle and…and…killed that horrible baron and that…that…that troll. But we need to get moving in order to accomplish any of it. Daylight's wasting, and those monsters aren't going to just kill themselves."

It was Uthiel's turn to shake his head, and the gesture brought a slight smile to Zander's face. "Don't even think about it, Briarlarn Dragonheart. You and the girls *will* stay well behind in the background like a good, obedient family should, for a change. That's an order, wife."

Briar glanced at Lara and Tawny. Immediately, both girls shifted, Lara into a sleek lioness, and Tawny into a very dangerous tiger. "I don't think so, husband. But," she smiled, "we will be very proud to fight at your side. It's our place, our right."

Uthiel's entire face turned red. "Now, do you see what you're in for?" he grumbled at Zander.

Zander couldn't help himself. He laughed, and it felt good. "Actually, I think I'm kind of looking forward to it, sir."

Uthiel snorted. "Well then, let's go kill ourselves some trespassers."

Ten folded his arms and spoke just four words. "Not Asla. She's ours."

Levin nodded.

Zander sighed. "I myself won't harm her if at all possible. I give you my word. Though I wouldn't say I completely trust her, she at least did aid us earlier. That, however, doesn't mean she won't turn against us when we threaten her father."

Briar's words surprised them all. "I don't believe she will turn against us. I've seen what that horrible man is capable of, what he's done. I've noticed remnants of the baron's handiwork. Scars so deep, so horrid, so plentiful, I've no doubt they're imprinted upon her soul forever. Asla needs our protection and rescue from her father, probably even more than Kitrina does from Marquart.

Zander wasn't the least surprised when Levin turned toward his brother. "Then it looks like the baron is ours also, Ten."

Ten nodded. "Most definitely, brother, most definitely."

Chapter Seventeen

Marquart paced the entry length of the dungeon like a trapped animal, her eyes darting back and forth and, every few seconds, stopping to glance up the stairs. She was obviously waiting for something or someone, and Kit didn't believe for the time it would take a single grain of sand to filter through the hourglass that what Marquart was waiting for was word that Kit's family was safe. On the contrary, the evil troll was probably expecting to hear that they were finally all dead.

It was all Kitrina could do to sit patiently and simply watch. Not that she wasn't concerned for the safety of her parents and her sisters, for she was. But really, only three troll soldiers against the leader of the Paladins of Albrath, his very magical wife, and his two shape-shifting daughters? The odds didn't seem even close to being fair. Add in the fact that Zander and the others were without a doubt in or very close to the castle this very moment? Oh, yes, her family was almost as safe as if they were in their very own beds...she hoped.

Marquart suddenly turned on her. "Shift and get into the cage, now."

Kitrina shook her head. "Not until I'm sure my family is in Landis just as you promised."

The troll growled. "Yout think youtself so smart, don't yout? Well, yout aren't." She grasped Kitrina's arm. "I'm tired of waiting. Yout will do as I say or else. I just realized something. I don't need yout family to bend yout to my will. I have dragons."

Kit's surroundings began to shimmer, and a heartbeat later, she found herself outside Castle Kuropkat in the very foggy, wet outer bailey, but still in the clutches of the commander Marquart and at the foot of the nest holding the magically restrained dragon's egg.

Kitrina shook her head to clear it as she looked around. "How?"

Marquart laughed. "Dark magic, of course. Very dark and very old. Now shift, paladin, or I'll use that same magic to crush this shell and the dragling within it before yout can take another breath." The troll once more growled. "That is what yout are, after all, isn't it, a Paladin of Albrath? Sworn to protect the dragons? Like yout daddy? Or didn't yout really mean the words of the oath?"

Kitrina gasped.

Marquart cackled. "Didn't think I knew about the paladin's oath, now did yout, my little Kit-ten? It's amazing what one reveals while talking in their sleep."

Kitrina was just about to shift and do as Marquart demanded when an almost naked Pierced Shortz with his blow-up sheep cousin, Baabette, bobbing up and down on his little gnome penis stepped through the cover of dense fog and rain.

He smiled up at her and said just one word. "Surprise!"

****

The great hall was deathly silent as they approached, and Zander motioned for the group to stop and await his signal. Then he heard it, felt it even, right through the unnatural stillness. Danger was on the other side of the doorway, danger and death. Not that it had been an actual resonance his ears had perceived. No, it was the sound, or really the lack of noise where at least an echo should've been, that put his spiritmaster sense on high alert.

With hand signals, Zander explained to his followers their roles in what was about to happen. Even little Tawny, in her tiger form, had no problem understanding the plan. She simply nodded her furry, striped head along with everyone else.

He mouthed the words "One...two...three," and as a unit, they moved forward. The moment they entered the great hall and were met face to face with the awaiting warriors, the battle was on. Swords swung from every angle, clashing loudly, scraping both stone and bone alike, as daggers flew through the air and fists smashed into faces.

Zander, Uthiel, Wally, Ten, and Levin tore a path straight up the middle of the room where the baron sat with Asla upon his lap. Trolls and Barbarians alike hit the floor in their wake. Their bodies still quivering, but their eyes dull and lifeless.

The girls were doing their part also. Any warrior, be they troll or barbarian, who managed to slip past the men, was quickly met and dispatched by the steel of Briar's dagger or the teeth and claws of her daughters.

When the last opponent lay dead at his feet, and Zander finally had a chance to look up, he was surprised. He stood so close to Baron Ambrose Fistslammer, he could've easily reached out and sliced the man's traitorous throat. And he would've if he hadn't already promised Ten and Levin the pleasure if the opportunity arose.

It was hard to resist. The baron was literally begging for it. He hid behind his daughter who he kept securely ensconced upon his lap, his captive, his shield. And the man was smiling with insanity shining in his cold eyes.

Zander very much wanted to wipe that smile from the baron's face, forever. Instead, he stepped back and motioned Ten and Levin forward. "I do believe the baron has something that rightly belongs to you two gentlemen?"

Ten nodded. "So it seems he does. That is, if she'll do us the honor of having us, of becoming our wife?" He knelt before her. "We both love you, Asla. Marry us and let us take you away from here."

Levin's cheeks pinkened as he nodded vigorously in agreement.

The baron laughed, and though he appeared to speak only to Ten and Levin, Zander knew his words were meant for him also. "Pretty little thing, isn't she? And talented if you know what I mean. After all, it was I who taught her everything she knows. But if you want her and truly don't mind receiving used goods, I'd be willing to part with her…for a price."

He chuckled. "If you two half-breed freaks of nature are willing to see me safely back to Halla and if King Adan can somehow be convinced to grant me amnesty for this one teensy-tiny transgression, I'll give her to you. If not, I'll kill her myself. I'll slice her throat from ear to ear, and you can watch her die right before your eyes." He sneered. "Try my patience, and just see if I don't."

Baron Fistslammer lifted a knife and held the blade to the pulse point of Asla's throat. "Tell them! Tell them you'll be more than happy to marry them in order to save your daddy."

Zander held his breath, not sure exactly what Asla would say or what she'd do. She looked as if she were in shock and she appeared beyond defeated. All he knew for certain was the hearts and futures of his cousins rested directly and entirely in Asla's hands.

Her eyes cleared as they filled with tears. She grasped her father's hand, the same hand holding the blade to her throat, and she sighed. "You're wrong, you know? It is I who would be more than honored to have you as my husbands, both of you. But my father is right, I am used goods. You deserve so much better. Forget about me. I don't matter. But please, I beg you, don't let him get away with what he's done here. Not this time, not this day."

The baron roared. "You ungrateful little tramp." He shook off Asla's hand and strengthened the grip on his knife. A drop of bright red blood welled as the point his blade made contact with her skin once again.

She winced.

Before another drop of Asla's blood could join the first, before even another beat of her father's heart had the chance to thump-thump in his chest, Levin, with a deafening roar, removed the baron's head with one quick, clean sweep of his sword.

At the same exact moment, Ten pulled Asla safely from the madman's grasp and into his waiting arms.

If it wasn't for all the blood and gore putting a damper on events, Zander would've thought what the two brothers had just done for the woman they so obviously loved to be one of the most romantic gestures he'd ever witnessed.

He faced Uthiel Dragonheart, his wife, his daughters, Wally, Ten, Levin, and Asla. "Let's get moving. It's time to put part two of this plan in motion."

****

Kitrina stared at Pierced, knowing if he was here in the bailey, acting like a fool with Baabette dangling off his private parts, then Zander and the others must be close by plotting, planning, biding their time, waiting for the perfect moment to strike.

She almost smiled, and she almost relaxed for a moment. Instead, she did as she'd pledged to do long ago. She fulfilled her oath to the dragons. She shifted into Cat as Marquart demanded and offered up her life in order to prevent further harm to the unhatched dragling and to hopefully buy time for Zander to put into effect whatever scheme the man had most assuredly come up with. For if there was one thing she knew about Zander Hammerstrike, it was the man had a plan. He always did, for everything.

"Don't just stand there starring, you unnatural creature," Marquart hissed. "Get into the cage, now."

Kitrina complied, and the metal latch on the contraption clicked shut, trapping her within the small enclosed space. Panic threatened to overtake her. Her heart pounded in her furry little chest, and her breath came fast and hard as if she'd run a very long race.

Kit strove to achieve calm. She couldn't allow fear to win the day. Even if she was merely a female, in her heart, she was just as much a Paladin of Albrath as any man ever born. She was also a VoT fine rogue if she said so herself and the eldest daughter of Sir Uthiel and Lady Briarlarn Dragonheart. She could do this. She wouldn't let them down, not any of them.

Instead of giving into her trepidation, she spent the next few moments glancing about, seeking a sign that her friends were indeed approaching. Friends who could also help protect the dragling from Marquart.

Then she saw it from the corner of her eye and through a gap between the throng of huge barbarian and troll guards surrounding Marquart and the dragon's nest. Movement. Not from where Kitrina expected but right out through the front doors of Castle Kuropkat.

Kit gasped as first Zander, then her father, followed by Wally, her mother, her two sisters in cat form, Ten, Levin, and Asla marched forward. At the same exact moment, a battle cry rent the air and, from out of the fog, strode King Adan, Uncle Sarco, his two sons Graydon and Gareth, Leeky Shortz, Talon, and an entire mixed contingent of barbarian and high elf warriors.

King Adan Hammerstrike spoke loud enough and clear enough that there could be no confusion as to the meaning of his words. "Do you really dare raise arms against your king? Drop them now, and I'll allow you to live. Fail to do so, and this will be your last day upon Albrath."

Kit wasn't the least bit surprised as the baron's remaining barbarian soldiers surrounding Marquart and the dragon's nest let their weapons simply clatter to the ground as they knelt before their king.

The troll soldiers, however, didn't move, and they didn't even flinch as the sound of Marquart's voice filled the bailey. "Yout would all do well to back away.

I now have what I came for, and I'm willing to leave peacefully. But if yout try to stop me, I'll be forced to crush this egg yout all seem to care so much about."

For emphasis, she held Kitrina's cage in front of her like a shield while with her other hand she pointed toward the golden egg and began to chant. "Power of darkness, power of night, fill me with yout evil and destroy this sight."

Blue flames shot from Marquart's fingertips, and the troll closed her fist around them before they could do any damage. "What will it be, paladins? The Kit-ten or the dragon? Yout choice."

Her mother stepped forward, though her father tried to hold her back. Pride filled Kitrina's heart. The woman, standing tall with her red hair flowing in the breeze like a blazing fire and her green eyes snapping and glaring right through the troll commander, no longer resembled the gentle, mild-mannered, soft-spoken housewife and mother Kit had come to know and love.

"You will release my daughter this very moment and step away from that egg, or I will kill you where you stand." Oh, no, this Briarlarn Dragonheart was more warrior than lady, and she'd come prepared to fight. Her voice was the same as Kit had always known it to be, calm, reassuring even. But the determination behind her words held a definite bite.

Marquart laughed. "Yout? Yout think yout can kill me? Bring it on, bitch." Again the troll commander began to chant, louder this time, faster. "Power of darkness, power of night, fill me with yout evil and destroy this sight."

The sound of the egg's shell cracking reverberated

throughout the bailey. Jade, the dragling's mother, screamed as Obsidian bellowed his rage. Swords clashed, thunder roared, fireballs flew through the air, and from the corner of her cat eye, Kitrina saw someone literally throw their own body over the egg, shielding it, but she couldn't take her eyes off her mother.

Her mother spread her arms wide and did what she was known far and wide for doing, she channeled. Her mother's powers were normally used to heal, but this time, Kitrina could not only see but feel Marquart's evil being repelled, being forced back inside the troll and away from the egg.

With an explosion of blue fire, Marquart suddenly loosened her grip upon the cage, and it dropped. Kitrina found herself tumbling through the air, and with a thud, the enclosure hit the ground, and its metal hinge gave way. In the space of a heartbeat, she leapt through the opening and shifted back into her human form.

Her eyes sought Zander and locked gazes with him, their eyes speaking in a language that didn't require words. Marquart focused all of her evil directly toward Briar, and her mother's arms began to tremble. It was now or never.

Kit held out her hand, and Zander nodded his understanding. He tossed a dagger straight at her. She caught it as easily as if they were merely practicing in rogue class. With both hands, she hefted the blade and plunged it beneath Marquart's outstretched arms, right between the third and fourth intercostal spaces of the troll's left side. Right where she knew there was no way in VoT she could miss slicing a huge chunk out of the commander's heart.

A blood-curdling scream bubbled forth from Marquart's mouth. It was the last sound she ever made. Then came silence, cold, calm, dead silence.

Kitrina bent and snatched the Dragonheart Opal from around the lifeless neck of the troll and placed it back around her own where it belonged. She took a deep breath and closed her eyes. It was over, finally over, and they'd all somehow survived intact.

Then, she heard it, the sound of anguish, and Kit turned toward the nest. There sat Sarco Sunwalker, the lord of the high elf nation, upon the cold, wet ground, and he held the body of his unmoving son, Gareth, in his arms.

"Why'd he do it? He's not human. He's not a Paladin of Albrath. He's a VoT high elf, for God Draka's sake," Sarco cried. "Why'd he put himself between the troll's dark magic and the egg?"

Obsidian's voice wafted through their minds. *"You are mistaken, Sarco Sunwalker. Your son has proven this day that though he may not be completely human, he is one hundred percent Paladin of Albrath. For, it is not race that determines a hero. It is the righteousness of his convictions that sets him apart from all others. And it is his ability to put the needs of the weaker above his own."*

Kitrina couldn't force her legs to move, but her mother rushed forward to kneel beside the young, high elfin fire wizard and placed her fingers gently against his neck.

"He still lives, barely," she sighed. "Graydon, hurry to Landis and bring back your mother and stop by Alaria and collect Lizbeth. I'll need both of their unique talents if I'm to have any chance of saving him."

Without a word, Gareth's twin nodded and left to do as she bid.

Her mother stood. "Let's get him inside so I can see to his injuries."

Immediately, Zander, Talon, Wally, and Pierced stepped forward. But in the end, it was only Uthiel Dragonheart's, Adan Hammerstrike's, and Leeky Shortz's help that Sarco would allow.

Kitrina understood why, and she knew the others probably did, too. Especially now, after what they'd all been through this last semester. Some bonds were closer than family or friendship. Some bonds could never be broken, no matter the circumstance, no matter the pain.

After all, bonds like the one her Uncle Sarco shared with her father, Adan, and Leeky had been forged by the interlacing of fibers of their beings over the period of an entire lifetime. Fibers torn from their very souls and given freely from the depths of their hearts.

Carefully they lifted Gareth, and once more Kitrina gasped. For there, directly beneath the high elfin wizard's body lay a perfectly formed, miraculously very much alive baby dragon. He opened his large black-as-night eyes and blinked up at them, then he slowly unfurled his black wings swirled with glorious patches of vibrant green and tried his best to follow after the man who'd just saved his life.

Words filtered again through the minds of all present. This time no more than a gentle whisper but obviously in Obsidian's voice. *"Malachite, no, my son, not yet. There will be time later to fulfill your destiny and do what you have need to do. This, I promise."*

The dragling nodded his little head, closed his eyes, and snuggled back into his nest. Jade and Obsidian surrounded their newly hatched son with their warmth, as Sarco, with the help of his friends, carried Gareth into the castle.

****

Kitrina paced. She didn't know what else to do with herself. Except perhaps, rack her brain once more seeking new ways to avoid Zander and the upcoming discussion they'd most assuredly have when the situation with Gareth was resolved.

What on Albrath had she been thinking when she'd shifted into Cat right before Zander's eyes? And even worse, how was she ever going to justify not telling him in the first place, when the reasons she hadn't now seemed ridiculously lame considering Gareth lay fighting for his very life while she worried over what some guy thought about her turning into a stupid cat? And then, of course, there was the little situation with the Dragon Heart Opal splitting, and that same guy being in clear possession of a substantial chunk of it. How was she going to deal with that?

Not that she'd had to *deal* with the barbarian in any capacity...as of yet. Zander hadn't so much as even looked her direction since they'd first entered the castle, let alone sought her out or touched her or demanded she stop what she was doing and speak with him. Why, if she didn't know better, she swear the dratted man had even forgotten she existed.

Kit shook her head. She couldn't worry about Zander right now. There would be time later for that confrontation. Right now, she needed to concentrate all her thoughts, prayers, and energy on Gareth, her unconscious high elf pseudo cousin, who without a thought for his own safety had shielded an innocent dragling with his body.

After Gareth had been carried inside the castle and laid upon a pallet before the fireplace in the great hall, there had been at least tasks to keep Kit's mind and hands busy. After all, a fire had to be built; water had to be boiled, bandages assembled, bodies of dead barbarian and troll warriors to be gathered up and disposed of, and the gore they'd left behind cleansed from every nook and cranny of the hall. Even Asla's father's remains had been collected, removed, and dumped into the same hole prepared for his followers. No marker was left to tell future generations where the Baron Fistslammer's remains rested. Some things were better long forgotten.

Kit and her sisters had helped the castle cook prepare a simple but filling meal of Alarian water buffalo steaks and Prescove Valley rice to feed everyone present. And she herself had been more than glad to pour not only the first round of mead into everyone's awaiting steins but had made sure she kept the liquid flowing freely throughout the meal.

But what to do now except fret?

It had been twelve long turns of the hourglass since they'd reentered Castle Kuropkat and the process of healing Gareth had begun. Twelve very long turns.

The second of the three moons of Albrath shined brightly through the hall's high windows, graciously lending its light to the dozen or so candles keeping darkness at bay. But still, Gareth, son of Sarco and Lark Sunwalker, high elf fire wizard and twin brother of Graydon, hadn't awoken, not once, not even so much as a twitch, a stir, or a blink.

Kit had the sinking feeling what they needed was more than whatever magic her mother could pull from her ever-present bag of herbs. Even with the help of Gareth's mother, spiritmaster Larksong Sunwalker, and his aunt, enchantress Lizbeth Hammerstrike, all their combined chanting, channeling, and spell casting was doing nothing more than lulling the contingent of barbarian and high-elf soldiers lounging about in the hall into a state of slumber.

Kitrina shook her head. At least, the volume of the warriors' combined snores served to keep her very much wide awake and alert. She sighed in frustration. Nothing was working. What they really needed, what Gareth desperately needed, was a miracle.

Suddenly, Pierced popped his head up from the tabletop where he'd been resting with Baabette cradled in his arms. "Look at the time." He pointed toward the hourglass. "Merry Yulemass everyone."

He lifted his mug high. "May the coming year find all—both warm-blooded and plastic—happy, healthy, and well loved."

Each man, woman, and child in turn raised their own mug and chanted, "Here, here." But it was Kitrina's mother's voice she heard above all others. She literally sang as she shouted, "Sarco, come quickly. Gareth's awakening."

From seemingly out of nowhere, Zander suddenly stood at Kitrina's side, his warm hand gripping hers. His heat infused Kit with a sense of safety, of solidarity. She was more than grateful for his presence and for his strength. Silently, they watched and waited just like everyone else.

Gareth struggled but, finally with Sarco's help, managed to at least lean himself up on an elbow and swallow a sip of water. Slowly, he opened his eyes. A look of first confusion and then horror crossed his face. And though his words came out sounding more like disjointed croaks, their meaning still rang clearly throughout the stunned silence of the hall with a volume to rival church bells.

"I can't see. I can't see anything." He shook his head. "What's wrong with me? Oh, my God Draka, I'm…I'm blind."

"No," Lark cried. "Don't worry. We'll keep trying, my son? We'll continue to channel, chant, and cast until you are whole again. There must be another spell, an herb, something we haven't tried yet?"

Briar shook her head. "His optic nerve was shattered by the dark magic, Lark. There's nothing, to my knowledge, that can repair that kind of damage."

Lark sobbed, and Gareth reached out a hand to comfort his mother. "Don't cry," he pleaded as he found her cheek and stroked it with the end of a finger. "Just tell me I didn't forfeit my sight for nothing. Tell me the dragling was saved."

It was on the tip of Kit's tongue to inform Gareth that, yes, he'd saved the baby dragon when a brand new voice filled all of their minds.

"Gareth Sunwalker, I am Malachite, son of Obsidian and Jade. From this day forward, and for as long as we both shall live, our destinies are now intertwined. I am your dragon and you are my paladin. It is my honor to walk by your side, protect your back, carry you where you need to go, and be the sight you sacrificed for me."

The young dragon walked right down the middle of the great hall until he stood directly before the man who had saved his life. Malachite nudged Gareth's hand.

One corner of Gareth's mouth lifted as he gently patted the dragling's small head. "Thank you, but that isn't necessary, little one. You're brand new, Malachite, and must remain here with your parents. They would miss you if you were to go away. And you don't owe me such loyalty. I did nothing special. Nothing that anyone else on Albrath wouldn't have done."

Again the voice floated through every mind present. "*My decision isn't up for debate or discussion. I do not possess the power to give back that which you sacrificed, elfin wizard. But I can go where you lead and be your eyes.*

"*You have a great gift, Gareth Sunwalker. From your mother's side you inherited the spiritmaster ability of feeling what others do. Since you have had this gift of empathy all your life, you have no idea how very rare your talent is. And now, without the barrier of normal eyesight and with the help of dragon vision, your empathic skills will hone quickly.*"

Gareth gasped. "VoT, you're right. I can see shapes?" He shook his head. "But not just shapes. I see...what? Auras?" He turned his head back and forth, scanning the room. "There are patterns of light, energy, something outlining everyone in the room. It's as if each person is cloaked within a cocoon composed of their life essence, and the emotions they're giving off is expressed back to me as a colored heat signature of sorts?"

Malachite nodded. "*You are correct. And as time passes and I mature, the more keen and sharp your second sight will become.*"

Leeky Shortz slapped his knee and cackled. "What the pink polka-dotted panties pulled down over the ears of an ogre orator giving a speech on masturbation ta a room full of drunk dwarf dandies do ya make of that? The lad's done gone and found himself a seeing-eye dragon."

Tears stung Kitrina's eyes, and she leaned in closer to Zander's warmth. He bent his head and nuzzled her neck as he whispered, "It appears things are well in hand here in the hall, my lady. Shall we adjourn to somewhere a little more private? There is much we need to discuss."

Kit didn't say a word. She'd been expecting, dreading this moment all evening, and it had finally arrived. She took a deep breath, squared her shoulders, and looked straight into the eyes of the man she not only loved with all of her heart, but also the very same man she had every intention of walking away from. With no more than a slight nod of her head to the right, Kitrina motioned for Zander to lead the way.

It didn't surprise her a bit when they walked down the long hallway and up to the door of her very own bedchamber. The same bedchamber she'd so happily led Zander to three years before when he'd been her deflowerer, her wonderful lover.

Kitrina sighed. There would be no love making of any kind going on behind that door this night, especially after he finished hearing what she had to say. As a matter of fact, after this conversation was over, touching her, kissing her, holding her, even being on the same planet with her was going to be the last thing on Zander Hammerstrike's mind. It was for his own good, though, and Kit knew it. But that didn't make the contemplation of the pain she'd intentionally cause over the course of the next turn of the hourglass any easier.

The moment the door closed behind them, Zander pushed her up against the wall and took her lips in a kiss that seared her to her very soul. Kit longed to cry out with the wonder of it.

Over and over, his mouth devoured hers, teasing, and tormenting, both giving and taking at the same time, but more than anything else, sharing a part of himself that she knew without a doubt belonged only to her.

And his tongue, oh my God Draka, his tongue was hot and hungry as it stroked, probed, tasted her, telling her in their very private language just how much he wanted her, desired her, had to have her, and right now.

This is what she would miss the most. This closeness. This feel of his body pressed snug against her own. This sensation of his rock-hard cock seeking to claim her, pleasure her. Her pussy tightened and her breasts became heavy with need. Her nipples hardened as shockwaves of excitement flowed through them landing with an unquenchable thirst deep in the pit of her belly. She tingled, she ached, she wanted. Fire coursed through her veins, igniting a burn only Zander had the means to extinguish. A fire he could stoke with just a look, a touch. And more importantly, a fire that she'd somehow have to get under control.

It took every ounce of Kitrina's will to push Zander away. Then, it took two deep breaths and even more of that will to force a chill she certainly wasn't feeling into her voice.

"I thought you wanted to come here to talk." She

folded her arms across her chest, and starred him straight in the eye.

Zander backed up a step and ran his fingers through his already mussed hair. "Of course, we need to talk. I just thought—"

Kit held up a hand. "How about if I make this easy for both of us. Yeah, I probably should've told you that Cat and I are one and the same, but truthfully," she chuckled, "it was my secret to keep as I wished and really none of your business."

"None of my business?" Zander roared.

Kitrina struggled not to flinch. She'd planned on making him angry, counted on it even. So she smiled. "Oh, please, lower your voice, Zander. Do you want the entire castle to hear you? I mean really, you've got to admit, you're being a tad dramatic, even for you. Wouldn't you agree? And was having a strange pussy underfoot all that bad?" She winked. "I did try ever so hard to behave."

A tick developed in Zander's left cheek, and the veins running along the sides of his bright red neck bulged. Kitrina swallowed hard.

"I'm being dramatic?" He shook his head. "You honestly think I'm upset about Cat? You think I brought you all the way in here to talk about something so…so unimportant as you not telling me you're a shape-shifter? Which, by the way, I'm very proud of you for. My God Draka, Kitrina, everything about you is impressive as VoT. You must know that."

Zander reached out and stroked her cheek, and Kit felt the heat, the gentleness of it all the way to her toes. "I couldn't care less about you keeping secrets, love. I'm sure you had your reasons. But what I do care about is where do we go from here?" He pulled his half of the Dragon Heart Opal from his pocket and held it out for her to see. "This is what we *need* to discuss."

It took everything in her power to pull away and turn her back on him. She couldn't say what needed to be said and still look him in the eye.

She forced a laugh. "It's just a stupid rock, Zander. It means less than nothing to me. You asked where we go from here. You'll return to Alaria or the Academy, of course, and I'll...I'll not. We both have responsibilities we can't simply walk away from, and they don't, in any way, shape, or form, coincide."

Kitrina shuddered but she couldn't help it. "There's nothing holding you here any longer, Zander. The threat is over. All three commanders are dead, the Dragon Heart Opal may very well be broken, but it's no longer in danger and my family is safe. So see, we can all just go back to the way things were before and live our very own versions of happily ever after."

She took a deep breath and turned to faced him once again. Slowly, Kit held out her hand, willing it not to tremble and give away the pain crushing her heart. "Thank you ever so much for all of your help. But really, Zander, I'm simply not interested in any kind of permanent future with you, and forgive me if I ever gave you the impression I was. Your services are no longer needed. You are dismissed."

Without a word, Alex Zander Collin Hammerstrike, heir to the throne of Alaria, turned and walked toward the door. But if the last glimpse Kitrina had of his face was any indication, she knew she'd accomplished her goal. She'd hurt beyond repair the only man she'd ever love, and she'd done it completely on purpose.

Now, Zander would be free without any false sense of duty or guilt to follow his true destiny, to become the next king of the barbarians after his father. Just as he'd been ordained before he'd ever held the Dragon Heart Opal or her heart in his hands. And now he'd even be able to do it with a clear conscience.

Then he surprised her. Instead of turning the door's knob and walking out of her life as he was supposed to do, Zander flipped the lock. Shutting them in together. Preventing the chance for any outside interference or help.

The sound of the tumblers falling into place echoed throughout the silence.

Chapter Eighteen

Kitrina gulped as Zander turned toward her, his expression hard as stone and just as unreadable. His lips were compressed, his blue-gray eyes shooting fire as his nostrils flared.

"I'm dismissed?" he hissed, then closed his eyes for a moment and took in several deep breaths. When he finally did speak again, his voice was so controlled, so calculated, so cold, Kit shivered. He chuckled. "Oh, I think not, Kit-ten. We aren't anywhere near to being done with this particular discussion. But then, simply trying to talk to you like two reasonable adults would hasn't work out too well either. At least not with that stubborn little smart-ass, know-it-all attitude of yours. Now, has it? He walked toward her. "Though I love your spunk, I do believe it's time for a different approach."

She opened her mouth, but Zander simply smiled. "Oh, no, you don't, little Miss Kitrina Dragonheart, Miss Rogue-Extraordinaire, Miss I-Don't-Need-Any-Thing-or-Any-Body. You've had your say. It's my turn now."

"No." She shook her head. "I don't think so."

And with that, Kit shifted.

****

"You little pain-in-my-ass ball of fur. Get back out here and fight fair!"

Though he couldn't see her, Zander had no doubt Cat had scooted beneath the bed as far as she could go and wedged herself into a corner. He wasn't sure which he wanted to do first when he finally managed to get his hands on her again. Break her scrawny little cat neck or pet her soft cat belly until she was helpless to do anything but purr for him again.

Then she'd shift and he'd really make her pay for the countless times she'd driven him crazy during the past semester. He'd kiss her silly and love her into submission. And he wouldn't let up for even the time it took a single grain of sand to trickle through the hourglass until he'd gotten *his* way for once.

Oh, yes, before this night was over, he'd have the stubborn-as-VoT, glorious female he'd fallen so deeply and hopelessly in love with finally agreeing to be his wife.

But first, he had to catch her.

Zander lay flat on his back on the floor and stretched his arm as far under the bed as he could, swiping up toward where he guessed she would be. The very tip of one finger came in contact with warm soft fur. A paw probably.

He stretched a hair more, wrapped his fingers around it, and tugged.

She bit him.

"Oww," Zander yelped as he jerked his hand away.

He stood, dusted himself off, and contemplated the situation. "You might as well come out from under there and face me, Kit. I'm not going anywhere until we settle this."

She peeked out from under the bed, and he grabbed her up. "Don't you dare bite me again."

She hissed at him.

"Stop it and shift, so we can talk."

She shook her head.

"Have it your way." He chuckled. "I've got all night, and I'm not going anywhere until we do."

Zander sat on the edge of the bed with Cat in his arms and petted her back with gentle yet firm strokes from the top of her head to the very tip of her long black-as-the-night tail.

She purred, and he smiled. "Like that, huh? Thought you might."

She rubbed her head against his arm, and he leaned over and kissed her on the top of it. "Come on, Kit, you've never been a coward before. Don't be one now. Shift and talk to me."

Suddenly she transformed, and Zander found himself with his arms full of very warm, very naked woman. But it was a warm, naked woman with big tears in her eyes. "Put me down and go away, Zander. We can't do this anymore. Please."

"Why?" He nuzzled Kitrina's neck, and she sighed.

"You were born to be a king, not just a mate to some silly human whose greatest claim to fame is her ability to throw a knife in a fairly straight line and turn herself into a stupid house cat."

He kissed her neck, both ears, her forehead, her nose, her chin, and finally her lips, long and deep. "I happen to like those things about you very much, silly human."

She shuddered in his arms.

"You, my love, are so much more than the culmination of your talents. You're my heart, my soul, my destiny." He kissed her again. "My everything. I'm nothing without you, Kit."

He ran a single finger over her left nipple, tweaked it, then leaned down, took it into his mouth, and sucked. It hardened and sweetened.

Kitrina shook her head back and forth. "No, no, no. I can't do this. You can't—we mustn't."

Zander placed a finger lightly against her lips. "Shh. For the love of God Draka, Kitrina, I need you to listen. I need..." He lifted his head and looked her straight in the eye. "It's going to take a lot more than just words to convince your sweet, stubborn, sexy little ass to see this from my point of view, isn't it?" He turned with her in his arms, flipped the coverlet back, and gently deposited her upon the bed. "Well, then, let's just see if I'm up to the task."

Zander stood, pulled his tunic up over his head, tossed it to the side, dropped his breeks to the floor, and quickly stepped out of them. His cock was already hard and heavy, aching for her touch, aching to fill her with his seed, claim her, brand her as his own, for always.

"I've been told I'm better at show than tell," he whispered. "Shall we see if that's true?"

Climbing onto the bed beside her, Zander wrapped his arms about her waist and nuzzled her neck once more. He breathed in deeply the ever-changing fragrance that was Kitrina. Today, she was a subtle mixture of spice and lust, courage, and...and...tangerines. It was a heady combination, and his cock spasmed in response.

"Let me show you, Kit," he pleaded. "Let me show you all the reasons why we're not only meant to be together, but it's our destiny."

****

She was on fire. A burn that scorched her soul and incinerated her heart, leaving in its wake a pile of unfulfilled ashes mixed with regrets.

Though she'd loved Zander Hammerstrike for as long as she could remember, Kitrina had never, ever, experienced this depth of both pleasure and pain while in his arms. Pleasure, because his was the one and only touch she'd ever craved, ever wanted, needed, lived for even. And pain, because, like it or not, this simply had to be the very last time she'd give free rein to her carnal desires with this man...ever.

After this one last time, she'd give him up. She'd finally push him away forever, even if it killed her to do it. She told herself she would. But first, she'd make sure Zander wasn't the only one participating in this little show and tell game of his.

She'd show him with every kiss, every touch, just what he meant to her, and she'd tell him with every single sigh, every cry of his name, just how much she loved him. And she'd do it without letting him see how much her heart ached. Hopefully, in the end, this one last time would be enough to see them both through.

Then he whispered close to her ear, "Remember the first time I was in this room, Kitten?" He kissed her nose. "Remember what I said about ravishing and how it can be quite barbaric and only for the experienced?" He kissed her forehead, and Kitrina smiled. "Well, my love, you and I are no longer strangers to the many facets of lovemaking, and I don't know about you, but I'm in the mood for a session of touching and tasting, kissing and fondling, pounding and plundering, and just downright, good old-fashioned fucking, of epic proportions. What say you?"

Kit leaned up and kissed the cheek of the man she loved as she made a grab for a handful of his rock-hard cock. Wrapping her fingers snugly around it, she stroked slowly, and he shivered beneath her touch. "Epic proportions? Hmm. Bring it on if you think you can, barbarian."

She lay back and sighed.

He chuckled, and his eyes twinkled in the low light of the room. Tingles of delight rippled through her belly in anticipation.

"Just relax, my lady, and prepare to be ravished, barbarian style." Zander smiled against the tender skin of her neck. He took her mouth in a kiss that made her forget to breathe and turned those very same ripples deep in her belly into outright explosions of intense desire between her thighs. Oh, yes, there was no doubt about it, Zander was definitely capable of bringing it.

His fingers, his hands, his lips, his tongue, and even his toes at the end of his wonderfully big feet attached to his long lean legs seemed to be everywhere all at the same time.

Kitrina gloried in the feel of so very much barbarian over her, touching her, melding with her, becoming one. And though he cocooned her within the safe confines of his arms, at the same time, he overstimulated every single nerve ending her body possessed with his very thorough exploration of her person. Spirals of pleasure ricocheted throughout her chest and belly as her pussy ached to be filled. It was an overstimulation Kit thanked the gods for.

His cock rested hot and heavy against her belly instead of where she wanted—needed it—as Zander took his frustratingly good old-fashioned time kissing first her lips, her neck, and then the cleft between her breasts before latching onto one or the other of her nipples and sucking. She bucked her hips against him in a silent plea, and he chuckled.

"Patience, sweetheart. Ravishing is an art form. We'll get there. We have all night."

She bucked against him once more and held his face between her two hands so he had no choice but look her straight in the eye. "I don't want art, Zander. I want, I need you inside me now."

Something in his eyes changed. Wariness perhaps? "Are you sure you're ready for this, Kit? Because there's something I very much need to tell you. When I—we do make love in a few heartbeats from now, I mean to take you for the first time as your husband."

Kitrina sucked in a breath. "You can't—we can't—not ever. You've a throne to consider, people counting on you, remember?"

In response, Zander suddenly spread her thighs with one of his own and positioned himself at her opening. Kit squirmed to get away but couldn't budge the big barbarian.

He leaned his head down until their foreheads barely touched and whispered, "All the thrones of Albrath would be cold as death without you by my side. It's already done, Kit. I've abdicated."

"No," she cried. "There's still time. You can take it back."

He shook his head. "I don't want to. What I want is to take you, now and forever." He held up his hand for Kitrina to see and pointed to the small slice in the middle of his palm. "I've already taken the Paladin of Albrath's oath with Obsidian. We've shared blood and words. All that's left is to make this union official with you. I hope you're ready to commit, because here I come."

With that, Zander thrust his hips forward until his cock was buried deep within her pussy, knocking upon her cervix. Her eyes crossed with the pleasure, the sweetness of it, and she couldn't help but answer his knock with an invitation of her own. She lifted her hips toward him.

He looked at her again and what she saw in the depths of his gaze had Kit holding her breath. Slowly, he moved, in and out, and with every stroke of his hot, hard, wonderful cock into her more than ready and willing body, he spoke the words of a promise she thought never to hear, let alone from him.

"I, Zander," thrust, "take thee Kitrina," thrust, "to be my lawfully wedded wife," thrust...thrust, "to have and to hold," thrust, "from this day forward," thrust, "for as long as we both shall live." Thrust...thrust...thrust. "So help us God Draka."

He grinned, and all Kit could manage to do was gulp as he plunged into her again and again, quicker each time and deeper if that was possible.

Her toes curled. Oh, my God Draka, he loved her, really loved her. And not just loved her a little bit but loved her enough to give up a throne. Could she live with herself if she allowed it? He thrust again, and icy-hot sparks of excitement shot all the way down her spine, exploding right between her legs. Her pussy clenched around him, the tender membranes of her sheath quivering along the path his cock forged. Her heart skipped a beat as a blinding white ball of euphoria formed in the pit of her belly, spreading outward, gathering momentum.

She kissed him hard, glorying in the salty-sweet essence of the man she knew Zander to be. The scent of that same essence filled her nostrils and clouded her brain to anything but this moment, this man, this version of their future together. This promise of the many nights to come spent in his arms, in his bed, as his wife. Nights of passion, nights of pleasure, and days filled with laughter and sunshine.

"What say you, Kit?" he demanded, his breath coming heavy, his cock stroking her very soul. "Will you have me as your husband?"

She couldn't think, let alone reply. Alex Zander Hammerstrike, the man who should've been a king, seemed determined to pledge his future to a mere human instead. She shook her head. Could she do it? Did she dare?

There would be so much to answer for and so many to answer to. But together, they'd get through it, wouldn't they? The alternative was too horrible to comprehend now that Zander had said the words and made the vow. Without him, life would be nothing more than a very long, very lonely, very miserable passage of time.

Kitrina stared straight into the eyes of the man she would love until the end of her days and said only two words, but they were the only two words that needed saying. "I do." She sighed.

After that, there was no talk, there was only his pounding into her, fast and furiously, his lips kissing hers and his sweat mingling with her own as she rose to meet each of his thrusts and kissed him back with the freedom only a wife knows. The freedom to touch and taste and pleasure at will. The freedom to love with abandon. Safe in the knowledge that never again would she be alone.

Only a handful of grains of sand had time to trickle through the hourglass before with a roar of satisfaction, they both shattered with ecstasy. Together, forever, just as destiny intended.

Epilogue

The first early morning beams of light filtered through the window of Kitrina's bedchamber, and Zander sighed. Soon they'd be forced to rise and face the challenges of the coming day. He wished he could put off what needed to be done for just a while longer. He'd much rather stay right where he was, snug within his bride's arms, and make love to his beautiful wife once more, and then again and again and again until neither one had the energy to even blink.

He smiled.

Had it really only been a matter of a few turns of the hourglass, and a few more bouts of intense lovemaking since they'd returned to the great hall, faced their parents, and declared their intention to wed, immediately?

Kit's mom, Lady Briarlarn, and his own mother, Queen Lizbeth, and even Aunt Lark had been amazing, and Zander had to give them kudos for carrying out his and Kit's wishes so swiftly, efficiently, and without question or comment. It was as if they'd all three known that if they didn't act with haste, the skittish Kitrina might yet attempt to bolt and run.

Zander chuckled. They hadn't given Kit the chance to consider fleeing. They'd kept her mind and hands busy with details and tasks. Not that he would've let Kitrina Dragonheart, now Baroness Hammerstrike go anywhere without him at her side. Not ever again.

But the mothers and the aunt, they'd all made quick work of pulling together an absolutely lovely little wedding, and they'd made it look remarkably easy. A man of the cloth had been hastily procured from the village, the hall had been cleared and righted back to its former greatness, stout ale had been brought up from the cellars, and food for the wedding feast had been prepared.

Even the fathers, Adan and Uthiel, along with Uncle Sarco and Uncle Leeky, Talon, and all the cousins had joined in the preparations. His father, King Adan himself, had taken up an ax and chopped wood for a fire to warm the hall. Sir Uthiel had gathered all of the Paladins of Albrath together to be witnesses, and Uncle Leeky, with the help of Obsidian, rounded up the dragons.

The cousins, Asla, Talon, and Kit's sisters, Lara and Tawny, probably had the worst job, but even they'd done what needed to be with smiles on their faces. They'd scrubbed every inch of the castle's main floor until it shone, and not a trace of battle or bloodshed was left behind to mar the festivities. Even Gareth, with Malachite by his side, had helped.

Though Zander appreciated all of their efforts, it was the look on Kit's face, the gleam in her eyes, and the strength of conviction in her voice when she'd finally said "*I do*" once more, but this time before their onlookers, that had truly mattered.

He leaned over and kissed his wife's forehead as he nudged her body with his hardening cock. God Draka, she was beautiful, beyond beautiful, exquisite, gorgeous even. It still surprised him how much he loved her, desired her, needed her, had to have her again, already.

She slowly opened her eyes and smiled. "Put that thing away and go back to sleep, Baron Hammerstrike. You've worn me out."

Zander laughed. "I'd almost forgotten. I really am the Baron of Halla now, and you truly are my baroness. Who would've thought?" He nuzzled her neck. "It's going to take some time to get comfortable with these change of titles, wife."

Kit gazed up at him, and it wasn't happiness he saw shining back. It was tears.

"Do you... have regrets?" she whispered. "I'd understand if you did."

He pondered the question for a moment. Did he? The thought of waking up beside this woman every morning, and falling asleep with her in his arms every night for the rest of his life filled him to overflowing with warmth. The thought of her growing round with his children, feeding them at her breasts, holding them upon her lap, and teaching them her rogue skills brought tears to his own eyes. The thought of a lifetime spent in her company, of hearing her laughter, of knowing her love, of belonging at her side, brought a sense of complete peace to his soul. Zander Hammerstrike knew he was exactly where he was meant to be.

He smiled and shook his head as he kissed his wife soundly. "I have no regrets, my love. Not about us. Never about us, Kit. Someday, we'll embrace our destiny completely and lead a brand new generation of Paladins of Albrath, and we'll do it together."

Kit sighed. "Not me, my lord. Only you can be leader. You're male. But I'll be proud to stand by your side."

Zander shook his head once more. "Times change and so do laws." He pointed toward the door for emphasis. "Just look at what's already transpired in the space of a day, let alone years. The Paladins of Albrath are no longer an all-boys club comprised of just humans. A whole slew of others, including barbarians, elves, gnomes, halflings, and even a troll or two have taken the oath. Not to mention the fact that, after today, the dragons will no longer reside only within the caves above Castle Kuropkat, they'll be scattered all throughout Albrath."

Kit opened her mouth to speak, but Zander stopped her with a quick kiss before continuing himself. "Though Carnelian is determined to stay here with your family and most of the older dragons, Obsidian and Jade are just as resolved to reside in Halla with us. And let's not forget, that purple female dragon, Amethyst, has already left for the halfling kingdom with Ten, Levin, and Asla. And of course, Malachite's going to follow Gareth to Landis."

Kitrina laughed then. "A dragon in the capital city of the high elves. Will wonders never cease? Though still just a dragling, I've no doubt Malachite will take Landis by storm." She sobered. "But Gareth...oh my God Draka, Zander, I...I feel awful about what happened to Gareth."

He rubbed her back. "Me, too, but it wasn't anyone's fault. Gareth chose his path and his own destiny when he put himself between Marquart and Malachite. He's strong, Kit. Stronger than we give him credit for. Gareth will come through this. Just watch and see if he doesn't."

He hugged her close. "What I was speaking of earlier, what I truly regret is that, instead of us going directly to Mia and explaining face to face why the burden of the throne now rests upon her small shoulders, we must travel to Halla and see to the castle, see to the people counting upon us, see to our new home, set it to rights."

Kitrina nodded. "She's going to be so angry with us, Zander. Mia was always happy and content being just the spare. She never, ever wanted the throne for herself."

Zander laid flat on his back and stared up at the ceiling. "I know she didn't, and I do feel bad for her."

He turned back toward Kitrina and pulled her within his arms until her cheek rested against his chest. "But, like it or not, want it or not, the throne of Alaria is now Mia's destiny, not mine. I'll do as my parents ask and give them time to speak with her, make her comfortable with the situation, and then I'm going to send Talon to her."

Kitrina pulled away. "Talon? Do you really think that's wise? We both know his reputation."

Zander chuckled. "Mia's going to need Talon's unique skill set. She's going to be required someday to choose a mate, and who better suited to help her with that choice than Talon? I trust him, he's my friend. He'll protect my sister with his life."

It was Kitrina's turn to chuckle. "But my dear husband, I think I probably know Mia even better than you do since we've shared confidences all our lives and she's my very best friend in all of Albrath. My question to you is who's going to protect Talon from Mia?"

A knock on the door prevented Zander from

answering. Instead, he stood, pulled on his breeks, strode across the room, and yanked the door open.

There stood Pierced, his gay Goth gnome pseudo cousin, stark-ass naked with Baabette, the blow-up sheep, situated so as to appear to be sucking his tiny gnome prick.

"Surprise!" Pierced shouted.

Zander simply shook his head and closed the door.

On the way back to their bed and his wife, he couldn't help but overhear Uncle Leeky. "What the purple-painted pasties glued ta the nipples of an ogre pole dancer's hanging-ta-the-bellybutton boobies do ya think yare doing, son? Ya call being nakey and covering that less than impressive willy of ya's with a cheap piece of plastic a proper surprise? Come on over here and sit down. I'll instruct ya on how ta really surprise folk."

Zander and Kitrina giggled. They had no idea what stories Uncle Leeky would tell Pierced, and they didn't care. They were too busy writing their own.

Tamed by the Fire

About the Author

Hi, my name is Maxine Mansfield, and I write fantasy, erotic romances. I live in the far northern state of Alaska where the summer days are long and the winter nights even longer. I have one very special man, his three equally special children, and our six delightful grandchildren in my life. Not to mention a very bossy African Grey parrot named Gabriel. Oh, and Gnomes! Many, many Gnomes!

Visit Maxine at
www.maxinemansfield.com

To chat with Maxine Mansfield and other Wild Rose Press authors of erotic romance, join us at www.groups.yahoo.com/group/thewilderroses.

Also Available

Touched By The Magic

by

Maxine Mansfield

Book One of The Academy Series

http://amzn.com/1612173705

New to The Academy of Magical Arts, Briarlarn Tumbleweed wants to learn the art of a True Healer, but her nerves get the best of her when she's paired in the sexually dynamic healing class with Uthiel Stoutheart, Paladin of the Realm. Between burning off his eyebrows and overturning a candle on certain exposed male parts, she isn't making a very good impression. But how can she focus when Uthiel is strong, brave, and touches Briar in a way that leaves her weak in the knees, quivering with pleasure, and begging for more?

Falling in love with the accident-prone but talented Briar was not what Uthiel had planned, but life with the sexy healer is adventurous, hilarious, mind-blowingly stimulating, and clearly his destiny. His soul awakens while taking her to new heights of ecstasy, yet he can't allow his own pleasure. There's no getting around it—he must leave The Academy and pursue his quest to right the wrongs done to his people if he can ever hope to find happiness with Briar.

But is their love strong enough to mend the magic so desperately needed to preserve their world, and that touches both their souls with a searing heat?

Also Available

Tempted By The Storm

by

Maxine Mansfield

Book Two of The Academy Series

http://amzn.com/1612177166

Larksong Hammerstrike has always been just the younger sister of Princess Aryanna. Never quite as pretty or as smart, always lacking, a mere empath whose power gets her into trouble more often than not. But at Carnalval, the festival of all things sexual, she unleashes her sensual side for a night in the arms of a masked stranger. When morning dawns, Lark can't resist a peek beneath the mask of her lover and is once again crushed by fate. The man of her lusty adventure is none other than the future Lord of the High Elves and destined to marry her sister.

As heir to the kingdom of Landis and current instructor of wizardry at the Academy of Magical Arts, Sarco Sunwalker is honor bound to rise above the temptation of the beautiful empathic student who invades his mind, body, and soul. But when sparks fly, lightning strikes, and thunder rolls, Sarco finds himself more than tempted by the storm of Lark's passion and vows to find a solution that will prevent a war between races, fulfill an infamous quest, and win Lark's hand.

Also Available

Taken By The Passion

by

Maxine Mansfield

Book Three of The Academy Series

http://amzn.com/1612177956

Lizbeth wasn't given a choice whom to marry. She'd been betrothed to the, stubborn, arrogant, egotistical, Adan Hammerstrike, barbarian prince, heir to the throne of Alaria, and...and...murderer, since the day she'd been born. But, did that mean she wasn't entitled to follow her own dreams? Especially if those dreams could keep those she cared for safe? And so what if Adan had grown from the troll of a little boy he'd been into a ridiculously handsome, sexy man. Her heart could resist him, couldn't it?

The last thing on Albrath, Adan ever wanted was to be saddled for all of eternity to the screeching, boring, lackluster, Lizbeth Soulenticer. Though her beauty's beyond compare, there are only so many turns of the hourglass in a night to enjoy it. The rest of the unbearable time, he'll be forced to contend with her silly, hero worship, and her stupid pet choices. But, Adan is a man bound by duty and honor, and he will do what he must, even though he longs for a mate who will challenge him in bed and out. Not that he'll give her his heart, mind you, at least not until they both find themselves Taken by the Passion.

Turn the page to read an excerpt.

Chapter One

Lizbeth glanced at the gorgeous barbarian standing nonchalantly with his well-defined arms folded across the expanse of his wide, bare chest, and cringed. Who would have guessed such a cold-blooded, vicious murderer could end up with the face and body of a god? Yet, somehow, he had. She balled her hands into fists, clinging desperately to the one emotion she'd fostered concerning this man for as long as she could remember...anger.

One of the barbarian's friends laughed at something he said and, with the shake of his head, a lock of hair the color of summer wheat dislodged from behind his perfectly rounded ear, and fell across his forehead. Lizbeth had the strangest urge to tuck it securely back in place. Her fingers tingled with the desire to go to him, reach up, and do just that. It wasn't fair.

Prince Adan Zeth Conner Hammerstrike wasn't supposed to be devastatingly handsome or brilliantly witty or muscled beyond belief from head to toe like the barbarian warrior he was. He was still supposed to be the horrid troll of a boy he'd been when last she had the misfortune to be in his presence.

At least one thing about the man remained consistent. If the tilt of his chin and the arrogant smirk on his face were any indications, he still possessed the same annoying, egotistical, pompous-ass attitude he'd always had.

Lizbeth sighed. Perhaps his body had changed for the better, but the important details remained the same. He was still the crown prince of Alaria and the man destined to be the next king of the Barbarians, and she was as she'd always been, nothing more than property.

Turning from him and the sounds of celebration, she walked to the floor-to-ceiling windows of his family's castle and glanced out and upward at the night sky. The three moons of Albrath, each in a different phase, shone down, illuminating the icy-cold, barren landscape and high mountains of the far northern kingdom of Alaria. So this was home?

Tears threatened, and Lizbeth scrunched her eyes tight to prevent their escape. She would not cry today of all days. It was a promise she'd made. Her entire life had been in preparation for this day, and she had willingly done what duty dictated. Now, all she wanted was to get through the rest of this evening, say goodnight, gather her valise, and be on her way.

A single tear escaped past her defenses, and Lizbeth quickly swiped it away before anyone had a chance to notice. She wasn't a little girl anymore. As of twelve turns of the hourglass ago, she was twenty-one and a woman fully grown. And not just any woman, either. As of two turns ago of that same hourglass, she was the signed, sealed, and delivered wife of Prince Adan Hammerstrike. On parchment anyway. And that was more than she'd ever wanted from the man.

Happily-ever-afters with someone you loved and who loved you back were fairytales for children, not the reality of a royal's life on Albrath.

Lady Lizbeth Claire Soulenticer, now Princess Lizbeth Hammerstrike, future queen of the Barbarians certainly didn't believe in anything as silly as fairytales. She never had.

****

Oh, God Draka, she wasn't crying was she? After being raised with four sisters, let alone his queen of a mother, he couldn't abide another moment of female drama. Adan sighed as he watched the slip of a girl wipe what looked suspiciously like a tear from her cheek. He shook his head and wondered, for not the first time this day, what he'd ever done to be saddled with such a wife. One who didn't have the capacity to be anything but what she'd always been—a whining, sniveling, pain in his arse, unwanted responsibility.

Not that he wouldn't still do her the honor of bedding her for, after all, it was his duty. And even if she wasn't the type of woman he would have chosen for a wife, had he been given the opportunity to choose, she wasn't horrid to look upon. As a matter of fact, she was stunning.

Hair the color of liquid toffee, rich and thick, hung well past her waist. Strands of copper with gold highlights danced in the glow of a hundred candles scattered throughout the room. Adan's fingers itched to gauge its weight. His chest ached to have it brush across his ribs and come to rest upon his shoulders as she gracefully rode him long into the coming night.

Skin the shade of warm cream, and lips, full and pouty with just a tint of peach, caused a stirring beneath his ceremonial kilt. The promise of breasts full and heavy below her lacey, white gown teased at his senses while her hips, just the right size to grasp with both hands, tormented his mind.

Surprisingly enough, however, it was her ears that totally enthralled him. They always had. All afternoon his tongue had been tempted to flick out and finally taste the crisp little points of her ears. Who would have thought dainty, pointed, half-wood-elf ears could be so damn sexy? Perhaps he wasn't quite as immune to his pretty little wife's charms as he thought.

Adan chuckled to himself. He didn't have to be immune. All he need do was crook a finger and beckon, and she would immediately come running to his side. It was her nature and in her training. All she'd ever known in life, from the moment she'd been born, was whatever Prince Adan wanted would one day be her duty to give. Every lesson she'd taken, every book she'd read, every single thing she ate, learned, and probably even dreamed of, had been for one purpose— to become the wife of and to please Prince Adan Hammerstrike.

For a fleeting moment, Adan wondered if she'd ever had more than a handful of thoughts in her pretty little head she could rightfully call her own. Thoughts that didn't revolve directly around him. Probably not. How boring.

Glancing about the room at his friends, Adan blew out a breath. To his right stood Uthiel Dragonheart, human paladin, protector of dragons, master of Castle Kuropkat, and husband to the beautiful Briar, an amazing elf-human healer. Not a happier man in all of Albrath could be found.

That is unless you took into account the equally jovial Sarco Sunwalker, across the way to Adan's left. Sarco, heir to the Lordship of the Elves, wizard instructor at the Academy of Magical Arts, and husband to Adan's youngest sister, Lark.

Both were strong-minded men with wives who complemented and challenged them. Opinionated, smart, sometimes sassy, never boring, always in the thick of things, passionate wives.

And what kind of wife did Adan now have? He glanced toward Lizbeth, and the touch of sadness that flickered in her soft hazel eyes made him almost feel guilty about what he had planned. After all, it wasn't her fault if she was ordinary, predictable, and boring. She was what she was, and nothing more or less than a product of her upbringing.

Like it or not, enjoyable or not, it was still his duty to consummate this travesty of a marriage before he took his leave of her. And leave her was exactly what he planned to do.

When the sun rose in the morning, he would bid farewell to his uninteresting little responsibility. His parents could contend with her. Allowing him the freedom to return to the Academy with his comrades and continue his carefree life, unfettered by the likes of an unwanted wife, at least until such a time duty forced his return.

No doubt she would cry and beg him to stay, but in the end, it would do her no good. His mind was made up.

With a gesture and bow goodnight to his friends and family, Adan headed toward his bride.

****

Down a long corridor, they walked in silence. Up a staircase, past two hallways, one to the right then another to the left, through a drafty archway, and across the width of an expansive open-ended room until they stopped before a door.

Lizbeth could smell a hint of wood smoke, alder she guessed, as Adan turned and cupped her chin in his big, barbarian hand. Try as she might, she couldn't stop herself from trembling.

"Don't worry your little head about my pleasure or anything else this night. I'm sure you're quite eager to use some of those techniques you've been studying over the past few years to please me, but for this evening, allow me to simply do what needs to be done quickly and efficiently. My pleasure will come in good time, Lizard."

If his smile hadn't been so genuine and if Lizbeth hadn't been certain the only thing between the big buffoon's ears was more of the same hot air he'd been spouting all evening, she would have smacked the condescending look right off his face. Don't worry about his pleasure? Eager to use techniques to please him? And...and...Lizard? Who did he think he was?

Instead, she smiled at him innocently. "Lizard, seriously, Adan? Do I really remind you of a reptile? And your pleasure? You mistake my distress, my lord. I'm simply not accustomed to the extreme cold here in your kingdom. Hmm, I hadn't given your pleasure a single thought. Was I supposed to?"

Adan's look of genuine concern was almost laughable. "I was under the impression husbands were supposed to come up with pet names for their wives. It's a rule, I think. I like Lizard. I mean, you don't look like one or anything, it's just...cute."

His eyes gleamed as he graced her with a smile she knew was meant to rattle her resolve and bring the fair maiden in her to her knees. "You have been adequately deflowered and schooled in all the arts of seduction, haven't you? You've taken the sex practices and theory classes all young people are required to take? I'm quite certain it was in the marriage contract your parents signed. You do understand what I'm talking about and what's about to happen, don't you? Please tell me you do, my lady."

It was all Lizbeth could do to respond with a straight face. "Yes, I've been properly deflowered and schooled in all forms of sexual functions. And as far as understanding, I know exactly what I'm about to do."

His smile gentled and became genuine. The sight of it almost made her feel guilty about the course of action she'd long ago decided upon...almost.

Adan opened the door to his room, and Lizbeth gaped and hesitated before stepping across the threshold. The parts of the castle she'd seen thus far had been bad enough with their stark walls of white stone and colorless decor, but this? This chamber was the most horrid of them all.

Her first impression of the room was one of ice. Cold, devoid of emotion or life, frosty, bitter aloneness. Lizbeth shivered and hugged her arms close to her body. From the white fur rugs scattered about the white stone floor to snow-white drapes hanging loosely open above the stark floor-to-ceiling windows, everything was devoid of color. Even the view was one of never-ending bleakness. And it was huge. No, huge wasn't the word. It was ridiculously huge for a sleeping chamber.

The only furnishings in the entire space consisted of a single, white, wooden chest against one wall and a white four-poster bed. The four posts were each carved in the image of fearsome dragon heads.

Lizbeth shuddered. The thought of dragons had chills racing along her spine. Let alone snow-white dragons with dead eyes and razor-sharp teeth. Words from a childhood poem came suddenly to mind and she shivered. When the sun doth set and dusk draws near, If ye've misbehaved, ye have reason to fear. For by darkness of night, wings take flight, And seek out the naughty to devour by next light.

Lizbeth shook her head to dispel the image. Knowing that even if she were standing here naked and freezing, the bed's coverlet of thick white fur wouldn't be enough to entice her to climb into that bed. Still, she couldn't force her gaze from the monstrosity. The thing was so big it took up most of the room. The horrendous sleeping space was situated in the very center and was large enough to accommodate an entire family of barbarians, and then some.

Lizbeth shivered once more. What kind of man could find peace enough to sleep surrounded by such…hopelessness?

There were very few things in the chamber that weren't white. Yellow flames licked at dark logs while red coals glowed like dragon's eyes in the fireplace on the far wall. The only other thing of any color was her one sad-looking, brown valise, sitting next to a white door across the room. The lone saving grace to the entire space was the familiar smell of wood smoke. It reminded her of home.

Lizbeth turned to Adan. "Is there somewhere I may change, my lord?"

Adan chuckled. "We're married, remember, Lizard. Feel free to change right here. I don't mind. As a matter of fact, why not simply slip off your gown and drop it to the floor. It will expedite things."

She hated herself for the rush of heat warming her cheeks. "I realize we're now wed, but I would prefer a touch of privacy. A bride looks forward to preparing for her wedding night. Surely even a barbarian can understand that?"

He raised an eyebrow but simply pointed to the door her valise set beside. "Suit yourself, and take all the time you need." He grinned wolfishly. "I'm a patient man, even for a barbarian, and I'll be right here waiting when you're ready to come out and play, Lizard."

Adan loosened the clasp holding his kilt together, and green and blue plaid wool slithered to the floor. For the space of forty-two heartbeats, Lizbeth stood frozen, staring at the glorious nakedness of her husband. Bronzed muscles rippled across his taut belly, while a halo of springy golden curls surrounded a broad, long cock.

The air in the room became agonizingly thin, and pinpricks of color floated before Lizbeth's eyes. It wasn't as if she'd never seen a naked man, but she'd certainly never seen one as marvelously made as this one.

His already more-than-adequate phallus began expanding until the veins running along its side pulsated. Lizbeth did the only thing she could think to do. She ran to her valise, snatched it up, opened the door, darted inside, and slammed the door closed behind her.

She wasn't sure how long she'd been in the small changing room, but she knew from her growing sense of claustrophobia it had been a while. God Draka, how she hated confined spaces, and it had already taken more than a few minutes just for her hands to stop shaking enough to manage the closures on her hideous white gown, let alone the ties of her corset or the multiple layers of snow-white petticoats. Manage them, though, she finally did. Then it took almost as long to rifle through her bag and find the garments she was searching for.

With a pounding heart, she slipped on her pale beige tunic and traveling pants, then stuffed her wedding gown with all its accessories haphazardly into the bag. Taking three deep calming breaths and blowing them slowly out, Lizbeth turned the doorknob, stepped out into the room, and faced her waiting husband.

If the look of surprise on Adan Hammerstrike's face hadn't been so priceless, Lizbeth knew she would've been tempted to lose her nerve as she nodded in his direction, walked right past the bed, and headed toward the door.

In his haste to rise, Adan became tangled in the white coverlet on the bed and, with a thud, ended up sprawled on the floor. "Where do you think you're going?"

Slowly, she turned and glanced at the angry barbarian. "To the portal, of course. Did I forget to mention I'm starting classes at The Academy of Magical Arts in the morning? I really must be going. I don't wish to be late." She forced a smile. "It was a lovely wedding and reception. I truly am sorry my brothers were unavoidably detained and couldn't be here. They would've especially enjoyed the Alarian ale. Please give my regards to your family and friends."

The silk coverlet was forgotten as Adan leapt to his feet. "The Academy? What the VoT are you talking about, woman? You didn't say a word to me about any classes, and you well know it. This is unacceptable. You are my wife, and this is our wedding night. You can't just…just leave."

Lizbeth stiffened her spine and glared. "Prince or not, don't you dare curse at me, Adan Hammerstrike. If you wish to speak of the Valley of Torment then call it as such, and not that vulgar VoT word. And as for being your wife, that's only a technicality, and we both know it. We've been betrothed since the day I was born. My parents signed a contract pledging I would be your queen, not share your bed while you're still merely a prince."

She paced back and forth before the door. "You aren't king yet, and until you are, I will have the life I've been denied thus far. I'm now of age, and I wish to become an enchantress. As God Draka is my witness, I'm going to do just that. I'm through spending my days studying you and living your life instead of my own. I'm sick to death of you. I know more about you than you could possibly remember about yourself. And anyway, I wouldn't spend the night willingly in the same bed with a vicious murderer like you until duty dictates I must for all the platt in Albrath, husband or not."

She stopped and glared at him.

Adan ran his hand through his hair and took a deep breath. "So, that's what all this is about, huh? After all these years, you're still upset over the stupid rabbit? Lizbeth, I was fifteen and you were eleven, for God Draka's sake. I was trying to impress you with my elite hunting skills. How was I to know you'd made a pet of the thing? Rabbits are food. They're meant to be eaten, not played with. How many times must I say I'm sorry?"

He balled his fists at his side. "I am the prince and your husband. You'll immediately forgive me once and for all and stop this foolishness. I demand it."

Tears burned the back of her eyes, but Lizbeth forbade them to fall. "Demand it? Well, that certainly doesn't make you sound any sorrier now than you did then. For your information, I wasn't allowed to have pets. Did you know that? It took me weeks to get Horatio to come close enough so I could feed him from my hand and even longer to actually get him to trust me enough to touch him."

Lizbeth held up three fingers. "Do you have any idea how many times I got to pet his soft brown fur before you...you murdered him?"

Adan gulped, and Lizbeth knew he didn't want to answer the question. She waited, tapping her toe impatiently.

"Three?" he finally said.

Lizbeth nodded as her voice rose another octave. "Yes, only three times, and then I had to stand there and not shed a single tear while poor little Horatio was skinned and stuffed in a pot with vegetables."

She lifted her chin and stiffened her spine. "I didn't dare tell mother why I was sick and couldn't possibly eat. I wasn't allowed to ever get dirty or play with creatures like other children were, let alone make a pet of one. I could never take the chance one of them might bite or scratch me and mar my perfect skin. Oh, no, the future queen of the barbarians, the future wife of Prince

Adan Hammerstrike had to be without flaw. It was in the damnable marriage contract."

The tears did come to the surface then, and Lizbeth knew from the look on his face Adan had seen them. He started toward her as if he were going to offer comfort.

She held out a hand. "Don't! I neither need nor want your pity. All I want is my freedom until you become king. I give you my word, the day you accept your crown, even though I dread the thought of it, I'll do my duty. I'll come back here and be your wife."

He stood in all his naked splendor with his arms crossed looking as if he were contemplating the situation. He rubbed his jaw twice, nodded a couple of times then spoke. "I realize you can't stand the sight of me because I am, after all, the evil bunny slayer. But we have a duty to consummate this marriage."

He held out a hand. "Spend this one night with me, Lizbeth, and if you still feel the same in the morning, we'll talk about you possibly going to the Academy and taking a few classes now and then. After all, how would it look to my family and friends if my brand new wife took off before the sun rises on her wedding night? I have appearances to uphold, we both do."

Lizbeth sizzled with anger. "I don't like you, remember? I couldn't care less how this looks to anybody, and…and…and, I won't spend this night or any other with you, until I have to, even on a bet."

Adan grinned. "Really? Not even on a bet? What if a bet was to get you exactly what you say you want most? A life of your own without a moment's interference from me until the day I do become king?"

Lizbeth shook her head and turned to leave, yet Adan's next words not only stopped her forward motion but had her turning and facing him once more.

"I never took you for a coward, Lizbeth, guess I was wrong. You say you know me better than I know myself. I say prove it, Lizard. If you can manage to answer ten...no, make that five questions about me correctly, you win."

His grin grew even bigger. "And if you win, not only will I escort you to the front gate and wave you through the portal on your way to the Academy, I'll be happy to inform my family and friends that you're leaving me. That you find a dusty, old institution more sexually appealing than you do your own husband, and rightly so."

The grin disappeared from his face. "But if you don't answer all the questions correctly, you'll spend this one night, this entire night, willingly in my bed, in my arms, as my wife, in every sense of the word. Deal?"

He held out his hand again, and Lizbeth stared at it. Her fingers itched with the temptation to take him up on his offer. A life without interference or being under Adan's thumb, even for a short while, was more than a little tempting. Could she trust him, though?

Lizbeth hesitated, weighing her options. Other than being a bunny killer, Adan Hammerstrike was known far and wide for his word. Once he gave it, he never took it back.

She'd spent the majority of every day, for as long as she could remember, learning everything there was to know about the arrogant barbarian prince. She couldn't lose, and this was an opportunity she couldn't afford to pass up.

Lizbeth smiled as she shook his hand. "Deal."

Thank you for purchasing
this Wild Rose Press, Inc. publication.
For other wonderful stories of erotic romance,
please visit our on-line bookstore at
www.thewilderroses.com.

For questions or more information
contact us at
info@thewildrosepress.com.

The Wild Rose Press, Inc.
www.thewilderroses.com